Dark Enough to See the Stars in a Jamestown Sky

Based on the true story of the women and children of Jamestown

Connie Lapallo

Llumina Press

F
LAP

ISBN: 1-59526-421-3

Printed in the United States of America by Llumina Press

Library of Congress Control Number: 2006928790

Dedication

To the Women and Children of Jamestown—

Especially to my 13th great grandmother Joan Phippen Peirce and 12th great grandmother Cecily Reynolds Bailey Jordan Farrar.

Your faith, perseverance, and courage inspire me across four hundred years.

To Nana and Mom,

also direct descendents of Joan and Cecily, with love.

To Papa Christian,

for always having time to walk with me, searching the fields for relics, and telling me about when you were a boy: "I found so many Civil War bullets I could fill a wheelbarrow, so I used them in my slingshot!" How I miss you.

And to my great-grandma Burgess,

for all the stories about "the olden days." I wrote them down, and I remembered. You made a century ago seem so close I felt I could touch it. You inspired me to learn more and see if the past would give over its secrets. I miss you, too!

Acknowledgements

With love and appreciation to:

My husband Chris, and my children Sarah, Michael, Kerry, and Adam Lapallo,

for the thousands of things you did to make this all happen.

Cathi Eubanks,

for the inspiration of true friendship—a gift from God that endures forever.

Therese Silberman,

for an artist's eye, a gardener's insight, and a friend's loving encouragement.

Richard Maida,

my cousin, but as dear as a brother, for the English West Country tour—an unforgettable trip back in time. Also, thanks to Tracey for the warm hospitality.

Nancy Blackburn,

for friendship and faith, and for spending a sweltering day researching with me in the 'tween deck of the *Susan Constant!*

They say to keep a green tree in your heart and perhaps a singing bird will come. To others whose song has inspired me through the years:

My dad and my brother Michael, Kim Colgin, Holly Boyle, Janet and Ricky Lee, Allison Mesnard, Kathy Lowry, the Germains, the Silbermans, Denise Del Prete, the Frasers, Stephen Leftwich, the Pratts, the Rugaris, the Lapallos, the Nettes, the Goldsmiths, Jean Weller, Parrish Mort, Kim Kremer, Traci Haden, Courtney Cranor, Barb Noll, the Caldwells, Jeanine Moore, Ruth Savino, Katie Huggins, Susan Owens, Carol Seeley, Lucy Pryor, Carol Ziolkowski, Allison Baldwin, Ali Schoolmeester, Rick and Jennifer Alvey, the Eubanks kids—Ali, Madi, and Bryon, Becky Shermer, Robert Holland, Lori Rockwell, Donna Chesson, Lois Jones, Donna Pritchett, Mom and Pop Lapallo, Aunt Mary, Uncle Vernon, my cousins, the Cultural Studies and Writing Group kids, and many others...

Thanks especially to those who so helpfully read and commented on the manuscript: Anne Westrick, Cathi Eubanks, Jean Weller, Sally Fraser, and Therese Silberman, as well as my husband and children.

To the Hanover Writers Club, including Joanne, Anne, Bob, Miriam, Jane, Sheila, Fran, Jean, Wayne, Lorraine, Laura, Sherry, Virginia, Liz, and Coleen—your encouragement and belief meant so much.

Thanks also to many wonderful historic interpreters, especially at Jamestown Settlement, Jamestown National Historical Site and Jamestown Rediscovery at Historic Jamestowne, the Citie of Henricus, Agecroft Hall, Roanoke Island Festival Park, the Elizabethan Gardens, the Fort Raleigh National Historic Site, and the Tudor House in Weymouth, Dorset, England.

Cover design and painting by Sarah A. Lapallo with suggestions from Kerry, Michael, and Adam Lapallo. Thanks, Peter, for the advice!

Back cover photograph by Beth Goldsmith.

Foreword

It is a strange thing, to sit in the pew on the site of a 400-year-old church and chat with your great-great-great-great-great-great-great-great-great-great-great-great-great grandmother, but that is what I did one winter day in 2000. Joan Peirce was there, and she and I sat together and talked. She had on her long kirtle and apron—period costume we would call it. Her woven basket of goods beside her, her hat tied around her head.

This was not the *real* Joan Peirce, of course, but an historic interpreter. She had just given "Joan's tour" at Jamestown National Historic Park, and I asked her afterward if we might talk.

Somewhere in the universe, an unusual stirring must occur when this happens. Somewhere a door opens, and the real Joan Peirce does enter—a portal is somehow breeched, left ajar.

What would Joan say if she and I really could talk? She would tell me her story, and, based on what I have learned of her life, I think it would go something like this.

– *C.M.L., February 2006*

To the Virginian Voyage

Britons, you stay too long;
Quickly aboard bestow you,
And with a merry gale
Swell your stretched sail,
With vows as strong
As the winds that blow you.

And cheerfully at sea,
Success you still entice,
To get the pearl and gold,
And ours to hold,
Virginia,
Earth's only paradise.

~ *Michael Drayton, 1606*

When it is dark enough, you can see the stars.

~ Ralph Waldo Emerson

Mulberry Island, Virginia

August 1649

Marking My Fortieth Year in the Colony

M ost times when folks come to visit Mulberry Island, they have questions. The first one is, "Begging your pardon, Mistress, but why are you toiling in the garden at your age, when you have servants to help you?"

Well, my bones do well for a body nearing seventy. Some women are embarrassed about their age—not me. When you've lived as long as I have, and seen as much as I've seen, you consider it a blessing to be here still. There aren't many walking this colony today who remember its founding. I do, praise God. There are less still who remember the days of our Queen Bess. I lived through her reign, and the reigns of King James and King Charles, even unto the tragic beheading of Charles this spring. I never thought I should live to see an England without a king or queen. I am nearly beyond my time, I suppose, like a relic.

However, not in the grave yet.

So I'm not shy about it. I tell all Virginia I shall be seventy in the spring. Moreover, I plan on being here to mark the occasion!

As for why I still work outside—I work outside because *I like it*. I believe in keeping oneself busy. Don't wait on me, I say. I tell them firmly, I work outside because I can. Because Virginia bird calls, the feel of the earth, and the tumbling river currents are soothing to me.

Now, forty years ago, I never would've told you any of this was soothing.

This always leads to their next question.

"Begging your pardon again, Mistress Peirce, but *how did you do it?*" they begin.

"You've no need to keep begging anything from me, young lass, but I appreciate your manners," I say. "And how did I do what?" It's a bit of a game, since I know exactly what they mean. But I politely wait for the second part of the question.

Now I have thrown them somewhat. "How did you, a woman alone with a young child, survive that horrible Starving Time when so many others—even so many men—died, back at James Town? And—pardon me if I'm prying, Mistress—but what made you decide to come at all back then? Virginia was but an outpost in the wilderness in those days—scarcely a woman to be found."

"You mean, why was I so foolish as to come, and why was I so lucky as to survive anyway?" I ask in return, feigning indignation.

They take a step back, fearing they have offended me.

Then I smile. I am not offended, for I have heard these questions many times before.

And if I am so inclined—if the weather is breezy, and I can hear the mourning doves and the river rushing past the fields, I might gesture to a chair.

"Have a seat, then," I say to my visitor. "Do you truly want to hear an old woman's tales of the upstart James Town colony, and what the Starving Time was truly like? Few enough remember it any more. Well, I am of a mood to tell my secrets today, and I will share them with you. I am marking the fortieth year since my arrival, and…well, it *is* right close to St. James Day, isn't it? Aye, the 25th of July is just past.

"Then indeed I will tell the story, because it was on that day forty years ago the great *hurricano* struck our ships bound for Virginia. I knew at that moment I'd made the mistake of a lifetime. That I chanced to carry a pilgrim badge from the tomb of St. James mattered not. It appeared the Spanish saint would devour our ships in the hurricane on his day. 'It is *Spanish* territory—go away!' he seemed to cry in the howling winds."

But I suppose I should start at the beginning.

To Make of This Earth a Garden
May 1592

Speak not—whisper not:
Here bloweth thyme and bergamot...
Dark-spiked rosemary and myrrh,
Lean-stalked, purple lavender...

~ Walter de la Mare

To know someone here or there with whom you feel
there is understanding in spite of distances or
thoughts unexpressed—that can make of this earth a garden.

~ Johann Wolfgang von Goethe

The spring I turned twelve in 1592, I learned my father would not be returning from sea one day.

I knew because he told me.

It was early in the season yet, an English spring of lilacs and field poppies and jonquils sprouting from amongst the hollyhocks. Pushing from beneath the ground, they seemed to say, "Good day! We are arriving now and it has all been worth it—the long wet winter, the grey afternoons. You shall be seeing more of us soon."

My mother was the best herbalist in Melcombe Regis, or so everyone said. I was the youngest child—and only daughter—so she determined I should learn too, and I soaked up her words like March downpours in the countryside. Flowers for color and sweet airs, she said, herbs for cooking and healing, and vegetables that healing might not be needed. I savored the feel of loamy earth and the contained wildness of our garden in Dorset, happy for any reason to dig my fingers in the soil.

This day she knelt, plucking weeds around the lemon thyme and cotton lavender in the knot garden. The green and grey plants marched in lines, one regiment neatly crossing another to give a startling woven effect in bursts of dark and light color. I ran my hand across the low boxwoods trimmed to form a protective frame around the winding herbs. The boxwoods were more than decorative, as their scent also discouraged deer, squirrels, and coneys.

"Joanie, cotton lavender is used for…?" Joanie was my pet name, as my parents christened me Jane.

"Poisonous bites of all types," I replied without hesitation.

"And when might you use sage?" Mother looked at me expectantly.

"For fevers, the palsy, headache, woefulness, the colic, and to strengthen the sinews," I recited.

"That is so. And the potency of sage is why we call it...?"

I thought a moment. I always wanted to say *king* but corrected myself. "*Sovereign Sage*," I said, pleased I had remembered. This was a game, but I knew its real purpose was to tutor me in medicinal herbs and flowers.

Beside the knot garden, another boxwood surrounded rosemary and lavender. In season, we draped drying clothes over this hedge to sweeten them.

The brick path wound through many plots, small but efficiently organized. I stopped to admire foxgloves, as tall as I was with pink bellflowers waving in rhythm to the wind. Bachelor's buttons peeked around them, as though shyly curious, petite but handsomely attired in blue. Nearby purple irises danced. Humble forget-me-nots played with snapdragons. I opened the dragon's mouth while studying the array.

Why do we call them *foxgloves*, Mother?"

She continued pulling weeds, her long dress draped across her knees, her straw hat buffering her from the sun. "Because of those naughty fairies." She said no more, and I waited. And waited.

Finally, I realized she was teasing me, so I pressed. "Fairies?"

She kept her expression nonchalant. "Fairies used to give these flowers to foxes to wear on their paws so they could sneak up on coneys and squirrels and the like. See? Fox gloves." At this, she smiled over her shoulder, leaving me to wonder.

I decided to play along. "Fairies scattered these daisies too, didn't they, Mother?"

"Aye, fairies scatter daisies when children die to cheer up their mothers. *Day's eyes*, we call them, because they open their sunny eyes to greet the morning. *Day's eyes*," she said again wistfully. She glanced at the patch of daisies and periwinkle planted in remembrance of my sister and brother. The loss of these two children left a broad gap between my grown brothers—Jack, Robin, and Tom—and me. I wrapped my arm about Mother's waist to show her I understood—that I too loved the sister and brother I had never met. She gave me a sad smile, saying, "How lonely I would be without you!"

Still, even the daisies and periwinkle had medicinal uses, and while she cherished these flowers, she wasted them not. My mother's garden was practical and orderly yet graceful, just as she herself was.

I took in the whole of it: the flowers in bloom, the ones to come. The honeysuckle would not arrive for a few months yet, but I learned early how to pull the stem to taste one sweet drop of nectar. And soon the roses would burst forth in unkempt glory—whites, pinks and reds—as they crept up and about the arched pergolas. Even all these did mother use for healing.

The kitchen herb garden contained parsley, mints, lovage, sage, fennel, garlic, mustard, and sweet basil. A second herb garden held remedies: monk's hood, wormwood, hyssop, rue, mugwort, lemon balm, belladonna, marsh-mallow, lungwort, marjoram, feverfew, chicory…. It was much for me to learn, particularly since some were poisonous. Not the sort of thing one should erringly add to pottage! Most of the flowers had healing qualities, as too the cooking herbs. Mother had remedies grouped by similar ailments, with separate plots for all poisonous herbs.

"Feverfew?" Mother asked, as we yanked weeds around bluebells.

"Those giddied in the head or with vertigo," I quoted.

"Aye. And pennyroyal also aids the dizziness," she added.

When we'd finished for the day, Mother placed her hands on her hips. "Lovely," she said, drawing in the wonderland of color and fragrance.

We had only just gone inside when the doorknocker rapped. Mother turned the key and heaved the great door open. There stood Wicker, my father's most trusted crewman. The *Anne* was home!

Streaming Splendour Through the Sky
May 1592

By command of the Duke, you rest here a King, O Harold, that you may be guardian still of the shore and sea.
> ~ Lord William Malet's epitaph for the Saxon king Harold—carved into a cliff overlooking Harold's final battle at Hastings by order of William the Conqueror

Though they fell, they fell like stars,
Streaming splendour through the sky.
> ~ James Montgomery

L ooking ruffled from the voyage, Wicker nonetheless politely tipped his hat to my mother, saying, "Good afternoon, Mistress. I'm pleased to bring you news that we've arrived safely within the port o' Melcombe. Master Phippen's tending his accounts dockside, but asks me to tell you he'll be here presently." I clapped my hands. Father home, a story for me, and exotic herbs or bulbs for my mother, no doubt. Another safe journey, another reunion after his two and half months away trading in Ireland.

We were used to my father's travels, since he was a merchant mariner just as his father, grandfather, and brothers before him. The sea had long lured the Phippen men. They knew the winds and the tides and the rigging and the merchandise they moved across one ocean, over this sea or that, to one port and then another.

The men in my family had three passions: ships, trading, and God. And those men, every one of them, desired to be either ministers of the Gospel or mariners—but the ministers still eyed the sea and the mariners still read the Book.

My father was the third generation to make his living importing and exporting across the Irish Sea. Both my grandfather and great-grandfather had relocated to Ireland. I think if the fighting had ever ceased we'd all be living in a Southern Irish port town, like Youghal or Waterford. My great-grandfather, a Cornishman, had owned an Irish mercantile business, until the uprisings cost him his property too many times. He'd moved through Scotland and Ireland wherever opportunity called, until at last it led back to England.

I couldn't wait to see my father and hear about the trip. Sometimes his men evaded Spanish privateers or battled a tempest—common threats. Algerian pirates cruised the Irish coast as well. Danger behind him, Father would tamp his tobacco, fire up his pipe, prop his feet near the hearth, and the storytelling began.

For my part, I wanted to show him our garden right away, but I also knew he'd ask after my studies at home. Greek and French I labored at, but Latin came naturally to me for reasons I knew not. I should never love arithmetic as well as poetry, preferring reading and gardening to household accounts.

As the door closed behind Wicker, we began working to make the house especially sweet and clean for my father. It was our customary routine, Mother sweeping as she hummed and sang, while I dusted.

My mother whisked her straw broom to the song's rhythm, sometimes murmuring the words, sometimes just the tune. Her wistful voice carried me back to my own task, dusting.

> *Greensleeves was all my joy,*
> *Greensleeves was my delight,*
> *Greensleeves was my heart of gold,*
> *and who but my Lady Greensleeves.*

I rubbed the ancient oak table and the large clock, both heirlooms from my mother's family, the Jordaines. I saw that the hour approached two as I ran the linen rag down the clock's panel, admiring its rich wood. Her grandfather was an horologer, and he had created this piece. He fled France for England during the Hundred Years War, over a century before I was born.

"The countryside ruined, his livelihood—clock-making—devastated by never-ending battles with the English. What was he to do?" Mother, quiet in her musings, was nonetheless quite proud of her Norman French heritage.

Our Jordaine family pronounced their name differently than the English Jordans did. Everyone in my family pronounced it *Jerrden*, whether they spelt it *Jordaine, Jourdain*, or *Jordan*. An old family legend held that the name derived from a Norse word meaning *earth*—but our preferred Christian explanation was that it originated during the Crusades when a knight, honored at the River Jordan, adopted it as a surname.

I lingered over my favorite piece, the Malet Crest. Little larger than my hand, it hung on the wall in gleaming—though at this moment, dusty—glory. As I polished, the sheen returned to its three silver scallop shells. *Tres escallops*, they were called in heraldry.

Now I wondered which of them took the pilgrimage?

Which of my ancestors journeyed to Compostela and saw the field of stars where the bones of St. James the Greater lay? St. James, Apostle of Jesus. Someone in our family, perhaps four hundred years ago, had traveled there according to my father. Scallops, I knew, symbolized a pilgrimage, *the* pilgrimage, to Spain. It must have been during the Crusades, I reckoned.

"Mother, do you know who went?"

She ceased her humming and glanced at me curiously.

"Who went where?" She smiled a little, being used to my head asking more questions than actually emerged from my mouth.

"Who went to Spain?"

She looked puzzled, and no wonder! Just three years after the Armada attack, Spain was a sworn enemy. Then she noticed I was dusting the crest.

"Oh, Child, Spain! The scallops, you mean?"

"Aye, please. I know scallops mean pilgrimage, but which grandfather went, do you suppose? Was it during the crusades?"

She blew her lips in an almost exasperated sigh. "I can tell you not, but perhaps your father knows, and I am quite sure he won't mind you asking!" This last was a joke, because we both knew Father loved any excuse to delve into family lore.

Mother went back to sweeping and singing.

> *I have been ready at your hand,*
> *to grant whatever you would crave,*
> *I have both wagered life and land,*
> *Your love and good-will for to have.*

I polished the crest a little longer than perhaps necessary. It was dramatic on the white lime walls surrounded by oaken supports. As the breeze stirred off the waters of Melcombe Bay, I considered those who had come before me. *They are like a river*, I thought, *and the river is me*. Like drops of water, their blood was mine.

Ye Mariners of England

May 1592

Ye mariners of England,
That guard our native seas;
Whose flag has braved, a thousand years,
The battle and the breeze!
Britannia needs no bulwarks
No towers along the steep;
Her march is o'er the mountain wave,
Her home is on the deep.

~ Thomas Campbell

My heart danced when he opened the door. He hugged my mother and then me, asking, "Joanie, my lass, what have you been doing while I was away? Well, growing, for one thing!" he added. I stood taller. "And helping your mother with the garden, I see." He wiped a smudge of dirt from my face.

"Aye, Sir. How was the voyage to the Irish Sea? Did you bring back a story?"

He usually did. How true they all were, I was never sure. Once he told me they bled him at Youghal and found seawater in his blood. "Nearly killed the leeches!" he'd added before laughing.

This time he seemed more pensive as he pulled off his boots. He looked at me directly, and the blue light in his eyes was captivating. Mine were blue also, but surely they did not have the look of sun glinting off water as his did. Perhaps the lines of his sunned face and black hair and beard deepened his eyes. Blue like the sea, I supposed.

"Hm, a story." He hesitated. Mother had fixed mutton, peas, and a loaf of fresh bread. "After supper, Joanie. I'm famished tonight." I was surprised, but nodded obligingly.

A verse formed in my head: *All their eyes are upon me. They* are *me.* I did not know exactly who they all were, but my father had told me enough to imagine vivid faces. Some had lived long ago.

Now we sat upon the modern age, the end of the sixteenth century. Even so, these ancient grandparents were real to me because the stories made them so. Crests like this reminded me they had once lived even as I did. This part of them I could touch. The metal was cold beneath my fingers, but, oh, how the scallops shone.

"Girls do carry the bloodline as well as boys. Isn't that so, Mother?"

"Hm?" Mother paused in her song. "What are you asking?"

"I carry the family blood—the Phippens, the Jordaines, the Malets—as much as any of my brothers?"

She shook her head, not to mean *no*, only to say, *why would you ask such a thing?* But she indulged this round of questions with a shrug.

"I am a Phippen now but was born a Jordaine." She paused to count back. "And your great-great-grandmother Phippen, or Fitzpen, as the name was then, was a Malet." She gave me a sideways glance. "But you know that from the endless stream of family tales. Of course you carry her blood, as does your father." She paused, eyeing the crest. "Such a stunning piece." Its workmanship had withstood the hundred years or so it had been in our family. My grandmother Malet had inherited it somehow, and her young husband, John Fitzpen, had altered his own family crest to include *tres escallops* in honor of his wife. Her name, I knew, was Joanna.

I imagined her a fair noblewoman, engaged to yet another merchant mariner—my great-great-grandfather. In my mind, Joanna sat astride a white horse, and her dress, I saw, was burgundy velvet. A sash swept behind, and I could hear her breath, the thudding hooves, the searing wind off the Cornish coast—and I knew she was me. Or some part of me. Of course, she rode well, for she—and I knew this to be so—was herself a granddaughter of the great Lady Godiva. How many *greats* this was, I knew not, but the Godiva of legend was born four hundred years before Joanna.

Everyone knew the legend of Lady Godiva, but my father told me her real name was not Godiva at all. That was the Latinized version created years after her death. No, her Saxon name was Countess Godgifu, meaning *God's Gift.* Godgifu was the last of the great Saxon women, the *only* woman allowed to own land after the Norman Conquest. Then it was true. We—my grandmother Malet and I—still carried her blood.

Legend says Godgifu's husband overtaxed the town. When the mothers begged her to have him lower taxes that their children might not starve, she presented the idea to him.

"Will you lower the fees? They are desperate," the young Godgifu asked her elderly husband.

He laughed her off with a challenge. "When you ride naked through Coventry at midday, I will do as you ask."

Godgifu must have smiled at that and thought, "As you wish." She struck a deal with the townspeople. Look away, she told them, and I will do it. They did, she did, and her husband removed the taxes—on everything but horses. To this day, the people of that town brag on their low taxes, and it has been over five hundred years since Godgifu died. What we remember less of her is how she gave money to the poor and founded a monastery that survived until recent years, when King Henry VIII destroyed it during the Reformation. A pity, that. We were no lovers of the Catholic faith—but that was old England reduced to rubble. Her monastery, her great landholdings, and her devotion to God and the Virgin Mary were also legendary, and that we knew to be true.

On the Norman side of the conquest came galloping another ancestor, Lord Malet, a friend of the Norman duke, William the Conqueror. Malet had a Norman father—a descendent of a Viking prince—and a Saxon mother, said to be a daughter of Godgifu. For this reason, Duke William ordered my ancient grandfather Malet to bury the rival Saxon king Harold, for Malet was a cousin of Harold's wife. So the Malet line held cordage to both worlds, the old and the new, the Norman and the Saxon. Perhaps this was why the Normans allowed Godgifu to keep her lands. We did not know. Some said the Saxons sainted Godgifu and made pilgrimage to her resting place, but the Normans put an end to that. The Saxons then created the legend around her to keep people coming. Godgifu herself was a granddaughter of Alfred the Great. And so I traced the river to its source, watching it wind, wondering of the souls that comprised it.

Now, I wondered, which grandfather made his own pilgrimage to the field of stars in Compostela, marking his journey with three scallops? I would ask my father if he knew.

On the cusp of the seventeenth century, England had changed much from the days of my ancestors. We had a charming, enigmatic Queen, one who proved beyond doubt that women could possess brains as well as good sense. I believed that. And England was testing its bounds in other lands, like Ireland and the New World. Yet there seemed little adventure a girl like me could have. One day I would marry, bear children—God-willing—and die in the West Country of England as so many before me had. Surely, even with new discoveries, there was scant opportunity for a woman to do more than wave a husband *God be with you* as he went into battle or sailed off for months at a time. Though I carried the bloodline, its adventure stopped here, I felt.

Still, Godgifu never thought Normans would overrun her home or that she would be the only Saxon woman allowed to keep her land—and Lord Malet didn't expect to have his feet in the soil of two countries.

Neither did I. It certainly came as a surprise to me when it happened.

"And for you," he said to my mother, handing her a wooden box of seeds and bulbs. "It's called *oleander.* Then there's bee orchid, husk cherry, and lantern plant, all from Amsterdam." She beamed in delight. Truly, this was a good arrangement, my father bringing home every curious flower and herb he could find, and my mother's love of raising them.

"Well, it looks as though my mother shall finally find her way back to Dorset, after all these years," my father said. His business in Ireland always took him to Youghal, the port city in County Cork where my grandparents had lived so long. "I do not think these Irish plantations are proving to be all the Queen had hoped," he said, a disappointed expression upon his face.

Across the ocean, the New World beckoned with loud supporters like Sir Walter Ralegh and Sir Francis Drake. Yet the Queen resisted the idea of transporting Englishmen so far away to this unfamiliar climate and continent. It made more sense to colonize Ireland, she felt.

The Irish did not agree.

Twelve years before, the Irish rebels had sacked Youghal, forcing the English to retake the town. As punishment, the Queen seized large parcels of Irish lands away from rebel sympathizers and gave them to those loyal to her—these were the first English plantations. Mind you, they were not there to plant gardens but to plant *English.*

My grandfather Phippen, or Thickpenny as he styled himself, had received warrants from Queen Bess to conduct business in Ireland. He was Vittler of the Garrisons, Impost Collector, and an importer and exporter of wine. Keeping the English soldiers and military posts stocked was good work, and my grandfather's business flourished. His ships, the *Ventura,* the *Roma,* the *Ascension,* and the one we inherited, the *Anne,* stayed busy trafficking between England and Ireland.

Queen Bess had first given my grandparents an old fortified merchant house, built about a hundred years ago by an Irish family who supported the rebels. A unique structure, it was a narrow castle between townhouses. The true innovation was the fortified upstairs to keep merchandise safe. In letters home, my grandmother said it was lovely, three stories with ample space to store their goods and to dwell. My father had seen it and said it was a marvelous idea, living so close to a bustling port in a house designed as a warehouse and storefront.

Later, the Queen had also granted my grandparents the old Dominican Friary—no Irishman was going to have that prize! The Queen also gave them other lands—even an island—with the understanding that they could keep and develop them for twenty-one years. The Queen required all new landholders to bring in English tenants, to build defenses, to provide soldiers, and to cultivate the land in the English manner.

"Your mother is coming home to Dorset at long last? Doesn't she like living at the friary?" Mother asked, as she served supper.

Grandfather had died when I was three, and my grandmother buried him at the friary. Yet my grandmother had prospered even after my grandfather's death. The Queen continued granting her lands in Meath and Waterford as a planter in her own right. She had since remarried a gentleman named Harding but still lived as a tenant at the friary, which the Queen had since granted to Sir Walter Ralegh.

My father sighed. "Famine and plague, although that seems much behind them now, have taken a toll on the countryside. The opportunities are not what they once were there, especially with the continued fighting. Ralegh himself is having difficulty maintaining tenants over his vast estates. Not only is he *not* bringing tenants in to his lands in Ireland, but the Virginia expeditions have been a disappointment to him as well."

Mother nodded. The Queen had not only given Ralegh thousands of acres in Southern Ireland, she had also made him Lord and Governor of all plantations he could settle across the waters in Virginia. It was in Virginia that Ralegh's best hopes were. He had even introduced a New World plant, called a *potato*, to Youghal. But one of Ralegh's Virginia colonies had failed, and the other had vanished after English ships were unable to resupply it during the Armada attacks.

"Still," my father added thoughtfully, "It is remarkable the quantity of lands that my mother, a woman, amassed even after my father's death. Although these plantations have not so far been a success, future ones surely will fare better— somewhere, somehow. If I were a younger man and opportunity ever opened up for another colonizing effort to Virginia..."

My mother shushed him. "You do just fine as a mariner. Besides, we were too young to plant Ireland and are too old to plant Virginia."

My father shrugged and, with a smile, feigned a helpless look. To me, he said, "You see that your mother will not allow me to permanently plant else-where. However, being a planter brings women considerable security, Joanie. Remember this if opportunity arises for you. Planting on foreign soil to import and export goods, as your grandparents did, is a sound strategy for advance-ment—one of the few where women may become wealthy in their own right."

"Leaving Melcombe is not something I would ever choose," I said. My home, my harbor, my garden...

14

"Ah, you think so. You think you love it here, but other lands hold charms all their own. Drake and Ralegh say Virginia is bountiful beyond an Englishman's imagination. I have never been to Virginia, of course, but I know Ireland is impressive. You walk through that Watergate into Youghal and think, *what a splendid location.* A pity we have to continually fight the Irish for it!"

All this talk of planting foreign lands reminded me of my pilgrim question.

"Father, you told me the cockleshells on the crest meant someone went on a pilgrimage. I was wondering if you knew who it was."

He thought for a moment and said, "I don't know specifically which of the Malets went to Spain. I *do* know your great-great-grandfather Phippen went, though."

"The one who married the Malet?"

"Aye. He had decided to put the scallops on his own crest to honor his wife's family. But something didn't feel right to him."

"Didn't he like them?"

"The shells or the family?" my father asked, eyes twinkling. "Never mind, for he liked them both. He didn't believe, though, that anyone in *his* family had ever made the pilgrimage. This was about a hundred years ago, the late 1400s, just after they married. And so he went. We don't know the route the ancient Malet took to Compostela, but my grandfather journeyed the English Way."

"The English Way to Spain?"

He nodded. "An Englishman is a mariner, so the English sailed to Corunna, Spain, there to walk to Compostela. The French Way, the *Camino,* was popular for walkers, but *sailors"*— he puffed out— "sailors take the English Way! Much shorter, and still being traveled a hundred years ago. Let me show you something."

He rose and walked to the secretary near the window, opening a drawer and pulling out a large key. With it, he unlocked our chest. "I also keep a family tree in here which I copied from one my grandfather drew. This is what I want to show you, though." He lifted out a metal object, several inches across. I saw it was scallop-shaped with a hole through the top. It appeared to be a pendant of some type.

"Here." He held it out to me. "The pilgrim's badge that belonged to my grandfather's grandfather." I sucked in my breath. I had never seen this before. "Others have belongings of his—a ring, his inkwell. I requested this, although my cousins scoffed. 'Why do you want that old thing?' they asked. Badges are not worth much, but somehow I liked it. Do you know what pilgrims usually do with them?"

"Keep them as treasures as he did, of course." That seemed obvious.

He laughed. "Oh, no. Not a bit. Most pilgrims found a good high bridge, and away with them!" He flung his arm, a tight grip on the badge, to demonstrate. I recoiled in surprise. "They toss them into the river and make a wish to the saint."

"If I had a badge such as this, I would never pitch it to the river!" I said defiantly. "I would skip the wish and keep the badge."

My father threw back his head and laughed. "You are the real treasure, Lovey."

"But that's what our ancient grandfather did too, didn't he? Else it would not be here."

"Just so. He was a practical man and treasured it, as you say, more than the wish. It certainly had value to *him*. It inspired his use of *escallops* on our family arms."

I leaned in to get a closer look at the grey molded metal. "What's it made of?"

"It's a mixture of lead and tin, so she's solid." He placed it in my hands, letting me gauge its weight.

"How did the bones of St. James get to Spain, anyway?" I asked, still holding the badge. I liked the feel of it. It felt sturdy—dependable somehow.

"Well, after the death of Jesus, his Apostles went around the world to spread the Gospel. You know that," he began.

I nodded.

"They say St. James went to Spain but did not have much luck converting *those people*."

"William!" my mother broke in.

He laughed. "Well, all right. But it was not a roaring success. James returned to Jerusalem, where Herod beheaded him, making James the first martyred Apostle. His followers spirited his body away to a ship, setting off for Spain to bury him in secret."

My father lit his pipe as he spoke, lowering his voice. "Angels guided the voyage, or so they say, because a ship was waiting for them and made the journey at supernatural speed. His followers placed the body in a tomb on a hillside. Eight hundred years later, a hermit was alone in a field at night when he had a vision of a great milky light with one large star ringed by smaller ones. Perhaps God was directing him to something, the hermit thought. But to what? He followed the light to a cave. The next morning he told some monks about it, and they returned to dig. When they did, they found the bones of St. James and his two disciples."

I made a face. "Father," I said, an eyebrow raised skeptically. "Bones are bones. How did they know they belonged to St. James?"

"A right fair question! Bones are bones, 'tis true. But *these* bones," he said, leaning in to me, "had a scroll buried with them declaring them the body of St. James. The Spanish made a shrine there, and it became second only to the Holy Land itself for pilgrimage. The field and the town the Spanish now call *Composé*-*tela,* meaning *field of stars*—the Spanish believe St. James protects them specifically, but I say this—the Apostles of our Lord protect all Christian men. No one shall convince me otherwise."

He continued, "So that's why on July 25, St. James Day, children use cockle-shells to make shrines, even in England, to honor James and Compostela. *San Tiago,* the Spanish call him. Of course, King Henry forbade pilgrimages to Catholic sites, but we have this badge to remind us of the days when we *could* travel there. Aye, it is quite a relic. Also a reminder of a bloody time in our history, when we became Anglican and no longer Catholic."

The Phippens were staunchly Protestant. Actually, they didn't so much care about the brand of religion. They simply wanted freedom to worship as they chose. That let Catholicism out, and Puritanism was too starched in its beliefs for their tastes. The Phippens said, in effect, "We have an English Bible now. Let us read it and get on with it! God will direct our paths."

My great-great-uncles had paid dearly for their support of the Protestant cause. King Henry's men brought them to the dreaded Star Chamber to answer for their actions. The Star Chamber was miserable, an inquisition, and Henry's men determined the punishments. Its purpose was to serve the King's whims, not to serve justice.

"Your uncle Will stood up for his brothers George and Kit when they got called to the Chamber, didn't he, Father?"

"He did. He was around fifty and an alderman when he stood on behalf of his brothers, who were Gospel ministers. Uncle George and Uncle Kit held services in private, which was illegal. Church services then, as now, had to be officially Anglican. Uncle Will's testimony may have shortened his brothers' sentences—but it did not keep them out of prison. Kit lost all his possessions and went to prison in 1533. They released him three years later, but he died just after that."

"What about your grandfather? Did they call him to the Star Chamber too?"

"No, he was younger than his brothers and out on the sea, traveling about. He lived his beliefs but never felt called to preach. When he returned to Dorset, he made his living as a merchant here. I remember him—I was about your age when he died. He talked about faraway places, letting me climb on his ship the *Seawynd* and ring her bell. That set my eyes on the ocean, just as it had my father. My grandmother and several of her sons died onboard and they buried them at sea. It's not an easy life," he added, looking at me. "But there is something about riding that ocean—the journey and the return. St. Augustine said all life was a pilgrimage," he added suddenly.

Now I knew I was confused. "But pilgrimages are forbidden. You said so."

He smiled, but this time I thought his eyes looked sad. "That kind of pilgrimage is rare now. First, the Black Death put an end to those traveling the *Camino*—too many falling sick in towns along the way. Then the Reformation ended most remaining pilgrimages. Why, when Sir Francis Drake landed at Corunna a few years ago, the Spanish hid the bones of St. James, so we don't even know where they are now." He looked mysterious. "But some things about pilgrimage will always remain. That's what St. Augustine meant."

"Some things? You mean like this badge?"

"The badge is only a symbol of something greater, a larger pilgrimage we all take. It is neither Protestant *nor* Catholic. Do you understand, Lovey?"

I did not. "If life is a pilgrimage, where are we going?"

"That is for you to figure out. Perhaps you are not traveling at all. Perhaps you are." Now his eyes were twinkling again. He held the badge so it caught the light of the candle.

Dream or Ghost of a Dream
May 1592

Is it a dream or ghost
Of a dream that comes to me,
Here in the twilight on the coast,
Blue cinctured by the sea?

~ Frank Dempster Sherman

O f course, when supper was over I had not forgotten to ask about his journey. He saw the expectant look and knew what I was after.

He studied me for a moment. "A story? Do you never tire of them, Joan?" I
didn't, and well he knew that!

Again, I saw his pensiveness. "This is a different kind of tale," he began
slowly. "It's actually a dream I had on ship." I saw my mother glance up as she
cleared pewter trenchers from the table. I leaned forward. He had my attention
with this most unusual of openings. Was this part of the story? When would he
tell me about the pirates he had seen, the storms off the Irish coast?

"Feels good to be home," he said, warming his hands around the candle.

"What was your dream?" I asked, eager for him to begin.

"Oh, that." His voice was casual. "In my dream, the sky was dark and there were
black waves wildly lashing the ship, as though the sea were angry. It was a tempest as
few men have ever seen. It was so vivid," he said, almost to himself. "Suddenly,
across the bow came a large wave, roaring over the main deck, over the top—over
me. I knew it had come for me, that I should not survive it. Then I awoke."

Now my heart, so light earlier, nearly stopped in horror. This was a *real*
dream, not part of a story. I had not expected this! I covered my mouth. "It's
only a dream, though, Father. It doesn't mean anything." I was desperate for him
to agree with me.

He did not.

"Joanie, I was born to the sea, and to the sea I'll perish. That is what the
dream signifies." He said this matter-of-factly, as though discussing nothing

more than the evening's mutton. "Don't waste grief on me when the time comes. I'll be in good hands." I could not understand his placid tone.

I put my arms around his neck. "Don't go back, then! Stay and be a land merchant. You don't have to return to the sea. You don't...owe it anything." I felt my logic was sound and expected him to agree.

He shook his head. "You can neither defeat destiny nor escape it, Joanie. You know that. Providence is the Lord's will made manifest. If He wills that I rest in the ocean as my uncles and grandmother do, then so be it." He shrugged. "Where the hand of God leads me, the hand of God saves me."

Now I was confused. "So you will not die in the ocean after all? You feel God will spare you?"

"No, I will die in the sea." He said this simply, without emotion. "But the hand of God is not the hand of misfortune, even when it seems so. Even in death, it rescues. It will pluck my soul from the sea and deliver it to another realm. There is no queen there, but a King. I'm ready for His Kingdom when He's ready for me. *Let me take the wings of the morning, and dwell in the uttermost parts of the sea. Yet thither shall thine hand lead me, and thy right hand hold me.*"

This was his oft-quoted Psalm 139. We had a well-loved and well-used Geneva Bible, which Mother kept on the Bible table near the stairs. Father read this verse often, saying it was the mariner and explorer's promise.

"So you see, Joanie, there is nothing to fear, for *uttermost parts of the sea* refers to its depths as well as its reaches. All must die, and if my body is to rest in the ocean, I'm content with that—so long as my spirit rests with God. Mariners often quote Thomas More: *He who hath no grave is covered in sky.*"

Again, I noticed the intensity of his deep blue eyes. Their light calmed me, even now. My father was devout, so I believed his eyes reflected God's presence itself, if that were possible. His serenity seemed complete.

"Is there pie for dessert? A treat after too many sea biscuits, too much salted pork?" he added with a broad smile at my mother. She had a confused expression and stood, still holding the trenchers. She appeared about to say something, but instead replied weakly, "Indeed, pie for you, Sir." Her light tone sounded forced, but it deepened the smile on my father's face.

The lines about his eyes were like drawings the wind had made, as he set his compass for the Isle of Portland, or Ireland, Scotland, or France, I thought.

There would be no talking him out of the sea.

On Yonder Island, Not to Rise

March 1594–November 1596

Where Portland from her top doth over-peere the maine,
Her rugged front empal'd on every part with rocks...
~ Michael Drayton

The star-filled seas are smooth to-night
From France to England strown;
Black towers above the Portland light
The felon-quarried stone.

On yonder island, not to rise,
Never to stir forth free,
Far from his folk a dead lad lies
That once was friends with me.
~ Alfred Edward Housman

Still, once I knew about his dream, I feared for him whenever he was out to sea. But as weeks, then months and even years went by, I decided that my father, who knew so much about so many things, might be mistaken about this. After all, it seemed out of character for him. Could a dream foretell? This practical man seemed to think it could. I hoped fervently it could not.

The spring of 1594 was to be the last that my mother and I gathered herbs together, for she developed a coarse and rasping cough with ague the following March while Father was at sea.

Anxiously, I fumbled with the apothecary jars in the cupboard. Why couldn't I remember what to use? I felt panicked as her fever raged. My mother had worked so hard to train me...

Weakly, and between phlegm-filled coughs, she called, "Licorice and comfrey for the lungs, lemon balm and marsh-mallow for the ague. And syrup of horehound."

Of course, of course.

Then she added, "Also, chamomile for you, to calm." I saw she smiled. Still teaching.

Spring without Mother was not the same. At first, I tried to ignore the garden. Not this year. I could not venture there so soon. The bulbs my father brought from his latest voyage lay idly in their sack. He had received at port the news she was gone.

Soon, though, the weeds thickened and the flowers, when they arrived, looked as forlorn as I felt, choked and untended.

This was not the way it should be.

At last, I doffed her straw hat with determination, lifted down her basket, and placed the bulbs inside. With a new set in my walk, I pushed open the back door and faced the garden. Flowers, herbs, and vegetables—they were my responsibility now.

Her passing left only my father and me, but within a year, he had married a widow named Latatia. Lattie, though good-hearted, could not replace my mother, but she was kind enough to recognize that. In turn, I tried to be mindful of her and her rightful place in our home.

Novembers in Melcombe Regis were always bleak, rainy and windy, as though the sun left us to sail to Spain. Yet—and perhaps it was the events that made it seem this way—November of 1596 was wetter, colder, and more dismal than ever I could remember. No fire could warm the house or dry it out, it seemed.

I was home alone when the sheriff pounded the door with the news—a ship had gone down in the Portland Race and they believed it to be the *Anne*.

The Isle of Portland sat off the coast of Melcombe Regis, at the bottom of Dorset. Portland was a craggy, ugly place, but its natives were smitten with it and few ever left, marrying only other Portlanders. We called them *slingers* because they pitched rocks at strangers to keep us away. Most of all, they were famous looters. Sometimes they helped the victims of shipwrecks before rummaging for goods—sometimes not. And Portland was the most dangerous coast in all England, so these were a people accustomed to wreckage. I wondered if my father had needed help, or if they had simply scavenged his possessions like so many buzzards.

22

The Queen's business had taken him to Portland that year.

Though small, the island was strategically important to England. A natural fortress, its rocky shores guarded the Dorset coastline and provided a place to watch for enemy ships. The Crown knew Spain or France would love to capture Portland, as then the island's advantages turned to nightmares for the English. Therefore, sixty or so years before my father went down, King Henry VIII built a castle there, fearing Catholic marauders would invade England and desiring solid protection on that island.

He was right about the Catholic invaders, but they did not come when he expected but nearly fifty years later in 1588. I was eight when the Spanish Armada came to the coast near Melcombe to invade England. We were able to keep the Spanish from reaching shore and assaulting us by land. We fought them in the sea and won, to the astonishment of all Europe. The Armada was the largest, strongest navy in the world. With one thousand men and 130 ships, they cut a swath seven miles wide across the sea—a fearsome sight, to be sure. How afraid we felt, how much we needed the protection of God. And how He smiled on us and struck them with terrible storms.

If our victory surprised Queen Bess, she did not show it. She had expected the hand of God to guide us to *gloriana*—and so apparently, it had. It was clear to us that God favored our newly Protestant nation, and the Spanish King could not force us to convert back to Catholicism.

In the summer of 1596, eight years after the Armada invasion, the Queen sent an expedition to ransack the port of Cadiz, Spain. It went well, but the effect was akin to putting a stick up a hornet's nest and banging it around. Now the Queen thought it prudent to make doubly sure the Isle of Portland was well fortified.

My father received a warrant to carry goods for improvements to the fifty-year-old fort. On return trips, he brought Portland stone or wool back to the mainland. He had done this for several months without incident, though he was aware of the treacherousness of the rocks—the dreaded coastline.

"You know what color the rocks are on that island, Joanie?" my father said to me between runs.

"Grey, aren't they?"

"Ah, that's not nearly descriptive enough. They are *dead-Spaniard*—that *is* in the grey family, but perhaps with just a slight ruddiness." My father's eyes crinkled as he said it.

Dead-Spaniard had an eerie ring to it. It suggested to me the windswept reaches, the crosscurrents, the uneven depths, the sudden storms—and the rocks. All these made mariners fear Portland. Sailors steered by sighting the castle, but kept a respectful distance from shore. My father made light of the crossings, but I knew he would be glad to start other runs soon. In fact, he was itching to return to Ireland.

He took pride in this mission, though—helping protect all England from Spanish invasion. In truth, we all felt the Spanish were whipped dogs, but one could never tell. Sometimes even a whipped dog used its last strength to attack.

The run Father began on Friday, November 22, was to be his last to Portland for the winter. It was simply too dangerous even for a seasoned mariner like himself. The weather did not appear overly menacing, and he expected to be home in a week or so.

"One more run, Joanie, and I am done!" he said as he departed, blue eyes shining.

"God be with you," I murmured, and he replied solemnly, "He always is."

The storm blew up in the early hours of Sunday, November 24, windy gusts driving my father's ship onto the Portland rocks. The sea always gives up its dead, the islanders say. Soldiers stationed there found the bodies of my father and his eleven crewmen near the wreckage of his ship, which lay, battered and skeletal, at the shoreline.

Because they died honorably in service to the Queen, the men received a full military burial, which meant my brothers and I could not attend. They placed my father in a lead coffin, like some cold metal seashell, and dropped the caskets overboard at sea.

Twelve cannon blasts sounded, one for each lost life.

With a cloak wrapped about me in a vain attempt to stay warm, I walked to the harbor the morning of his burial. At fifteen, I had lost my mother and now at sixteen my father, causing something inside me to go very, very numb. Had it only been a few years before that we had gardened and woven stories together by firelight? I was not prepared to make my way alone so soon.

Finding a black scallop shell, I impulsively picked it up and pitched it as far as I could across the water, out to sea.

"Godspeed to you in your journeys," I whispered as it vanished from view.

My Scallop-Shell of Quiet

December 1596

Give me my scallop-shell of quiet,
My staff of faith to walk upon,
My scrip of joy, immortal diet,
My bottle of salvation,
My gown of glory, hope's true gage,
And thus I'll make my pilgrimage.

~ Sir Walter Ralegh

"Your father wanted you to have this," Lattie said to me several weeks after my father died. She pulled something out of a little drawer. The pilgrim's badge?

I looked at her in surprise. "But, Mother Lattie, this is a family heirloom. It should go to one of my brothers—surely not to me, a youngest daughter."

Lattie smiled and pushed it toward me again. "No, no—it is for you. Your father specifically asked me to give it to you should something happen to him." Here we both turned our eyes to the floor. She added, "Your brothers will receive far more in terms of property, but this token is something he thought you would appreciate. And I am sure you know its story. He enjoyed so much telling you the old tales." Her eyes were wistful. I felt a sudden surge of love for Lattie. My father had made a wise choice in marrying her.

I gave her a hug, one hand still clutching the badge. "You are a dear soul. If I have never said it, thank you for all your kindnesses since my mother died." One thought occurred to me. "But why me? Why not my brothers who will carry on the family name?"

She looked a bit puzzled before replying, "Your father said he had a…a feeling about you. About you being your own sort of pilgrim, about a journey. He said he made a point of telling you about his grandfather's pilgrimage, because the Spirit led him to do so. You asked, and he felt that was significant." She did not seem to understand the words any more than I did.

"Did he say anything more?"

"Aye." She stopped, collecting his words. "I believe he said, 'Tell her we are all pilgrims in a sense, going wherever the hand of God leads us. We never know what our journey will be, what path we are to follow. The Word is a lamp we follow with trust. Joan will take the winding path in ways she may not expect. I've tried to teach her this. Remind her, though, Lattie,' he said to me." Latatia finished. "And so I have honored his request."

"If I am to sojourn, I sojourn in Dorset. I love my harbor home," I said defiantly. In truth, I was not sure whom I was defying.

Lattie gazed at me a moment, and then said, "Providence may have other ideas for you. Your father was a very religious man and he seemed to have some…insight. He would not have said it if he did not feel impelled somehow."

I closed my hand around the badge with sudden trepidation. *I do not want to go*, I thought. *I do not want to go*. Then it struck me. I had no idea *where it was* I didn't want to go.

All in My Youth and Prime
March 1599–March 1600

I wish the Queen of England would write to me in time
and send me to some regiment all in my youth and prime.
~ The Rock of Bawn, traditional ballad

T om Reynolds was a distant cousin of mine with dark hair and freckles and
eyes with a shimmer that reminded me of a pixie, or piskie as the Cornish
called these magical beings. Now, I knew not what a pixie looked like, but if I
ever glimpsed one, I imagined he'd have Tom's eyes—an upward turn to the
edges, a sparkle, a dance of mischief. You couldn't help but love a man with eyes
like that. I did.

Tom and I married in the spring of 1599 before he departed for Irish soldiering duties. Soon he would return on leave with other relatives, all soldiers,
including my oldest brother Jack, Sam Jordan, and Will Peirce. Sam was my
mother's first cousin, while Will and my father were second cousins. We were all
blood, though it did run a bit thin through cousins and cousins of cousins.

Marriage we understood to be an alliance between families. The bond between the Phippen, Peirce, Reynolds, and Jordaine families went back
hundreds of years. We were an extended family linked multiple ways, like
threads on a spider web. Weave enough threads, and the web would with-
stand tragedy of every sort.

The New Year—and in fact the new century—rang in with huge celebra-
tions in Melcombe Regis and all across England, still in the glory days of Queen
Bess. I listened to the pealing bells and festivities outside my door with anticipa-
tion. I could not wait for Tom to get home, although I was not sure when that
would be.

I nearly fainted when he appeared at the door that March day.
"You're home!" I threw my arms around him, and he lifted me up.

"Uh, Joanie, I don't want to be rude but you are a mite heavier than when I left in the fall. You must have enjoyed pork and pease porridge and all the good things from your garden. And you are a lovely lass, with your cheeks so full and rosy." His smile was genuine.

"Well, Tom, there is another thing that thickens a woman's waist very quickly."

"Goose?"

I rolled my eyes. I did love the man, but he could be dense as a lilac thicket sometimes.

"Goose? You're a goose. I meant a baby!" I said.

"A baby? Is it so? When is he due? I mean, when are you due? Wait 'til I tell the fellows in my regiment!"

"We're expecting in the summer, perhaps the end of July or beginning of August." Now that he was home, I could let myself feel the excitement I had carefully restrained through the winter.

Tom grabbed me again, his face lit with joy. "A baby—me to be a father! A splendid start to the new century," he cried ebulliently. Then he added, "Do you have ideas for names?"

"Well," I said slowly. "If it's a boy, I would like him to be Thomas like you. And if it's a girl, I'd call her Cecily after my grandmother Cecily Jordaine, if it pleases you."

He kissed me and said, "It pleases me. You please me. And a new baby pleases me most of all!"

Between the Crosses, Row on Row

June–July 1600

Courage, boys, 'tis one to ten,
But we return all gentlemen
All gentlemen as well as they,
Over the hills and far away.
Over the Hills and O'er the Main,
To Flanders, Portugal and Spain,
The Queen commands and we'll obey
Over the Hills and far away.
~ Traditional English Ballad

In Flanders fields the poppies blow
Between the crosses, row on row
That mark our place; and in the sky
The larks, still bravely singing, fly
Scarce heard amid the guns below.
~ John McCrae

om's regiment, led by Sir Thomas Gates, was now in Flanders fighting alongside Holland's Maurice of Nassau. The Netherlands were trying desperately to maintain their Protestant independence against another Spanish Catholic invasion. English mercenary musketeers such as Tom provided the perfect manpower.

He had written me in June, telling me all about this new offensive, adding that he expected his company to go to Flanders soon. He added some surprising news.

I have been dreaming lately about coming home to be a merchant. A life by the hearth! I think I should like that. What would you say to the babe having a father nearby, not off battling Spanish pirates in this wet country?

29

What did I think of it? I knew what I thought. A hearthside dream, warm and bright like his face. Sweet, as the babe would be. My heart fluttered in the hope of it. How right the 1600s were beginning!

Will Peirce's name was scrawled on the outside of a letter which arrived from Flanders in July. Strange, I thought. I had not expected a letter from Tom's comrade, my cousin Will. Perhaps Tom was returning soon. I ripped open the seal to see the words I most dreaded. *"...not coming home...valiant to the last...an honor to the regiment...spoke so highly of you...excited about little Tom or Cecily...most sincere sympathy....Your brother Jack...same battle at Nieuwpoort...terrible loss..."* Jack too. Jack too.

My mind darted in blind grief, picturing first Tom's face then Jack's smile, so much like my father's. It settled at last on Tom, unable to take in the loss of both and needing to focus on the one that affected me most directly.

I dropped the letter to the floor, a hand upon my belly. I was barely twenty, soon to be a mother, and my husband was not coming home. I felt myself grow dizzy with nausea, as I realized Tom would never see his own child.

I rushed to a chamber pot and vomited again and again, 'til there was nothing left inside me. Except my baby, which gave a kick as though reminding me she was there. "I know you are, little one," I said quietly. I dropped into a chair. "It will be just the two of us for a while." I was young and certain to remarry, when I felt ready. But I would need a little time.

The flowers waved in my backyard; the robins perched here and there. All the natural world, it seemed, celebrated the new year, this bright era of the seventeenth century. All but me, that is.

My heart was back in the old one, mourning my boy with the pixie eyes.

Under an English Heaven

September 1600

If I should die, think only this of me:
That there's some corner of a foreign field
That is for ever England. There shall be
In that rich earth a richer dust concealed....

And laughter, learnt of friends; and gentleness,
In hearts at peace, under an English heaven.

~ Rupert Brooke

September rains. The grey matched my spirit the day Will Peirce and Sam Jordan came calling.

I had been expecting them.

The two soldiers looked grim, wiping the mud from their boots in the foyer and then joining me in the great room. Sam had a sack, which he dropped beside his chair.

The babe slept in a cradle nearby, so that I could hear her when she wakened.

"This is Cecily. Is that right?" Will asked softly, walking over to the cradle. "Tom told us you had names picked out. He was excited either way, boy or girl. I'm sorry he..." Will's voice trailed off. He shook his head. "It's not right that he never got to see his daughter. You had such a loss in both at once—Tom and Jack." Will's expression bore deep sympathy.

Sam stepped over by Will and squatted near the cradle. "Hello, there, little babe. Hello." Cecily, sleeping, made a cooing sound and smacked her lips. They were tiny and pink, like a rose set into her round cheeks.

Sam stood and both men cast their eyes to the floor. There was a moment of silence, so I gestured for them to have a seat. We had three chairs and each of us chose one quietly, so as not to disturb the baby.

Sam felt obliged to explain a little more. I tried not to flinch while listening. "Maurice sent us all to Nieuwpoort, in Flanders, where dens of Spanish pirates

31

raid Dutch ships in the North Sea. We had hundreds of English musketeers on the north flank on the beach, along with eleven thousand Dutch infantry and riders in the center and on the south flank, going against the Spanish *tercios*." I knew enough to understand the implication—the *tercios* were highly skilled pike and musket formations, both dreaded and respected by all European armies.

Sam continued, "Maurice put the Spanish in a position where they'd have to squint into the afternoon sun and the sand would blow in their eyes. His chaplain prayed for Protestant victory, right in front of the troops. Despite our losses..." His voice caught on the word. "Despite our losses we drove the Spanish Hapsburgs back. 'Tis a rare feat to drive the Spanish backward on land. This one battle may have secured Dutch independence."

Was that supposed to make me feel better? That Tom and Jack's loss were not in vain?

"We wanted to pay our respects to you, Joan, and to let you know how much Tom loved you. His death was very honorable, as was Jack's," Will said.

That was enough, and my eyes welled up. "Would that it had been a dishonorable life than an honorable death so soon!" Where had that come from? I had not meant to say it.

"Well." Both men looked away uneasily.

"I'm sorry, Will, Sam. Will, I do appreciate your...your very kind and thoughtfully written letter." Was I mistaken, or did he color slightly? It could not have been an easy letter to write. "I thought we had our whole lives in front of us. I was not expecting this. Tom was charmed; he was charming. Maybe I just thought he would *charm* his way through every battle."

"The fault wasn't his. He did everything he could," Will said. "He was planning to come home to stay because he thought he had the prize of Melcombe in you."

Now it was I that blushed slightly.

"Oh, there's one other thing," Will said. "Tom told us he planned to bring you some special Dutch flowers when he returned home next."

"He said you kept a fine garden," Sam put in.

Will looked a little shy. "So we took the liberty of bringing you some bulbs. They're called *tulips*, and the Dutch are enchanted with them."

"Tulips?"

"We're not much into flowers ourselves..." Will began. In spite of myself, I couldn't help being amused by the thought of these two soldiers choosing bulbs for me. "But they come in all colors. Did you know the Dutch have even managed to get them speckled and striped?" Will finished earnestly. "We got you the brightest, most cheerful ones we could find."

"The best!" Sam said enthusiastically, as though speaking of a new matchlock musket. He obviously felt badly for upsetting me.

"You're so very thoughtful," I said, touched. Tulips! I wondered what they looked like.

The baby began to stir, and the gentlemen said they should take leave so I might care for her.

"Thank you for all you've done. I know you have little time home and your visit means much to me," I told them. "I do appreciate the...information. Cecily will want to know one day."

"We're all cousins," Will said. "We are of the same blood line, and it's a good one. I have faith in you to carry on. And as for the babe—" He stole a glance at Cecily. "There is yet another fine generation, up and coming. The future is there, in that cradle."

"A fine future in her indeed!" Sam added. Sam was red and solid and even his words had a solid sound to them.

"She has his eyes," I said wistfully. I saw them opening, dark with a slight upward turn. Little pixie eyes.

"May we check on you from time to time?" Will asked.

"Of course. I'm obliged to you for remembering me." I gave each of my cousins a quick hug, shut the door behind them, and went to our daughter—my daughter—who was now squirming.

"It is you and I, Cecily. I hope we two women have the fight in us we need to get through."

Cecily held her fists near her chin, and our eyes met.

Wherever Sorrow is, Relief Would Be

December 1600–May 1601

Wherever sorrow is, relief would be:
If you do sorrow at my grief in love,
By giving love your sorrow and my grief
Were both extermined.

~ William Shakespeare, *As You Like It*

True to their word, both Sam and Will called on me whenever they were home from Lowlands duty. Sam was married to Frances, a woman I knew slightly, and their first child had arrived not long before Cecily.

Will, himself not married, took special interest in how Cecily and I fared. Sam lived in Melcombe Regis as I did, but Will was from Wiveliscombe, in Somerset, the county next to Dorset. I appreciated the effort he made to visit me, but he assured me that his ship landed at the Port o' Melcombe anyway. Eyeing the town one day, he said, "I do believe I could be comfortable here on the edge of the Narrow Sea."

I smiled and said, "I certainly am. This harbor town has always been my home, and I hope to have no other."

One thing I asked of him when I knew him better. "You have training as a barrister at Gray's Inn." Gray's Inn was one of four Inns of the Court. Will had studied there before going off to fight. "Why do you not pursue law?"

He shrugged. "I am a soldier at heart, although perhaps one day that will change. I am interested in the law, but also in the strategy of battle. England's future is beyond the realms of her borders. She must defend against the Spanish and the Catholic threat, and she must find new territories. It is an exciting time in which to live, Joan."

All I heard was *I am soldier*. Were all of these men just *soldiers at heart?* I wondered.

Each trip, Will faithfully produced a sack of tulip bulbs for me. "I'm collecting all the varieties I can find," he said proudly.

34

Once he brought Cecily a Dutch wooden doll and surprised me with two Chinese porcelain wine cups, white with festive blue lines. Another time he gave me something else I would long treasure.

"See what everyone is talking about?" he said, holding out a book. He seemed very pleased with himself. "It's John Gerard's *Herball, or Generall Historie of Plants.*"

I sucked in my breath. Gerard! I had heard of his work. "Wouldn't my mother have loved this," I said softly, setting it on the table and flipping its leaves. "Remedies, folklore, descriptions—and lovely prints of the plants, so I can see what each one looks like!" I was impressed at Will's thoughtfulness and his belief in my ability to learn from such a distinguished volume.

"Your specialty," he said. "It seems to me that the knowledge of remedies is a great help to a family." I was still admiring the bright pictures of flowers I'd heard of but had never seen when Will remarked casually, "I was wondering if you'd like to attend a play with me Saturday. A company of actors is touring the countryside and will be in town then."

In truth, I had missed certain things, and the idea of an outing appealed to me. "Aye, that does sound pleasant, Will. But what shall I do with Cecily?"

There was a sparkle in his eyes when he replied, "I'm sure Sam and Frances wouldn't mind keeping her for you so we could go."

Sam and Frances! "You've thought this out, haven't you? Have you already asked them?"

He cleared his throat a little shyly. "Yes, and it does seem they're amenable to the idea."

I had to admit, this soft-spoken gentleman, my cousin, was growing on me. By the time we'd finished seeing Mr. Will Shakespeare's *As You Like It* on the village green, I had agreed to become his wife.

The Sword, the Horse, the Shield
May 1602

A new mistress now I chase,
The first foe in the field;
And with a stronger faith embrace
A sword, a horse, a shield.

~ Richard Lovelace

"Will, no!"

"Joan, this is the best opportunity available."

"More mercenary work?"

"I am a soldier. You knew that when you married me."

"Soldiers!" I slapped my hand on the table, startling Cecily. I turned away and covered my eyes.

He came behind me, touching my shoulder. He seemed surprised by my tears.

"It's just that I...don't want to lose you, too." I pleaded with my eyes. Perhaps if he saw my distress...

"Joan, you will not lose me," he said deliberately.

"How can you say that? Tom thought he would retire to the hearth, a merchant!"

"Tom's death was sad, tragic—a good man and a solid soldier. But we can't shrink from life because of what happened to him. Many's the good man that died, but many more's the good Englishman who has not. We must think to the latter. We're in God's hands—our future is only to trust in Him."

He was right, I knew. His words rang eerily similar to those of my father.

"It's just that..." I started but did not finish.

"Just that, what?"

"It's just that you are soon to be a father. I would like this child to know you."

Will's expression was priceless. This was not the way I had meant to tell him. However, now that we were making such decisions, he must know.

36

He hugged me, and we sat on the window seat together. "I will return home well before my child is born. I promise you."

Will was true to his word, returning home on leave in October of 1602 when the baby, Jack, was born. He was determined that he should live to see his son grow up.

Yet there was another card fate played on us.

A Thoroughfare Full of Woe
October 1602–October 1603

This world tis but a thoroughfare full of woe,
And we been pilgrims passing to and fro.
~ Geoffrey Chaucer

Ring a ring of roses,
A pocket full of posies,
Atishoo, atishoo,
We all fall down.

~ Rhyme describing the plague

L ittle Jack grew suddenly ill as autumn arrived in 1603. He had just learned to say a few words and to walk but suddenly was too weak to even pull himself up.

The Black Death had been racing through London and some other large towns that year. I feared the worst when the fever came on him, as there was a minor outbreak going on in Melcombe just then. As a town, we were not immune—no one anywhere seemed to be—but it never hit us as hard as the crowded cities. In fact, story was that the plague originally entered England through the port of Melcombe in the middle of the 1300s. On and off for 250 years we had lived under its grisly threat. When the merchant-tailor and Mrs. Collier down the street both succumbed to the plague, I held my breath and prayed God would not take either of my children—or me, because Will was away fighting and I was all they had.

For a few days, the baby suffered with an ague so severe he was limp. Poor drenched little boy. I put rags to his forehead and frantically flipped pages of Gerard's herbal book.

He recommended sorrel: *Sorrell doth undoubtedly cool and mightily dry; but because it is sour it likewise cutteth tough humors....The leaves of Sorrell taken in good quantity, stamped and strained into some Ale, and a posset made thereof, cooleth the sick body, quencheth the thirst, and allayeth the heat of such as are troubled with a pestilent fever, hot ague, or any great inflammation within.*

To make a posset, I knew I needed to use hot sweetened milk, curdle it with ale, and then spice it with sorrel. With relief, I realized I had sorrel on hand.

I supported Jack's head, so he could sup of it. His eyes drooped from weakness, and as he drank, I prayed.

When the first red boil appeared, I panicked and scrawled a note to my brother Thomas:

My loving brother, I pray you help me. Baby Jack has taken very ill. Please keep Cecily until I send for her, this I beg. She herself is well, pray God she remains so. If I should die, please raise her until Will returns. You are a Godsend for your mercy. May God bless your household. I remain your devoted sister, Joan.

I dared not mention—even to my brother—that I suspected Little Jack had plague. I did not want the authorities to lock us in our home with a red cross painted on the door.

I gave a neighbor boy three pence to take Cecily with the note to my brother's home. Perhaps it was not too late to protect her from catching it. Cecily, just three and understanding only that the baby was sick, obligingly said goodbye to her little brother.

It was the last time she saw him.

I watched helplessly as my son vomited blood for three days until he died.

Dutifully, after his burial, I scrubbed the house. I opened the shutters, letting in as much fresh air as possible. I burned his clothes, his bedding, and his toys.

Within a day, it was as though he never existed.

I pulled out my scallop shell badge and studied it. *Thou shalt not fear the arrow that flies by day, and no plague shall come nigh thy dwelling,* said the Psalms, but plague had come near—in fact, into—my dwelling. All I knew was that by twenty-three, I had lost my parents, a husband, a son, and a brother. I slammed the badge back into its box.

Then I lay down and cried for three days.

Every Tear Should Turn a Mill
December 1603–January 1605

I'll go up on Portland hill,
And there I'll sit and cry my fill.
And every tear should turn a mill.
My love has gone for a soldier.

~ Traditional 17th century ballad

C ecily might have felt I was a different mother than the one she had left behind two months before. When she returned, I was considerably thinner as I had lost all appetite. In fact, the very thought of food sent me into waves of nausea. I still cried a great deal and had done little to lift myself up and start anew.

Despite the lack of food and the plethora of tears, I did not catch the plague. The days were shorter and the nights had grown chill. That meant the plague was likely to wane for another year—perhaps to reappear in the spring or perhaps not. We never knew.

We had lost Queen Bess just months before, and sadness lay over the realm like a burial shroud. The casket with the Queen's effigy draped in purple had rolled forlornly through the streets of London, and crowds wailed before it, or so I heard. The sense of loss was profound and affected every member of the kingdom, even as James VI of Scotland took his new throne. He would now have the title King James I of England as well.

I, for one, thought my heart should burst with all its sadness, the kingdom's loss fueling my own grief. For months, I smiled little. The winter leading to 1604 was the darkest I could recall. Sometimes I cried simply because I could think of nothing else to do.

I found Cecily remarkably perceptive for a small child. "Mama, eat," she said one day, holding up her bread.

"No, Lovey. You eat. Mama's not very hungry." I knew my face was ashen with deep creases beneath my eyes.

40

"Jackie's gone. He's gone with the angels," she said, her eyes filled with concern. Then I realized her concern was not for Jack; it was for *me*. She had every confidence Jack was safe with the angels. I felt a pluck on my heart, touched by her innocent belief. Who was I to doubt such faith? It was my first twinge of hope.

Will was home on Christmas leave, but the air hung heavy with our loss. There felt little to celebrate, although another inkling of recovery came when Cecily brought me a doll she had made. The stitches were crude, but the dark cords for the hair were unmistakable.

"So you won't miss baby Jack so much," she said simply. "See, he's smiling 'cause he's in heaven."

Will and I glanced at each other. Cecily's smile was radiant. I gave her a hug and thought maybe, just maybe, a little of the sadness lifted. After all, God had taken baby Jack but spared Cecily and me, and here was Will safe from the Lowlands fighting once more. Perhaps there were tasks yet undone He had in mind for us. It was important I live and live well, if for no other reason than my daughter needed me. We had not lost both of the children, after all.

"It is lovely, little lass," I said as Will held the child over his head, swinging her around.

In the spring, I learned I was expecting again. Jane, whom we called Janey, arrived in January 1605, and gradually our life resumed its usual rhythms.

Spain called a truce with England, lessening our fears of another Armada invasion, yet the Spanish continued battling in the Lowlands. The Netherlands defied Spain to continue ruling them, and that still provided good work for English mercenaries.

Will and Sam headed back to Terthol, Holland, under the direction of Sir Thomas Gates and his assistant, George Yeardley.

I sighed and prepared to continue raising my children alone. A sailor, I had learned, could not stay long from the sea. And a soldier could not be swayed from battle.

More than four years passed before change blew in like an ocean squall, sudden and unexpected.

The Fruits of Hope
April 1609

Brother, we shall make
Incredible discoveries and inherit
The fruits of hope...
> ~ Charles Langbridge Morgan

I truly think this day, there is not a work
of more excellent hope under the Sun.
> ~ Robert Jonson, *Nova Brittania*

In early April 1609, the two warring countries reached an accord. Spain signed a truce with the Lowlands rebels, agreeing to back off and give the Netherlands their hotly desired independence for twelve years.

But twelve years was too long for a horde of English mercenary soldiers to be unemployed.

The middle of April found Will and Sam and a few of their comrades-in-arms at another set of arms, the Kings Arms Pub in Melcombe Régis.

The Kings Arms sat on the corner of Bay Street and the Main Thoroughfare, close enough to the harbor that salty air drifted in through the doorway and, on less busy days, patrons could hear the seabirds. This day, however, the pub was full, every table and every bench. Many of the men inside were soldiers just returned from Lowlands duty.

Pubs in Melcombe in those days were much as they are even now, dark wood and smoky from the Caribbean tobacco in the gentlemen's pipes. King James himself hated *that stinking weed*, as he called it. He was in the minority, as most other gentlemen were enamored of it. Both Will and Sam loved a good pull on the pipe.

The barman clomped pewter mugs onto the long thick table. The men, shoulder-to-shoulder on benches as they had been shoulder-to-shoulder in battle, toasted one other. They toasted to the end of their long run in Holland with a raucous cheer, and they toasted to their leader, Sir Thomas Gates, whom they could thank for such good soldiering experience. They even toasted Maurice of Naussau for agreeing to a treaty with which he was not wholly pleased. Of course, the mercenaries knew this treaty put them out of work, but every one had no doubt missed home and family in England. Will, for one, was ready to decide where the course of his fate would take him next.

It was soon in coming.

Sam threw a pamphlet down on the table, and announced with his usual flourish, "Gentlemen, I give you Virginia."

I give you Virginia.

And just like that, everything in my world changed. I was not there but heard the story from Will.

"It's not you giving us Virginia, Sam. It's the King. God save the King!" And another round of toasting went up. The soldiers were in a festive mood, and if a rat had run across the wood floor, they probably would've toasted even that.

"God save the King!" they cried together, clinking the pewter ware before taking a swig of beer.

Sam, who had come prepared, gave every man a copy of the broadside, the same one he had slapped so ceremoniously onto the table. *Nova Britannia,* the title read, *Offering Most Excellent fruites by Planting in Virginia. Exciting all such as be well affected to further the same.*

"I say we plant Virginia!"

Virginia: the word fell from the lips of Englishmen more than any other that spring. Virgin-ee-a! The cry went up from the pulpits, neighbors buzzed on street corners, even the butcher asked his customers about it. Boys talked of signing on as indentured servants. Soldiers considered it a career opportunity. Young mothers rocked babies and heard the word: *Virginia.* From every pub and every pulpit, in every conversation, came the question, "They say the King will soon sign a new charter for the Virginia Company. Are you going? Have you signed on? How about your brother, your cousin, your wife? Will you adventure there, or just invest?" Entire companies were signing on: the fishmongers, the grocers, the weavers, the haberdashers. Lords and knights and farmers were investing. Everyone, it seemed, who could pull together twelve shillings, ten pence—the cost of one share—wanted in.

And then there were those who, rather than venturing their money, ventured themselves—seven years of living and working in the colony for one share of stock: a piece of land and part of the profits.

The Virginia Company thrilled to the publicity, because they, of course, had started it. Robert Jonson, the author of *Nova Britannia,* was the son-in-law of Sir Thomas Smythe, treasurer of the Virginia Company.

43

There in the Kings Arms, Will leaned back and stroked his beard. A thoughtful man, not one to do something because others did, he picked up the broadside with one hand, rubbing his chin with the other.

"I say if we go, we go together." Sam squinted around the table at the others. "Here's to God, Gold, and Glory. God's a Protestant Englishman, after all!" Sam was all grins. He knew how to rouse a table to action.

"Aye, 'God, Gold, and Glory!'" cried several of the men, and the mugs flew upward again.

All but Will's, that is. He was still reading.

He shook his head. "I want to think this out," he said at last.

"What's to think out?" That was Henry, a musketeer like Will. "They say this new charter will give men their *own land* after seven years. Fifty acres at a minimum! Where would you get that here?" He looked around the inn at the crowded room as though it symbolized the whole bursting countryside. "Every square inch of England is filling up."

"Why," he continued, "you can't dump a chamber pot out the window without drenching some man's head!" The soldiers laughed, but it was true. Conditions were tight, unsanitary, and miserable, especially in the big cities like London.

"There're no jobs!" Hugh Deale put in, snuffing out his pipe. "What're we old soldiers going to do next? Off to France? More fighting in Ireland? Virginia has all the land we could hope for, so when we're ready to put down roots we can truly *put down roots*. I, for one, am going!"

A cheer went up, followed by more clinking.

"We've scant time to think this over," John Dewbourne was saying. "They're planning to send the expedition out in May, maybe even the *first* of May! We have five weeks, maybe. *Maybe*," he said again for emphasis.

"What's your hesitation, Will? Joan and the young ones? There are women and children aplenty signing on this time. Bring them with you," Sam said, giving his cousin a pat on the back.

Bring them with me...bring them with me.... Will's mind was racing. He did not expect to make a commitment that night, even if the others did.

"Let's see what we got on the positive side," said Hugh. He held out his hand and began ticking off fingers. "There's wood and lots of it. We've got no wood here for burning, much less for shipbuilding!" He was right about that. Creating the large fleet to fight the Armada had taken whole forests down. "And if England doesn't solve the timber issue, we'll be Spain's handmaid before you know it." He drummed his finger with each word as he proclaimed, "No ships, no defense."

"Don't forget jobs," Hugh went on. "We need the work."

"Fish, fowl, fruits, nuts, berries—everyone who's been there says you've never seen such...such *abundance,*" Sam put in. "It's like Eden! And who deserves Eden more than Englishmen? The Spanish?"

"God send bloody King Philip to a miserable grave!" That was Henry again. His brother had perished in the Netherlands, and his father died during the Armada attack. No one at the table hated the Spanish more than he did.

"We need a way through that continent to the East! *Someone* will find the Northwest Passage soon enough. Will it be us or *the Spanish?*" Sam knew what all there did—the spices and teas of India would be lucrative indeed, if Englishmen could procure it themselves. Everyone had a theory as to where that passage was, the northern or southern part of the country, but one thing was certain. Only those planted in Virginia would have a chance of finding it. Sam knew these soldiers thrilled to the adventure of the chase, just as he did.

"Gates says the New World is amazing!" John added. They had all heard Gates's stories of the vastness he had seen when he accompanied Sir Frances Drake to rescue the first colony on Roanoke Island. "He says it; I believe it." Gates's word was gold as far as his men were concerned. "And he's to be the Governor in charge until the actual Governor, Lord De La Warr, comes next year." That was the gossip on the street, anyhow. It seemed credible. Gates had been the first signer of the original charter in 1606 before heading back to action in the Low Countries.

"Say, how many you got there, Hugh?" Henry asked.

"What's it look like? I got four fingers up. Or can't you count that high, Son?" The others laughed and somebody slapped Henry's back.

"Add Gates in charge too," John said again.

"We haven't even started counting yet!" Sam said, pounding his mug for emphasis. "There's iron ore, potash, tar, minerals, sassafras, grapes for wine, flax and hemp, sturgeon, mulberry trees to feed silkworms, and..." Sam was talking so fast he was breathless.

"You've forgotten the most important one, Gentlemen." Will had spoken. He'd been so quiet until then that the others stopped and looked his way. Will's words, always thoughtful, commanded attention by their sparsity.

"Conversion. There are heathen savages who have never seen the light of Christ and never will unless we show them. Word is they worship the devil, yet they are peaceful and follow their kings. *Go ye into all the world and preach the Kingdom of Heaven.* A new King can be theirs. But how will this occur before the Lord's coming unless we do it? We've seen the way of the Spanish! They kill those they would convert, in their brutal way. Englishmen bring an Englishmen's conscience to that New World, as the Romans did to us. We were but savages ourselves then. God will give us the land so that we may bring light to the naturals thereof."

"Protestant light!" Hugh put in.

Will had marked a spot in the broadside and now looked down and read, *"I should say no more but with Caleb and Joshua, the land which we have searched out is a very good land. If the Lord love us, he will bring our people to it, and will give it us for a possession."*

Silence fell upon the table as Sam said, "Hands in for a vote."

Hugh's hand went in first. John reached in and grabbed it, as did Sam and then Henry. All eyes looked at Will. "In?" Sam asked.

Will hesitated, took a moment and reread the line his finger rested on. Virginia sounded very much like Canaan to him.

"In," he said at last, reaching atop the men's hands and grasping the top one.

All raised them, forming a tent of arms and hands above the men's heads and a cheer went up.

"Virginia!" Sam cried. "To the Virginia Adventurers!" and all heartily, but not surprisingly, grabbed their mugs for a toast.

Will, of course, still had to figure out how to tell me about all this.

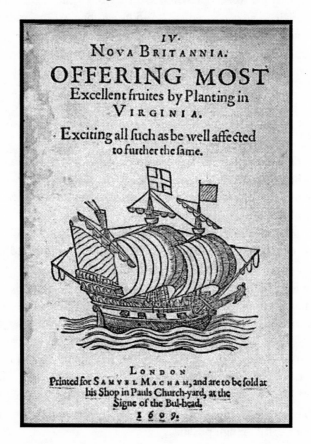

The Steady Trade Winds Blowing
April 1609

...the sleepy tune
Of the quiet voice calling me,
the long low croon
Of the steady Trade Winds blowing.
> ~ John Masefield

The large oak door groaned as Will pushed it open. It was later than I had expected, but I smiled as he came in. I knew how Sam could get Will laughing, and I was glad he had met with his friends from Gates's regiment. How wonderful to have him home for a while! There had been so many years of him off fighting.

He studied me with serious eyes, though he tried to appear nonchalant.

I knew him better than that.

"What is it? Are you all right? How was Sam?" I leaned my head to the side and looked at him. Why did I suddenly feel uneasy?

Will kissed my cheek and sat down. "Sorry I'm late for supper. We all...got into an extended discussion."

"Whatever about? Old battle stories, valor and glory?" I smiled again, searching for a spark of lightheartedness in his expression, but there was none.

"Glory, yes. And my guess is there will be some valor involved, too." He looked away.

I was not used to Will being mysterious and said so.

"Blast, Joan. I am not ready to discuss it yet, and you've pegged me in an instant."

I smiled and shrugged. I hated to let him know reading him was as easy as reading my Bible, or the Book of Common Prayer, or....a broadside posted on every corner.

Suddenly I knew, without knowing how I knew, and I felt my heart sink into my stomach.

Virginia.

Why had I thought God would spare us this decision? I loved my home and my town. My mother lay buried here as well as my infant son. I had never imagined living anywhere else. Or was Will planning to include me? Had he made a final decision yet? I glanced at Janey, just four. Cecily was sitting on the bench with her legs swinging. They did not quite touch the floor. She was spooning her pottage out as carefully as a nine-year-old could.

I walked to where Will sat at the head of the table and said, "Your discussion was about...Virginia, wasn't it?"

He dropped his head and stroked his beard, as he always did when pensive.

"Indeed." Then he looked up at me and said, "I have not formally committed to anyone, haven't signed anything." I felt a surge of relief.

"I have, however, committed to my cousin and friends."

My heart sank again. Will's word was serious business to him. He would not give it, or retract it, lightly.

"Let's have the supper blessing and we can discuss this more once the children are in bed," he said, reaching for my hand.

I sat down wordlessly to the beef pottage that had smelled so good to me earlier.

I was no longer hungry.

Fear | to Fall

April 1609

Fain would I climb, yet fear I to fall.

~ Sir Walter Ralegh, etched in a
windowpane for Queen Elizabeth

If thy heart fails thee, climb not at all.

~ Queen Elizabeth's etched reply

After evening prayers and singing a Psalm together, I tucked Janey and Cecily into the big bed they shared on the second floor. Sometimes I heard them giggling before they fell asleep, but not this night. Cecily seemed to sense the tension between Will and me, the size of the decision, perhaps. She asked no questions and I volunteered nothing. After all, what did I know yet myself?

As I descended the spiral stairs, carved into a corner cove of the great room, I saw Will sitting at the table. A candle burned nearby, and papers lay in front of him. He smoothed them and rested his forehead on his fingers, looking first at the papers, then over toward the window. The harbor was still visible in the light of dusk. His expression was distant and he appeared not to notice me as I entered the room.

He had said we would talk, but I chose instead to leave him to his musing and allow him to approach me when ready. After all, I had guessed his thoughts when he was not yet prepared to discuss the venture. This obviously was not an easy choice for him, and I could almost see him calculating and weighing alternatives in his mind.

He rose, pulled a sheaf of paper and quill from the secretary's drawer and returned to his big armchair at the end of the table.

I sat in the other chair, closer to the fireplace, and took up my mending— the only sounds the rustle of his papers and squeak of my chair as I shifted.

At last, he heaved a sigh, folded the papers, and unrolled a map. He glanced over his shoulder at me. Was he grateful I had not interrupted him? I thought so.

"Joan, I can't think of any reason not to go."

My heart fluttered, and I stood, coming over and seating myself on the bench. I touched the corner of the documents nearest me.

"Well, at least there are no dragons on this map!"

He did not smile at my attempt at a joke. We both remembered the maps of our grandfather's day, every one trailing off into nothingness guarded by dragons. *Beware!* the maps seemed to say. *Here is unknown territory, and beasts of the sea may lay in wait!*

"No dragons, Joan. But much unknown, nonetheless."

"Tell me about Virginia, Will. Tell me why you think we should go." I slipped the "we" in, and he did not correct me.

"It's every good reason in God's earth—land and minerals, medicinal herbs and plants, forests and timber, trading opportunities, even spreading the Gospel to the naturals there. The new charter—and it appears King James will sign it— will give us perhaps fifty acres and a share of all profits and minerals after some seven years there. I am hard-pressed to say what England holds for us with so much offered in Virginia, so much opportunity. The climate is mild and Gates talked endlessly of its size, charm, and abundance. It is teeming with life. We don't even know how big this country is. It could even be..." He hesitated. "It could even be the Promised Land of the Bible."

This startled me. I had never considered that.

"There are those who think so. Reverend Symonds described it at his White Chapel sermon to the Virginia Company. I've been reading a broadside with the text of it, and his words have struck me somehow. He compared Virginia to the land of Canaan flowing with milk and honey. Just as Caleb and Joshua encouraged Israel to go and take possession of Canaan, Englishmen should go to the colony in Virginia, a land brimming with fish and fowl."

His voice was excited now. "See here?" He pulled a broadside from beneath the map and read from it God's commandment to Abram: "*Get thee out of thy Country and from thy kindred and from thy father's house, unto the land that I will show thee. And I will make of thee a great nation, and will bless thee and make thy name great and thou shalt be a blessing. . . and in thee shall all families of the earth be blessed.*" He looked at me searchingly but I could only put my hands to my cheeks. I did not know what to think.

"I cannot get the idea out of my mind that God is providing this land to us just as was promised in the Bible," he continued. "How is it such a vast continent has lain idle for so many millennia when all of Europe is overcrowded? It makes no sense. It sits as though waiting for us to come to it. If so, it is Providence in every way. And if it is Providence, we should trust God to lead us there safely and believe in every good outcome."

Speechless, I looked from him to the papers on the table. He made a convincing case, to be sure. For a moment, all was silence except for the large clock my great-grandfather Jordaine had made. Its rhythmic pendulum seemed mocking, as though egging me to a decision I was not prepared to make.

At last, I said, "So you do think I should come with you?"

"Yes." His answer was firm, without a trace of doubt. I wondered how he could be so certain. I knew several families where the wife and children planned to stay behind, and the husband would send for them later if conditions were good. Why did Will want me to go?

"Help me understand, then, what you are thinking." I was pleased at the evenness of my voice. I would hear this out.

He took a deep breath and then said, "Reading the proposed charter carefully, I see that you too will be allotted land and profits after seven years, the same as a man. That means as a family we would get twice the acreage than if I were to go alone."

"Couldn't I come later and get my acreage then? You could try this and see what you think."

"No, that wouldn't be the most strategic plan. Early adventurers will have more privileges than later ones, according to what Gates and the leaders expect the charter to say. This gives us both the highest chance at all opportunities. It will give us seniority as colonists at James Town. There will be ample work for soldiers such as myself there—but this time you and I will not have the North Sea between us." At last, there was a smile. "Let us not discount your ability to work with healing herbs either, Joan. You can plant us a garden in the settlement. We'll consider carefully what seeds and bulbs to bring."

I thought I understood. "Then you and I and the girls would sail together to the New World." The idea did not sound as frightening suddenly. At least we would be together.

He pursed his lips and gave me that pensive look again. My stomach dropped once more, as I could always tell when he was about to give me news I would not like.

"Joan, you know I love Cecily as my own daughter."

My eyes widened in fear. Cecily! Why was he bringing up her name?

I said cautiously, "Yes. And she adores you. You're the only father she has ever known."

51

"Exactly. She is a wonderful child, bright for a girl, and deserves the best opportunities in life—which James Town could provide her." He said the last words with deliberation. I breathed a sigh of relief. We would all go then.

"…if she waits in England a year."

"What?" I could not believe what he was saying! He was asking me to leave my daughter a continent—an ocean—away?

"Why? She's a good girl and a great help to me with Janey. Oh, she can be a bit of a handful sometimes, but she…"

"Joan, wait. Let me finish."

I glared at him but ceased talking.

"Janey is only four years old, not even close to the age of attainment, of receiving acreage. But Cecily…." He pointed his finger as he spoke. "Cecily is only a year away. Ten-year-olds who sail will receive the same land as an adult and a share of all profits and minerals. This means Cecily herself will inherit—inherit nothing, she will earn—her *own* fifty acres, profits and Company shares. And if she marries a man who is also a shareholder, she will have a fine plot of land. But if she should somehow become a widow or not marry, all these rights and privileges will still be hers, and no one may take them from her! Do you see that holding her back a year could improve the lot of her entire life? We'll use this time to obtain some additional tutoring for her too, which will not be available in a frontier outpost like James Town."

Will had thought this out as only Will would do. He was not only looking toward the best future for himself, but also for Cecily and for me, should we ever find ourselves alone again. It was a security I lacked, but which would have served me well, when Tom died. In Virginia, we would have our own land and our own shares—female or not. My grandmother Thickpenny flashed through my mind with my father's words about opportunities for women as colonial landholders.

"Wait, what about Janey?"

"Janey will have to come. She's not close enough to the cut-off age and won't reach it before the deadline, but that's fine. Cecily, at least, will have benefit of receiving her own land. The charter may at some point change to give it to Janey too. She will undoubtedly have some sort of seniority as an early colonist, however young."

This was a great deal to take in. Still, the thought of receiving my own land, my own fifty acres, of having a share in the Company, was exhilarating.

"How soon?" I asked suddenly.

"Right away. They may sail as early as the first of May, but by the end of May certainly. The Virginia Company is gathering supplies and organizing ships even as we speak. Do you agree, then, that we should go?"

My reply was so swift it startled even me. "Yes. Yes, I think we should go." I scarcely believed the words as they came from my mouth, but here I was agreeing to this. What was I thinking? Was it the correct decision? "I think we should go, but allow me to pray about it." I would go to the harbor and pray tomorrow. That would ease my mind.

Then I considered my girls sleeping soundly together upstairs. One would come. One would stay behind. How would Cecily feel? Would she understand?

Little Jack would never come, but I would not think about that.

The Chiding Sea

April 1609

I heard or seemed to hear the chiding Sea
Say, Pilgrim, why so late and slow to come?
Am I not always here, thy summer home?
Is not my voice thy music, morn and eve?

~ Ralph Waldo Emerson

I walked the beach at Melcombe Harbor with a heavy heart. This place had offered me solace after my father and mother's deaths, and I had walked here often in the months following the deaths of Tom and Little Jack.

The initial thrill of Will's proposition had worn off, and now doubts bombarded me from every side. I did not want to leave Dorset. I had *never* wanted to leave here. The New World—while sounding promising on paper—held terrors all its own. First, we must survive the sea voyage of perhaps ten weeks. Then we did not know exactly what awaited us in Virginia. We could not know for sure the Indians wanted us there. The Virginia Company told us they were gentle. Were they?

Beyond that, I was leaving my friends, my home, my nieces and nephews, the grave of my little son, all that was comforting and familiar in exchange for all that was unknown. I understood Will's reasons, his passion—but what if he was mistaken? I did not want to discover that *there*. Yet I knew he had made his decision. Only an equally passionate conviction could overturn this one—and that was unlikely to happen.

There remained the biggest question of all. "How do you..." I began, feeling my heart crushing beneath what my words conveyed. I tried again, speaking aloud to the God I hoped would hear. "How do you give up a child? How do you leave her behind?" It was not a conventional prayer, filled with Biblical language and Anglican ritual, but it came from deep within my heart as none had ever done before.

My words hung in the harbor air, and I wondered if I had been too bold, perhaps even disrespectful, in this prayer.

Yet in the span of that moment, remarkably, I felt a voice whisper to me that He did understand this pain, as He had Himself given up a child.

"Is it you, Lord?" I whispered in awe. I had never felt Him so close, so strong, so loving. I paused. The Presence was palpable. Natural. It emboldened me to continue talking.

"I don't know how to leave her a continent away, an ocean separating us. I do not know if I will ever see her again."

I will keep thy family whole. The voice seemed to speak firmly but with overwhelming gentleness.

"I believe You, but my heart doubts."

Doubt not. Leave the child.

Leave the child.

In truth, there *were* sound reasons. It was only a year, and she would enter as a full planter at James Town. The additional tutoring before departure would strengthen her skills in reading, writing, and her ability to manage a household. She would continue her Latin and Greek, completing two years as I had. Although not all women received an education, I had, and I praised God for it. I wanted her to have the same chances as I had—the ability to read well and understand much.

Truly, this was one advantage of having a queen, not a king, on the throne for so long. Educational opportunities for women had never been stronger, since Queen Bess proved that women were as capable of learning as men. Wiser, forward-thinking men, such as Will and my father, saw this and wanted *all* their children to complete some education. The boys, of course, might go on to college, but the girls could at least get ample home tutoring for their future role as household managers. Besides, Cecily would likely be a landowner herself. She would need this education.

I understood suddenly that if I truly loved Cecily, I would have to let go. For a little while. God had promised, or I felt He had. Taking her with me and trying to hold her close would not serve her best, as she grew older. After all, we did not even know if *we* would still be there beyond a year. If we were, we would send for Cecily. It seemed simple enough. Many widows or widowers, once remarried, sent children of previous marriages to live with others to give the new union a fresh start. While I would never choose that, it was common for a child to live with relatives.

I studied the harbor, grey and threatening, as though the weather mirrored my own sadness. I thought about Cecily. This plan was not what I wanted to do, but it is what I would have to do.

"Cecily, it may be hard on you, but you will see why it is best. One day, we'll both see why." I spoke aloud with only the herring gulls to hear my words. Perhaps it was I who needed the reassurance.

I took a last look at the far, far horizon and thought, *I cannot even see France, yet it's so close. How much farther is the New World than this?* I did not need an answer to that, for I knew.

Sketches of the New World had replaced the dragons off the Atlantic. We knew what lay across the ocean. Or we thought we did. The New World was there, but its true nature remained the great unknown.

How much farther? Worlds and worlds away, or so it seemed to me that April morning.

If only I could be certain.

The waves lapped around my feet, calming my spirit with each gentle nudge.

A moment passed.

Then two.

A stillness and silence came over me as I closed my eyes. The sounds of the harbor and village drifted away.

My peace I give unto you. My peace I leave with you. Not as the world gives do I give.

A voice spoke to my heart, and it was unmistakable. I *did* feel peaceful. I felt whole.

Lo, I am with you, even to the uttermost parts of the sea. My father's Psalm! A voice seemed to whisper it straight into my soul.

I did not open my eyes for a moment.

"Is it you, Lord?" I whispered at last. "Are you speaking to me, even me?"

Yes, the silent assurance seemed to say. But what did it mean? *I am with you to the uttermost parts of the sea* could only mean He intended for me to go. But how could I be sure?

Lap.

The water washed against my ankle, and I felt something hard. I opened my eyes and looked down.

There, as large as my hand, still joined at its hinge, lay a perfect scallop shell.

The Crest of England

April 1609

A seashell should be the crest of England,
not only because it represents a power built on the waves,
but also the hard finish of the men.
The Englishman is finished like a cowry or a murex.
~ Ralph Waldo Emerson

The largest scallop shell I had ever seen—pristine and whole. I had never found one still attached as this one was. I lifted it up in awe. "Thank you, Lord," I whispered.

The shell was rosy and dappled brown, at once soothing and cheerful.

This I have carried from some unknown place in the sea, and it has not broken. Whole have I kept it. Whole will I keep thee and thy family.

If I had not felt peace before, I felt it now.

Suddenly, Will's words echoed in my mind. *The Promised Land, the land of Canaan*, he had said. Virginia's abundance would bless England, while England would bless Virginia with God's Word. We were meant to settle there. How did I know this? How did I understand as never before?

My heart felt light as I scooped up the wondrous shell—the pilgrim's shell. The shell of St. James, of James Town on the James River! "Yes, Lord, I will go. When I am afraid, I will trust in Thee. *Even to the uttermost parts of the sea.*"

I had to go find Will and tell him. My answer was definitely *yes*.

The Whitewash'd Wall

Early May 1609

The whitewash'd wall, the nicely sanded floor,
The varnish'd clock that click'd behind the door;
The chest contriv'd a double debt to pay,
A bed by night, a chest of drawers by day.

~ Oliver Goldsmith

Who has not felt how sadly sweet
The dream of home, the dream of home,
Steals o'er the heart, too soon to fleet,
When far o'er sea or land we roam.

~ Thomas Moore

A week after finding the shell, I walked to the harbor once more to take in the spring breeze, to pray, to begin the process of saying goodbye to my home. I found the water healing somehow, and it helped me think. Without knowing why—to comfort me, perhaps—I carried the scallop shell along too.

Will had brought the Virginia Company's documents home, and we were officially on the list of adventurers. We had paid our fees to purchase shares in the joint stock company, and we had signed our Oath of Allegiance to the King.

I, Joan Peirce, do utterly testify and declare in my conscience that the King's Highness the only supreme Governor of Great Britain and of all the Colony of Virginia....as well in all spiritual and ecclesiastical things (or causes) as temporal.

It went on to swear me to renounce any foreign prince or powers, recognizing they had no authority in James's realm, including his colony of Virginia. I swore allegiance to him and to defend him if necessary. I would have Will there to protect me. Having to fend for myself, or to defend the King as the case may be, seemed only a formality. Of course, we would always be loyal to England, wherever our house might be.

Saying goodbye to my actual home was harder.

I walked from the harbor in a sort of daze, feeling neither the cobblestones beneath my feet nor the touch of spring in the air. With the signing of the papers, it had become very real and very final. Fear ebbed and flowed in me like the tides of the Narrow Sea. *When I am afraid, I will trust in Thee.* Easier said than done! For there was a great ocean between me and the place I had been called to go.

When I arrived at my front door, I was almost startled. How had I arrived here? I looked behind me. Had I truly walked all that way, and no memory of doing so?

I wondered if Will were home yet from conducting the business necessary for us to depart. I let the brass knocker fall several times, listening for his key to unlock the door from the inside.

As I waited, I saw that everything—*everything*—looked different to me now that I was leaving it. The door—I studied its rich brown color, its thickness, the vertical panels of oak—even its gentle archway. Just a door—but my door. My home.

I rubbed the stone walls, looking up. Three stories, gabled windows at the top. A steep pitch to the roof. The house next to it nearly touching mine.

We were not the richest people in Melcombe by any means, but we lived better than many. Will's position as a Captain in the Lowlands, and his service in Ireland before that, had given him some prestige. He was careful with his money but happy to purchase the things we needed to live comfortably. Our home was not some grand manor, to be sure, not such as an earl or duke would possess. But many were the wives at the market who would trade their homes with mine. Its three floors gave me all the room our family needed.

I stepped over to the front window and peered in. No Will that I could see, which was just as well. I needed this time alone to ponder it all. I reached in my waist pocket and pulled out the iron key. Its head was a Celtic cross as large as my palm. What kind of key would I have at James Town? Were there even *doors* at James Town? Doors. Of course, there were doors. Now I was letting my fears get the better of me. There would have to be doors to keep out the—

There I went again. Wild animals. Savages. Thieves.

Yes, I thought wryly, certainly there would be doors at James Town—as well as a *pallisado* around it.

I opened the door carefully and stepped over the threshold, which allowed me a glimpse of my own pale face in the foyer mirror. My eyes were wide, with dark circles beneath them. I had not slept well the past week, and it showed. I hung the key on its hook beneath the mirror and stood there studying the great room.

To my right and in front of the large front window was our big, sturdy table. It seated eight very nicely. The chairs stood straight and proud. They were family heirlooms and must have been 150 years old. I had reupholstered the seats myself. They would have to stay behind, I reckoned. I looked at the tapestry on the floor—a present from Will in celebration of our first year of marriage. It too would stay. The pewter candlesticks—they would go. I found myself inventorying the room rather than admiring it.

I breathed deeply—English air, my air, my home. The sights and smells of my home. The scent of oak, the smokiness of the morning's fire, the lingering smells of the day's bread. The panes in the big window, making "x's" that pointed to the window seat. The lovely red velvet curtains hanging on either side. The square chair we had purchased only recently to place near the sideboard. The lime-washed walls, brightening and cheering the room, white and a contrast to the dark oak supports that framed them. The grand fireplace I had so loved—my dream of a hearth.

Well, they had hearths in James Town too, and soon enough I would make one my own. I looked at the Bible table, with its ever-present Geneva Bible upon it. Certainly the Bible would come. We could not manage without the Word. That was certain.

But the Bible table? I began to wonder how much we could, or should, bring. What did the Virginia Company allow us in provisions and personal items? I would have to discuss all this with Will. The pots and pans hanging around the fireplace, the iron hooks and pokers for laying them atop the fire, the heirloom rocker from Will's family. More questions, more unknowns.

I climbed the curving staircase to the second floor where our three bedrooms were. There was so much...*comfort* in this house. It was only about fifteen years old, still retaining its patina of newness, of freshness. Around and up the stairs I went, thinking, calculating, worrying, wondering. So many emotions. So much to decide.

The ship.

The ship was small, I knew, but surely we would be allowed *some* of these items, and we were two passengers. Would they permit us double cargo space or would they consider us "one family, one set of belongings"? I knew not.

Some things I knew would go in our trunk. We would need herbs, bulbs, seeds, remedies, and my Gerard's *Herball*. A sheaf of writing paper, a quill, and inkwell would be necessary. A few small, sentimental items I would bring, such as the little Chinese wine cups and several simple pieces of Delftware. Janey would need a few playthings, such as marbles and her doll, Bessie. I planned to bring my scallop shell—I must! I would wear the pilgrim's badge around my neck and under my kirtle. I had also heard that the Company permitted each passenger one gallon of *aqua vitae*, which would provide us a little fermented drink.

Other ships would come later, making deliveries. Could we not, in stages, have some of our more prized possessions sent to us? And, in the end, were the possessions what truly mattered? I thought of my two girls sleeping side by side.

I sat upon our high bed with its elegant carved wood and the quilt made by Will's mother. I ran my hand across it. So many things, so many memories, so little time to choose.

I will never leave thee nor forsake thee.

I stopped, as a new thought occurred to me.

"Where the hand of God leads me, the hand of God saves me," my father had said. Surely, there was only one great comfort and that was God—one great promise and that was His. One great mission—to follow as He led.

Had I so soon forgotten? He had *told* me He would be there. He had promised me with.... I looked down and saw I was still holding the shell.

Odd, I thought, *how one can hold an answer in one's hand and forget it is even there. Pilgrims travel with little, yet God meets their needs along the way. He will meet ours, too. The rest we will figure out as need be.*

I rubbed the graceful shell, and prepared to set it upon my dresser where the antique pilgrim's badge, shaped as a scallop, lay. They belonged together.

Together. This gave me an idea, and I brought the shell with me to find Cecily, for we had to talk.

The Dividing Sea
Early May 1609

The Lord watch between me and thee,
when we are absent one from another.
~ Genesis 31:49

Mother and child! Though the dividing sea
Shall roll its tide between us, we are one...
~ Florence T. Holt

"Lovey, look what I have for you." I opened the door to Cecily's room and saw she was stitching her needlework. She pulled and sewed, the brightly colored threads twirling between her fingers.

She looked up to find me holding an opened scallop shell. She gasped and held her hands out. "Mother, it's so fair! It's lovely, that." She ran her fingers around its edges, gently, being careful not to break it in any way. "Did you find it at the harbor today?"

"It washed ashore last week. See, it used to be one cockleshell, or scallop. Then it opened and now is in two parts. Yet it is still part of one whole. A hinge keeps each half together. Do you see that?"

She turned the shell over, studying it. "It was one, but now it is two."

"We could close it together again, like so," I said, easing it back together.

"But it used to be sealed all the way around, didn't it, Mother?"

"It used to be. But it didn't serve the animal that lived here to be enclosed any longer. It had to break free. When it did, it became two shells."

"Oh." She was still running her fingers along, feeling it, enjoying the shimmering pink interior, the beige and peach ridges pointing outward like a sunrise.

"Come, let's sit in the garden a while and talk." We strolled out the back door and nestled together on a stone bench. The jonquils and irises had begun to open. A sparrow landed on a twig, which wobbled beneath his weight. Everything seemed so cheery. Everything but the news I had to give Cecily.

"We are like that, you and I. Like that shell. Did you know the scallop shell is the symbol of the pilgrim? The traveler to other lands?"

She wrinkled her face for a moment, partly in confusion and partly because the sun was in her eyes. She looked up at me. "Why are we like a shell?"

I felt queasiness in my stomach, as if I might be ill. I drew a deep breath and forced myself to continue.

I cupped the shell like a basket. "We are like it, because this part is you," I said, tapping the side closest to her. The sun glinted off its pearly inside. "And this side is me." I tapped the other.

Her trusting face was too much for me, and I felt I would cry. But then I remembered—her land, her future. This, God willing, would ensure her prosperity, even if something should happen to Will and me.

"Father and I are going to Virginia. Do you know that Virginia is across the sea?"

"Of course I do. Everyone talks of it. It is vast, with Indians, deer and big rivers. That's what I hear."

"And that is so."

"Will Janey and I go too?"

Here was the hard part.

"Janey will go, because she is so young, but you..." I felt a sudden surge of inspiration. "...you are nearly old enough to go as your *own* adventurer!"

"I can adventure there? But Janey is too little?"

"Yes. But...you must wait until you're ten. And you are not quite there yet! When you are ten, you will get your own land one day."

Her eyes widened.

"You are quite the independent young lady, so you must bear up for just one year, and then we will send for you."

Suddenly, land did not seem so enticing to her. She did not want to be an adventurer when she understood what it meant. "I will be away from you for a year? Where will I stay?"

"You will live with Uncle Tom, Aunt Elizabeth and their children as you did when baby Jack was sick. Their two girls are not much older than you are. Bess is thirteen now and Elinor's eleven. You remember they also have three boys about your age. Perhaps you will all come over together, next summer. Father, Janey, and I will depart this year. You are bold and brave. Can you do this?"

Her eyes clouded with concern. She looked at the scallop and up at me. Then she asked the question I least expected.

"Mama, I don't understand. What is the difference between an adventurer and a pilgrim?" Her eyes were trusting—she was certain I knew the answer.

What should I say? How could I put it into words she would understand when I wasn't sure I understood it myself? I chose my thoughts carefully, wrapping my arm about her shoulder, feeling her smallness.

"An adventurer goes to a faraway place to see what is out there. But a pilgrim goes to a faraway place to see what is in *here*." I patted my heart.

"Oh." She considered that for a moment. "Then may I be a pilgrim and an adventurer at the same time?"

I mulled that, and then shrugged, "I don't see why not. Come to think of it, I guess your father and I will be. Can you do it?"

Her lip quivered and I thought she would cry.

She did not.

Suddenly to my amazement, she said defiantly, "I can, and I will!"

It took me aback. Perhaps I expected her to be more upset that she would not be with me. Still, her independence could only be a good thing. It would serve her well later, whatever the future might hold. Where did she get her fire, I wondered. Her father's side or mine? No matter. Fire burned, and fire, in this instance, was a good thing. I hugged her close. "That is my little adventurer—and pilgrim!" I added quickly. "Now, here is the important part. I will take half of the shell—my half. And you take the other half. And when we are together again in James Town, we will put our two halves together to form one shell! May I snap it apart?"

She nodded.

I twisted the two halves until the scallop gave way. "Which would you like?" She studied each side and chose the one closest to her.

"Now, hold your hand up like so." I spread my fingers outward, in a fan shape, palm facing her.

She looked at me curiously, and placed her own hand up, palm facing mine. "Like this?"

"Spread your fingers!"

"Aye!" She was obviously enjoying our game.

"Now, see." I carefully touched my palm to hers. My fingers were just longer. "See the scallop we have made?"

Understanding lit her eyes. "I see it!"

"When you feel alone, hold your hand up and remember that soon we'll join them together again, just like this. But 'til then, we're still parts of the same whole."

"May I bring my scallop when I come?" she asked tentatively.

I smiled and touched her hair. "Oh, yes," I said, as though it were a very serious matter. "You have to, so we can put them back together." At that, my own eyes welled with tears. Perhaps I was not pretending as much as I thought. "They must not be apart too long," I said hoarsely.

I thought of the sea, how wide and deep it was. Two halves of a shell separated in the sea never found each other again, even on the same beach. Once apart, all was lost. But we were not shells. We had ships, and a means of finding one another again. Maybe it was a silly game and without meaning.

Then I saw that Cecily, who had been admiring her shell, held it against her chest. It had become her treasure.

No, it was not silly after all. I, too, clasped mine to my heart.

The Girl I Left Behind Me

June 1, 1609

How sweet the hours I passed away,
With the girl I left behind me.

~ Traditional English ballad

That last day spun with so many faces and whirring activity. Noise and crowds filled the portside street at Plymouth Hoe in Devon. I felt small in so large a gathering and my heart thundered with apprehension. Cecily wore a fearful expression, as though she thought we were forsaking her. It was nearly more than I could bear. Saying we would do this was easy—carrying through with it was not. I wanted to grab her and sweep her in my arms. *Safe with me,* I thought. Maybe we should take her after all. We could probably make hasty arrangements. Were we risking too much?

My brother Tom had brought her to wave us off and assured me she would be fine—sharing their tutors, helping his wife with housework as if she were his own daughter. Over the next year, she would continue learning homemaking skills, French, Latin, Greek, and sums. As a future landowner—I puffed at the thought—she would need these skills in Virginia even more than here. If we found mines or minerals, she would own a share. And she would own a portion of any profits the Virginia Company made. I relaxed. It was a good plan, a solid plan. *Yes,* I told myself firmly. *It is a risk, but one must risk to achieve anything worthwhile.* Risk went with achievement, perseverance with reward. My father had taught me that.

I knelt down in front of Cecily. "Look at all this excitement," I said with more confidence than I felt. "You are just as much adventurer as we are! You are equal to Father and me. Janey counts as a child in this, but you will be an adult. You do understand?" Did she understand we were not choosing Janey over her?

Cecily glanced for a moment at her younger sister, whose hand I was holding, and then up at me. She looked over at Will, who was checking arrangements with several Company officials.

66

I saw resoluteness enter her eyes. "I understand."

Then to my surprise, she knelt before her little sister, as I had to her. Janey knew we were moving to a new land across the sea and that we would be on the ship for many weeks, but all else was foreign to her. Of course, I admitted to myself, all else was foreign to me too.

"Janey, you will have to take care of yourself in James Town until I get there. Then we will be together again. Show me your hand, like this." She held up her palm to her sister. Obediently, Janey lifted hers up also. As my fingers had been just longer than Cecily's, Cecily's were just longer than Janey's.

"There," Cecily said, smiling. "See how we make two halves of a whole?" Janey nodded, understanding this as a game.

"When I see you again," Cecily continued, "I will put my hand to yours and we will touch them just like this, just like two parts of a cockleshell!" Janey's chubby cheeks filled out in a smile.

"Aye, Sissy," she said. "But I want you to go! I want you to go with us." Her eyes fairly pleaded to her sister. This was all beyond her understanding.

I waited, giving Cecily a chance to handle this.

Cecily put her arm around her sister. I was touched to see this gentle side I had not noticed before. "I want to go too." She looked at the ships wistfully. They were impressive with their shining brightwork and lofty masts. "But I have to stay here until next year, when I'm an *adult*. Then I will come. Aye?"

Janey nodded sadly. "Aye."

"Show me your hand."

Janey held it up.

"'Til then!" Cecily said, touching it with her own. "Don't forget." She kissed her sister's cheek, and then smiled up at me.

"I won't forget, Sisley!" Janey said, pronouncing the name as best she could and wrapping her arms around her sister's waist. For a moment, both girls embraced and I turned away lest my sadness overcome me.

Cecily reached for my hand. "When I come, I'll bring my cockleshell, Mama." Suddenly, she looked tentative. "You won't forget? You won't forget your shell? You won't forget...." She paused. "You won't forget *me*, will you?" Her eyes suddenly searched mine for reassurance.

"Cecily, you are one person I can never forget," I said firmly. I took my little girl, who did not appear quite as little as she did before, and wrapped my arms around her. "I am very proud of you," I said, trying not get choked up. "I wish your grandfather Phippen could have seen you. He would have loved you so. And..." I started to say, "And so would your father Tom." But at that moment there seemed no reason to remind Cecily that Will was not her real father. He had raised her, and Cecily, though carrying the Reynolds name, had never even met Tom. Sweet Tom. But he was the past, and today was all we had. "And...your father and I love you too," I finished.

I was proud of the little girl I left standing on the dock that day. I knew it would be a long year, but I had faith we would be together again. After all, what could happen in a year?

To Sail Beyond the Sunset

June 1, 1609

The lights begin to twinkle from the rocks;
The long day wanes; the slow moon climbs; the deep
Moans round with many voices. Come, my friends.
'Tis not too late to seek a newer world.
Push off, and sitting well in order smite
the sounding furrows; for my purpose holds
To sail beyond the sunset, and the baths
Of all the western stars, until I die.

~ Alfred Tennyson

A s departure time grew near, more people crowded onto the dock and the street facing it at Plymouth Hoe. The famous Plymouth Hoe! It was here twenty-one years before that Sir Francis Drake had bowled until the Armada arrived, so the story went.

I took it all in—the tall homes with their pointed gables, the inns, the shops, and the cobblestone streets, visitors dressed in satin bodices, doublets and hosiery of every color. How long would it be before I saw another town like this, I wondered. James Town seemed so primitive, so wild, by comparison.

Plymouth too was getting a look at something much different than it had ever seen. This was the largest expedition ever sent by the Virginia Company or any colonizing group anywhere. The flotilla had embarked from the Thames in London, working its way here to meet several more ships. Now comprised of nine vessels, it was at its grandest—quite a spectacle for this port town. The ships wore festive paint in red, blue, and green geometric patterns and their brightwork glinted in the afternoon sun. Dominating the line was the flagship, the admiral *Sea Venture*, two or three times grander than the others in the fleet. One quarter, or perhaps a third, of the adventurers would ride in this single behemoth, with the rest divided amongst the other seven ships and a ketch.

The fleet had dropped anchor in Plymouth Sound on May 20, five days after departing London. Many of the adventurers were from counties surrounding Plymouth. Some were from Devon or Dorset, as we were. There were those from Cornwall and Somerset and Wiltshire. The Virginia Company had permitted adventurers to choose the most convenient port. For those of us from the English West Country, Plymouth was it.

The Virginia Company had decided to group its most illustrious men on the *Sea Venture*. They could not be in better hands than those of Admiral Sir George Somers, a celebrated naval hero, and of Vice Admiral Christopher Newport, both of whom had outstanding reputations.

The Company had indeed chosen Sir Thomas Gates Interim Governor until Lord De La Warr finished getting his affairs in order. Gates would also travel on the *Sea Venture*, where a locked iron box contained the new charter and instructions from the King. Gates would implement the change in government the charter required—a Governor-for-Life replacing the President and Council at James Town.

George Yeardley, Gates's assistant in the Lowlands, was now Captain of the Governor's Guard. Will and Sam, comrades of Yeardley's, were soldiers in the guard along with some twenty others, so they would also travel on the *Sea Venture*.

Our cousin Silvester Jourdain was another *Sea Venture* passenger. Silvester, Somers's friend and business associate from their hometown of Lyme Regis in Dorset, would document the voyage for future Virginia Company promotionals. Silvester was a travelogue writer as well as a merchant specializing in husbanding ships' provisions.

I yearned to be a passenger on this grand ship with my husband and cousins, with these famous men, and in such capable hands. A few wives had managed passage on it, but most traveled on separate, smaller ships as I did. The Company had relegated Janey and me to the *Blessing*, which sat seventh in the fleet.

Just then, Will's comrade John Rolfe passed us with his wife Sarah. John greeted us warmly, although I noticed Sarah seemed anxious. She, I knew, had received permission to ride the impressive *Sea Venture* with her husband.

"Good man, that Rolfe," Will commented to me. "I hope you will become well-acquainted with his wife, once we are all settled in Virginia." *She gets to travel with them*, I thought bitterly. Yet she appeared so sweet in countenance that it was hard to hold the resentment. And I was powerless to change my ship, anyway.

"Will, I don't understand why all the leaders are traveling together and why Janey and I can't be with you," I had asked when he told me the arrangements.

"Three reasons," he said. "First, the Company thinks it's best to put most of the women who have children on the *Blessing*. There will be few children on the *Sea Venture*. Then too the Company wants all the leaders together to minimize squabbling. They also reckon that an eight-week sea voyage gives them time to finalize plans and become familiar with one other. Most importantly, the leadership will then all make their entrance to James Town together. A few men gained the privilege of bringing their wives and children on board with them, but I did not have seniority for this. I did ask, however. I'm sorry." He frowned and shook his head, his distress obvious.

Lowering his voice, he added, "Personally, it doesn't make much sense to me, putting the leaders together. Yes, they will have a contingent of soldiers to protect them, but what if the ship goes down? Then what?"

"Will! Don't speak so!"

"Joan, it's the reality of the situation. Ships sink. None of these is likely to, and George Somers is the star of the English navy, as you know. *A lamb on land, a lion at sea*, they say of him. We have England's most exalted mariners with us, but loss of life at sea happens. You know that from personal experience."

I grimaced, as images of the Portland Race, the rocks, the battered *Anne* flashed through my mind.

He leaned close to me so that the children could not overhear. "Truly, Joan, 'tis better we're on separate ships, even though we have no choice. If we are on the same vessel and something should happen, Cecily becomes an orphan like that." He snapped his fingers. "The odds are slight that *both* our ships would go down. Also, if there's plague or illness, it may strike one ship while the other remains unscathed. That has nothing to do with sailing ability, either. A smaller ship like the *Blessing*, even with all the women and children, has less chance of illness than we do. I want you to arrive safely," he said with tenderness. "I am willing to give you up for a couple of months for just that reason."

I knew it was useless to argue. The men made the decisions or complied with officers' commands. We women did what the men told us to do. The *Blessing* it would be.

At that moment, a commotion from the dock caught our attention. The *Blessing's* crew was pushing the capstan, a giant wheel with a rope used to hoist the heaviest cargo onboard. A terrified mare dangled in the air, as sailors cranked the great wheel, which lifted her higher and higher.

My mouth dropped open, and I turned to Will. "A horse! We are going to be onboard with a horse?"

"I only learned today or I would have warned you. Aye, all the horses will be on the *Blessing*."

"*All* the horses? How many?"

"Eight."

"I shall be without you *and* upon a floating stable?" I cried in disbelief. "While you will have the comfort of the flagship? Well, I certainly hope the *Blessing* lives up to her name!"

"And the *Sea Venture*, or *Sea Adventure* as she's sometimes called—may she *not* live up to her name," he said with a laugh.

"Well, the smell's going to be horrible on the *Blessing*," I said under my breath. Of course, it wasn't going to be a bed of pansies on any of the ships— certainly not my mother's flower garden.

Just then, Will raised his hand in greeting to a well-dressed gentleman, who returned the wave.

"George Yeardley," Will said to me, by way of explanation. Yeardley was making his way over to us even then.

"What's his wife's name?" I whispered, eyeing the young woman at his side.

"Temperance," Will said quickly. "She's very well-connected. She was a Flowerdieu, and her mother was the daughter of Lord Stanley."

"Oh." My eyes widened. There were noblemen on this journey, but not too many noblewomen. She was young, too. I reckoned her to be in her early twenties. I wondered resentfully if she had a choice spot on the *Sea Venture*.

"George!" Will was saying, with his hand outstretched. "May I present my wife Joan and my daughters, Cecily and Jane? Also, my brother-in-law, Tom Phippen." We all smiled and graciously nodded our heads while George introduced Temperance.

Then Temperance stooped down to Janey, "Hello, little lady. Are you excited about your ride on the ship?" Janey giggled.

Cecily, however, looked pained and turned away. I reached for her shoulder and stroked it, wishing there were something I could say to her.

The men began discussing business, leaving Temperance and me alone.

"I suppose you're on the *Sea Venture*," I said, trying to hide my envy.

"No," she said simply. "George thinks it's safer if I travel on another ship, so I'll be on the rear admiral *Falcon* with Captains Nelson and John Martin."

"Oh." Her reply took me aback. I had just assumed… although admittedly I would not have expected a woman of her breeding to be traveling to Virginia at all. Still, she didn't have a presumptuous manner.

"Where are you going to be?" she asked.

"The *Blessing*," I said ruefully.

Temperance grimaced. "Horses?" she said with a raised eyebrow.

"Aye."

Perhaps seeing my discouragement, she added quickly, "So you can just pretend you're on a farm in the Devon countryside instead of on a long sea voyage. A farm with a great view of the water." I saw she was joking and trying to ease my discomfort, so I laughed along with her. She had a spark about her that appealed to me. She certainly was not stuffy.

The ringing of ships' bells indicated we needed to move toward our own vessels. Temperance and George rushed away, she with a goodbye wave. "Farewell until we meet again in Virginia!" she cried. I felt a strange sense of assurance in that, although I could not say why, as I waved in return.

We began our walk toward the gangplanks. I tried to identify the other ships I saw: the *Lion, Unity, Swallow, Falcon, Diamond* and a most interesting little ship, the *Virginia*. They called her *Virginia* because she was Virginia-built, in the now-deserted Popham colony. Finally, the *Sea Venture* would tow a small ketch for later use as a river vessel.

The sun was beginning to set over the western waters, its orange triangle on the Narrow Sea seeming to point in the direction we should go. Six hundred persons, a true cross-section of the city and countryside—peers, knights, doctors, ministers, Captains, esquires, gentlemen, merchants, tradesmen, and ordinary citizens—were boarding.

"Captain Peirce!" cried another soldier, as he gestured to the plank.

"It's time, Joanie." Will said, giving me a kiss goodbye and kneeling to hug Janey. He shook Tom's hand, and then gave Cecily the longest embrace of all. I did the same, trying to etch into my mind each contour of her small body, hoping to remember it in Virginia. I did not want to let go, but finally I knew I must.

My stomach dropped and my heart fluttered. The moment had come. I reached for and squeezed Will's hand, and he disappeared into the crowd.

When my turn came to board ship, I placed one foot hesitantly onto the gangplank. It shook with the weight of its passengers. It was, after all, just wood and iron crafted by men. As I peered beyond the ship to the ocean, I felt the *Blessing's* insignificance to the great water in which she sat.

Only a second passed as I glanced at my other foot still planted on Plymouth Wharf. Cecily's voice echoed in my ears. One foot in each place—my heart and soul on the threshold of the unknown.

Will promised me that, even if his duties did not allow him to return, I might come back if I found the wilderness too daunting. And yet, in that moment, I knew. Without knowing how, I knew that if I left, I would never call England home again. Somehow, it seemed that by placing both feet upon this bridge, I gave up claim to the Old World and committed to the new one, forever.

With that realization, a rush of fear shook me, and I wobbled like the plank. And with that fear came a sudden, terrible urge to turn around, to step off, to trust that Will would return safely. *To stay.*

With that fear came also strength, its source unknown to me, and in that strength, resolve. I took a deep breath of salty air, letting it fill my chest even while tears blurred my vision.

But God too is upon the threshold, I told myself, *bridging the gap between two worlds.*

And so I lifted my other foot from the dock, placing it on the plank. And the first I lifted beyond the second, taking one step, then another, climbing higher and higher. Until the ship itself rose to greet me, until my feet rested upon it, until its sails whipped overhead—beating out a greeting, pounding in the wind, pounding like my heart—urging me to go.

Woven Wind

June 1 – July 25, 1609

Our life is of woven wind.
~ Joseph Joubert

Never had I seen such chaos as aboard the *Blessing*. Everyone was struggling to find a place to be, all wanting to watch the departure and trying to catch a final glimpse of loved ones.

Pulling Janey along, I rushed to the edge to peer over. The crowds below were thick, however, and, try as I might, I could not spy Cecily. I scanned the dock, until at last I found her blue kirtle, her little straw hat, her hand tucked in Tom's. She would be his child for the next year. Tears streamed down my face. *What was I doing?*

My tears only lasted a moment, as a crewmember, whose name I later learned was Harrison, chided us with, "Below! Below!" He then turned to a shipmate, grumbling, "Look at all them women and children! We got us a ship-load o' hens!" I saw about eight or nine women and as many children scrambling about the deck.

The sailor shuffled us toward the 'tween deck, between the main deck and the hold. The crew busied themselves with preparations, unfurling sails and loosening ropes that held us in port. Already, three men cranked the windlass to draw up the anchor. It was hot, heavy work in June. Several sailors scaled the rigging, high over our heads, struggling with ropes and sails. We were in the way, and the crew's disdain made that clear.

I gripped the rope ladder, quickly turning to savor the last view of unobstructed sky I'd see for some time. I eased myself down the hatch to the 'tween deck, just in front of Janey. If she tumbled, I hoped to catch her or at least to break her fall. She proved more agile than I did, however, and we both made it down easily.

The crew had closed the gun ports and sealed them shut with beeswax to keep water out. These would stay sealed the entire voyage, unless the Spanish attacked and we needed to fire ordnance. Our only sources of light and air were the scuttle and the griddled center hatchway—and the crew would even batten that down in foul weather. The 'tween deck did have openings at the bow and stern, which would allow in a little water and, we hoped, much wind as the ship sailed.

Once below, I managed to find a spot against the wall for Janey and me—a prized location, a little out of the way but not too far from the scuttle. Salty air was not too healthful; everyone knew that. Still, with this many people in cramped quarters, any air might be a good thing, I reasoned. Certainly better than foul vapors, which were the least healthful of all.

The aft, or stern, of the ship would cause less seasickness, but being between the hatch and scuttle would allow most air and light. Against the ribs of the ship were mattresses, each about four by six feet, made of linen and stuffed with straw. There was one mattress for every two passengers, so Janey and I would share one. Cargo was not only in the hold below us—with the horses—but stacked on the floor beneath our feet.

I tried to get my bearings. This would be our home for the next eight to twelve weeks, depending on winds. What could we expect?

The ship was perhaps seventy-five feet long and twenty feet across. It could transport a burden of about 120 tons. I guessed there were some seventy passengers all together—and, of course, eight of those were horses. I was still not beyond the fact that I was living above a floating stable for several months.

Janey was all wide eyes and questions. I was glad I knew something about sailing from my father.

"Can we climb back up to see the water some more, Mama?" Janey asked, pointing to the scuttle.

"No, Lovey. The crew has much work to do, and we would only be in the way."

"What do we do then?"

"We wait, we sleep, we sing, we play games, we tell stories...all on the 'tween deck."

"What's a *'tween deck*?"

"It's the *deck between*! Between the main deck, where the crew is, and the hold, where the horses and supplies are."

"What are we?"

"Do you know what *cargo* is?"

She shook her head.

"Cargo is something that moves from place to place. That's what we are." These were all private merchant ships, leased to the Virginia Company. The design of these—and all ships—was to transport goods, not passengers. There-fore, we must remain stowed—out of the way with the hogsheads of sea biscuits, small beer, and salt fish. And the horses. They considered us, like the stallions and mares, *living cargo.*

"Do we ever get to go back up?"

"On calm days when the ship is at a standstill, perhaps. The Captain does not want anyone to topple overboard! That would be frightening, wouldn't it?"

She nodded, and I continued. "When the wind is quiet the crew's work is also lighter, so we would not be so much in the way. Even then, the Captain will only let a few folks up at a time." I knew it could be weeks before we had that opportunity, if we went up at all. It was much at the whims of the ship's master, Gabriel Archer, and its Captain, Robert Adams. We would be an afterthought for these men and their crew. Their main task was to deliver us to Virginia.

At last, I felt the *Blessing* ease out of port. I imagined the dockside crowd blending into a distant swarm, their waving and cheering becoming a dull roar until the winds muffled it and all contact with shore ended.

We were on our way to Virginia.

The ships got off to a slow start. The winds pounded us from the South-west, forcing us to seek shelter in Falmouth Harbor, tucked away on the Cornish coast.

"This is not a good omen!" said Elizabeth, one of the women whose pallet was next to my own. She didn't look like a pleasant neighbor, but perhaps her disposition would improve once the journey began. Then it occurred to me that *no one's* disposition would get jollier being so long at sea and in such tight quar-ters. "Ah, well," I said to myself with a sigh.

For six frustrating days we sat, waiting for the winds to turn. Now that we were going and committed to it all, I wanted to see progress. Instead, all I saw was the rocky Cornish coast. And all I heard were Elizabeth's complaints. Eliza-beth shared a pallet with another woman, Maggie Deale, the wife of Will's comrade Hugh from the Lowlands. Both women's husbands were on the *Sea Venture* with Will. At voyage's beginning, none of us knew each other. In close quarters for so long, that changed rapidly.

On the eighth of June the winds turned favorable, and we were able to edge out of Falmouth Harbor. Captain Adams pointed our bow west, following the six ships in front of us. Two more trailed our stern. "Seventh sail," he called us, to indicate our position in the rank.

The sails billowed, bold and strong, and I felt a surge of optimism. The horses caused us to rock by their stomping sometimes, but we all began to settle in. There were a few other children too, so Janey found playmates in them as well as in the ship's cat. We had more women and children than any of the ships, with most of us congregated on the same side.

"If we truly are *a hen's ship*, we can call this section *the henhouse*, eh?" observed Maggie.

Maggie's spirit contrasted with Elizabeth's pallor and dread of each day's event, and I enjoyed her from the start. Like me, she'd been surprised by her husband Hugh's desire to go to Virginia, though she was not necessarily opposed to it. Her attitude, like mine, was just to get through. "A day passes quickly and it's gone. My grandfather always said, 'Don't wish your life away.' So I intend to make the best I can of this journey. Two months will be behind us soon enough. A life is short. Every day's a journey, on land or on sea," she told me early on.

"You sound like Humphrey Gilbert. When he was on his way to claim Newfoundland for England, he called to another ship, 'We are as near to heaven by land as by sea!'" I said, remembering the story.

"Aye." Maggie gave me a shrewd look. "But as that was just nigh of him falling overboard, perhaps we can find *another* verse to steer by!" We both laughed. I found her smile hearty, her enthusiasm genuine.

It was through Maggie we got our best news of what was going on aboveboard, as she had managed to befriend the crewman Harrison our first week out.

"We need us an ally up there, among the sailors. I got my eye on him," she said to me as we were nosing through the Narrow Sea to open ocean. She gestured toward Harrison, who brought our meal rations each day. He seemed to find the task distasteful—we were certainly more nuisance than cargo. But he performed his duty faithfully.

As Harrison was making his way through the 'tween deck, Maggie, Elizabeth, and I held out our tankards. I held two, one for Janey. Water, of course, was foul, so small beer it was for all but the nursing babes. Since small beer was brewed three times, we could down our gallon-a-day allotment without staggering.

With practiced hand, Harrison poured the beer as the ship rocked beneath his feet.

"Thank you ever so much!" Maggie said to Harrison as though she were receiving the finest wine in His Majesty's palace. He looked surprised by the acknowledgement. He cocked one eye wider than the other and wiggled his mouth so that his grey beard shook.

"Welcome," he said, moving on.

I pulled out a pinch of orange powder and added it to Janey's and my beer.

"What's that?" Maggie asked. "Magic potion? You're not a witch, are you?" She laughed at her own joke.

"It's ginger, for the stomach. I brought a supply of herbs and spices as curatives or preventatives. My mother taught me all about them, and I grow me a fine garden." I hesitated. I supposed I had enough to share, if the voyage did not stretch too long. I hoped ginger would keep Janey and me well from seasickness. "I can give you some too, if you'd like. And you, Elizabeth," I said, not wanting to leave her out. We were all bunked close together and would be for many weeks. Perhaps the time to start working together was now.

"I'll be right pleased to take you up on that!" Maggie said. She held out her tankard.

Elizabeth said, "I don't see the use in mucking my beer. Thank you, anyway."

I shrugged. The more for us.

Rations came four times a day, as was the practice at sea. These came in precise four-hour shifts signaled by bells, aligned with the changing of the ship's watch. At each one, we received a portion of some meat, like salt pork or beef, dried fish, oatmeal or peas, and—without fail—sea biscuits and two pints of small beer. The biscuits were flour, salt, and water, baked until stone hard. Not my fresh loaves, surely, but we made do. The worms and weevils we spied, we flecked away before taking a bite. The ones we didn't see simply became an unsavory crunch in the biscuit. The amount of mold on the biscuits progressed with the voyage.

On days when the winds were quiet, the cook lit a charcoal box to warm our supper. Ship's rules forbade passengers to have fire of any type. That was too dangerous. Only the ship's cook had permission to use open flame in his quarters aboveboard. He prepared meals for the Captain and sailors in a large cauldron up in the fo'c'sle of the ship. Before this journey, I had never thought of fire for meals as a luxury.

"Rations!" cried Harrison as he scaled the rope ladder. He worked directly for the quartermaster, serving at two of the four shifts. He balanced wooden buckets, each one containing provisions for four or five people.

One day, as Harrison came through, Maggie whispered to me, "Stay with me. I have an idea."

"Master Harrison," Maggie called politely. Harrison, of course, was not used to anyone addressing him as "Master." In Maggie's Devon twang, it came out *Maister.*

"What be it?"

"We just wanted to thank you for taking such good care of us, down here in the *hen's house.*"

He scowled and grunted in response.

"Mistress Peirce here has brought her quite a good supply of the finest medicinal herbs from Melcombe Regis. Why, Mistress Peirce," she said, throwing an arm around my shoulder for effect, "is quite famous around her parts for her surgical ability."

I looked at her, shocked. I was no more a doctor's assistant than a billy goat!

Harrison shook his head and said, "What? That's poppycock."

"Not poppycock," Maggie said, lowering her voice. "She's very skilled and brought her prime stock aboard. Now, not many know this—" I wondered if *I* knew this, but listened to hear her finish. "Not many know she is a fine and practiced herbalist and healer. We thought if you should ever be feeling poorly on this voyage, she might be able to fix you up with some of these herbs. 'Tis special, just for you, since you are taking such good care of us down here in the 'tween deck. Now," she cautioned him sternly, "don't be telling all the other crew about this. She doesn't have enough for all."

Harrison looked warily from Maggie to me and back again.

"Aye, I'll remember that. Thank you, Mistress Peirce." I saw a trace of smile behind the hard seaman's face.

"Thank *you*, Master Harrison," I said, feeling the role.

After he walked away, I turned to Maggie. "What was that all about?"

"Simple," she said. "We may need information. We need a friend aboveboard, someone who knows what the Captain has told the crew, if there are changes or alarms. Now we have one. Cheers!" she said, holding her tankard up to mine.

Maggie boldly, but always pleasantly, asked Harrison about the goings on up above. He informed us that Governor Gates sent word from the *Sea Venture* that the fleet should catch the trade winds. We would sail southwest toward the Spanish Canary Islands, while still staying well away from them. No one wanted to antagonize the Spanish.

"At the Canaries, we head due west. We're to steer away from the West Indies and straight toward Virginia. If winds separate us, Gates says to go to

Barbuda and wait seven days until his flagship arrives. If they do not come, we continue on to Virginia without them," Harrison told us, gesturing in a forward motion with his hands.

This puzzled me. I had seen Will's map and knew that most voyages to Virginia went through the Caribbean, making a layover at one of the islands in the Bahamian Sea.

"That seems a strange route." I said.

He shrugged. "It's a trial. By turning west at the Azores and sailing straight through, they expect to shave weeks off the voyage. They believe it can be done."

They believe it can be done. The words echoed in my thoughts. "Well, I certainly hope belief can make it so!" yelled Elizabeth from behind me. I rolled my eyes at Maggie and she laughed. "Aye, don't we all!" she said good-naturedly.

I found, agreeably, that I had only mild seasickness, and when my stomach rose, my herbs and remedies settled it right quickly. That was fortunate, for those that brought no remedies, or found no relief in them, spent considerable time with their heads hung over chamber pots. Their ashen, green faces were, as my father might have phrased it, the color of a dead Spaniard.

We relieved ourselves in these same chamber pots as well. We women could slip the pots under our skirts—not exactly a privy, but something.

When the pot filled, a sailor such as Harrison hauled it up the scuttle, dumped it over the side and gave it back to us. We kept each 'til it was full, so I need not say, with the limited air, how horrid the stench was. If the movement of the ship did not turn a stomach, the smell did.

As it happened, Elizabeth was sick more than most, and I began to feel sorry for her. When she was done after one particularly grueling episode, I pulled out my satchel of herbs and remedies. "Don't you want to try one of these?" I asked.

"What have you there, Mistress Herbalist?" Her voice was almost nasty.

"Well, I have conserves of roses, clove-gillyflowers, wormwood, green ginger, burnt-wine, nutmeg, mace, cinnamon, and raisins of the sun, amongst other things," I said, ignoring her tone. "Try the conserve of wormwood. I take a little every time I feel it coming on, and thus far, Janey and I have been fairly well. I can't wait to get my garden planted in James Town," I added.

"Oh, you're mighty confident."

I gritted my teeth. It could be a long voyage with this one.

"I have this *confidence: that he who began a great work in you shall complete it at the time of Christ Jesus,"* I said. The words were out of my mouth so quickly I scarcely knew from whence they came.

To my surprise, Elizabeth began to cry.

"I never wanted to come on this stinking voyage, but my husband insisted, and I miss my home and my family and how to God am I going to stand it if I'm *retching* the whole time?" Her words came out in a stream, and she put her head down.

I wrapped my arm around her shoulder. "Well, I wasn't thrilled about it either at first, but it could be a great opportunity for all of us." I said the words carefully, hoping they sounded encouraging but not *too* cheerful.

She swiped her hand into the air and pushed me away. I took a deep breath. I wanted to like her, but she wasn't making this easy. Of course, I reminded myself, being horribly sick on a voyage one never wanted to take would be far worse on her than on anyone around her. I considered what to say next, but before I could open my mouth, she grabbed for the bucket and vomited again.

I reckoned Elizabeth was right. It would be a long voyage for her. I slipped the wormwood onto her pallet and went to check on Janey.

Later, Elizabeth came over to me. She was wobbly on her legs, but said flatly, "Thank you, Joan. I believe the wormwood is helping."

I smiled. "I'm glad it could settle you some, Elizabeth. I also have some little cakes of sugar and gum-dragon. The cinnamon and ginger in them helps becalm a seasick body. If you brought none, I'll share the cakes," I said gently.

For a moment, she looked genuinely touched. Then she scowled and turned away. She was determined, it seemed, either not to like me or not to like anything at all. I could not tell which.

Most days were much the same on the *Blessing*. I told Janey stories, remembering ones my father had recounted to me so many years before—stories of our family, of the sea, of days long past. Some days she rolled marbles with the other children or played dolls, always accompanied by the rock, rock, rocking of the ship. There were chess and draughts, dominoes and Nine Men's Morris, backgammon and, for the men, cards and dice. Sometimes, James Henderson played his recorder, and Robin Partin brought his lute. Music distracted those whose tempers flared due to tight quarters, seasickness, or sheer monotony, and so it brought welcome relief.

Maggie, we soon learned, had a haunting voice. Evenings she would burst into song, accompanying herself with the bright tap and trill of her tambourine. If James or Robin knew the tune, they played along. Grateful for the diversion, even the children hushed to listen. Strains with her unmistakable lilt filled the 'tween deck.

I wish I were on yonder hill.
'Tis there I'd sit and I'd cry my fill,
And ev'ry tear would turn a mill,
And a blessing walk with you, my love.

His hair was black and his eyes were blue.
His arms were strong and his words were true.
I wish in my heart that I were with you,
And a blessing walk with you, my love.

I'll sell my rod, I'll sell my reel.
I'll sell my only spinning wheel
To buy my love a sword of steel,
And a blessing walk with you, my love.

Then the King, he was forced to flee,
Took my love across the sea.
I wish in my heart he were here with me.
And a blessing walk with you, my love.

I'll dye my kirtles, I'll dye them red,
And 'round the world I'll beg my bread,
Until my parents shall wish me dead.
And a blessing walk with you, my love.

Come, come, come, O love,
Quickly come to me, softly move,
Come to the door and away we'll flee,
And safe forever may my darling be.

I wish, I wish, I wish in vain,
I wish I had my heart again,
And vainly think I'd not complain,
And a blessing walk with you, my love.

But now my love has gone to France
To try his fortune to advance.
If he e'er come back, 'tis but a chance.
And a blessing walk with you, my love.

I glanced up to see Harrison standing partway down the rope ladder, a basket of sea biscuits under one arm. He stood quietly, listening. Yet when he caught my glance, he said quickly, "Bah, hens!" He made an exaggerated motion of rolling his eyes. As he walked back up the steps, though, I noticed he was humming.

"Well," I said to Maggie over my shoulder. "The *roosters* might complain about us. Then again, if cargoes of flax don't need to be fed, they don't sing, either!"

We went on a southerly, then westerly, course from the Tropic of Cancer. The sun was almost directly overhead, and the wind blew only mildly as June sweltered into July. If I thought England had hot summers, this heat was beyond what I had ever imagined possible. It was relentless, such that I sometimes felt I had a wet woolen blanket wrapped across me, when in fact there was none. Janey squirmed uncomfortably most nights, as did I. Sometimes the winds did mercifully pick up in the darkness, and a ghost of a breeze might blow through the hatch, scuttle, or one end of the *Blessing*. We lived for those.

During the day, if the winds were at a dead calm, Captain Adams might allow us aboveboard. Then we stood on deck to catch whatever breeze there was. It was hot in the direct sun, but a welcome relief to breathe fresh air and escape the stifling stillness of the 'tween deck.

Aboveboard, I could see the other ships, sometimes closer, sometimes more distant, as though we had our own little crowd in the middle of the ocean. Yet seeing them, even though I could not make out individual faces, made me feel we were not so alone here in this vast nowhere.

I always wondered how they fared, information Harrison supplied when Maggie sweetly asked him. He shared a rumor that one ship had plague in her. Maggie and I recoiled, until he added he didn't believe it was the *Sea Venture*. On other ships, there had been deaths due to the calenture, caused by the suffocating heat. The crews were tossing bodies overboard. Remarkably, outside of the many seasick souls such as Elizabeth, the *Blessing* had no seriously ill passengers. Harrison told us he heard Captain Archer say he expected to have the puniest of all the fleet because of so many women and children, yet we were all well. Perhaps the ship truly *was* living up to her name.

Temperance Yeardley flashed through my mind. I wondered how she fared on the *Falcon*. As days crept by and July moved toward August, I reckoned to see her again in a few weeks, as well as my husband and Sam. We pushed closer to

Virginia each day—with Maggie singing, children playing, sharing cold meals, downing ginger beer—and we thought surely we had seen the worst this voyage had to offer.

However, to our surprise, we found there was indeed a dragon lurking on the map near the Bermudas—also known as the Island of Devils.

Between the Dragon, and His Wrath
July 25, 1609

Recommend me to God, my friend!
> ~ Medieval pilgrim's prayer to St.
> James upon reaching his tomb

Come not between the dragon, and his wrath.
> ~ William Shakespeare

On July 25, the day of St. James, the morning began calmly enough. As the first light of dawn crept through the hatch and scuttle, bow and stern, I said a silent prayer, a little different from my usual one.

St. James, you know I am Protestant, yet I believe all the saints of heaven and Apostles are there for us. On your day, I wear about my neck a badge from your shrine. I wonder, what have you in store for us this day?

It was a question I would later regret asking.

Perhaps the Apostles were not partial to the Protestants but to Catholics only—though this did not make sense to me. And the Spanish did claim St. James fought on their behalf. Some said they had seen visions of him, heading up armies against the natives down in the southern parts of the New World.

It made me curious. In a battle, which way would St. James fight? Would he fight for the Spanish only—their *San Tiago* they called him—or would he also remember the Protestants, so many of whom carried his name? I supposed only St. James knew the answer to that.

I slipped over to the opening in the bow, and gazed out. It was blue in every direction I could see, ocean and sky, and the clouds billowed up in sheer whiteness. The sun seemed to cast a yellow glow to portions of the 'tween deck it reached, as though it came at us from a different angle somehow. I could not remember a more glorious day on this ship.

In the distant horizon, breaking the blue expanse, I could see the grey and white outlines of other ships. I believed I could see the *Sea Venture* in the distance. It was most obvious because it was so large. I would still have preferred being on the great ship. We were within weeks of James Town and the fleet had managed fine. I wished I could have been aboard the *Sea Venture* all this time and been privy to the proceedings. Not invited in, of course, but perhaps able to overhear, to watch, to learn. I would like to have seen the great Admiral Sir George Somers at work.

Nearer us were four of the other ships. It was hard to tell which they were at this distance, but I thought I could make out the *Diamond*, the *Lion*, the *Falcon*, and the *Unity*. It also seemed the winds were picking up pleasantly. The flapping of the sails became more rhythmic, and I had a hand against the ship's ribs to steady myself.

I knew from Harrison we were nearing the Bermudas—bewitched, bedeviled islands—haunted and uninhabitable. Everyone knew that the screeches and moans drifting from them were cries of demons, ghosts and lost souls. There wasn't too much the Spanish and English agreed on but that—none dared go close or they should never return. I felt goose pimples rise on my skin and realized I would be glad when we were safely at James Town.

Sitting on a mattress, Maggie and I had settled ourselves in for a good game of draughts.

"King me!" she cried merrily as she slid her piece to the front of the board.

I was about to lay a red one atop it, when Maggie murmured, "That's odd. What's Harrison doing down here? It's early for rations."

Peering over my shoulder, I saw him at the base of the scuttle. He clenched his fists and scowled. His eyes adjusted to the low light, and he squinted as though searching for something. At last, his gaze settled on the two of us, and he bolted over, grabbing each of us roughly by an arm.

"Master Harrison!" Maggie cried indignantly, pulling away. "What do you think you're doing?"

"Quiet!" Harrison hissed, leaning his face close to ours. I jerked my arm away. Who did he think he was?

"Where is she?" he snapped at me. The winds roared now, and it was suddenly hard to hear.

"Who?" I yelled.

"Your girl! Where is she? Get her, *now!*" he ordered with a fierceness I had never seen in him.

Maggie and I stared at each other in confusion.

He yanked my arm again, pulling my shoulder closer to his face. His fingers clamped so tightly that my arm throbbed. Wild and unflinching, he forced me to meet his gaze. My heart pounded.

"It's blackenin' fast—the Cap'n thinks it's a *hurricano*! I ain't even supposed to be down here, but I come to warn you! Get your girl, get her now, and rig yourselves in tight against something, anything. Grab a mattress! Hatch is going down in a minute, and I gotta get up there 'fore I'm missed!"

"But…" *Hurricano?*

"Listen—ain't nothing can save a ship from a hurricane if the hurricane wants her—but prayers might help, so say 'em. And if we don't get through, pray your drowning's quick."

Before we could respond, he had turned to grab hold of the ladder, his feet barely touching the ropes as he scaled it. My heart raced and I trembled in every limb, ill with terror.

"Janey!" Maggie had already started to the stern where we had last seen her playing marbles. The light from the sky was dropping. I searched for the safest spot, concluding there was none. We didn't want to be where anything heavy could hit us. "Brace with mattresses!" I cried to Maggie as she carried the squirming child.

"Put me down!" Janey screamed, uncertain why we'd snatched her.

"Janey! Danger! Stay with me," I yelled. Others were murmuring of an on-coming storm, but only Maggie and I knew the truth.

We heard the low throaty rumble of thunder in the distance, coming closer—the tail of the dragon, brushing waves as it approached in a path toward us.

Elizabeth lay near the ribs of the ship, weaker than ever. She had been sleeping, but the violent rocking woke her and sent her into dry heaves. I put Janey beside her and upended a mattress against the two of them. The ship pitched furiously and the hatch above us fell with a slam. One of the crew secured canvas atop it. Besides two widely swinging lanterns, casting ghoulish shapes, the only light now entered from the bow and stern, and that light dropped ominously. Through those openings, I could tell the skies must be growing black, as though night had been born of day.

Already the winds whistled around the ship, shoving it. *Get out of my way!* they seemed to cry, and in response, the *Blessing* creaked and groaned, as water lashed through the openings. The other passengers were shrieking and disoriented now. They understood. No ordinary tempest pummeled a ship as this. The thunder banged in ever deepening tones and waves slammed us from all sides.

Either St. James would slay this dragon, or St. James *was* the dragon. I knew not which. *Recommend me to God, my friend.*

Neither Sun nor Star

July 25, 1609

When neither Sun nor Star appeared for many days,
and no small tempest beat upon us, all hope of being
saved was taken away.

~ Passenger Silvester Jourdain,
quoting Acts 27 to describe the
hurricane, July 1609

My father spoke of this king of tempests called *huracan*. The Spanish learned its name from the Indians, and they, in turn, named it for their god of thunder, wind, and rain. This, they believed, was the god who created these sea dragons. *Huracan, hurricano.* Columbus battled one and lived to report that no European had ever seen the likes of such a sea beast. *Hurricanos* were all but legend, yet mariners still dreaded the Bahamian Sea. Could *this* be one of them, bearing down on us?

Large drops splattered the ship and ocean. The gales churning the water joined rain drilling it. The waves reacted in fury. The sky, the little we could see of it, had grown eerie black, as though the devil himself had thrown his cape over the sun.

How right this was, I was not to know yet, for surely we had entered the Hell of the Ocean. We had passed its gates near the Bermudas and now we descended into its depths—deep, dark, and terrifying. The devils from the island—or the Spanish-sympathizing ghost of St. James, I had no idea which—had come for us.

Never had the ship seemed so small and the ocean so vast. Above the rising din were screams. Close to my ear was Janey's cry of terror. The wind shrieked around the *Blessing's* mast. "Mama, scary sounds! A ghoul!" Janey cried.

At last, the battle between ship, wind, rain, and ocean drowned out all else, even the clattering and whinnying of the confused horses.

I wrapped my arms tightly around Janey and pushed with my legs against a chest to keep Elizabeth from rolling away. I hoped holding my body close to the frail woman gave her some comfort, even if I could do no more than that, for I reserved both my arms for Janey. Maggie was near, but I could not see her.

We had crossed storms on this voyage—but how much more violent this *hurricano*. Even its name sounded like death.

I realized that from somewhere, from some great center of calm within myself, I must find the peace of God. Only then could I impart it to my child. It must come from me first.

The winds whistled and sang and moaned, rolling the ship with great invisible hands. The storm shook the *Blessing*, and the *Blessing* shook us, and our own trembling shook us even harder. The *Blessing* rolled, and the wind howled as though laughing at us. We were like babies in a cradle rocked by a dragon and about as helpless.

I knew something of how mariners handled tempests. The Captain would aim the bow into the storm, which I thought seemed to rage from the northeast.

I will walk with thee through the winds and the rains and the storms....

An image of Paul in the storm on his missionary work sprang into my mind. *Lo, I am with you always.*

Dear God, be with us now.

The winds blew the rain, smacking us from the sides and with such craziness that it was impossible to tell whether it rained up or down. It seemed to beat the ship from every angle—pounding and thudding—and I swear the ship screamed in pain. The power and fury of such a thing was unimaginable.

My grip on Janey's waist seemed strong enough to choke her, but I dared not release her. I gritted my teeth thinking, *if we go, we go together!*

Janey's mouth was open and she was heaving her small body with everything she had. I knew she was screaming and I knew I was too, but I could not hear our cries over the war outside. Elizabeth was ghastly white and I wondered if she might die right there. My eyes adjusting to near darkness—the only light from the lantern—I could see shadows of those grabbing poles and holding on. I saw them jerked around, I saw their eyes wide and their mouths open—but I heard only the dragon. I felt the ship listing and things not battened down sliding to starboard, then port. I saw men trying to toss cargo out the openings of the bow and stern in the 'tween deck. Wind and water slapped it back in their face.

Take that! it seemed to cry.

The terror went on for hours. Violence knocked the lanterns out. The darkness was complete. It would not end, but the dragon lashed, shaking us with its clawed hands, ripping us with its teeth, banging us with its tail.

We had descended into Hell.

The winds and the rains obey His commands, and the ocean hearkens unto Him, I thought. "Help us, Jesus!" I cried, though no one, not even Janey could hear my words.

"You promised! You promised!" I yelled, not sure if I were reminding or reprimanding Him. Why had I done this? Why had I ever agreed to sail from my harbor home? Why had I brought my daughter into this? She had trusted me.... Thank God, Cecily was safe in Melcombe.

Still, the *whys* were of no use now. We were here, the storm was here, and there was nothing to do but endure it.

The dragon tore Janey from my grasp.

"Janey!" I screamed, but in a moment she was gone, tumbling across the 'tween deck. "Janey, Janey," I murmured. I could not save her now. I could see nothing but blackness nor hear anything but wind and rain.

Again and again we felt the *Blessing* rise and drop—the waves must have been as tall as cathedrals. We teetered to port then starboard, aft and bow.

It battered us and threw us and knocked us into one another. It rolled us and beat us and slammed our few possessions into us and onto us.

Our screams drowned in the wind, even unto our own ears.

I felt the bruises on my body and the warm, salty liquid trickling into my mouth. *Blood.* Janey was somewhere, and I could neither find her nor help her.

I lay on a mattress and made my arms and legs loose. It was helpless to fight, hopeless to stand. I would have to allow myself to roll. I gripped the mattress and went over and over, feeling boots in my face, heads in my stomach, elbows in my eyes.

The ship rose and fell, rose and fell. Waves pounded it, and the wind howled like some great demon. It roared like a monster seen by no man's eyes. *Death, be merciful,* I thought. Swift and beneath the cold water, as Harrison had said. Take us quickly; take us now. It was no longer a matter of *if,* only when.

The Blessing *shall hold.*

Words, firm and assuring. Who had spoken them? Surely not any of the other passengers, whom I could neither see nor hear, only feel as they rammed into me and I into them.

Hold your blessings.

Again, words unbidden, insistent, commanding. My head tossed, but my mind raced. What blessings had I? My husband, my daughters, my health. A good life so far. The memory of my parents. Friends such as Maggie. Songs and music. I thought of Maggie's sweet voice.

Yea, though I walk through the valley of the shadow of death, I will fear no evil, for Thou art with me, said the voice.

Yes. I repeated Psalm 23 in my head, over and over. *The valley of the shadow of death.* We dropped what felt like forty feet on a wave. *Into the valley.* "I will fear no evil. I will fear no evil!" I screamed the words in my head, determined and resolute. "I...will...fear...*no...evil!*"

At once, a great calm settled over me, even as the wind beat us without mercy. Perhaps I truly did fear no evil. Suddenly I thought, *we are lost.* I saw the events about me as though detached. *That poor woman and her child,* I thought, referring to Janey and myself. *They shall die. They shall be tossed into the sea.* And I surprised myself because I felt no emotion, but hoped only that it would happen soon, for their sake.

And Will...would survive, or he wouldn't. It was amazing how serene my thinking had become, as though the more vicious the storm, the less I was able to react. Perhaps the *Sea Venture* fared better than we did. Will had been right to separate us—for all souls in this ship were surely lost.

Did Beat All the Light From Heaven
July 25–July 29, 1609

The clouds gathering thick upon us, and the winds singing and whistling most unusually, . . . a dreadful storme and hideous began to blow from out the Northeast, which swelling and roaring as it were by fits, some hours with more violence than others, at length did beat all light from heaven, which like an hell of darkness, turned black upon us....

Windes and seas were as mad as fury and rage could make them...The sea swelled above the Clouds and gave battle unto heaven.

~ William Strachey, describing the hurricane, July 25, 1609

Could I have known that the terror on the *Sea Venture* exceeded even ours? I envisioned it many times afterward—what Will must have thought, what he felt, how he suffered. How it happened.

With a shrill pitch, winds whipped the sails and drove the clouds over the sun. The ensuing darkness was as ominous as it was sudden this day of St. James, 1609.

Will wasn't sure when he began to sense that *this* storm was different, something neither he nor any of his comrades had experienced before. Well, he wasn't a mariner but a soldier. The seamen knew their trade, and they were under the direction of the best—Admiral Sir George Somers and Vice Admiral Christopher Newport. With military man Governor Sir Thomas Gates on board the *Sea Venture*, and the best military, political, and strategic leadership bound for Virginia in this one ship, Will felt there wasn't too much cause for concern. If anyone could see this expedition through a tempest, these were the men. Captains Archer and Adams on the *Blessing* were able as well. He would have to pray they understood tempests—even this most peculiar one.

Will had made a business of keeping his mouth shut and observing. Standing at a distance, Will glimpsed Admiral Somers's face. The old mariner was nearing

93

sixty, England's greatest naval hero. Called out of retirement to lead this largest-ever colonizing effort, Somers had risen to the occasion, leaving his comfortable Dorset estate to head across the Atlantic.

Christopher Newport had been admiral of the original three ships landing in 1607 and had visited Virginia once since. He had traded with the natives, searched upriver, and made a trial of finding gold. Of course, he was still embarrassed about that shipment of fool's gold he had brought home to the Virginia Company, but such things happened, even to the best. Even with one arm lost in battle, he was a commanding sight. Neither the sea nor Virginia daunted him.

Will could see that Somers and Newport were conferring. The winds menaced those aboveboard. The storm looked to be outrageous. Will understood the look of concern. The two men, with Gates, were responsible for the lives of five or six hundred colonists and an incredible array of property, including seven privately owned ships and two pinnaces. Their reputations, their lives, and the lives and fortunes of hundreds depended on them.

Will saw now that Gates had joined the group, and Newport gestured to the pinnace they towed. They would have to cut it loose. The winds were banging it so hard that a tether to another ship was not safe for either vessel under these rising conditions.

The sky darkened to midnight blue, then black, while wind pounded the sails. The rain pelted the deck from above at first but quickly shifted, grazing the men from the side, stinging their faces.

"By God, man, this is sudden!" Sam cried to his cousin above the growing storm.

"Aye!" Will yelled, as crewmen scurried up the rigging to draw in sails. The sky gushed rivers of water upon them. He had never seen a storm such as this where in an instant up was down and down was up. The winds, snarling, whipped them from every angle.

"Below, below!" cried the mate, and Will and Sam scrambled down the hatch. Seawater was slopping onto the women and passengers, who howled in terror. Will, like other soldiers and mariners, was helpless to intervene. Children cried, women screamed, and the men pled to God for deliverance, for now the ship was shaking in the winds, winds so loud that every cry was lost.

Lost but to God's ears, Will thought, his heart hammering his chest. The booming, cracking thunder overtook the wind's shrieking as though competing. And then it hit Will with devastating certainty: *this was a hurricano!* The ship groaned as a wave slapped her hard. *She shall split*, he realized in terror. But she didn't. And again he thought, *now, that rocking shall split her!* But again it held. It would capsize this time, surely—but it did not. It held, it held, it held. Every minute he waited for the salt water to swallow him. Will was not a fatalistic man, but swift death was God's mercy in this situation, he felt.

"Oh, my God!" cried a passenger, and Will turned to see what was in the hatch.

The sea. The sea was in the hatch, and it looked to be about five feet over the ballast.

The winds rose and fell and Sam cried, "The oakum's come loose!" A mighty leak had opened somewhere, and almost every joint spit out its oakum. *Where was the leak?* Will felt his blood running cold, as cold as the rising seawater.

"Every man search for leaks!" cried Gates, and every able-bodied man responded. None too proud or below his station. There stood the master, the master's mate, and the bosun, quartermaster, cooper, carpenter, and soldiers such as Will and Sam, shoulder to shoulder. All grabbed candles and crept along the ribs, viewing the sides, searching every corner. Listening for moving water.

The gunner handed out beef, and they stuffed every crack they found. But none found the gaping wound. Was there one? Or so many small ones it mattered not?

All pumps ran at maximum capacity now, chugging and sputtering. *Thank God!* Will thought—only to see them clogged with sea biscuits. Ten thousand weight of biscuits.

"The big leak's got to be in the bread room!" yelled the carpenter. Making his way in, he ripped up the bread room and found nothing. Still the pump clogged on biscuits and the water rose.

Will saw, to his horror, that the great ship had suffered a mortal wound, and, as blood would gush from a battered man, so water rushed into the battered ship. Will knew, as he was sure Sam did, that all hope was lost.

Yet, remarkably, the ship stayed afloat.

Through the night they worked. Tuesday morning the storm showed no signs of abating, so Governor Gates divided all 140 men—no exceptions but women and children—into three parts, opening the ship in three places: the forecastle, the waist, and hard by the binnacle. Then he appointed each man the post to attend.

"Take bucket or pump, and work one hour, and rest one hour!" Gates ordered. He and Somers were in the mix, too—Gates on the pump near the capstan while Somers rested. Then the aged Somers took the pump while Gates rested.

By God, they are an inspiration! Will thought, sweeping up water in his bucket with fury. He saw in astonishment that every man, even those who had never done a day's labor in their lives, worked without fail. No one missed a shift. An hour turned into two, four, eight, twenty. Still they worked their stations. There was no sleep, no food, no drink. Some of the common sort stripped naked so their clothes would not hinder them. Salt water sprayed into their eyes and kept them awake. Will considered the irony. *We drown a little moment by moment to prevent one massive final end by drowning.*

The hurricane sometimes raged more violently than it did at others—but never did it stop. Tuesday turned into Wednesday without sun or pole star in sight. When the men tried putting up a storm sail, the winds shoved the ship in such fury that it took six or eight men to hold the whipstaff—normally a one-man job.

Wednesday wore on, the men nearing complete exhaustion. Every part of Will's body ached, a burning numb feeling. He had swallowed, God only knew, how much salt water. His hands bled from blisters and the blood washed quickly into the water, leaving only the sting. His back blazed in pain. He prayed Psalms while he bailed. He said the Lord's Prayer. He developed his own prayer: *God with me, God save me, God our protection, God our keep.* If he could think of nothing else, he thought of that. He must keep his mind on *"God is our refuge and our strength, an ever-present help in time of trouble."* He was glad he knew so many Psalms and Bible verses by heart. He remembered how Luke told of the great storm in the Mediterranean, and how God promised Paul he'd save them. He swept, poured, swept, poured seawater. Endless.

Each time his rest hour came, he handed the bucket to his partner, a carpenter named Michael, and, more sore and wet than he had ever been in his life, tried to doze. It was not possible. Some hours he wandered around the ship, encouraged by the united effort but discouraged by the magnitude of the job, the vastness and anger of the sea.

At last, the mountainous, breaking wave froze every man's heart in his body, quenching the fire of their spirits. *It is over,* Will thought in resignation. *We gave our all. No man can say we didn't try.*

The water slammed across the quarterdeck and poop deck, covering the ship like a shroud, filling her to the brim from within—from the hatches up to the spar deck. It wrested the whipstaff from the helmsman's hand, and so knocked him that he banged first against port, then against starboard. The ship did not split in two, and, blessedly, neither did the man. Beaten and bruised, the helmsman lay off to the side, but a new sailor came up and called others to add their strength to holding the whipstaff. What typically required one crewman had five subduing it, and yet it still seemed alive.

When the monster wave hit, Gates was below the capstan, urging the men around him to keep fighting, to stay heartened. The wave knocked him over and left him groveling, while all those about him went down on their faces. Stunned, the ship, which had been making nine or ten leagues in a watch *without sails*, sat in eerie stillness amid the raging ocean.

Surely, we are sinking, Will thought. Faces of his family raced through his mind, and then his tattered dreams for life in the New World. "Yea, though I walk through the valley of the shadow of death, I wilt fear no evil," he said to himself. "The Lord is my shepherd, I shall not want." He hoped, he prayed God the *Blessing* would make it to Virginia.

He heard Gates say his one ambition was to die in *aperto coelo*—in open sky—and in the company of his friends. *What a tragedy*, Will thought. *England's best and brightest—Somers, Gates, Newport, so many fine soldiers—dying together beneath the waves*. He felt suddenly detached. If they were dying, why not him? He was dying amongst the best, amongst friends, as Gates said. It was a noble death at that, for they had done their utmost for their country. They had sought the New World—Canaan—even if it was never to be theirs. He understood in an instant that the loss of the *Sea Venture* would likely mean the end of the Virginia colony—perhaps the end of all England's dreams of colonization.

No one could bear the cost after this.

Yet, again the *Sea Venture* did not split; she did not capsize—even as the water level within her continued to grow. The enormity of the last wave pitched the battle further in the ocean's favor. Numb, the men kept bailing, but each knew. Every inch the water level gained, the *Sea Venture* grew a little heavier, rested lower in the Atlantic. They were losing the war.

Thursday night, a curious spectacle appeared. Somers was the first to spot the apparition. "St. Elmo's fire!" he called out. Will saw the lights he indicated. Some sailors called them *Corpus Santos*—body of the saint.

Oblivious to the suffering and hopelessness of the men, the blue lights chased and danced merrily. They resembled faint stars, trembling and streaming along with a sparkling blaze half the height of the mainmast. Sometimes they shot from shroud to shroud, settling on one, darting about. The masts looked like candles tipped in blue flames. For three or four hours, the phantom lights kept with them, running sometimes along the mainline and then returning.

On the morning watch, they vanished suddenly.

"A good omen, that!" Sam cried to Will. "The Spanish say no ship sinks if St. Elmo is with them. On his watch, no ship goes under."

Will, ever practical, replied, "Well, the saint has not pointed us in any due direction with his darting hither and thither. We set sail on June 2, St. Elmo's Day, and the storm struck on St. James Day. Between those two saints, one should point us home but neither is being all too helpful at the moment."

Sam, bloodshot eyes and lined face, laughed wearily, slapped Will, and said, "Old mate, I'm glad to die with you."

By now, men below had thrown over much luggage, many a trunk or chest and staved butt of beer. Hogsheads of oil, cider, wine and vinegar—all heaved over, as well as all the cannons and ordnance on starboard side. As each item bubbled from sight beneath the waves, the dream of Virginia grew dimmer, dismantled piece by piece.

The next—and final—step was to cut off the mainmast to lighten her more. The ship by now was so shaken, torn, and leaky that water covered two full tiers of hogsheads above the ballast. The men, including Will and Sam, stood in water up to their middles with buckets, barricoes and kettles, bailing. The pumps never stopped except when jammed.

As he pumped, Will ran quick figures in his head. Every hour they freed some 1,200 barricoes of water, consisting of six to eight gallons each. Besides that, three pumps were going continually—two beneath the capstan and the other above the half deck. At each pump, there should be around four thousand strokes in a watch, so every four hours they were sending *one hundred tons* of water back out of the ship. How was it possible the water levels continued to grow? No one could find the major leak.

The third day and night passed—it was now Friday morning—without any pause or respite, and still, still the water rose. Higher, despite all bailing. Higher, despite all pumping. Higher, despite all repairs to every found leak. *Two thousand tons of water thrown back to the sea, yet still this was not enough.*

There comes a moment when each soldier knows his effort is futile. These men knew it. The Captains knew it, and the mariners knew it as well. Even Gates and old Somers, nobly heroic to the last, understood. Time to let go. Their hearts failed with their strength, and Will, together with his comrades, mariners, and passengers, felt the hope within his spirit extinguish.

Now the men, finding any unspoiled beverage left on ship, began toasting their last goodbye. Three days of relentless storm and bailing. Two weeks from Virginia, with all the leadership, the charter, and the settlement's food—the *Sea*

Venture was going down. The men, many of them soldiers who had fought the Spanish so bravely, were now losing a war with sea and storm, inch by watery inch.

To Will, Sam cried, "See you in a better world!" Sam always bore a trace of smile, even under such circumstance.

"We did our best for England." Will choked out the words. "We tried."

Sam, at least, had the assurance of knowing Frances and his children were safe at home. Will had no such peace. *I have failed her,* he thought. *Joan trusted me, trusted my decision and judgment. I convinced her to come, and I, and probably she and Janey as well, shall perish here in the sea. Her own gravest fear, come to pass—dying in a storm at sea.* He pictured the terror, the horrifying end for little Janey. *Pray, God, St. James, help us.*

Hugh approached, then Tom, and finally John and Henry. "Together!" Hugh shouted, throwing in his hand. "We made the choice together and we share a farewell together." The other men reached in and clasped hands. Their clothes drenched, water droplets clinging to their beards and eyelashes, their faces lined with exhaustion, their hands cold and wet, but their grasp no less firm.

It had been a grand dream. A valiant battle, but at last the *Sea Venture's* mortal wound was taking her under.

The Forget-Me-Nots of the Angels
July 25–July 27, 1609

Silently, one by one, in the infinite meadows of heaven,
Blossomed the lovely stars, the forget-me-nots of the angels.
~ Henry Wadsworth Longfellow

On the *Blessing*, each minute seemed an hour. Yet huddled in the darkness, we waited for a death that never came.

We waited for an end to the storm that never seemed to come either. The tail of the hurricane whipped us for forty-four hours, nearly two full days—there was no day, no night, no sleep, no food, no water, no light, no air—no peace. No hope, yet remarkably, no death.

When at last it moved from us, we were stunned, like prey that discovers itself released. Had we truly survived? Even the weakest among us, like Elizabeth, had made it through.

But what of the Captain and crew above? Calm settled the ocean, and the skies turned shimmering blue as though wiped clean. A seaman rolled back the canvas on the hatch, and blessed light and air entered. A face peered down, a grin as wide as the expanse of blue sea. Harrison.

Taking stock of our situation, we discovered all the fleet separated and our own ship badly battered. It had been impossible for the fleet to stay together or even communicate over the incessant din of the storm. We could only imagine how the others fared, for we could see none of them now. Were all nine still afloat?

Janey, Maggie, and I had bruises, scrapes, and gashes, and we ached in every part of our body—as did everyone else. Yet, no one had fallen overboard and no one had died, praise God. It was a miracle of Providence, so we were not of a mind to complain. We were alive, and life appeared different because *it was*. It simply was.

For the first time in nearly two days, the scuttle opened, the rope ladder dropped in, and down came Harrison with rations.

100

We were shaky with hunger and thirst such as we had not known 'til then. Elizabeth was pale and quivering. She seemed too weak even to throw up. She had eaten little in the days before the storm, growing very thin, and appeared unable to eat even now. She took a small bite, then curled into a ball on her mattress. Sea biscuits and ales and dried meats were not much in the way of fine cuisine, but I was glad that Janey and I could keep them down. For small things grateful.

When he got to us, Harrison said nonchalantly, "You ladies fared a-well, I see, and the girl too. Some bloody knocks. They'll heal. Eat hearty, then."

"We fared just fine," Maggie said, pretending indignation. "What? Did you come down here expecting *scrambled eggs* in the henhouse?"

Harrison laughed as he mumbled, "Aw, hens."

Night approached and darkness crept over the *Blessing*—a true dark, a natural dark—and how wondrous to see stars again, however briefly, before we all collapsed in sleep.

The Port, Well Worth the Cruise, Is Near

July 27–August 15, 1609

Lowly faithful, banish fear,
Right onward drive unharmed;
The port, well worth the cruise, is near,
And every wave is charmed.

~ Ralph Waldo Emerson

For a week, the *Blessing* sailed alone on a wide ocean, a speck in the vastness, wondering which ships besides herself had survived.

Each time Harrison brought rations, he'd pet Janey's head. "How's my little lady?" He'd taken a liking to her and she to him—"the biscuit man," she called him. And each time as he handed us our trenchers and tankards, Maggie and I would touch his sleeve. He knew what we were asking. His expression was kind, but he'd shake his head. "No, Mistresses. She ain't been sighted. None of 'em has—not yet," he'd add.

The "she" he referred to was the *Sea Venture*, the grand dame of the fleet, the floating home of both our husbands. Pray, God, she still *did* float. None spotted? Could it be that only *we* had survived? We gave not into that thought.

The storm had lasted an eternity, it seemed, striking on Monday and not relenting until Wednesday. When finally the seas calmed, Maggie and I took to praying for the other vessels. All through Thursday, Friday, and Saturday we prayed for the other ships. *Lord, hear our prayer.*

Maggie loved the Psalms, and she sang every one she could recall.

"I *wish* we had a *Sternehold's and Hopkins Book of Psalms!*" she said. She had brought one on the voyage, but it had been so severely water-damaged in the hurricane it would no longer function as a hymnal. The Psalms and tunes we remembered, though, we sang together holding hands. My song nothing unto hers, but perhaps God could use even a poor voice like mine? I wondered if God believed nightingales sang sweeter than raspy blackbirds? How about the plain sparrow? I asked Maggie what she thought.

"Don't you think God created you just as you are? My gift may be singing, but yours is in the garden, bringing God's fruits up from the earth. Mighty handy talent, that. Besides, I think if all birds sang like nightingales, He'd get a mite bored with 'em! Say, did I ever tell you about *my* extensive yard garden in Devonshire?"

"No," I said with sudden interest.

She laughed. "That's 'cause there wasn't one! It's not my gift."

"But your gift brings hope," I said with a touch of regret.

"And yours brings healing and sweetness," she said without pause. "Psalm 91, then? Wasn't that one your father loved?"

And so sang the nightingale and the sparrow.

> *For why? Unto his Angels all*
> *with charge commanded he,*
> *That still in all thy ways they shall*
> *preserve and prosper thee.*
> *And in their hands shall bear thee up,*
> *still waiting thee upon*
> *So that thy foote shall never chance*
> *to spurn at any stone,*
> *Upon the lion thou shalt go,*
> *the adder fell and long:*
> *And tread upon the Lion's young*
> *with Dragons stout and strong*

"Now," said Maggie, "we would prefer *seeing* the *Lion, Falcon,* and *Swallow* to treading on any of them!"

"But we wouldn't mind treading on the *Dragon,*" I put in.

On August 3, with a burst of joy we spied the *Lion,* and soon after the *Unity* and the *Falcon* caught up to us. I didn't know why I felt compelled to see Temperance again. I looked forward to comparing her voyage to ours and prayed she were both alive and free of sickness.

Within the *Blessing,* hope swelled that shortly the *Sea Venture,* the *Swallow,* the *Diamond,* and the *Virginia* would also appear in the distance at any time.

Of the four ships now banded together, the *Unity* had taken the worst beating. Less than ten of her seventy adventurers were still healthy. Of the seamen, only the master, his boy and one sailor were well enough to steer the ship. A few of our crewmen rowed over to them in a shallop to climb aboard and help.

It appeared that, like us, the *Falcon* and the *Lion* were battered but had no severe leaks. Captains Archer and Adams discussed it with the masters of the *Lion*, the *Unity*, and the *Falcon*, and announced we would not head to Barbuda, far to the south, to wait for the Admiral *Sea Venture*. We were simply too close to the mainland of Virginia for that.

Now we four ships set course directly for James Town. Perhaps we would find our leadership—and our husbands—already there when we arrived, for the *Sea Venture* was nowhere in view and had been out front when the tempest hit.

As days passed and we drew nearer Virginia, all the things my father had taught me about approaching land returned to me. I saw a thin strip of cloud on the horizon, an early sign of land! The water changed from deep blue to a green-brown. Seabirds, like sentinels of the coast, hovered and swooped. Debris in the water made our hearts leap as though it were gold dust washing up to us.

Pines sweetened the salt air. Before we could even see Virginia, she welcomed us. It smelled healthful! We had been on board ship for over two months now, about nine weeks, I reckoned.

Still in the 'tween deck, we *living cargo* craned forward, edging one another for a peek out the bow's opening, as though we might glimpse the Promised Land by sticking our necks as far forward as possible. Wishing could not bring her into view. Not yet. And so a few more days passed.

"Land ho!" cried the lookout, and I froze on my pallet. Had I truly heard what I thought I did? The cheering up top told me it was so. Then we all whooped, the relief a people could only feel when they have been so long at sea—especially when a dragon has grasped them in its claws and shaken them on the voyage.

"Janey, land!" I said. "Perhaps Father is already at James Town." I longed to be with Will again and know he was safe.

Janey clapped. "Land, Mama, land!"

Green and brown horizon rose in the distance. The ocean did have an endpoint in the New World after all.

We yearned to be free of this smelly, stifling box, as the sun continued to pummel us with its sweltering heat. I wondered if August in Virginia always felt so tropical. It would be wonderful to get off this ship, to feel solid earth, and to have a good meal. I could scarcely remember anything but sea biscuits and small beer.

At the same time, I felt my insides jump with unexpected fear. The ship was cramped, true, but it was also familiar. Virginia beckoned us…but to what? Our ship was but a dot on a coastline that stretched in both directions until it faded into grey. One knew somehow it traveled on and on for untold miles.

It was August 11 when Captain Archer edged the *Blessing* into the mouth of a broad bay. The Chesapeake Bay was far more expansive than I imagined—almost as large as a sea—and even the mouth of the river stretched wide. Gradually, we nosed into the King's River, also called the James. The Virginia Company said smaller rivers crawled up into Virginia like veins in a man's hand. Witnessing how grand this one was, I could imagine it were so.

The hurricane had made our journey unusually treacherous. That may be why the Captain took pity on us and gave the command to open the hatch while we were still in the river, rather than waiting until we actually anchored. The winds were light, and we moved gently through the river, the *Blessing* cutting through water with quiet confidence.

My heart raced with excitement, and my palms grew sweaty—this time, more from nervousness than the heat. We made our way up the scuttle toward daylight into open sky, the sweet river breeze, wind rustling past our ears, and the cool spray of water. Along the banks, the calls of birds and frogs seemed primeval in their simplicity. Exhilaration swept away fear.

Now I understood the attraction of this land, even with all its unknowns and challenges. *This is what the pamphlet writers meant. This is what drew the imagination of Sir Francis Drake and Humphrey Gilbert and so many others.* There was something elegant and Edenlike here.

The trees—how immense! These forests were different from the English countryside, with thickets so dense they appeared impenetrable. Yet there were open fields, too. I understood the natives to be farmers as well as hunters and here their clearings indicated that.

Large grey seabirds circled. Others passed overhead—amusing birds that looked as though they had stretched their beaks holding something far too heavy. These flew in long formations, occasionally ducking into the water to scoop fish. I had never seen any bird like this—its beak more a pot than a bill! *Pelicans,* Harrison called them. Janey laughed and pointed with one hand while I clasped the other, and Maggie patted my back happily. *Behold, Canaan.*

The sun dropped lower, deepening hues in the sky, and casting fiery orange onto the surface of the water. As if signaled, the chirping, creaking and croaking from the forests pitched louder. So this was August in Virginia—exuberant with the sounds of life in the swamps and woods. It was warm, lush, and fragrant. "Perhaps Will was right," I said to Maggie. "Perhaps this *is* our Promised Land."

"We can hope. We can pray," she replied. "We will never know 'til we try it."

Whosoever puts his hand to the plow and looks back is not fit for the kingdom of Heaven flashed through my mind, and I thought, *You are right, Lord. We can look only forward, never back.*

I strained my eyes far west down the river, wondering if I could see the fort yet. Or the *Sea Venture.*

No, I could see neither.

At last, after four days of traveling upriver, the wooden *pallisado,* some fifteen feet high, came into view. I drew a sharp breath upon first sight of this impaled log fort. *James Town.* Each corner had a rounded bulwark where heavy ordnance were poised, barrels aimed at the water through portals.

Near the palisade, moored to a pine, was a docked ship. It was not the *Sea Venture*—or any of our expedition—and my heart fell. Well, the others would follow in a matter of days.

I was amazed that ships of this size were able to get close enough to shore for the mariners to rope them to the trees. Apparently, the depth of the river was one of the reasons the leaders had chosen this site two years before.

Getting a look at the James Town marsh, I supposed deep-water access had seemed more important than healthfulness, for everyone knew stagnant water was not good for a body. Apparently, Captain Archer thought the same thing, because I heard him say to the navigator, "You see what I meant when I pointed out that plot of land they call *Archer's Hope?* Wasn't it preferable to this brackish mess? But I couldn't persuade the Council when we were selecting a fort site."

Slowly the *Blessing, Unity, Falcon,* and *Lion* edged near the fort.

At that moment, we were startled when the gates swung wide with a clank of chain mail armor. Soldiers, wearing helmets and fully armed, aimed their muskets at us and prepared to fire.

Among Unknown Men,
in Lands Beyond the Sea
August 15–August 16, 1609

I traveled among unknown men, in lands beyond the sea;
nor England! did I know till then what love I bore to thee.
~ William Wordsworth

"Halt fire!" commanded a man, a Captain, standing near the front of the fort. "They are English." He said the word *English* with disdain and a scowl he did not even attempt to hide as he studied the fleet of four bedraggled ships. They must have mistaken us for Spanish warships. Obviously, we were unexpected—and it appeared, unwelcome—arrivals.

I wondered if this could be Captain John Smith, President of James Town. Will had spoken of his reputation for belligerence. I knew many of the leaders, including Captain Archer, complained of Smith's arrogance and vanity, which they found especially offensive from the son of a common yeoman farmer. Many of the leadership were returning to James Town, so old rivalries were sure to flare—which they did immediately.

"Captain Smith!" cried Captain Archer from the deck. "What a pleasure to see you again." His over-emphasis of the word *pleasure* sounded as sarcastic as he must have intended it. His hatred toward John Smith was well known. And, truth be told, each of the four ships contained some enemy or another of Captain Smith. That would account for the sneer in Smith's voice. The Spanish might have been happier news for him.

Smith had his hands on his hips, a cocky lift to one brow, and struck me as all red—red beard, hair, and face. Archer disembarked while the rest of us took in the scene from the deck.

We received the word with profound disappointment: all would sleep on the ships tonight. They were unprepared for us, and Smith needed to study the situation.

The next morning, at first light and after one more meal of sea biscuits, Harrison directed us back up the scuttle. Single file, we came down the gangplank. My heart pounded and my legs trembled with each step.

When my leather shoes first touched Virginia, I felt dizzy and stumbled because the land did not rock beneath me. I reached for the arm of Maggie, who also was unsteady, as was Janey. I noticed others staggering. What a sight we were, unkempt and foul smelling from months at sea, many of us still with gashes from the hurricane.

Dreamlike, it occurred to me that the soles of my shoes had last touched solid earth in Plymouth, England, two and a half months ago. Now we were an ocean away. We had been ten full weeks at sea, counting the week we sought shelter from the winds in Falmouth Harbor.

My next thought was how eager I was for food! Real food, English or Virginian mattered not to me, nor to any of us. I glanced at Elizabeth, making her way down the gangplank, and noticed she was little but bones.

When Temperance came down the *Falcon's* plank, I saw she looked well, if a bit apprehensive. She was as acutely aware as I was, no doubt, that no one had sighted our husbands' ship yet.

No worry, it would be here soon with the rest of the fleet.

The unfamiliar ship we had seen, the *Mary and John*, belonged to Captain Samuel Argall. Apparently, the Virginia Company had sent Argall to scout a more direct route to Virginia, an improvement on the roundabout one through the Torrid Zone of the Caribbean, which forced a stopover in the Bahaman Islands. The Virginia Company had instructed him to sail the Azores route, south to the Canaries and then due west as we did, directly to Virginia. Once here, he was also to study the fishing grounds. At the top of his list was the sturgeon, a ten-foot long delicacy that lived in the James River and in the bay.

Argall had been here about a month, informing Captain Smith that our huge expedition would arrive later—however, this was considerably sooner than either man expected. Argall told him too that we would bring with us a new charter, instructions, and a change in leadership. The Virginia Company was initiating a new system of government, with an all-powerful Governor-for-Life instead of a weaker President and Council. The Company was tactfully sending Captain Smith to supervise Point Comfort.

What Captain Smith saw that August day caused him much concern, when he was having trouble feeding the two hundred settlers already present. We were four ships arriving earlier than he anticipated, with an expected total of five hundred additional mouths to feed.

We could be little help, arriving too late in the year to do any corn planting, and we were not seasoned, either. Most settlers needed to get through that critical first summer to adapt to the new climate and illnesses borne of the swamp. We'd have no seasoning time before winter set in.

Beyond that, the Captains of the ships—Gabriel Archer of the *Blessing*, John Ratcliffe of the yet-to-arrive *Diamond*, and John Martin of the *Falcon*—were enemies of Captain Smith from the first year at James Town in 1607. Their return was obviously *not* welcome to him since they would no doubt undermine his leadership. They might even blame him for the deaths of the other Council members. Hadn't they nearly executed him once before when some of his men died on an expedition? He had felt the scratchy noose around his neck. Captain Newport's timely arrival in the First Supply had halted his execution scheduled for that night. Smith had a grudging respect for the one-armed Captain who pardoned him.

Yet, *none* of these Captains knew how to deal effectively with the natives, as far as Smith was concerned. Even Newport was an Indian-pleaser. Catering to the natives was poor strategy in dealing with them, Smith felt. The natives respected a show of strength, but when they perceived an English weakness, they were keen to exploit it. These Indians were shrewd and knew how to play feuding English leaders against one another. Feuding—there was going to be some of that. And sickness would claim many of the new, unseasoned arrivals. Hunger remained the harshest threat. If the Indians played these circumstances against him as he suspected they would…

The fact that the Virginia Company planned to remove him as President was the least of his worries.

Yes, he was no doubt distressed about our arrival, especially when he learned a hurricane had spoiled most of our provisions and supplies. The *Sea Venture* held most of our victuals, however, so perhaps they had fared better. We would see when they landed.

I can only say we felt about as welcome as the *hurricano* when we blew into James Town that sweltering summer day. We were a hungry hurricane at that, finding a town ill prepared for us in terms of shelter or food. Added to Smith's worries were the four missing ships—one of which carried the new charter, all the leadership, and hundreds more people.

Travelers in the Wilderness of the World

August 16, 1609

We are all travelers in the wilderness of the world, and the best that we can find in our travels is an honest friend.

~ Robert Louis Stevenson

Temperance and I found each other across the several hundred people there that morning. We embraced as though we had always known each other, and in some ways, it felt we had. It was wonderful to see a familiar face.

"How was your voyage overall?" I asked.

She grimaced. "Ten very, very long weeks. But I was only mildly seasick, praise heavens, and few on our ship had any real illness of which to speak. How about you? Did the hurricane hit you hard? I myself am still nursing wounds and bruises." She pushed up the sleeve of her kirtle, stained and worn from the journey, to show me a particularly bad cut with black all around it.

"I think the heel of someone's boot decided to scale my arm." She laughed. "How did you fare?"

"About the same. That we survived the hurricane at all is a miracle. And the whole voyage, some poor souls never stopped retching." I nodded to Elizabeth Mayhew. "She, for example, had an extremely rough time of it." Lowering my voice, I said, "Frankly, I'm surprised she's still alive."

Temperance nodded sympathetically.

"What do you suppose we do first?" I asked. It felt strange to be without Will, Sam, Hugh, and George, but their ship would land in a day or so, I reckoned.

Just then, Maggie wandered over, and I introduced the two women. "Mistress Temperance Yeardley, please meet Mistress Maggie Deale."

To Maggie, I added, "You may recognize her name, as Temperance's husband has commanded our husbands in the Lowlands."

Maggie bowed her head courteously. "A pleasure, Temperance."

"Pleased to meet you, Maggie. And my friends call me *Tempie*."

110

Maggie smiled warmly. "Aye, then, Tempie."

"On the ship, Maggie sang like a nightingale," I said, still impressed.

"And had a voyage like a seadog. But we managed, didn't we?" Maggie said to me. "It's good to find solid earth." She touched a pine tree, relishing the sturdiness of it. "It doesn't rock!" she laughed. We all looked upward to its spire, and then leaned around it for a glimpse inside the fort.

There we saw cottages with timber frames and wide country chimneys. I could not place this design that appeared to be a strange mix of English and Indian construction.

"Have you ever been to Lincolnshire?" Maggie asked absently, studying the cottages from afar.

"No, I don't believe so." I thought I knew what she was driving at. Smith was a Lincolnshire man.

"This is reminiscent of the cottages there, in a peculiar sort of way."

What was peculiar was that, rather than thatching the roofs, the men had covered them in fine woven mats and...tree bark. On the walls, where we might have expected whitewashed mud daubed between woven branches, were also mats and tree bark.

Maggie said no more, and we three simply stood for a moment, taking it in. No one spoke, but we were no doubt thinking the same thing. These cottages were a distant cry from the spacious homes we left behind. I could only imagine the estate in which Tempie had grown up.

Some cottages were within the walls of the fort, and others were outside of it. We could see the largest building in the center, which we gathered to be a church and meeting place. A wooden cross marked its roof.

This was no Melcombe, nor ever would be. At the thought of my protected little harbor town and Cecily, I felt a pain run through me, but I dismissed it quickly. That was an ocean away and what seemed a lifetime ago. In particular, the image of Cecily's face stabbed me, so I pushed it from my mind.

While waiting to find out what we should do next, we had time to view our other surroundings. We could make out what appeared to be a pitch and tar swamp to one side of the palisade walls, some cleared lands, and the forest itself.

"So this is Virginia? The fabled land o'plenty?" Maggie said, glancing about.

The variety of birds, and in so many colors, fascinated me. A red one with a peaked cap cried *cheer cheer* from the brush. (*Indeed, we could use some cheer*, I thought.) There was a great blue and white fellow, noisy and aggressive, also wearing a peaked cap, and a great black woodpecker with white on its wings and

111

a grand, festive red crest. ("Virginia birds do like their fancy headwear," was Tempie's wry comment.) Ravens and cawing blackbirds we recognized at once. A small black and yellow bird made me laugh with joy in its brilliance. I felt the deprivation of being on blue sea for so long, I suddenly realized. There were small brown birds with arched backs, which gave their tail feathers a happy tilt. Another one looked like a sparrow wearing a black cap, calling *chick-a-dee, chick-a-dee, chick-a-dee-dee-dee* from the brush. We later learned the settlers had simply dubbed this noisy crier *chickadee*. Perhaps this *was* an Eden, and we its Adam and Eve, naming creatures.

"Now that is an odd bird!" Tempie pointed to what looked like a crow with orange and yellow stripes across its wings. "Do you suppose he knows he isn't matched properly?" Later we spied orange and black birds with black wings. "These two must get together and straighten out their wardrobes!" Tempie said, leaving Maggie and me grinning. Tempie, I had begun to understand, used humor to lighten her distress.

We had never imagined there could be so many squirrels. They were nearly as large as our hares—and grey, not red as English squirrels were. We had heard of squirrels unique to this country with folds of skin such that they soared from tree to tree, catching the wind like a grey furry sail. Flying squirrels!

The country brimmed with the stunning as well as the mysterious. We knew the forests contained small lions, bears, red wolves, and foxes. There were musk cats, black with a white stripe down their back, which sprayed a foul scent when threatened. The Indians called these *shigak*. There were other small animals the natives called *arakuns*, which had black masks and dexterous hands. And little grey pig-like animals they called *opossums*.

The air was humid, and buzzing insects made bold sounds as the sun dropped lower. The sky was clear and wide, and the smells were glorious—so fresh and dramatic compared to the stifled air onboard ship. I thought I should never get enough of plants, the richness of leaves and berries and wildflowers drying from a mild late afternoon rain.

"Virginia is alive," I murmured.

I saw Tempie had a skeptical eye raised my way. "Let's hope *we* stay alive in it!" she commented, and Maggie laughed.

"I think I shall like her," Maggie said to me with a nudge.

"Who exactly is in charge, then?" cried a man's voice, pulling us from our reverie. We turned in its direction. Captains Archer and Martin had squared off with the current President, Captain Smith. The two men, obviously in agreement, glared at Smith with disdain they did not attempt to hide. Apparently, Archer had begun giving commands as soon as he stepped off ship, as had Martin. Smith was having none of it.

"I am the President," said the cool Smith, "Unless you show me orders otherwise."

Martin took a step toward him. "See here, you plebian fool! You know the new charter is on the *Sea Venture,* and Argall has told you its contents." He indicated a blonde man standing off to one side.

"Your leadership command is over," Archer said with narrowed eyes. "Martin or I shall take over until the *Sea Venture* arrives."

Smith, all red—beard, hair and face—stared down the other two men. His look was contemptuous and he spat on the ground.

"You two were useless in the first Council. Then you sailed back home and coddled yourselves. Now you *dare* to return after *I* turned this fort around by the sweat of mine own blood these two years? Get away from me," he said with a shove, pushing his way through them. "Produce a new charter and we shall talk. 'Til then, *I* remain President unless *I* decide otherwise," he said over his shoulder. "And may I remind you, my term as President is not up until the tenth of October. You are under *my* command until then, or until that charter appears over that blue horizon." He pointed downriver. "I have no time for your useless strutting. Right now my priority is feeding—and housing—280 new arrivals with two hundred more on the way, late in the season, with not enough corn stockpiled and winter coming hard in on us. We don't have markets here, Gentlemen. We grow it, we catch it, or we barter for it. And the natives are not much in a bartering mood at the moment. Were you aware that rats and rot destroyed all our stored grain this spring? No? Talk to me about surviving a wilderness with this hand of cards, and then talk to me about leading. Show me the charter, Gentlemen. Right now, I have a responsibility and some quick decisions to make. Or hadn't you noticed there are women and children without men here?"

Archer cursed Smith, but Smith kept walking. Soldiers, tense, stood behind each faction.

Maggie, Tempie, and I looked at each other helplessly. Our military husbands would have been appalled at this display. The crowd was milling and tired, and the sense of chaos grew.

Sounding worried, Tempie observed, "Well, as the proverb says, *delays are dangerous.* The delay of the *Sea Venture* is certainly dangerous to James Town."

"Aye," Maggie agreed, casting a sharp eye at the officers. "They also say *fish always stink from the head downward.* I do believe we are downwind of a stench right now. But, never you mind, Governor Gates will set this lot straight, right quick. We need that charter. We need those men."

She was right. And the men we needed most were our own husbands—mine, Tempie and Maggie's. Until they arrived, we would have to fend for ourselves.

An hour later, Captain Smith called a meeting in the church, and Reverend Meese performed a prayer service. Meese was new to the colony also, replacing the saintly Reverend Hunt who had died the previous year.

With its strange matting and tree bark exterior, the church was primitive compared to the beautiful stone and brick chapels of Dorset. We were the largest congregation this humble church had ever seen.

Tempie, Maggie, Janey, and I managed to get a seat in one of the tall, straight cedar pews, but folks were spilling out everywhere. Some crowded into the back, while others stood outside leaning through the windows.

Janey squirmed in discomfort in the heat. Her leaning against me only made us both stickier.

"It is unbearably *hot,*" Tempie whispered to me. We dripped sweat and swatted at stinging insects the soldiers dubbed *mayflies.*

"If they are indeed *may*flies, they are three months overdue their stay," she added. "They appear to me to have the worst characteristics of a fly and a bee," she said, killing one on her arm. I tried to maintain my reverent pose, but a chuckle escaped me.

It was not clear who was in charge, but since both the leadership *and* the new charter were missing, it appeared Smith was still President. Smith stood at the end of the last prayer and announced firmly to all congregated, "My one-year term of Presidency is due to expire in three weeks." He cast a sharp glance at Archer and Martin. "I intend to hold it until then."

The two opposing Captains rose to their feet as well. Archer, a finger pointed at Smith, fired back, "You hold it *only* until the new charter arrives. Officially, that charter carries the King's signature, and we are under its authority this very moment!"

Smith glared at Archer, disgust evident on his face. In a surprise move, Smith said, "Have it, then. I commend it to Captain Martin—the lesser of two evils." He shot a piercing look at Archer. "I resign." Smith stomped from the church.

Everyone fell into a stunned silence, even Martin—clearly not expecting to receive what he had demanded.

The next morning we learned that Martin kept the Presidency for three hours—and then gave it back to Smith. There was too much for him to learn too quickly, and without a charter backing him, he had no real authority anyway. Until the *Sea Venture* landed, probably within a few days, Smith would remain President.

The next question was how Captain Smith would house all of these new inhabitants, since the confines of the fort could not hold so many. Smith thought he had a solution.

James Town was located on a piece of land that was nearly, but not quite, an island. It was about half marsh and half forest, with cleared fields also. The massive James River formed one shoreline and the fort stood along that. Another waterway branched off the James River and created a second shoreline. Being of a practical nature, the soldiers had simply called this smaller river the Thorofare. The Thorofare gradually blended into an even smaller waterway called the Back River, which ultimately widened into Sandy Bay. A narrow land bridge cut across this small bay and provided the only overland access from James Town Island to the mainland of Virginia.

A three-story blockhouse stood at this strip of land, with a garrison of soldiers keeping constant sentry. No one, English or Indian, was to pass beyond the blockhouse without the President's permission. It was here the Indians conducted their trade with the town, going no further inland unless accompanied by soldiers from the blockhouse.

This meant that the entire island was fairly secure from prowling natives, even outside of the fort's palisades. Therefore, Smith felt comfortable erecting tents near the cornfields.

Captain Smith created hasty living arrangements for all of us. There were only about forty or fifty cottages, so besides putting some in tents, he assigned others to continue sleeping on the ships.

Fourteen women had husbands on the missing *Sea Venture*, so he assigned seven each to two cottages. Apparently, Captain Smith felt it was not proper to leave us to our own devices in the field without husbands to protect us.

Our cottage measured no more than twenty by twenty feet. Maggie, Elizabeth, Tempie, and I were in a house with three other women and three children besides Janey. We could look forward to Maggie's voice, but with Elizabeth, well, we would have to find patience.

Our quarters included a large but crude fireplace with a bread oven to one side, clay floors, a table, two benches, two stools, and three beds. There was one pot and skillet, a door and three windows. A ladder led to a small loft where some, including the children, might sleep. There was a cellar, and space beside the house for a small garden. The previous owners had a few plants growing.

Tempie was unimpressed. "Well, I'm glad I left Scottow for this!" she said, referring to her village in Norfolk. Tempie was the niece of Baron Stanley and was used to manors and privilege. I had to agree. Even my home in Dorset was a manor house compared to this one, which was smaller and more primitive in every way—including its dirt floors.

Yet, I told myself that there were those in tents in the field, so I supposed we should be grateful to have this much.

Whether Man or Woman
Be the Most Necessary
August 16, 1609

...in a newe plantation it is not knowen whether man or woman be the most necessary.
~ Petition of the Virginia Assembly, 1619

That first evening, Captain Smith sent Annie Laydon over to the two houses of single women to help us understand the ways of James Town. Barely fifteen, Annie had managed as the lone female in the settlement for nine months.

"Oh, I am *glad* to see you!" she said to us, when we had let her in. "Women folk! It does a body good!" Her smile was large, and her few missing teeth beamed at us. Yet she was attractive in a hearty, likeable way. She appeared to be with child. I marveled at her—little more than a girl herself, with child, and without female companionship for so long. Yet she seemed confident in herself and in this new world.

"Well-seasoned, I am! What questions do you have?"

The seven women searched each other's faces. There were so many questions we didn't know where to start.

I remembered Maggie's strategy of learning from those who might have an inside story. "So you're the only woman besides the new arrivals?" I asked. I wondered who would have midwifed her if we had not come. Bringing babies into the world was not the task of men!

Annie grinned again. She was sitting on one of the stools, her legs braced on either side of her dirty kirtle, her boots planted firmly.

"Aye, I'm the only woman *now* since my mistress died," she said with emphasis. "I wondered how I would have the baby without women to help me through the birth. Up until the spring, an Indian girl named Pocahontas used to come 'round. I thought maybe she could be the midwife."

Seeing our surprised expressions, Annie went on, "No need to fear her. She won't no wild animal. She's about my age and the daughter of their *werowance*, the

117

Powhatan. I liked her. I liked her a lot. Mistress Forrest died within a month of us arriving last October, so Pocahontas was the only woman around. She showed me Virginia ways, taking me to the woods and fields. She'd always bring corn with her, if they had any to spare. I miss her. I don't know why she stopped coming, but I 'spect it was problems between the tribe and us, as usual. The men folk fight and the women folk bear the brunt."

"What's a *werowance*?" Tempie asked.

"It's a leader, a chief. Pocahontas was fascinated with us, and we learned from her. She adored Captain Smith, so she visited the fort a couple of times a week—until those visits suddenly stopped. Cap'n Smith thinks the Powhatan moved their village somewhere further upland where we couldn't get there as easily and that her father won't allow Pocahontas to come here now. Would you believe the Cap'n says she saved his life *twice* when he was at the Powhatan's village? One time, says he, she put her own head over his when the braves were about to stone him."

Annie was a natural storyteller and the women drank in every word. Tempie was the wife of the soon-to-be Governor's assistant; Maggie and I were Captain's wives. We were all well older than she was. Yet she was our superior in every way, because she, already, was a Virginian.

"What happened to your mistress, Annie?" Maggie asked

"Mistress Forrest was a sweet lady, but the voyage about done her in. Once we landed, she got the bloody flux and scarce survived a month. We were with the Second Supply." We nodded. We knew ours was the third group of supply ships since the founding expedition in May 1607.

"The Second Supply was a small lot compared to yours—just one ship, the *Mary and Margaret*. Our timing was good, because we arrived last October, so we didn't have to start out in the heat of the summer like you folks." Tempie and I exchanged glances. That didn't sound good.

"What's wrong with the heat of the summer—besides the blasted *heat*, of course?" Tempie wanted to know.

"You ain't seasoned. You're not going to get time to adjust to Virginia before the summer fluxes hit you. Whereas me, I had the whole, icy winter to get used to the climate and ease into it during the springtime. When you make it through one summer, we say you're *seasoned*. That first Virginia summer is hardest on a body. On the other hand, summer's nigh closing, so it might be all right."

Even as she spoke, we were fanning ourselves against the muggy heat.

Seeing how hot we were, Annie added, "Before any of you get to complaining about these odd cottages, be thankful they are what they are and not mud and stud."

We looked at her quizzically. She continued, "Mud and stud is just fine for English summers and winters, but after the big fire in January of '08, Smith had all the houses rebuilt this way. He said a house with a thatched roof and mud walls in Virginia might as well be a bread oven." She laughed at the allusion. "The Indians use mats and bark, and their houses stay warm in the winter, dry in the spring rains, and cool in the summer. It's more bearable in here than it would've been the other way, even if it's not as fancy! And let me tell you, the winters get cold faster than you would reckon after such a scorching summer."

"When does the season start to cool down?" Maggie asked.

Annie thought for a moment. "We arrived the last day of September and disembarked October 1. It was growing cooler by then. They have some hot days in October, though. The old settlers call it *Indian summer.*"

"Who is your husband?" asked Maggie.

"I married Jack Laydon after the Mistress died. Jack's a carpenter who came in the First Supply. We were the first wedding in James Town," she added proudly. "In fact, the *only* wedding in James Town so far." She patted her belly. "Now we're expecting our first child long about Christmastime. Another first for James Town!"

The women began murmuring. This was much to take in.

We drew straws for the few beds. Tempie and I had not been among the lucky few to win a bed, but I was pleased that Maggie—and even Elizabeth—did. Elizabeth had now grown so scrawny that I thought a good night's rest would do her good.

"Oh, what is this scratchy, filthy linen made of?" she cried, banging it with her hands. I rolled my eyes at Maggie across the room.

"With so many new arrivals sleeping in tents in the field, I am *so* thankful for a cottage in which to sleep, aren't *you,* Elizabeth?" Maggie nearly sung out.

Elizabeth glared at her. "Nothing short of a four poster bed planted on Cornish soil is where I want to sleep." She climbed beneath the sheet, and as she did, I noticed she trembled with the effort. I felt a measure of compassion for her in spite of myself.

"Elizabeth, is there something I can fetch to soothe you?" I asked, almost afraid of the answer.

She did not reply, but rolled over, and I could see that the effort taxed her. I shrugged and said no more.

The whistling, creaking, and groaning from the marshes and woods sounded like ghouls surrounding us on every side. There were rhythmic hooting sounds from higher above and a startling cheeping that rang through it all.

"What on God's earth is *that commotion?*" Tempie asked in her very direct way.

We women were settling ourselves in. Tempie and I had mattresses on the floor, and Janey was nestled next to me. But I was too exhausted to be afraid. Even the crooning of forest frogs and insects and the buzz of mosquitoes 'round my ears—another delight we had discovered—could not keep me awake that evening. I had not slept on solid land in seventy days.

"It is Virginia, saying hello and good night," I murmured to Tempie, my head on the musty linen mattress, my eyes closing before the words were even out.

I Awoke and Found Me Here

August 16–August 25, 1609

And I awoke and found me here,
On the cold hill side.

And that is why I sojourn here,
Alone and palely loitering,
Though the sedge is withered from the lake,
And no birds sing.

~ John Keats

We were gradually growing accustomed to the ways of James Town, but politically much of it remained unbridled. The absent charter, leadership and food were tremendous blows.

President Smith had no support from the leadership already in James Town, as there *was* no other leadership—all of Smith's fellow Councilmen had died before our arrival. Only he, its President, had survived. His enemies were the Captains Archer and Martin, as well as Captain Ratcliffe on one of the still-missing ships. Smith was also enemies with George Percy, the youngest son of a nobleman and another early Council member.

Although none of the erstwhile leadership liked Smith, they could not deny Smith's experience in dealing with the Indians and in planting. We needed a respected figure such as Governor Gates to balance the bickering Captains while taking advantage of Smith's knowledge. The charter on the *Sea Venture* afforded Gates powerful authority as a Governor—not subject to the whinnying of a Council. Newport and Somers lent additional dignity to the enterprise and loyal soldiers onboard would keep peace between political factions.

Each day, all eyes were on the river. *Where were the missing ships?*

Finally, two days after our landing, a lookout spotted a vessel coming up the river. This time the sentry did not sound the alarm for a possible Spanish attack.

121

We were expecting the straggling ships any time. I craned my neck hopefully, as did Tempie, our baskets still under our arms from a morning spent collecting roots and berries.

"What do you think?" she asked me.

I sighed and shook my head. "Too small."

"I think you're right."

When it got closer and docked, we recognized the vice-admiral *Diamond,* delivering Captain John Ratcliffe.

Everyone knew hatred flared between Smith and Ratcliffe, yet they nonetheless feigned courtesy. Smith doffed his hat. "Captain Ratcliffe, a pleasure. Welcome!" He was not smiling.

Ratcliffe had been President once, the previous year, and well Smith remembered *that.* While Smith negotiated with Indians, back at James Town President Ratcliffe had ordered all house construction halted so that his men could build him a grand palace—a *state capitol.* There had been a devastating fire a few months before, so, in Smith's opinion, rebuilding the necessities—not palatial estates—should have been the order of the day. Meanwhile, Ratcliffe made no secret of enjoying the better victuals, as befitted *a President.* The rest of the Council had taken notice of Ratcliffe's excesses as well. About that time, the Council had rather unceremoniously ousted Ratcliffe from office and Smith had taken over. He had been President ever since.

Bygones were obviously not bygones. Ratcliffe, likewise, took off his hat and gave a bow. "Captain Smith. So good to see you again!" The men glared—a very courteous glare, however.

"Where's the *Sea Venture?*" Ratcliffe asked, surveying the ships lined up at shore.

"Not here, not yet, so *I* am still President until Gates brings himself and the charter naming him Interim Governor." Smith obviously understood the question implicit in Ratcliffe's remark. *Who's in charge?*

Ratcliffe shuffled, clearly unhappy with that news.

"What's the *Diamond's* condition? How are the sailors and landsmen?" Captain Smith continued.

Ratcliffe shook his head. "She's got the plague in her." My stomach fell. So the rumors were true; here was one disease I had hoped would not cross the Atlantic. The *Diamond,* I recalled, had departed from London and must have brought the plague from there. "We lost a considerable number, with many others deathly ill—though I myself am well."

It was hard to tell whether Smith was pleased or not to hear that Ratcliffe was in good shape.

"Keep the passengers on ship, then. You too," Smith ordered flatly. "We will not add plague to our growing list of concerns."

Ratcliffe, uncomfortable taking commands from Smith, nonetheless complied. "As you wish, *President* Smith." There was a hint of sarcasm in his voice.

"Any sighting of the *Sea Venture?*" Smith asked before Ratcliffe departed.

Ratcliffe's eyes widened. "None."

Several days later, another ship made its way upriver. The *Swallow*, Captain Moone's ship, was heavily storm-damaged. The whole mainmast had gone overboard during the hurricane.

We learned that between them, the *Diamond* and the *Swallow* had thirty-two deaths along the way, and two baby boys were born—and died—on the journey. It was clear that despite hardship, the *Blessing had* indeed lived up to its name.

Five days after the *Swallow's* arrival, I stood scanning the water, looking eastward downriver. The sun rose little by little, and I squinted in its glare. *God has promised, God has promised,* I thought restlessly. Had I heard Him wrong? *Whole will I keep thee and thy family,* He had said. Perhaps if those words *did* come from God, He meant He would rejoin us and make us whole in heaven. Perhaps I had not heard Him at all—but only the whispering waters of Melcome Bay. I put my hand to my chest, feeling the pilgrim's badge. I no longer knew what to believe.

I felt a hand upon my shoulder. Tempie had come up quietly behind me.

As though reading my thoughts, she said in a hushed tone, "It is not coming, Joan."

I bit my lip, eyes squeezed shut, knowing she was right but as yet unready to accept it. The truth hung in the air. Each day hope for the survival of the *Sea Venture* grew dimmer. Each hour the river lay empty, the stakes crept higher. An image of my father—the storm, the rocks, his body—came to my thoughts but I shoved it away. *No!*

"It *is* coming!" I fairly screamed at her. "It's just straggling somehow. Perhaps it lost its mainmast like the *Swallow.* That's what's slowing it down. It's…it's…" I was talking in a fast, desperate tone. "It will be here tomorrow then, certainly! Tempie, you know as well as I do that miracles happen *every day.* If it takes a miracle, a miracle it will be." I said this with every ounce of faith and defiance in my soul—faith I neither possessed nor believed.

Tempie flinched but nodded, her eyes sympathetic and glistening with tears. "Of course you're right," she said slowly. She shrugged. "If it did lose its mast and its other sails tore, it could be weeks before it comes upriver." Her tone said she would not deflate me, however bleak the outlook. She would give me time to accept it on my own terms, in my own way. I appreciated that.

There was a pensiveness to the stony quiet then. Wayward seabirds faced the wind, making their way back down the James, and the water softly jabbed the shoreline, rhythmically, as though taunting it. I would have sworn the river, wide and empty, felt bereft. So, too, did I.

"I'm sorry for my outburst." I felt contrite. After all, she had her own loss to mourn, as did Maggie. Wordlessly, Tempie placed her arm around me and touched her head to mine. And so we stood as the sun inched higher, faces to the east, arms wrapped about each other's waists. Together we watched and waited, as though this moment, this time, distant sails would appear.

They did not.

To Strive, to Seek, to Find, and Not to Yield
August 29, 1609

Come unto these yellow sands,
And then take hands.

~ William Shakespeare

Though much is taken, much abides; and though
We are not now that strength which in old days
Moved earth and heaven, that which we are, we are—
One equal temper of heroic hearts,
Made weak by time and fate, but strong in will
To strive, to seek, to find, and not to yield.

~ Alfred Tennyson

James Town continued to be crowded and chaotic—not enough living quarters for so many colonists, and open hostility between the old leadership command of Smith against Ratcliffe, Martin, and Archer. Captain Percy was ill and hoped to return to England, so although he did not care for Smith, he had avoided the fray.

We had been in Virginia for several weeks, and each passing day dampened our hopes for the *Sea Venture*. She was not coming. This we all knew, and this no one spoke aloud but uttered only in whispers amongst one's closest friends. It was hard to know who was the ablest gentleman to be in charge—a thought that was downright frightening.

Smith had spent considerable time on the ships with the sailors, celebrating and blowing off powder. The loud, smoky bangs from the ships' ordnance shattered morning silence at best and seemed wasteful at worst.

"Why does he do this?" Tempie asked, echoing the question on everyone's minds. "It is annoying and squanders our ammunition!"

"Smith woos the uncommitted and hopes to sway them to his cause," Maggie said. She, Tempie, and I trudged the woods in the late August heat, gathering whatever we could find in the way of roots and berries.

125

"So if the sailors side with Smith, he creates more allies?" I asked Maggie.

She nodded with a frown. "Or he may be trying to ensure that the Indians both *hear* us and *fear* us," she added.

"Certainly they have heard us by now! When is enough, enough, then?" I asked, irritated with Smith, as another shot split the air.

Obviously troubled by the Captain's actions, Maggie shook her head in disgust. "Yesterday was enough," she said.

"Those fish are stinking from the head downward again," Tempie murmured, and we laughed despite our agitation.

This day we had baskets slung across our arms and hoped to fill them. We'd found the woods speckled with shrubs of just-ripening blue berries called *huckleberries*. These grew underfoot everywhere and we eagerly collected all we could. We were becoming familiar with the forests and waterways around us.

Besides the two rivers, we had several smaller creeks. These were all brackish fingers of water, which flowed into and out of the Thorofare or the James River with the tides. To the right of the fort was the Pitch and Tar Swamp, and near the Back River lay the Back River Marsh. These, besides Lower Point and Black Point, formed our major landmarks outside of the fort. Black Point was where the Thorofare split from the James River, and Lower Point was the corner where our island jutted into the James. In all, the island had some thirty miles of shoreline and miles and miles of creeks and streams.

In the narrow offshoot ridges upland near Goose Hill were groves of oak and maple. Beech and walnut trees grew amongst the groves, and the underbrush was so low Captain Smith swore one could gallop a horse through there.

We continued making our way beyond Goose Point uplands into the groves where the huckleberries were prolific.

Some of the women went searching as we did, while others never went at all. Elizabeth Mayhew, for example, was still unwell from the voyage. She had an excuse. Others, like Mary Tompkins, felt roving too far beyond the fort was frightening. Some said they didn't want to get their hands dirty. A few felt the Company Store would meet all their needs.

Yet that seemed unrealistic to anyone who truly considered the logistics. Much of what the Virginia Company sent had been on the huge *Sea Venture*. When we landed, Smith had seven acres of corn planted, but the ones camped in the field fell upon at least a third of that and had already devoured it.

I left Janey at the cottage with those who stayed in. Tempie, Maggie, and I tramped the woods and fields faithfully each day and delighted in the plants, both strange and familiar, we discovered.

Wild blackberries were just coming into season, and we expected to enjoy them until Michaelmas day. Tradition held that the Archangel Michael tossed the devil from heaven on Michaelmas, causing Lucifer to land squarely in a bramble bush. The poor berries withered and were not edible after that date each year, but we expected to enjoy them for another month or so.

Virginia sassafras charmed us with its diverse leaf shapes, like soft green hands. Normally obtained from the Orient, sassafras was a medicinal blessing of the New World, and we dug up what we found.

"Do you remember hearing of colonists at Roanoke who survived off of only sassafras pottage?" I asked Maggie and Tempie as we rooted it out.

Maggie nodded, a shrewd eye cast about her. "It will do us well to collect, dry, and store all we can against the coming winter. *What can't be cured must be endured,* as they say."

"They also say *poverty is no disgrace, but it is a great inconvenience,*" Tempie added ruefully, her hands and apron blackened with dirt and mud. Maggie and I chuckled as we all continued our search.

Sassafras roots we would dry to make remedies and oils while using the dried leaves for beverages or seasoning. The Virginia Company had ordered us to ship sassafras oil home as soon as possible. In the meantime, it was a precious commodity for us here.

It was never wise to tarry in the woods. Although the natives were not supposed to be on the island, occasionally they paddled their canoes across the Thorofare or Back River. We had not seen any Indians since we landed, but prudence urged us to gather efficiently and scurry back inside the palisade walls.

Absently, we troweled the cluster of sassafras we had found. Another blast split the morning air, causing us to jump.

Maggie said firmly, "When we finish here, we must talk."

We slipped into the church between services. Placing our baskets on a pew, we huddled together in the back, wiping perspiration beads off our faces. We chose a seat beneath a window, hoping to catch any breeze. The church had large, airy windows, but like the rest of the island, it remained stifling. Virginia had a pervasive heat beyond our imaginings. Biting mosquitoes replaced the stinging mayflies at sunset, as though they had arranged shifts in doling misery. Already, some of the newcomers were falling ill with summer fluxes, though we three and Janey had thus far been fortunate.

"We need a plan," Maggie began, her voice low. There was no one near the window, but it didn't hurt to be cautious. As on ship, she saw that we women could—must, in fact—take charge for ourselves.

"Agreed," Tempie said.

"Aye," I added.

"First off, we know there have been *no* sightings of the *Sea Venture* since the storm hit. Have we accepted that it is likely...lost?" Maggie asked. Her tone was softer. She looked from one of us to the other. In the ensuing silence, she continued, "I do not expect to see my Hugh again." The tears in her eyes belied the conviction of her words. "This side of heaven, I mean."

Tempie and I glanced at each other and then dropped our heads. *Was Will truly gone? And Sam?* Unlike Maggie and Tempie, I had a child to tend and one expectantly waiting in England to join her half of the scallop shell with mine. I touched the pilgrim's badge around my neck. Even in this heat, I kept it on for the security it gave. It reminded me of my father, of a time when life was not nearly so complicated—when I made pottage and waited for fanciful bulbs and herbs and a story of Algerian pirates. When tulips in every color burst into my life, and Mr. Shakespeare's plays were the street corner babble. I had wished for adventure like the women of old in my family—but not truly. All I had truly desired was a hearth in Melcombe, my husband safely at my side, and my little girls giggling in an upper room.

James Town seemed part dream, part nightmare. Only the scallop badge seemed real, a link to another time and another place.

"Joan?" Tempie touched my arm.

I covered my eyes and began crying. "I was willing to give this a try, my best, my all, but could we have imagined it so awful?" At that instant, a mayfly stung my arm, and I slapped it hard in anger, inflicting a bruise worse than the welt. "Little beast!" I was beginning to appreciate Elizabeth's sentiments of this *stinking place*, as she called it.

"Who took the harsher blow, him or you?" Tempie asked, and I laughed in spite of myself while the tears rolled down my sweaty cheeks. "Say, don't you know water is valuable here? Yet look at you wasting it," she said kindly. She gave my cheek a wipe and placed an arm about me.

"You are right, Joan. We didn't know, but we do now," Maggie said. She shrugged. "What we have, we have. We need to plan as...widows." Even Maggie, for all her strength, faltered on that word.

We three took hands, Maggie reaching across Tempie to grasp my right hand while Tempie held my left. Together, our arms formed a circle. I felt their clammy palms and their trembling. In truth, we were all afraid. I drew a deep breath and composed myself.

"We gain strength from one another. We cannot forget that," Maggie continued. "Let us work together as friends, even family."

"We are all we have," I said. I squeezed their hands, and each squeezed in return.

"We know food is scarce," Tempie said tentatively. A frightening thought, that.

"Did your plants and herbs book survive the storm?" Maggie asked me.

I nodded. "I have it." It had gotten wet but was yet readable.

"Good."

"There *are* some Virginia species in it—from the Roanoke expedition twenty years ago and plants procured from the Spanish," I ventured. "Plus I have the herbs I brought with me. A few damaged by seawater, but many of them salvageable."

"Aye," Maggie said firmly. "And all your roots and seeds to plant."

"Yes, most of them." A few I had lost, but I was getting the idea. "And I know something about what to gather from the woods."

"Then you have much to offer."

Thinking aloud, I said, "We need to find out from Annie Laydon if she knows when last year's frost was. She arrived the first day of October, she said. Much of what I have, I still can plant as a fall garden—beets, carrots, radishes, and peas. It's a start. It's something."

"Good," Maggie continued. "Without leadership, we can expect continued fighting from the men. Prior to our landing, the food had already dwindled— thanks to the rats and the rot in the storehouse. And Smith did not receive enough notice of our arrival to adjust planting. Not to mention many of our best provisions were lost with the *Sea Venture.*"

Every time she said *lost* and *Sea Venture*, my heart dropped to my stomach. I swallowed but nodded. We must face this reality, because survival depended on it.

"By God, where is our hope, then?" Tempie asked, brow furrowed in concern.

"I know!" I said suddenly. "These ships will have to return to England soon—they're only leased from merchants. They'll inform the Virginia Company about our plight and the *Sea Venture's* loss. They'll send supply ships."

"Perhaps not." Tempie spoke quietly, and she too was correct. If there were a war going on, as happened to the Roanoke colonists, England would need all vessels to fight. Or if the Virginia Company could not raise funds in the frenzy of the staggering loss of the *Sea Venture*—one hundred fifty souls, all that property, and the country's brightest stars. "No funds, no ships," she said with finality.

"Even with relief arriving, it will take, let us say, three months for these ships to arrive back in London, at least another month for the Company to garner support and refigure strategy, and then three more months for them to return to us," Maggie added.

"If they come," Tempie said.

"If they come," Maggie concurred.

"March, at the earliest, then," I said, counting out the months. And the ships had not even departed James Town yet.

We were still holding hands, and Maggie breathed, "Pray, God, see us through the fall and winter alone at James Town. Our hope is in manna from heaven. Oh, Lord, give us this day—and every day—our daily bread."

We had no time for grief. We would have to organize our planting and gathering at once, this day. For even in the blistering heat, the summer hours grew shorter and winter's threat edged closer.

Danger's Troubled Night
August 29–September 7, 1609

The meteor flag of England
Shall yet terrific burn,
Till danger's troubled night depart,
And the star of peace return.

~ Thomas Campbell

Never, never, never believe any war will be smooth and easy, or that anyone
who embarks on the strange voyage can measure the tides and hurricanes he
will encounter. The statesman who yields to war fever…is the slave of unfore-
seeable and uncontrollable events.

~ Sir Winston Churchill

In the end, it was hard to say whether the natives placed a noose about our necks or we had done it ourselves. But one thing was certain: our necks were in one, and it rapidly tightened—first with this yank, then with that one. Within weeks of our arrival, even the women began to sense a constriction of native relations, a strangling sensation. A growing unease settled over the town.

Despite his bluster, or perhaps because of it, Smith seemed successful in holding the Indians at arm's length. They appeared to both respect and fear him, a strategy that kept relations mostly civil. Perhaps *that* was the reason for the firepower emanating from the ships. Let the natives, who were sure to be watching, know that this was a powerful fleet that had arrived—not a weak and disjointed band of milksop leaders with hostile men and untrained women and children.

And, yes, we were all aware that from the bushes, from the forests, from the swamps across the Back River, dark eyes studied us.

Some of these dark eyes no doubt belonged to Nansemond bowmen, seething as a result of an expedition to negotiate with them gone very, very wrong. How this came about we would soon learn.

131

Days after we landed, Captain Smith had dispatched Martin and Percy with sixty men downriver to the Nansemonds to purchase an island from the tribe. At the same time, he had sent Captain West with 120 men upriver to the falls to establish a fort.

The Virginia Company had ordered new settlements to strengthen our defensive position against the Spanish and the natives. In Smith's eyes, another necessity was lessening the crowding at James Town. However, Smith's most impelling reason for establishing these settlements was the potential food sources they provided. With 180 men sent elsewhere, close to half the population would have means of food besides that on James Town Island. However, organizing outlying settlements presented a unique challenge for Smith, as it was hard to protect the men further out.

All that we women knew was that it sounded positive at the outset. With nearly half of the men dispersed, crowding and flaring tempers lessened. The idea that winter might not be as lean as we had first thought was great encouragement.

However, we did not understand that, marshy and forgotten, James Town island was wasteland as far as the natives were concerned. We could have it. But West's fort was to be built near an Indian town called Arsetock, prime farmland and the birthplace of Chief Powhatan. And the island we hoped to purchase from the Nansemonds they considered sacred.

The first indication we had that all was *not* well was Percy's return from Nansemond territory. Smith had ordered him to report back to James Town once Martin was situated on the tribe's island in the Nansemond River.

The morning that Captain Percy returned with a small group of soldiers, Tempie and I were coming home from the Company Store, having just collected our day's ration of cornmeal and a few peas. Percy's demeanor caught our attention—still physically unwell, he was also flustered and angry. He approached the sentry at the fort's river gate, and the sentry gestured toward the *Blessing.* Smith was onboard, and that was no doubt whom Percy sought. A steely glint in his eyes, Percy marched up the gangplank, yelling, "Smith!"

"What is that about, do you suppose?" Tempie asked nervously.

I didn't know but wondered how we could find out. Of course, Smith spent much time on the ships with sailors. *Harrison!* Would he still treat us kindly?

Several days later, Maggie and I made an excuse to wander over near the river. We asked a mariner if he knew Harrison's whereabouts. "Sailed up to West's Fort with Cap'n Smith," he replied curtly without looking up.

Disappointed, Maggie asked, "Do you know why they've gone, Sir?"

He shrugged. "Check on the new settlement, I reckon." He said no more and we realized we would have to wait and hope Harrison was more helpful.

Days passed, then a week. At last, we saw the *Blessing* making its way back downriver. After they had roped it to the pines and furled the sails, Maggie and I tried once more to locate Harrison.

Maggie pointed toward the bow with excitement. "I see him!" We found something reassuring in his familiar old seaman's face.

Harrison spied us at the same time, touching his cap with a smile and a nod.

"Sir!" Maggie called up. "Could you help us?"

His face clouded. Were we disturbing him? I wondered. Then I saw that his expression bore concern. "Faring well, me hens?" he asked as he disembarked. "How's your girl?" he said to me.

"Janey's fine, Sir," I said. "And how fared you at West's Fort?"

He spat on the ground and shook his head in disgust. "A mutinous company of soldiers there, Mistress. Smith could do naught with 'em." He moved to continue his work, but I grabbed his sleeve.

"Master Harrison, as women alone, Maggie and I hear little of politics. Yet this knowledge is vital to our safety and to the safety of my...my girl. Can you tell us anything more? Please, Sir?"

Harrison hesitated, then he nodded in sympathy and pulled us aside. "You understand, Mistresses, there's a considerable amount at stake in getting these additional forts up and running."

"For defense?" Maggie asked.

"For *food*," Harrison said with emphasis. He need say no more than that. This confirmed for us that Smith had deep concerns about winter provisions. "Pickings on the island will be lean. Too many folks, too small an area. The crowded conditions ain't healthy either, Smith says." Harrison cocked a jaundiced eye at us. "Now I happen to think Smith also wants to get these *would-be Presidents* upriver or downriver of wherever he himself might be. But he *is* worried about sparse victuals, no denying that."

"So although these forts are important, something went askew both places?" Maggie asked with apprehension.

Harrison nodded. "Many a-thing went askew, Mistress." He lowered his voice. "As we were on our way to the falls, we passed Cap'n West sailing back to James Town. 'West must consider the fort in good stead,' Smith said. 'It had better be.'"

"And was it?" I asked.

"Not a bit. The men there were talkin' about nothin' but gold. Meanwhile, there won't no discipline, they were raiding the Indian villages and gardens—even holding a few Indians hostage at the fort. That tribe up there is called the Powhatans. That's chief Powhatan's home tribe, and his son is the *werowance*, you see. Smith said this was not a tribe to trifle with. But the men jabbered on that the Indians kept raiding *them*. Well, Smith accused the soldiers of fouling relations mightily if the natives were attacking, since they were a tributary tribe."

"A *tributary* tribe?" Maggie was collecting information, and I could almost see her mind sorting through it.

"When a small tribe agrees to live in peace with a larger one, they pay what's called *tribute* to the higher chief. Tributes are corn, generally. In return, the high chief protects that smaller tribe. Most all the tribes around here pay tributes to Powhatan. Smith has some tribes agreeing to pay *him* tributes of corn as well. So when Smith arrived, the Indians wanted to know where their protection was? And who was going to protect them from their *protectors*?" Harrison laughed and spat again. "Smith dealt with West's men his own way—which, when Cap'n West returned, weren't pleasing to *him*." Barely twenty, West was a young nobleman, the brother of Lord De La Warr, and probably considered himself superior to Smith.

Harrison said another problem, as Smith saw it, was the location of the fort. West had chosen a marshy site, but Smith had other ideas. He approached Parahunt, a *werowance* at the falls, son of the great Powhatan, and—Smith claimed—a friend of his. Would Parahunt consider letting the English purchase the palisaded Indian town for the winter? Located on higher ground, its cleared lands stood ready to plant while its houses, called *yehakins*, were in move-in condition. No fool, Smith understood that for generations—no one knew how long—Powhatan's people had inhabited these woods and knew where to build and how to keep their homes comfortable through all Virginia weather.

Smith himself had been in their homes many times and observed them to be warm and dry. He was quite impressed by the way they pulled saplings across a frame to form an arched structure, which they covered in mats woven of marsh reeds. A central hole in the roof allowed smoke to escape. Built under trees that acted as weather shields, the *yehakins* afforded protection from the near-tropical sun of Virginia summers and the deep snows of winter. Besides, a purchased town saved the English the extraordinary time and man-hours required to build from the ground up.

Smith and Parahunt struck a deal. Smith would pay for the town, and Parahunt would in turn continue paying tribute to the English for protecting his people from their enemies, the Monacans, to the west. This seemed a bargain for all, Smith offered. Parahunt agreed.

West, however, balked. He had a different view of the little Indian village Smith had renamed *Nonsuch.* ("There is none such place as this!" Smith had said.) As soon as Smith departed, West returned his men to the marshland fort. Perhaps the nobleman was too proud to live in an Indian house, or perhaps West knew more about the Indian relations than he was telling.

"Cap'n Smith said he feared for his life amongst that lot and that West would not respect his knowledge of the natives or his friendship with Parahunt," Harrison continued. "West's men had their *gilded hopes,* as the Cap'n said. They were too interested in gold and the route to the South Seas, when any fool could see food and dry housing were their greatest needs for the winter. That's when West and the Cap'n got in a ferocious argument. West said if Parahunt was Smith's *so-called friend,* why was he attacking West's men? Smith said to keep 'em closer in, that wandering too far afield searching for gold got the Indians edgy. To which Cap'n West retorted that the Company *ordered* them to search for commodities to send home. 'Feed yourselves first, then search for commodities. The Virginia Company wants you alive and able to search, not dead upon a mountain of gold!' Smith shot back at him."

It was clear that Smith's enemies were accumulating—Archer, Ratcliffe, Martin, Percy, and now West.

Harrison continued, "West swore by the King's crown that Smith *himself* set the tribe on West's men by telling the Indians the English had just one volley of powder left."

Maggie shook her head. "That makes no sense. Smith wouldn't set the Indians on his own people." She paused. "Would he?"

Harrison made a face. "The bad blood between all these Captains runs thick and scarlet—and mighty deep." His clear blue eyes met ours. "Mistresses, it's hard to know where the truth be."

The air was still warm with summer, yet a chill coursed through me.

How much would Harrison share? Maggie pressed him. "You say the soldiers at West's fort are mutinous, but we also observed Captain Percy's angry arrival from the Nansemonds. Do you know what happened there?"

"Aye, indeed, Mistresses. Percy *was* angry—with both Smith *and* Martin! Percy said Cap'n Smith desired him and Martin to fail, that Smith *knew* the Nansemonds wouldn't sell the island with their sacred temple on it."

"Was it sacred? Why?" I asked. Until then, it had never occurred to me that anything might be sacred to the natives. "Sacred to devil worship, you mean?"

135

This was the story the Virginia Company had promoted in its pamphlets. The true beliefs of Virginia Indians were more complex, we were to learn, as old soldiers like Smith and Percy already had.

"It's sacred to Okee—their highest god or devil—and to their dead kings. The Indians have a burial temple on that island. They put images of Okee with the bodies of their kings stacked on scaffolds yonder high." Harrison gestured upward in the air. We learned later that the natives disemboweled the bodies of their chiefs and stuffed them with sand, then wrapped them in skins and mats. They laid the bodies atop platforms reaching two stories high inside these temples.

"Oh," Maggie said with sudden understanding. "Martin and Percy attempted to buy this island with a Nansemond temple on it. The natives refused and Percy felt tricked?"

"Won't as simple as refusing, Mistress. Percy said that Smith deceived him and Martin was a coward. Smith argued that the Nansemonds were a tributary tribe and should have been agreeable."

"But, like Parahunt's people, they were far from *agreeable*?" I asked. "Depending on who tells the story?"

"Just so. Lieutenant Sicklemore took most of the three-score soldiers ahead overland, while Percy and Martin followed in the ship." Harrison shrugged. "When Percy and Martin arrived, there won't no sign of Sicklemore's men. So they asked the Nansemonds—but the Indians won't talking. Percy says he told Martin they should disembark right then and search 'em out—despite the stormy night. But the delicate Cap'n Martin preferred not to muddy his breeches." Harrison's voice was tinged with sarcasm. "So Percy left with his company and discovered the men with good fires and in safety. Only when Cap'n Martin heard there was no danger the next morning would he leave his secure ship. Percy said if Martin had a spine, he won't sure where it was—'cause it won't in his back!" Harrison laughed at his own rendition of Percy's words.

"If this is so, then praise God Martin resigned the Presidency quickly!" Maggie said, and I nodded.

According to Harrison, Martin and Percy then sent two messengers with copper and hatchets to commence negotiations with the Nansemond chief Weyhohomo for the island. The messengers, however, failed to return.

Fearing the worst, Martin proposed they take the island by force. Before they could do that, the Captains managed to question the natives. "The Nansemonds confessed to killing the messengers by—pardon me, Mistresses— scraping their brains out with mussel shells."

Maggie and I recoiled in horror. These were the people as gentle as deer, the Virginia Company had said?

"So Cap'n Percy told Cap'n Smith he beat the savages off the island, burned their houses, ransacked the temples, took down the kings' corpses, and carried away the pearl and copper bracelets they use to decorate the tombs."

Martin, on the mainland, seized the King's son and another Indian, bound them up, and brought them onto the island to find Percy. Percy said a ship's boy picked up a pistol that suddenly fired, shooting the King's son in the breast. The prince, in fear and agony, burst through the cords and swam to the mainland, streaming blood behind him in the river.

"Percy had orders to return, but he told Martin to go raid the mainland for corn. Percy says Martin bucked because he was *terrified*. He didn't have no hostage, and the Nansemonds were out for war. So Martin told Percy he just wanted to save his *men's* skins." Harrison's laugh carried a sarcastic bite. "He's a good sort, ain't he—making sure *his men* was safe!"

Then Harrison continued more seriously, "But, Mistresses, Percy says there were *one thousand* bushels of corn there for the taking."

Maggie's mouth dropped open. "Martin let a thousand bushels of corn slip through his fingers—without even trying?"

"That is so, Mistress."

By the little I heard, I doubted Martin capable of running a fort—especially one surrounded by inflamed and warlike Nansemond and without adequate food stores. Boding worse for us was the injured prince and the desecrated kings' burial sites. The great Chief Powhatan would surely hear about these events.

Meanwhile, relations with the Indians at the falls sounded like they'd turned disastrous under West's leadership.

Perhaps Captain Smith was our most able leader after all.

But not for long. Before we could even bid our farewells and thank Harrison, Smith's boat joined the ship already in harbor.

On it was Captain Smith—bloodied, near bereft of his senses, and in extreme pain from a gunpowder wound ten inches square that had seared most of the flesh from his leg. His leg afire, Smith had jumped into the river and nearly drowned trying to snuff it out.

Harrison looked genuinely distraught as we watched Smith's men carry the injured leader off the boat. Harrison pushed his cap back, wiping his brow. "Now I can wager you that won't no accident," he muttered, hurrying back to his post at ship.

September Blow Soft

September 21, 1609

September blow soft till the fruit's in the loft.
~ Late 16th century English proverb

*G*unpowder? *Burned legs? Purchasing an Indian town? Brains scraped out with mussel shells?* I knelt in the small garden beside our cottage, pulling weeds with Janey at my side. There was much brewing in the settlement that I could not fathom, but this I knew—the feel of the earth, the gentle wind on my face. The comfort of the familiar in the vastly alien. Virginia soil was sandy in places, but rich in others—and where it was rich, it was deeply dark. I could, for the moment, forget the uncertainties and focus on the refreshing dampness inside the ground, even as the sun beat upon my neck and straw hat. September in Virginia had some cooler days, but most were still muggy as this one was.

Watching Janey swept me back into my mother's garden at Dorset. I could see myself as she was so many years ago. Janey raked at the soil, content to watch it furrow and to pattern the ground. How little she understood of our situation, how innocent she was. I put my around her, more for my sake than her own. Although I missed Cecily, in many ways I was thankful that she remained safely in Melcombe with my brother Tom.

I had used the Virginia method of sowing, and, to my relief, the plants were beginning to sprout. How pleased I was that the seeds had not fared badly in the hurricane. Will and I had chosen them and packed them carefully in a chest. Now I studied my garden—here beets and radishes, there turnips, carrots, peas, and mustard greens.

Annie Laydon had been most helpful in trying to recall the date of the previous year's frost.

"Well, let's see. We docked the day after Michaelmas, and the frost came in about a month after that," she had said. Michaelmas fell on September 29, so I reckoned I had until early November before the first frost hit. Annie confirmed that it *had* been the first week in November, she thought.

She also shared what she had learned from Pocahontas about how the Indians planted. In the spring, the Indians put two crops of corn in the ground. In late summer, they planted two more corn crops to help them through the winter.

"Pocahontas said the land was parched and had been for several planting seasons, more parched than her people could remember for generations. So their crops haven't been doing all that well. We ain't the only ones who've been hungry," Annie added. "And another thing. They don't broadcast their seeds like we do." I looked at her in surprise. We always tossed them out in a grand sweeping motion.

"What do they do, then?"

"Pocahontas laughed when I told her we threw the seeds. She wanted to know why we gave them to the birds to eat? She was a fine friend." Annie was momentarily distracted and gazed into space. "I sure do miss her." Then she continued, "Here, the Indians use a stick to make a hole. They put corn in it and beans around it, and then cover it over. Beans wrap around the corn for strength to go higher."

As I worked, I thought of the leaders. They were wasting valuable sailing time, holding the ships in port while they drafted formal charges against Smith. Smith, already onboard, was returning to England due to his injuries, and it was not at all clear he would survive the voyage. Meanwhile, the six ships lay listlessly in port, waiting on the compilation of these charges.

What's the man done, I thought idly. Probably the other Captains did not want Smith to speak freely to the Company without their own rebuttals in place. Meanwhile, a choice month for any kind of planting—howsoever light a winter crop might be—escaped them. Escaped us all, in fact, except for those of us who had come prepared and now took matters into our own hands.

We three women had not waited on orders from anyone to do what we knew intuitively must be accomplished. Even as I pulled at weeds, Tempie and Maggie were scouring the woods. We determined to lay up as much store as possible against the coming winter.

As I tugged weeds and worked the soil, I wondered what Will would have made of these so-called leaders. Will was an eminently practical man, so he likely would have respected Smith inasmuch as Smith *appeared* to have the best interests of the settlement at heart. Smith was a soldier and a doer, as Will was. *Yes*, I thought, working the soil, *Will probably would have liked Captain Smith.*

As for West, he had the puffery of the young and inexperienced, despite his noble upbringing. When he had a few years and battles behind him, West might become a capable leader. That would not help us at the present moment, however.

Will would have scorned Martin's cowardice—the way Martin first demanded the Presidency, then resigned it three hours later. And then his fear of disembarking in Nansemond territory, forcing Percy to venture out alone. Finally, Martin's most glaring act of cowardice was the one thousand bushels of corn he let slip through his fingers—fearing for his life if he confronted the natives! That would only feed native ideas that we were *all* cowards.

And the grandiose Ratcliffe was too eager to have an empire in the Virginia wilderness. Will would have hated that, too.

Archer and Percy I was unsure of, although Archer's willingness to form a triumvirate with Martin and Ratcliffe made him suspect.

Smith, whose term was expiring, had hastily appointed Percy our next President. Percy had planned to sail home because his health was poor, but he had agreed to stay on and accept the post. The other Captains had few issues with Percy, either, particularly since he was the son of an Earl. So Percy, although sickly, might have promise. It was hard to tell just yet, but he had been in Virginia from the beginning and was well familiar with the country. I laughed at the thought that I, a woman, felt qualified to judge them.

Then, still working the ground, I reconsidered that notion. After all, I had a brain in my head as much as they had—maybe more so! I, at least, knew enough to get the planting done. Parchment accusations we could not consume. But turnips....I touched the plant with my hand. It tickled me to picture Ratcliffe having a supper of salted paper in his James Town *Palace*.

At that moment, Isabel, one of the women who shared our cottage, burst through the door. "Joan, come! Elizabeth has not yet risen and seems to be faltering. She asks for you."

"Will you watch Janey, Isabel?" I asked, my heart suddenly thudding in my chest. She nodded and stepped over to Janey, as I dashed inside.

These Things Shall Never Die
September 21, 1609

So shall a light that cannot fade, beam on thee from on high.
And angel voices say to thee—these things shall never die.

~ Charles Dickens

By loving the unlovable, you made me lovable.

~ St. Augustine

hurried to Elizabeth's side and touched her forehead. She lay very still, and this time she did not push my hand, or me, away. Ashen, she lifted her eyes. Her breathing was ragged and her skin had a peculiar odor with a yellow cast to it. It struck me that her haggard face belied her age, for she could not have been more than thirty.

"Joan." Her voice was gentler than I had ever heard it. She coughed and sputum gurgled in her throat. I saw that she had been collecting it in a rag she kept beside her. "Have you...any remedies that might help me?" Her eyes pleaded, and I recognized genuine fear in them. With a sinking feeling, I knew remedies would do her no good now, but I did not tell her so.

"The very best remedy I know is a Psalm," I said with forced brightness. How I wished Maggie was here to lead it! But sensing Elizabeth's time was short, I lifted my sparrow's voice alone in the 23rd Psalm:

The Lord is only my support,
And he that doth me feed:
How can I then lack anything
Whereof I stand in need;
How doth me fold in coats most safe:
The tender grass fast by:
And after drives me to the streams,

That run most pleasantly,
And when I feel myself near lost,
Then doth he me home take
Conducting me in the right paths,
Even for his own name sake
And though I were even at death's door,
Yet would I fear none ill:
For with thy rod and shepherd's crook
I am comforted still.

Elizabeth lay with her eyes closed and did not seem to mind the cracks in my tune. I did the best I could. When I had finished, she opened her eyes and gazed at me thoughtfully. "You braced me."

"What?"

"With your body, you braced me from the storm."

I had forgotten. "Yes. You were so weak."

There was a humility in her I had never seen before. "It comforted me in the darkness. Thank you," she said with dignity. For once, her eyes were serene.

I nodded, eyes brimming. A voice in my head seemed to say that seeds of kindness *could* be planted during a frost and take unexpected root.

Then with a tone of acceptance she added, "Our husbands on the *Sea Venture* aren't coming back. And I won't see the month out. This heat, these flies…" She paused, drawing a few deep breaths. Then, trembling, she pulled from one skeletal finger a ring, so loose it nearly dangled.

"For you, Joan. See, it has a delicate rose carved on it. I love gardens too, but I wasn't as good at them as you were. Just never could get me the knack. Too ornery, I suppose. Scared the blossoms right off the vines." Still holding the ring out to me, she laughed with a crackling that started her coughing. I motioned to demure, but once she caught her breath she said hoarsely, "Don't make me scold you again. I have done enough of that."

"Bless you then, Elizabeth," I whispered, letting her give it to me.

"No, bless *you*. You're going to see the winter here while I shall be in other pastures with the Shepherd. My lot is easier than yours will be." Was that concern I read in her eyes?

Suddenly it dawned on me how little I knew of this woman. Viewing her only as cranky and complaining, I had stayed as far from her as possible—not easy on so small a ship and with our pallets close. Nor any easier in quarters as tight as this house. Yet I had found ways to keep a distance between us. Now, oddly, as she lay dying I wished we had more time. She was not as unlovable as she had seemed. Perhaps Providence had simply dealt her blows from which she could not recover.

I reached for her hand, which was as cold as death itself. I hoped some of the warmth from my own might seep into it, making her more comfortable if only for a little while.

At last, she drew in a final breath and released it with a shudder. Elizabeth had her wish. She would spend the winter months in another realm.

As for my daughter and me, we would trudge on and see what the coming months held for us.

Upon the Horizon's Verge

October 4, 1609

Between two worlds life hovers like a star,
twixt night and morn, upon the horizon's verge.

~ Lord Byron

When I think of my own native land,
In a moment I seem to be there;
But alas! recollection at hand
Soon hurries me back to despair.

~ William Cowper

I t was an odd grief, watching the ships depart. All were preparing to sail except the *Virginia*, the *Swallow*, and the *Mary and John*. The *Virginia* had finally arrived the day before, in sore shape and with her mainmast lost in the hurricane. It was good news that Captain Davis had come with his sixteen men, but when even his little *Virginia* limped in, hopes extinguished for the *Sea Venture*. Surely if she were still afloat, she would have made greater speed than a helpless little pinnace without a mainmast. Captain Davis confirmed that his crew had not sighted her since the hurricane struck. It was official, then. All of the other ships were in, and none had seen the *Sea Venture*. She was gone. I tried not to dwell on it, concentrating instead on things I could control—my gardening and my gathering.

At the least, these ships would carry word back to England of our terrible tragedy—the *Sea Venture's* loss with all our leadership, our husbands, and our supplies. Three of England's top men gone: the naval hero Somers, the military leader Gates, and the expert mariner Newport. The blow would be devastating, and the Virginia Company would have to send help and provisions. *They will have to,* I thought again.

As the sailors loaded up and made final preparations, Maggie and I spied Harrison. He rolled a barrel over from the well.

144

"Ah, I'm lookin' forward to this voyage. No hens!" he said. There was a sparkle in his eyes.

"No hens, is it?" Maggie said, a tilt in her chin, a play of mischief in her expression. "And where will you get your remedies, Master Harrison? And whose singing will calm your bejangled nerves? Not your own, that's for certain." She rolled her eyes.

"Aye, having none of it. Hens clucking, keeping an honest seaman from his work," he replied with a chuckle. "Take care of yourselves, Mistresses," he said more seriously. "You have no mates here yet to care for you. It's dangerous for women to be alone."

With a stealthy expression, he motioned for us to come aside, which we did. He lowered his tone and pointed a thumb over his shoulder at the ship. "You know we got Cap'n Smith on board."

We nodded. That was no secret, although we hadn't realized which ship he was on. The *Blessing,* then.

"Well, he's been talking with the sailors about what's going on around the settlement. And I been making it a point to listen." He paused to give us a meaningful look, his concern for us obvious.

He continued, "Smith thinks that with the harvest newly in and the current number of settlers—close to five hundred—the food in the store can last about ten weeks. Even at that, it'll be a meager portion, but every soul can have half a can of cornmeal a day. It would've been enough for about thirty weeks or more—into early May, probably, except for the timing of you new arrivals. Late in the season, losing most provisions in the storm, and then the lion's share lost with the *Sea Venture.* This puts the settlement at risk for the winter, unless them fellows"—he pointed his thumb over his shoulder at the larger quarters where the leaders bunked—"get it right."

"Get it right?" Maggie asked.

"He means they can't afford no mistakes. They got to watch the livestock, get the fish in when they're running, and not let the natives know times are hard. Those Indians look for chinks in the armor. They only keep peace now because Smith keeps 'em thinking we're stronger than we are. Keeping outlying settlements is important, for food's sake. More hunting grounds, more fishing grounds."

I felt my body go cold with fear as I began to understand. *No mistakes,* Harrison had said. My insides began to churn and my palms tingled with clamminess. What were the chances of *no mistakes* with this bunch of inept Councilors? Our hope was in Percy, whom I did feel to be an able man.

"One more thing," Harrison began. He looked around cautiously, lowering his voice. "Smith says his gunpowder burn was *no accident,* and…he won't name names, but says one of those other Captains came into his room at night to finish him up. The intruder held a pistol to Smith—him, helpless on his cot—but either the weapon failed or the coward's heart did. He's not sure which."

As one, Maggie and I both gasped. *Attempted assassination?*

"Anyhow, that's why he reckoned he'd better get back to England. He's in no position to defend himself. As it is, he might not survive the voyage home."

Reflexively, Maggie and I grasped one another's arms. The leadership situation kept growing more dismal, the outlook more frightening.

Harrison continued, "Ratcliffe's drummed up a slew of charges against Cap'n Smith, even promising some they can travel home to testify against him. Others have signed oaths of complaint at Ratcliffe's urging. Smith says the poorer soldiers are pleased to distort the truth—even outright lie—especially the ones he had punished for laziness. A bit o' revenge for being made to work." Harrison paused to study the two of us sympathetically. "So mind yourselves. The sailing life is no child's play, 'tis true, but we face *known* dangers. This place is a different kind of wild."

A different kind of wild. Those words knocked around my brain and gave me goose prickles.

I stashed the anger I still felt at the irresponsible leaders wasting weeks of provisions feeding mariners so they could drum up these charges. And they had used what could be the last of the mild weather arguing political factions rather than preparing for winter.

As the *Blessing's* master, Captain Adams, wandered over, Harrison stood a little straighter and raised his voice. "So as I was sayin', you ladies need to get on with your business and let me get on with mine." Captain Adams continued walking. Then with a look over his shoulder, Harrison reached in his pocket and pulled out a coin of some type, handing it to me.

"What's this?"

He ducked his head a bit shyly. "It's a Spanish *reale,* called a *bit.* It's for your girl. It'll bring 'er luck. I plucked it off a Spanish galleon myself! Been carrying it around in my pocket ever since. Well, what's an old seadog like me got to needin' a beat-up Spanish coin for luck?" His voice softened. "But a little girl in a strange land, without a father even. Things not looking so good all around. She might could use some luck, I reckoned. I had me a girl like her once, but the plague got 'er when she was seven. My wife too. I was out sailin' a privateer and didn't find out 'til I got into port." He straightened and cleared his throat. "Take it," he said more firmly, closing my fingers around the coin with his grizzled hand. "Give it to the lass for me, won't you? Tell 'er it's from *the biscuit man.*" He winked.

I reached over and gave the old sailor a hug. "Master Harrison, thank you for everything you've done. Have yourself a safe voyage back to England, aye? No hurricanes this time!"

"I'm prayin', Mistress, I'm prayin'!"

Maggie pushed herself taller with head high. Yet she looked as afraid as I felt when she said, "And as for us, I'm reckoning we can take care of ourselves. Isn't that so, Mistress Peirce?" She patted Harrison's arm, adding, "God be with you, Sir." There was no forced respect in this exchange, I noticed.

"And also with you," he replied with a serious nod. "With both of you—and your girl." He touched his hat in farewell and walked toward the *Blessing*, glancing back once to give us a parting smile.

I felt a peculiar sense of isolation, without the *Sea Venture* or Will and with Harrison's return to England. I remembered the reckoning we had done in the church. We had estimated that once the ships departed we might expect help in seven months. Now it was October. That meant May at the earliest, unless they sent an unexpected supply ship. Not likely with winter on its way and the Company believing us in sound shape. So for the duration of winter and most of spring, we would have to fend for ourselves.

As I watched Harrison climb the plank onto the *Blessing,* something childlike deep inside me wanted to cry out, "Take us with you!"

That being impossible, we had no choice but to make the best of the lot at hand.

We Hope to Plant a Nation

October 4, 1609

And to th' adventurers thus he writes,
Be not dismayed at all,
For scandal cannot do us wrong,
God will not let us fall.
Let England know our willingness,
For that our work is good;
We hope to plant a nation
Where none before hath stood.

~ Richard Rich, writing on the
Virginia Adventurers, 1610

After saying our farewells to Harrison, Maggie and I wandered through the fort back to our home. Harrison's words caused me to be more observant than previously, and I considered the hand Providence had dealt us.

Although there was political turmoil in the air as Captain Smith departed, our situation was by no means dismal. In fact, to all appearances James Town had the look of a thriving village, albeit primitive. As we walked, I took it all in.

To one side was one of our two blacksmiths, hammering away at a molten piece of iron. He was making a hinge or hook of some type and its tip glowed, a furious orange. His shop was shady, yet sweltered from the furnaces that blazed inside. He looked as though he had taken a dunk in the river, I thought, and I wagered he wished he could! Nearby, Jack Laydon, the only skilled carpenter, braced a spinning lathe as he shaped a cedar plank. He pumped his foot rhythmically. A pottery wheel whirled as the town's potter created tin-glazed earthenware trenchers and mugs for the settlement.

Against the palisade wall, two older boys played a game of skittles. One suddenly raised his arms in triumph as his ball toppled all the pins. "Match!" he cried in delight.

Reverend Meese wandered past, *The Book of Common Prayer* tucked under his arm. He was deep in conversation with Captain Dan Tucker, the Cape Merchant whose task was to manage the Company Store. Tucker was listening earnestly, intently. He was, in fact, so intent on the Reverend's words that he nearly bumped into two women crossing his path. They leaned in to each other conspiratorially, and then gave a raucous laugh that shook their shoulders. Behind them tagged a boy, playing a jew's harp. Suddenly, Captain Tucker came up short. His attention had been so fully on the Reverend that he had almost tripped over the boy. All through and around them roamed several dozen chickens, a portion of the five or six hundred wandering the town.

Chained just inside the gates were several enormous mastiffs, their rumbling growls showing why the Indians feared our dogs of war. In hunting skills and in battle, these animals had no superior.

Over in the far corner of the bulwarks were the raised platforms where the ordnance stood. Each bulwark contained four or five pieces, from the smaller falconets and minions to culverins twelve feet in length. Altogether, they were an impressive show of defensive power, and we could direct them to Spanish or Indian attackers.

By the gates, soldiers stood sentry. All these were reminders that James Town was a village *and* a fort. Near the gate, a soldier knelt cleaning his musket and singing a ballad of Drake's Adventures.

> *Oh, there was a ship that sailed, all across the lowland sea*
> *And the name of the ship was the Golden Trinity*
> *And we feared she would be taken by the Spanish enemy*
> *And they'd sink her in the lowland, lo,*
> *They'd sink her in the lowland sea.*

Among the nearly five hundred persons who had arrived and were still living, we had a hundred soldiers, skilled in the native's language and customs as well as in military tactics. Smith had shepherded and trained them well. Firepower we lacked none. Besides two dozen pieces of ordnance in the bulwarks, we had nearly three hundred muskets, snaphaunces, and firelocks as well as sufficient powder and match. There were more curats, pikes, swords and morions than men, and so we were well armed there also.

We had ample commodities to trade with the Indians—trinkets such as copper, beads, shears, brass casting counters, pots and pans, pennywhistles, glass toys, and bells. We were never to trade arms of any type, of course. That was a fast rule.

Provisions of meal in the store would see us only through December—a frightening thought—but that did also depend on how many died. Yet the death rate for most of 1609 had dropped considerably from the first one and a half years of settlement.

As supplemental victuals, we had farm animals—chickens, goats and sheep. But most reassuring of all were the five or six hundred swine living on the aptly named Hog Isle. The island formed a natural pen and the hogs readily bred there. Hog Isle was across the river and just three miles east of James Town, a simple jaunt by boat to bring pork as needed.

Fishing was another promising food source, since along with our three remaining ships, we had seven boats and a supply of nets. Although the sturgeon wouldn't run until the spring, when they did, each of these fish could feed dozens of men. We prized their roe as well.

Then there were the horses, the legacy of a very smelly voyage on the *Blessing*. In a pen behind the fort, we stabled six mares and a horse. All but one had survived.

Well stocked in tools, we also had ample apparel for a cold winter.

All told, it should have been a lean but not an impossible situation, I reassured myself. The town certainly *looked* vibrant enough, despite the political upheavals. Yet Harrison's words echoed in my mind. *No mistakes.*

After that, mistakes began mounting right away.

We Gather Together
Mid-October 1609

And on the banks, on both sides of the river, there will grow all kinds of trees for food. Their leaves will not wither nor their fruit fail, but they will bear fresh fruit every month, because the water for them flows from the sanctuary. Their fruit will be for food, and their leaves for healing.

~ Ezekiel 47:12

We gather together to ask the Lord's blessing;
He chastens and hastens His will to make known.

~ Traditional 16th century
Dutch hymn

"Do you think that is so, Joan?" Tempie asked me as we picked our way through the woods, baskets slung across our arms. "What Reverend Meese was saying in sermon today, I mean? Do you think we will be blessed by the labors of our hands?"

Because Maggie and I were both about ten years older than she was, Tempie occasionally looked to us for answers. Sometimes they were on our tongues; sometimes not. How much of life she had not experienced! At her age, although I had been a young widow with a baby, at least I had been in familiar surroundings. I admired her for being here at all.

"Well," I said, shifting my basket toward me so I could better see its contents, "I think it *is* true, yes. We have been out here every day, from first light, seeking, digging, searching." I looked down at my hands. They were red and cracked, permanently brown-stained and raw. I had always loved gardening, but foraging was a bit different. We were like little squirrels, hoping for acorns, sassafras roots, and wild berries. Each day, two of us started out early, directly after morning prayers at church.

I poked the ground with a stick, dislodging several acorns. Into the basket they went. Nearby, Tempie was on her hands and knees, digging at a root. It would do. As she pulled it, it went deeper and deeper and she groaned, letting out a cry as she fell backwards.

Still sitting in the leaves, she said suddenly, "I was born in a manor house. How did I end up here? Troweling for barely edible roots?"

Typically, we did not dawdle in the woods. Although the blockhouse provided a measure of safety, it did not prevent stray Indians from getting onto the island. Still, her indignation distracted me and struck me as humorous.

Feigning seriousness, I said, "In some kind of nightmare, are you? Dreamed you were on a continent, an ocean away from Scottow, the victuals growing scarce, frightening savages, and you didn't have a clue as to what you'd do for the upcoming winter? Is that it?"

"Aye." She wrinkled her face and raised her brow. "That would be about the size of it. Don't laugh too hard, *Mistress Peirce*, because...I believe you're having *the same dream!*" And she picked herself up and dusted off her bottom.

"Same dream," I nodded, and we laughed. It was a laugh tinged with bitterness, but laugh just the same. Any smile, any lightness we could find we grasped, especially in such a place. Because it had occurred to us that we were going to have to make the best of it. As Maggie said, it was what it was. All the wishing and hoping and praying could not send that ship of leaders here to us, could not bring our husbands back, could not induce the Virginia Company to get us supplies or, better, to get us home!

Tempie was just scooping up the toppled contents of her basket when we heard a rustle in the woods. My heart raced and we looked at each other in alarm, but it was only several fat squirrels running through the underbrush. The woods remained frightening, but we continued coming each day, despite our fear. Somehow, in some fashion, it would pay off. Surely, our work was not in vain—although in England, only the very, very poor would ever consider eating an acorn. We had discovered we could each collect about a bushel an hour.

"Pocahontas said they are the deer's favorite and her people devour many acorns between harvests of corn," Annie had told us, as she demonstrated how the Indians turned them into meal. Over a course of weeks, we had mastered this technique, although it was very time consuming.

"Well, I never thought I should become a miller," Tempie had said, an amusing scowl on her face, as we had converted the cottage into a little acorn mill over the past month.

We first soaked the acorns to wash away dirt, plucking out the floating ones. "Hollowed by the bugs," Annie explained. Out those went. Next came shelling, which required us to break the shell with a hammer and retrieve the little white ball from inside. Using a mortar and pestle, we ground the meat into coarse meal and then boiled that until it was pleasant to the taste, which took long hours and many changes of water. The water at first turned dark brown, but lightened each time we poured fresh water in. "This leaches away the bitter, leaving the sweet," Annie said. Once they were thoroughly dry, the final task was to grind them once more into a fine meal.

It was slow, arduous work, but after doing this daily, we were becoming rather skilled at it. Although the acorns were small, the insides were solid meat. To our great pleasure, we found the acorn meal tasty, even sweet, and we were accumulating a considerable surplus. We stored this securely in our cellar, and we let no day pass without gathering as many acorns as we could bring home. Thereafter we were able to stretch our rations using half acorn meal, half corn-meal. It was our own private provision, from the labors of our hands, as Reverend Meese had said. It gave me a measure of comfort to have work to do, especially in the midst of the turmoil all about us.

At that moment a wind whipped past, jostling tree limbs and forcing us to grip our baskets and to hold our kirtles down. It blew through the woods with a whistle, and as it did, I heard what sounded like marbles tapping the ground all about us. Acorns, falling like noisy rain. A few even pelted us on the head.

"Tempie, this must be a mast year for acorns. Virginia is bountiful, I know, but never have I seen so many!" It was difficult to walk without our shoes rolling around on them as though we were on wheels. Suddenly a realization struck me. "Tempie, *this is it!*" I nearly screamed.

She squinted and tilted her head. "This is what?"

I grabbed a handful and held them out to her. *"This* is the manna from heaven, our daily bread for which we prayed! God has provided us a mast year in acorns! Do you see? They fall from heaven. And by faithfully turning the acorns into flour, we have provision for bread! Probably it will be a mast year for wal-nuts, too!" I was fairly certain that mast, the dry fruits of trees, came in good years together. Some years the trees produced well, others they did not. "Hogs get fat off acorns! The deer, squirrels and wild turkey eat of them and stay healthy all winter during mast years. The Indians love them. Why *not* us?"

She gave me a dubious look and held one up. "You think *this* is our manna? The lowly acorn? I thought we were only supplementing provisions with it."

I did not respond but filled my basket as quickly as I could. I wanted to re-turn to the woods for more. Suddenly I understood that we must stockpile these while they were fresh and available to us. If this truly *were* our manna, we must treat them not as lowly, but as our own bread from heaven. A mast year!

With full baskets and in good spirits, we walked back into the fort. As we entered the town, Tempie and I glanced at Ed Goodwin, playing skittles in the street, and we rolled our eyes at each other.

"Don't you think some of these men would get the idea that *now* is the time to be in the woods gathering? Not when the ground is all frozen and the plants dead? They pin their hopes on a supply ship and that is downright foolish!" Tempie said indignantly.

She was right. Some of the men worked at preparing what they could, hunting and fishing, working gardens—but many did not. It was fortunate, I thought, that we could amass our private stores as well as eat from the public storehouse, because that meant those of us who worked harder would have something to show for it. We three intended to start the winter with as much tucked away as we could. The leaves were beginning to redden, and each day their color deepened, I thought of winter and wondered what it would bring.

At that moment, we saw a company of perhaps 120 soldiers coming through the opposite gate. At their head was Captain West.

"Why are *they* back?" Tempie whispered to me. "Weren't they supposed to be settled up at the falls of the river?"

I nodded, a basket brimming with acorns over my arm. I also wondered why they had returned overland since they left on a ship.

Wearing a resolute expression, the young West pounded on the door of Percy's quarters. The President continued to be so ill he could not even stand. Hearing Percy's weak response, West went inside, his hat in his hands but his expression unchanged.

One of the soldiers standing nearby squatted and laid his musket on the ground. To his comrade he said, "Cap'n West was wise to pull out of that fort with all the men we were losing to the Indians. *Parahunt's a friend,*" he said, mocking Captain Smith. Then he spit. "Well, we sure don't need enemies then!"

The other soldier grunted approval. "Smith thought we were going to live in Indian huts," his friend agreed with disdain.

Tempie and I glanced at each other in concern. No one need tell us that this meant an additional drain on the fort's food supply. The return of these soldiers increased by a third the number the Company Store and surrounding woods must feed. West's men had taken six months provisions when they left for the falls in August. Where, I wondered, was the remainder? And where was the boat?

We scurried back to the house to find Maggie rinsing yesterday's finds. She had a bowl filled with water on the table and was swishing acorns around in it.

On a piece of muslin lay the ones she had already washed. A kettle of acorns boiled over a fire that also warmed the autumn chill from the cottage. Janey stood beside her on the stool, helping.

Maggie glanced up as we came in, her round face lit in a smile. A strand of hair drooped across her eyes. She brushed it away with the back of a wet hand, but it tumbled down again. "Happy hunting?" she asked. Before I could reply, Janey ran over to me, throwing her arms around my waist.

I set my basket down quickly to scoop her up, kissing her cheek.

"Walnuts and 'corns!" she said, peering over my shoulder into the basket.

I laughed at her child's enthusiasm, for this was essentially what we brought each time. I let her choose a few to play with.

We had comfort in our routine, even as the politics left us uneasy. In the mornings, two of us scoured the woods and river's edge, while one stayed behind to watch Janey. The one at home fetched water from the well, tidied the cottage and prepared whatever provisions we received from the Company Store. She also tended the previous day's sorting, rinsing, boiling, grinding, and drying, and did as much acorn preparation as possible. The rest we finished in the evenings. Acorns in various stages of the process were stored in the cellar. They kept well and we reckoned we had the whole winter to continue working on them.

In the afternoon, two more of us ventured out—we would not squander the season of nuts—while the third woman stayed behind. In this way, only one of us had to brave the chilly fields and woods twice in a single day, and we took our turns in shifts. We found that the three of us, all industrious by nature, worked well together and had become fairly self-sufficient.

The small cellar held the fruits—and nuts—of our labors. Besides the acorns and acorn meal, we also had black walnuts. A third kind of nut the Indians mixed with water to make a drink they called *pokahichary,* so the English had dubbed this the hickory nut. It was more compact than the fleshy walnut, which was big as a child's fist. The walnuts stained our hands black, but the abundance of sweet meat inside was well worth it. We also had sassafras roots, and we had enjoyed wild blackberries until they at last dried up a few weeks before.

As Maggie rinsed and ground acorns, she was singing "Greensleeves." For a moment, it reminded me of my mother, though she never sang this melodically.

Tempie dropped her basket noisily onto the table beside Maggie, saying, "I fought me a squirrel for these. I hope they meet with your approval, Mistress Maggie."

Maggie looked into the basket. "Just one squirrel or a tribe of squirrels, Miss Temperance? Well!" She looked impressed. "That is quite a stock of acorns!" She put her hands on her waist. "Go on. Tell me how bravely you fought. Was he armed?"

Tempie threw her head back and laughed. "Well, he was plump, but he was no match for the likes of *me*." She narrowed her eyes playfully. "I let him live, but he and I shall meet again on the forest battlefield. Next time I hope not to have to wrestle him to the ground as I did this time."

Sitting on the floor with her acorns, Janey looked up and giggled. "Missus Tempie's funny."

I explained to Maggie my idea that acorns might be our manna, the answer to our prayer in the church several months ago. I wondered if Maggie would consider it foolish, but instead she wore a thoughtful expression. "He is faithful to provide to them who ask, in ways we may not expect. I believe you are right, Joan."

Tempie widened her eyes playfully at the little girl rolling acorns by her feet. "Well, Miss Janey, *I* thought our manna would be chunks of ginger cakes raining upon us—not squirrel food! Didn't you, Missy?" She heaved an exaggerated sigh. "But I guess I was mistaken." She winked at me.

"Aye, Missus Tempie," Janey said with a grin.

Then, turning the subject more serious, I said to Maggie, "Did you see that West's men have returned?"

Her face clouded. "Returned? All of them?"

"They gave up the fort and are apparently here to stay," Tempie added.

"Hmm." Maggie dried her hands on her apron and dropped onto the bench. She stared away into space, wearing a worried expression.

Finally, she said, "I don't like it."

"No," I said. "Neither did we. Perhaps Percy will send them back."

"Perhaps," she replied. "Perhaps." And she resumed washing the acorns, but her brows furrowed in concern.

Even When They Offer Gifts
Mid-October 1609

Trust not the horse, O Trojans. Be it what it may,
I fear the Grecians even when they offer gifts.
                              ~ Virgil, in the *Aeneid*

Noiseless as fear in a wide wilderness…
                              ~ John Keats

Janey's mouth stood agape, her eyes wide. This was her first sighting of Indians, and she—as well as I—felt a strange mix of wonder and fear. It was like seeing ogres from a fairy tale, frightening yet mystical with all the colors of paint and feathers. Janey hugged my hips, her cheek pressed against my kirtle, her eyes fixed upon the five natives.

Tempie and Maggie had just returned to the fort from gathering acorns, nuts, and roots. I spied them across the marketplace. The two women stopped short when they saw the procession of Indians, and Tempie huddled closer to Maggie.

Annie Laydon had emerged from her cottage and was staring at them also.

"You never get tired of the spectacle of it," she said, shaking her head as they moved past. The natives, in regal bearing, were casting sideways glances at us as well. For a moment I had the unsettling thought that perhaps *they* never tired of the spectacle of us either.

The sight was unusual all the way around. A soldier from the blockhouse escorted them into the fort. Also accompanying them was an English boy—at least, he appeared English with blonde hair and delicate features. The boy wore native clothing and seemed at home in it, and his skin had a hearty color.

"Annie, who is that?" I asked. He looked to be about fourteen, just younger than Annie herself was.

"That's Tom *Savage*." She had a merry twinkle in her eyes, as she added, "Ain't *that* a name for an Indian interpreter?"

"Oh. How…?"

"Captain Newport and Chief Powhatan made an exchange about six months before my supply arrived. They traded Tom for an Indian boy called Namontack, so they could be adopted sons and learn the strange tongues. I think Tom came on the First Supply."

Now I considered the whole scene. Four of the braves carried a large buck, hanging lifelessly upside down on poles between them. The deer swung slightly with each step the men took. The fifth bowman walked beside Tom Savage, towering over both him and the soldier.

I had heard the Indians were a giant race, and these men were powerfully built and taller than most Englishmen, towering over Annie and me by at least a foot. Their very presence suggested strength.

Their hair and eyes were as dark as midnight. On the top of their head, a cropped ridge of hair resembled a rooster's comb, and each brave had his hair shaved on the right side. "So it don't interfere with their shootin' arm," Annie explained. Yet on the left side, their hair was perhaps three feet long, and this they had decorated most unusually. The milder sort had used beads, shells, and copper, but one had an entire wing of a bird tucked in it with rattles tied to the feathers. The fourth had the strangest decoration of them all. I leaned in and squinted to be sure I saw it correctly. Was that a dried human hand?

Reading my expression, Annie said, "'Twas from an enemy, not a friend!"

The effect was altogether dramatic.

They wore shell necklaces and had large feathers and claws hanging from their ears. The claws must have been from huge birds of prey, and this too gave the impression of enormity and ferocity.

The men had painted themselves black with some yellow and blue, but mostly red. They had even rubbed their faces and shoulders in color. In some places, they had attached what appeared to be the down of colorful birds so that their bodies seemed rainbow laced. It was striking, exotic.

"The red man! Pocahontas smeared herself in that fashion. She said it was *puccoon* root mixed with bear grease and walnut oil."

"*Puccoon?*" I asked. All of these native terms were strange in my ears.

"We call it *bloodroot*."

"Oh." Smeared in *blood*root. Everything sounded savage.

"The downy feathers stick to the oils," Annie went on. "Pocahontas especially favored bluebird down for the color. The oil protects them from the weather and keeps flying pests away."

I could imagine Tempie's comment: *I should rather be stung!* Yet it was obvious that these people knew how to live in Virginia. They were frightening, wild, and fascinating all at once. No doubt, we could learn from them. In fact, we already had. We had a growing cellar of acorn meal to attest to that. If a tribe such as this could produce a kindly Pocahontas, surely there was more to them than the fierceness they projected.

The men had cloths wrapped around their waists, breeches partially covered their legs, and they were barefooted. They each had a quiver of arrows slung over their shoulder, their bows across their bodies, and a knife tucked in their waistbands. The bow itself was nearly five or six feet long. Finally, they wore a leather bag.

As they passed, one of the braves cut his glance toward me. I had been studying his appearance and looked up to see the dark eyes intent upon my own. My heart raced with fear of something I could not name, and I averted my eyes quickly. But not quickly enough, for I had seen the glint within the darkness of his eyes, and I felt strangely violated by it. As with any other people, there were the kind and the unkind. *As too with us*, I thought.

"Which way to Captain Smith?" Tom Savage asked the soldier in a forceful voice. He obviously enjoyed his youthful leadership role.

"Uh, Captain Smith is no longer at the fort. Captain Percy is President now."

Was it my imagination, or did I see Savage exchange a glance with the bowman?

"Is that so?" the boy asked. "My father Powhatan had heard this distressing news, but will be greatly saddened by its confirmation. The Captain is resupplying, I suppose?"

"No, you suppose wrong." The soldier shifted, looking uncomfortable in the conversation. His expression said clearly that he was unsure how much he should divulge. Yet he had an eye on the buck—venison would be a welcome treat.

"We heard he was injured," Savage pressed.

"Aye, that is so. He's likely dead by now. He had a vicious burn that consumed most of his leg."

Savage wore an expression of concern, then turned to speak with his "brothers" in their native tongue.

"Wonder what they're saying?" Annie whispered to me. I couldn't imagine, but I had a foreboding I could not explain.

"To President Percy then!" young Savage announced. "We have brought the President a gift of venison, as you can see."

The soldier nodded and walked them toward Percy's house.

When the Indians and Savage left the fort a day later, I saw that Harry Spelman and a Dutchman named Samuel accompanied them. Harry was a charming and educated boy about Tom's age. He had arrived with us in the summer.

Annie dropped by the cottage, telling us, "Tom requested that a couple of his countrymen be sent with him, so they asked Harry." Captain Smith had already sold Harry to Parahunt once up at the falls as part of the barter for the Indian town. Neither the town nor Harry's exchange actually occurred, and Harry had been reluctant to become an interpreter at that time. But now, having just returned to James Town with Captain West, he understood how tight victuals were. Indian venison any time he pleased wasn't sounding so bad.

Harry went, and we wouldn't see him again for nearly a month.

Let Us Not Despair or Mutiny
Mid-October to Late October, 1609

Do we not see in the firmament the lights carried along the shore by night, as Columbus did? Let us not despair or mutiny.

~ Henry David Thoreau

Just after the natives' visit, Percy decided to establish a new fort at Point Comfort for fishing and observation of passing ships. Coupled with the Nansemond Island fort on the opposite side of the river, this would give us sound sentry against our greatest fear, Spanish attack. Besides, hadn't Smith said outlying settlements were strategically important? The Company at home supported this move as well, so it seemed a sound move.

George Percy called a meeting at the church and announced those whom he would send to build the new fort, which he planned to name *Algernon* in honor of his oldest brother. Captain Ratcliffe would lead the group. Jack Laydon's name was on the list, probably because of his carpentry skills. Still, I was disappointed that we would lose Annie from our town. Her seasoned insights had been helpful, and I had hoped to aid the midwifing of the baby.

"Other volunteers?" Percy asked the congregation. A few hands went up. Tempie, Maggie, and I conferred with one another.

Maggie shook her head. "I don't quite trust the leadership of these smaller forts. Truth be told, I'm not sure I trust the leadership here either! But I think our prudent course is to stay close in, especially as women living alone." She was correct that Percy sought to enlist soldiers, artisans, and laborers, whose wives and children would accompany them as a matter of course. We, however, were on our own and probably most secure in the confines of the main settlement.

Soon after, Captain Martin returned from Nansemond Island. *Just* Captain Martin. He had left Lieutenant Michael Sicklemore in charge of that fort. Apparently, sporadic Indian attacks had made the yellow-livered Martin skittish. He feigned business but fooled no one.

"Coward!" Tempie whispered to me disdainfully when we heard the news of his retreat.

Then, late in October, to our surprise, remnants of Sicklemore's company returned without the Lieutenant. The story they related chilled every soul at James Town.

Lieutenant Sicklemore was a good man and a diligent soldier, but Martin had abandoned him with his hands full. First, seventeen of Sicklemore's men mutinied and stole a boat. They went to the Indian village of Kecoughtan, pretending to trade for food. We never heard from these men again, nor found the boat—all Indian casualties, no doubt.

Sicklemore and some of his men had gone in search of them, but neither did they return. When others from the fort ventured out, they discovered Sicklemore and his men murdered, their mouths gruesomely stuffed with bread.

This marked the end of the Nansemond Island fort, and with it came a grisly message from the natives. Just as Indians had murdered Spanish soldiers seeking gold by pouring the molten metal down their throats—a story we had heard from our military husbands—the Virginia Indians relayed similar sentiments. The message was all-too clear.

If you want bread, we'll give you bread.

Sounds and Sweet Airs
Late October 1609

Why should I feel discouraged, why should the shadows come,
Why should my heart be lonely, and long for heaven and home...

I sing because I'm happy, I sing because I'm free,
For His eye is on the sparrow, and I know He watches me.
~ Civilla D. Martin

Be not afeard; the isle is full of noises,
Sounds and sweet airs, that give delight and hurt not.
~ William Shakespeare

The ghastliness of Lieutenant Sicklemore's death left everyone shaken. The four of us—Maggie, Tempie and I, plus little Janey—settled into the house that evening. No one spoke of it. No one knew what to say. We had cooked up our paltry day's ration, a half can of cornmeal for each of us, supplementing it with a pottage of wild herbs and roots. Pork rations provided a welcome accompaniment, and as always, we stretched our cornmeal with acorn meal. Isabel and Mary, the other two women who had shared our home, had moved to Point Comfort, so we now had the cottage to ourselves.

Janey sat cross-legged on the bed playing with her rag doll Bessie and her wooden marbles. The nights had a cooler edge, and the leaves slowly turned orange and yellow. We might have thought the leaf colors spectacular had they not heralded the coming winter. Feeling disquieted, we busied ourselves with chores.

We had pulled the table close to the fire this night, and I sat upon the bench mending my kirtle as best I could. I had gotten a gaping hole by catching it on the door earlier in the day. I used the opportunity to take it in a little, as I had grown just a mite thinner. On the table sat two candles, flickering in their pewter stands. Inside our home, at least, there was peace, even if all about us was turmoil.

163

Maggie sat nearby at the table, quill in hand. She thought, wrote, thought, wrote in a little book she had brought from home. It had survived the hurricane with only minor damage. Sometimes she paused in her writing to gaze toward the candle, tickling her chin with the goose feather quill. Then she scribbled some more, the quill making a scratching sound as it crossed the page. She had a faraway look in her eyes.

"What do you write?" I asked her. Lost in thought, she held up a finger to indicate she needed a moment.

When she finished, she looked up. "It's verse, I suppose you would call it. Sometimes I hear musical words in my head. I am no poet, to be sure, but I love the sounds the words make. I have not written in a while, but lately I've felt the desire. It helps me in my thoughts sometimes."

"Maggie, I didn't know you were a poet!" I said, surprised.

"Now," she corrected me. "I just said I was *not* a poet. I only like the sound of the words. There is a marked difference!"

"I'm not sure I see what it is," I pressed.

"Poets produce poems, with meaning. I simply produce words, with sound."

I was not convinced. But before I could speak further, Tempie asked, "Won't you share your verse with us?"

Maggie colored and again stressed there was little to share. Yet, seeing our hopefulness and not wanting to disappoint us, she relented.

"All right then, if your expectations are suitably low." We told her they were *very* low, before wondering how that sounded. She shrugged with a smile, and then read:

> *Hope, the brilliant lady fair,*
> *A shimmering flame through dark Despair.*
> *Breeze may tickle her, and she may quiver—*
> *But Despair can never long her shiver.*
>
> *Old Fear would gladly her to snuff,*
> *But even he can ne'er stifle long enough.*
> *She shall endure, may slightly tremble—*
> *Yet see that mighty Spirit kindle.*
>
> *So burn you brilliant candle fair.*
> *Fight the sorrow, fight Despair.*
> *You shall endure Hoary Ones of old,*
> *Not falling to Bitter, nor succumbing with Cold.*
> *For what can conquer Hope when strong?*
> *But Faith shall hold her, all along.*

Tempie said in a hushed tone, "Why, Maggie, that was lovely! I should never have thought to compare hope to a candle as you did."

"Oh." Maggie seemed a bit embarrassed. "I told you. I like the sound of the words, and we have little else here but our own entertainments."

A shadow crossed Tempie's face and she dropped her head. "I'm afraid I owe you both an apology, especially you, Maggie. I have kept something from you."

"Kept something from us? Not a side of pork, is it?" Maggie asked with a laugh. "That is the only transgression we could not forgive."

Tempie did not laugh, but instead walked deliberately over to her chest, which had little damage from the hurricane. She knelt beside it and turned the key in its lock. Maggie and I waited wordlessly, our curiosity piqued. Reaching into it and rifling for a moment, Tempie found what she sought. Silently she held up *Sternehold and Hopkins Book of Psalms.*

"*Sternehold's!* Why have you not said so before?" Maggie asked, looking a bit hurt. We all knew the hurricane had ruined her own Psalms book, so she had been straining to recall ones from memory.

Tempie shrugged with a guilty expression. "I'm sorry. It's just that..." She hesitated. "My mother gave it to me, and it reminds me of our last conversation."

Tempie and her mother had not parted on the best of terms. Mistress Flowerdieu had not thought it appropriate for her daughter to come to a wilderness settlement in the New World. But Tempie had argued that her husband was coming since it was important to his soldier's career and that she would be at his side to support him. She would go where he went, *even to Virginia.*

"I believed I should sail with George, and my mother vehemently said I should not. Yet we come from a family with tragedy in marriage. Just see the fate that my aunt Amy endured for not attending her husband!"

Her great aunt had been the ill-fated Amy Robsart, wife of Robert Dudley, the Earl of Leicester. Gossip held that Queen Bess herself might have ordered the bride, barely twenty, pushed down the stairs to free Dudley to be *her* husband. Then again, the distraught young woman *may* have simply fallen or even thrown herself down the stairs. No one knew and, of course, propriety demanded that no one spoke of it above a whisper. Propriety—and the threat of treason. However, once Dudley had the stigma of being a possible murderer, the Queen could not marry him anyway. This had all occurred fifty years before, yet a smudge remained on the family name.

"I'm sorry. I didn't mean to be selfish. It only reminded me that my mother was right about coming here. George has gone down at sea, and here am I alone—and to what end?"

Neither Maggie nor I replied, but we were sympathetic. Few were the souls—especially the widows—who believed we had chosen well in coming. We had ventured in faith and what had it gained us?

Tempie opened to the flyleaf where her mother had inscribed: *Dearest Tempie, may God sojourn with you as he did with David.*

She made a face. "Well, there is *every other* horror out in the Virginia woods. I would not be at all surprised if Goliath weren't out there too!"

At this, Maggie and I burst into laughter, picturing Tempie with a sling bringing down the largest Indian—or squirrel—of them all. The tension broke for the first time since we had received news of Sicklemore.

"Let the past be the past, and let us sing, then!" Maggie said, taking the book from Tempie. She chose the 91st Psalm. "*Thou shalt not fear the arrow that flieth by day,*" she quoted. "That seems appropriate!"

"Well, Tempie has her sling, so I personally feel very comfortable with the situation," I said, and this time she gave me a wry smile.

Sternehold's was wonderful—the first complete compilation of all the Psalms set to music, as well as the Lord's Prayer and prayers of St. Augustine with musical notes. With Maggie to lead us in them, we were truly blessed.

Every night after that, we sang several hymns from there and often a ballad or two along with them. This, despite Sternehold's printed admonishment against secular songs. He wrote that his English Psalms and music were for people to sing *in private houses, for their godly solace and comfort, laying apart all ungodly Songs and Ballads, which tend onely to the nourishment of vice, corrupting of youth.* Ballads we could not forsake, for Maggie's rendition of them reminded us too well of home, especially as she played along on her tambourine. Her clear, bright voice drifted through the windows and soothed us, as did the crackling of the fire as autumn settled in.

Perhaps music could chase the sense of dread we were beginning to feel, the sense of something about to go terribly wrong.

The Blood of an Englishman
Early November–Late November, 1609

Fee! Fie! Foe! Fum!
I smell the blood of an Englishman.
Be he 'live, or be he dead,
I'll grind his bones to make my bread.

~ English fairy tale

Captain Ratcliffe was no one's favorite about town. He was pompous and arrogant, certain he could handle all the affairs of Virginia better than George Percy could, John Smith had, or anyone else ever would. It was he who had spent so much time dilly-dallying, drafting charges against Captain Smith when the ships should've been on their way back to England. Time in port cost us sorely needed food. And it was he who had ordered his men to build a Governor's Palace while the burned-out town required basic shelter. And finally, it was he who felt sure enough of his negotiating skills to put himself and thirty-six men in mortal danger.

That act of arrogance would be his last.

It all started when young Harry Spelman returned from his stay with the great chief Powhatan. Harry, the nephew of a noted scholar by the same name, apparently had inherited a prowess with words, as he had already acquired significant knowledge of the Powhatan's language.

Harry had been with Powhatan for three weeks and reported that the natives had treated him well. He had given Powhatan the copper and hatchet he'd taken along as gifts, which the old *werowance* received kindly. Then the chief had invited him and Tom Savage to join him at supper.

Now, Harry was pleased to bring a promising offer back to the fort, to President Percy. The chief was willing to trade! Send a ship with copper and in barter Powhatan would fill the ship with corn.

For Percy, this was most excellent news on the heels of the near panic he had been feeling, now that West's men were back in the fort and Indian relations seemed to be breaking down quickly. He'd sent Captain Tucker to inventory the Company Store, and the tally was just as Captain Smith had said. The corn would hold out three months. Now, with help from Powhatan, there burned a small torch of hope.

Captain Ratcliffe loaded up a pinnace with fifty men and headed to Powhatan's capital up the Pamunkey River at Orapax. They would have to leave the ship behind partway up the river, and tow a barge to the King's new—and deliberately difficult to reach—capital.

Things appeared congenial at the outset. Ratcliffe captured the King's son and daughter as hostages and delivered Harry back to the chief. This was common practice on both sides. Deal fairly—no ambushes—and the hostages would go free.

But Captain Ratcliffe felt confident in his own ability with the natives, so he released the prince and princess prematurely. Then, leaving Captain Phettiplace and fourteen men on the pinnace, he marched his thirty-six men into the Powhatan's largest town.

Around sixty years of age, Powhatan was the most statuesque in a country of burly Indians. He was tall, athletic, and wore a serious expression. He surrounded himself with fifty of the most imposing men of his country, and even other natives deferred to his grandeur.

The wily chief received Captain Ratcliffe warmly enough, providing the men bread and venison. As a return gift, Ratcliffe gave the Indians some copper and beads. Powhatan then offered the soldiers houses for the night, not far from his own large house and half a mile from the barge.

The next morning Powhatan came into the homes and greeted the Englishmen, leaving Harry, Tom, and the Dutchman with the English. Bowmen then escorted the soldiers to the central storehouse where the chief stored his provisions. The house brimmed with impressive numbers of baskets, all filled with corn.

Trading commenced, with Ratcliffe offering copper and beads in proportion to the amount of corn he received. Things seemed to be going smoothly enough. Baskets and baskets of corn! The bounty would certainly make Ratcliffe a hero when he returned.

But what was this? An English soldier whispered to Ratcliffe that the natives were pushing the basket bottoms up with their fists—not a square trade. An altercation broke out, and the chief departed, taking his wives, Harry, and the Dutchman with him.

Now Indian battle cries went up all about the town—frightening screams of *oulee* and *whoopub* that would freeze a man's blood in his veins.

Ratcliffe and his men made a move to escape with their corn, hoping to make it to the waiting barge. As they rushed from the storehouse, the soldiers began falling to the ground, shot through with arrows. Bowmen had hidden amid stalks in the surrounding cornfields and ambushed them with deadly accuracy.

One by one the English fell, the only one to escape being Jeffrey Shortridge. He had tried to get to the ship, but that was gone. The Indians had driven it off almost immediately after Ratcliffe left on the barge—pummeling it with arrows.

Captain Phettiplace had already arrived back at James Town with the pinnace and his fourteen men, bringing word that Captain Ratcliffe and his men were in serious danger. Even on the pinnace, Phettiplace and his men had barely escaped. We all knew what this meant. This was not trading gone poorly but calculated treachery. Powhatan had used Harry, who was unaware of the intent, as a pawn in the dealings.

On the day Shortridge returned on foot, panting and alone, Maggie and I were digging for tuckahoe roots at the edge of the marsh. The hems of our kirtles were wet and muddy. Annie had said these plants were like potatoes to the natives, and we were eager to give them a try. The days continued to grow shorter, our hands more raw in the cold. A pottage with these roots sounded worth tasting. As we walked, Maggie and I debated. Should we dry them first? Annie had warned us that we should. Though we shivered, we had filled two baskets with roots, so we felt pleased with ourselves. How wonderful it would be to get home to the fire!

We were not even to the door when Tempie flung it open. Her eyes were wide and she looked terrified. Before we could speak, she cried, "Ratcliffe and his men were all murdered! All but Master Shortridge, who escaped and brought the news. He watched them kill Captain Ratcliffe in a most horrific way. They tied Ratcliffe to a tree…" I saw that she flinched in the telling. "And then they scraped the skin off his bones with sharpened mussel shells—and cast his flesh into the fire while he *watched*."

Maggie shook her head in distress. "The poor Captain. These native men are so…brutal."

Tempie stopped her. "No, Maggie, you don't understand."

Maggie looked at her quizzically.

"The ones who did this were the Indian *women*."

No, Captain Ratcliffe was no one's favorite—but his horrifying end shook us all. Furthermore, Powhatan's Confederacy had spoken. All was *not* well with Indian relations. No corn—not now, not ever. Certainly not this winter.

Brown Skeletons of Leaves

Late November–Christmas 1609

Brown skeletons of leaves that lag
My forest-brook along...

...This soul hath been
Alone on a wide wide sea:
So lonely 'twas, that God himself
Scarce seemed there to be.

~ Samuel Taylor Coleridge

We have cried in our despair
That men desert...

~ William Butler Yeats

Once he received news of Ratcliffe's death, Percy ordered Captain Davis to Point Comfort to command the fort there in Ratcliffe's place. Percy himself continued to be seriously ill, barely able to get out of bed. Captain Archer was also not a well man.

With this latest development, George Percy was now sick of heart as well as sick of body, and he knew the food stores were critical. He took one last, desperate chance at trading, sending Captain West to the Potomac tribe farther north. They were in Powhatan's Confederacy, but far enough away that perhaps there might yet be some goodwill.

West loaded the *Swallow* with thirty-six men late in November, his sights set on heading down the James River to the Bay, then north to the Potomac's River. The Potomacs lived on a little peninsula there.

Janey and I were walking through town bundled in our woolen shawls, having just retrieved our day's corn rations from Captain Tucker. We observed the mariners loading the *Swallow* and paused near the gate to watch the men rolling

171

hogsheads onboard and setting the sails. I thought again how young Captain West was. He looked like a boy next to some of these soldiers who had ten years on him. He was, however, in fairly sound health compared to Percy and Archer.

Late November in Virginia brought a grey lifelessness with it. There was a dampness I had not expected, a foreshadowing of the winter to come. A few dead, brown leaves clung to branches in the surrounding forests. The woods brown, the skies grey, the river grey. All the colors of death and hopelessness, it seemed to me. The wind bit our fingers, even with gloves on. This place! Could it truly have been so hot our clothes clung to us with sweat in August just three months before—yet so cold and dreary now? I drew a long, deep sigh, the cold air filling my chest uncomfortably. I let it go in a slow puff of white. It was sad when it hurt to sigh.

At that, the wind picked up a little with a ghostly rumble. It ruffled the few remaining leaves with an eerie rattle, like the rattle of bones.

I looked down at the little girl who held my hand trustingly. She had large brown eyes and the cheeks of a cherub, round and rosy. Her mouth was small with a curve of sweetness. Her little cap was pulled down and tied around her ears leaving her all eyes and cheeks. My little angel.

"Mama, it's cold," she said simply.

"Yes, dearie. It *is* cold." I reached down and picked her up. I did not do that much any more. She was now five and getting big for me to lift, but somehow, this day, I wanted to feel her warm little body next to mine. I wanted her to wrap her arms around my neck, as she did almost instinctively. I wanted her to place those darling cheeks against mine. She did.

"I love you, Janey Sweet. And we are going to—" Here I hesitated. I felt my voice give way with emotion, with fear, things I did not want her to see. She was calm and trusting. She believed in me to care for her, even in this faraway place. We had survived the terrible hurricane, but a winter with little food I could not imagine. I squeezed her tight. I remembered I had not finished my sentence. "We are going to be just fine here!" I said brightly. *God, make it so,* I added under my breath.

I kissed her check and put her down, swinging her legs as I did. "There you go!" I said, and she smiled at me. Her eyes held such light that I felt mine well with tears.

Suddenly all pretense of brightness was gone and the tears were coming quickly and hard.

Her eyes grew cloudy as the sky and she said, "What's wrong, Mama?" The seriousness of her tone showed she understood perhaps more than I thought she did. It only made me cry harder, and I began to sob.

I knelt down and put my arms around her, and she took her hand and wiped the tears away. "Don't cry, Mama. It's all right."

No! I wanted to scream. It was not all right at all! It was all wrong. It was wrong to come, wrong that we were struck by the hurricane, wrong that we lost Will, wrong that all the leaders were drowned, wrong that John Smith had been injured and left. It was wrong to be at the edge of the world with a five year old I might not be able to feed, and a nine year old who might arrive to find she had no family left. No, it was definitely all wrong.

Lo, I am with you, even to the ends of the earth. Well, I thought, if James Town in November wasn't the ends of the earth, I didn't know where was.

I wiped the tears away and said as heartily as I could, "Oh, cold air is just causing my eyes to water. Let's get this cornmeal back to the cottage where it's warm!"

November turned to December, and the temperatures continued to drop. The Potomacs were a considerable distance to travel, but all hopes were on the *Swallow's* return. *We needed that corn.* Yet once again, all we could do was wait, knowing it would take weeks or a month or more for them to sail back to us.

Tempie, Maggie, and I bundled ourselves warmly and continued to gather what we could from the fields and woods, but we found less as time went by and the seasons changed. As before with the *Sea Venture*, we all kept one eye on the river, which was washed in grey-blue reflecting the winter skies.

We knew Christmas would be only what we made it. We dared not mention, but all could envision, spit-roasted meats with plum pottage, marchpane and gingerbread, Christmas ale and mulled wine. The spicy sweet warmth of the wine and pottage, amidst laughter and festivities and decorative greenery. Christmas in England.

But for us in James Town, the sweet and warm were not to be had—only the bitter and cold. The day felt hollow, as wind whipped down the river and across the settlement. The sky darkened to a threatening grey, and so fell our first Virginia snowfall. White lace decorated the trees, as the forests grew hushed and still. Not so much as a deer rustled in the woods, and the ground on both sides of the river lay in muffled whiteness. Snow covered the mat on our roof, but as the Indians had shown us, the cottage stayed dry. We might have felt a glorious purity in this season, had it not all felt so bleak instead. Try as we might, the best we could do was laying sprigs of red holly berries about the cottage.

We also considered whether the berries were edible.

"I saw a flock of brown birds with black masks greedily stealing them off the bush. They should know—they are Virginia natives," Tempie suggested with a wry smile. "And I see the squirrels devour them too."

Maggie wasn't so sure. "They are so brilliant red—they make me think of poison. What do you think, Joan?"

I mashed one between my fingers and smelled its insides. How could we know? Here was where we sorely missed Annie, as she might have the answer.

"Let's collect them but save them against the day when all our other provisions might be gone," I suggested. This we did.

Finally, late in December, a messenger arrived from Point Comfort bringing news from the bay about the *Swallow*. He first relayed the tidings that Annie Laydon had delivered a healthy little girl named Virginia. Ginny Laydon was the first white child born at James Town, and how uplifting to learn that both Annie and her baby had survived childbirth. This followed with happier news—the Potomacs, he said, had given Captain West an *entire shipload* of corn!

He interrupted our cheering to continue. Somehow, relations had broken down and our men had chopped off the heads and extremities of two Indians. No one ever quite knew the circumstances, but there went our chance of ever trading with that tribe again. Yet the corn the *Swallow* procured would ease conditions slightly—stave off the worst of the hunger, at least for a while.

When the ship had neared Point Comfort, Captain Davis flagged her down.

"There is severe want at James Town! Do not dock here. Make for the James River with all haste!" cried Davis.

Dutifully the ship hoisted sail. However, it did not bear right into the mouth of the James—but made instead for open ocean. The crew of the *Swallow* had mutinied against the young Captain. Either they had become pirates—or decided to return to England. There was not enough corn to save everyone—but it was enough to save themselves and to get home, taking with them our best ship.

Now our spirits as well as our hopes broke with a last, loud snap—like the limb of a great tree falling into the forest.

A Sojourner, as All My Fathers Were
Early January to Mid-January, 1610

Hope withering fled, and Mercy sighed farewell!
~ Lord Byron

Hear my prayer, O Lord, and hearken unto my cry:
keep not silence at my tears, for I am a stranger with Thee,
and a sojourner, as all my fathers were.
~ Psalm 39:12

January 1610 commenced with this most devastating and final blow, and all hopes went out to sea with the *Swallow*. The natives now struck at every source of victuals we had.

They chased off our deer.

They slaughtered all our swine on Hog Island.

They loosed our boats, sending them downriver.

They held us in siege, shooting us through with arrows if we went but a stone's throw beyond the blockhouse.

The fish were not biting, and in our fear, we left the nets to rot in the water.

The storehouse rations were near expended, and we were eating precious little each day as it was.

We ate whatever we could find, scavenge, or dig up.

Nothing more, nothing less.

In frigid cold, we were prisoners of our own island.

And we began to starve.

Praise God that we had spent so many hours in the forest, fields, and marshes during the months since our arrival searching for food. Praise God that we had dried it and stored it against the coming winter. And Praise God that our little cellar, while not full by any means, at least held *something*. Now Tempie,

Maggie, and I realized the importance of all that we had done, gathering the trifles of the woods, planting the little fall garden.

Captain Tucker was an honorable and honest man. That was critical, for as the Cape Merchant, he was in charge of distributing provisions. Primarily this was corn, but there were peas and a little oatmeal also. With his careful stewardship, the Company Store was still holding out beyond the time he had estimated it would. But it would not go much longer, probably only into February at best.

The Captain was firm on the rules too. We must retrieve our rations by a certain time each day. After that, he closed the store. He did not want to take a chance of anyone slipping in for double rations.

Turned away too many times for tardiness and finding the Captain rigid in his rules, some of the men created a taunting ballad:

> *Get out the way, old Dan Tucker!*
> *"It's too late to get your supper!"*
> *Old Dan and I we did fall out,*
> *And what do you think it was about,*
> *He tread on my corn, I kicked him on the shin,*
> *And that's the way this row begins.*

Now a frightening lawlessness began to take hold, as it became apparent that the little cornmeal we would receive was not nearly enough to keep us fed without any other sources of victuals. Several men tried to rob the Company Store, and Percy executed them. The President, still ailing, demonstrated by this action what we all felt. *Survival had become a life and death battle for food.*

Once we understood that the Indians had chased the deer from the island and slaughtered all the hogs, men began looking hungrily about them. We ate the chickens first, then the sheep. Next came the horses, slaughtered one by one—settlers even devoured their skin. With eyes on the river and no relief in sight, some began eating cats until there were no more of them. Gradually I noticed the chains swung loosely where once we had tethered the mastiffs.

Occasionally, some of the men managed to shoot squirrels or raccoons, beavers or muskrats. Mice, rats, foul musk turtles, and snakes—even poisonous ones—were next. Anything that crawled, crept, or moved was fair game. Anything dead was too—even if it were rotting.

In our relentless toil during the better weather, Tempie, Maggie and I had set aside more than most—maybe more than anyone else. We were cautious to tell no one, for food had become a commodity men would steal—and kill—for. We were three innocent women with a child, so we hoped no one would pay us any mind. We strove to keep a low countenance, and this we did. The pact between us was one of absolute trust. Our lives depended on it.

We cast up the amount we had in the cellar. We reckoned it split three ways, with an additional half share allotted for Janey. We estimated that we needed enough to see us through to early June, as that was our best guess as to when we might reasonably expect help. This was nearly five months—seemingly an eternity. We would continue foraging each day, as had been our arrangement, because it kept us occupied and less prone to despair. We would continue processing the scores of acorns, our manna indeed.

We made a further pact between us. We would avoid those things that seemed unclean to us, no matter how hungry we might become. Rabbits, squirrels, and songbirds—if we should have the great fortune to catch any—we would consume. But we would rather eat plants of the ground than any filthy rodents. We all knew that the time might come when we would stoop to this in our desperation, but we would start with this ideal. We had been faithful to our daily collections, whether the day was cold and wet or sweltering as in August. We had made no excuses, and now we prayed to God that we had done enough.

As we served our portions one evening in January, still stretching everything with acorn meal, Maggie shook her head. "My stomach is troubling me so. Save mine, and I will try to eat it later." She also declined to sing with us that night, preferring instead to lie down. I felt a pang of concern but shook it off. She was simply discouraged and would be her old self tomorrow. It must be that way, for I would not accept otherwise.

Now the Nightingale
Late January 1610

Now the nightingale, the pretty nightingale,
The sweetest singer in all the forest's choir,
Entreats thee, sweet Peggy, to hear thy true Love's tale:
Lo! yonder she sitteth, her breast against a briar.
~ Thomas Dekker

You'd be so lean, that blast of January
Would blow you through and through.
Now, my fair'st friend,
I would I had some flowers o' the spring that might
Become your time of day.
~ William Shakespeare

So far . . . so low . . .
A drowsy thrush? A waking nightingale?
Silence. We do not know.
~ Edward Shanks

From my apothecary jars, I administered lemon balm, rosemary, and sage oil to help relieve Maggie's colic and settle her insides. *Sovereign sage*, I thought. Stroking Maggie's hair fondly, I smiled at the allusion. My mother had believed sage a cure-all. Maggie seemed to have fallen into a quiet sleep, so perhaps it was helping.

Within a day, she seemed much improved, though she slept a little more than she usually did. Recuperative time was like that, I reasoned. Tempie and I alternated going to the woods to forage while one of us stayed with Janey, allowing Maggie to rest.

178

Yet the pallor of death hung over the town. The skies wore a winter grey shroud, which matched the mood that settled upon us all. Each day the soldiers dragged the ones we lost from their homes. There went young Nat, one of the blacksmiths. The next day, it was the Parks boy, but four years old, and just a few hours later, his mother. Some went to bed in seeming health, not to waken.

At first, the soldiers gave each his own grave, until that proved too much. Then they reminded themselves of the Bible verse, *but Jesus said unto him, "Follow me, and let the dead bury their dead."*

Let the dead bury their dead. Proper burial was too much hardship on those still living—weak and dying themselves. Another reason burial needed to be hasty was so the Indians might not see how many fell. And fell. Thus as the winter took a higher toll, we cast our friends into a burial pit behind the fort. It was brutal, and my heart wrenched each time I witnessed it, but there was little choice left to us in our besiegement. When I saw the little boy's body taken from his home, I ached with grief for him and his parents.

"Lucky we can bury 'em at all," I heard one soldier say as he dragged another body across the common area, past the church to the gravesite. I supposed he was right, though I felt something wither inside me when he said it.

Those were the days when I was sure I would not see spring at all. The flame in my heart burned low and my spirit flickered. Still I did all I could to keep my eye on the horizon and not upon the events I witnessed each day.

Late in January, I was returning from the woods. My feet trudged, but I tried to keep my faith alive. *When I am afraid, I will put my trust in thee,* I prayed as I walked. It was icy cold and my breath hung in the air in little white clouds and burned my chest. Had Dorset ever been this cold? The extremes of temperature in Virginia bewildered me, I thought idly as I made my way home. My weakened ankles, scratched and bleeding, gave way here and there on the uneven path and crunched the frozen ground. My knuckles reddened and my fingers ached. This was the thinnest I had ever been, and so I had little flesh to keep me warm. I was wearing several layers, but the cold gnawed through them all. The wind blew across the James River, sweeping the town in gusts. Sometimes we planted our feet so that the gale would not blow us over. Some days, as today, the river even froze. A frozen river! How much colder the settlement felt beside this enormous block of ice.

I longed to get my basket home and warm myself in front of the fire—first the front, then the back, then the front again. During wintertime in Virginia, no one was warm all over at once.

My heart lifted when I came within sight of our house—but quickly fell when Tempie raced outside. She had obviously been waiting for me, and I knew at once something was wrong. Her eyes were large and pleading, and she broke down at the sight of me.

"Joan, Joan, it is so terrible! So terrible!"

I dropped my basket and ran to her. "What? What is it? Is Janey all right? Tell me!" I nearly screamed at her.

She wiped her eyes with the back of her hand, and said haltingly, "Janey is well, as well as can be anyway. But Maggie—" She stopped. "She has the bloody flux and has no strength for it. She is barely awake even now."

"So fast," I murmured, pushing around her to the door.

"She suspected it yesterday but told us not, wanting to spare us worry, knowing there was naught we could do."

I barely noticed the warmth of the house with the inner chill of seeing Maggie's face. Gaunt and the color of parchment, her very aura said death. Her eyes were closed, and Tempie had bundled her well.

"My little nightingale," I said quietly, cradling her head. "We need your songs and your spirit. You shall pull through this—you must!" I whispered to her. In England, a nightingale heralded spring with low, sad crooning. I wondered if there were nightingales here? Probably not, so far from home. The only nightingale in Virginia was sweet Maggie, and I prayed to God that she would live to welcome the spring with us.

Tempie and I spent the evening praying over her, but we realized with wrenching certainty that she was slipping away.

I could still hear her ballads on ship, songs for a safe reunion with our husbands. With the *Sea Venture* lost, it was not to be. Still, the words of the song lingered in my memory. *I wish in my heart that I were with you.*

"I suppose now you will be," I said to her, stroking her hand. Her round, jovial face now lay so ashen, so still. Could it truly be that her voice, her soul, would be taken from us? Her breathing was ragged and labored and there was a slight whistle in it. *Never to sing so sweetly again.*

Tempie and I each held one of her hands, which barely pulsed with life. We had not even been able to say goodbye.

With tears stinging my eyes, I whispered, "Fly 'cross the river, little nightingale." And she did.

It Is the Hour

Late January 1610

It is the hour when from the boughs
The nightingale's high note is heard;
It is the hour when lovers' vows
Seem sweet in every whispered word;
And gentle winds, and waters near,
Make music to the lonely ear.

~ Lord Byron

Everything perfect in its kind has to transcend its own kind,
it must become something different and incomparable.
In some notes the nightingale is still a bird;
then it rises above...
and seems to suggest to every winged creature what singing is truly like.

~ Johann Wolfgang von Goethe

As the last of the sun slipped behind the river, Maggie drew in a long, deep breath and let it go. We perched on the edge of her mattress, still holding her hands as they grew stiff and cold.

"Do you think she knew she wasn't alone?" I asked, my voice wavering.

"Aye. Surely she did. We have been together since we landed, and you two were companions on ship. She has always had you."

There was little time to mourn as we prepared her for burial, though our tears spilled around her as we combed her hair and washed her face gently. We were about to undress her as was custom, but Tempie said, "Joan, we have plenty of women's clothes." She was right. It was customary to bury the dead wrapped in a shroud, but we had lost so many women that we now had abundant clothes. I hated the thought of wrapping her only in a shroud, without a coffin, in the bitter Virginia winter.

181

Because she had not yet risen for the day, Maggie had on just her white shift, which would do.

"She looks lovely," I said. "I only wish we could hear that voice one more time."

"One day we will," Tempie said with assurance.

I remembered Maggie's poem. "She never gave up hope, did she?" I said. "We could do no better than that."

Tempie retrieved her *Book of Psalms* and, after saying the Lord's Prayer, we knelt at her bedside.

Before we could commence, Tempie cried, "Wait!" She rose to find a candle, lit it, and carried it to Maggie's side. "We can hope with her and for her, can't we? Let this be *a shimmering flame through dark Despair.*"

I nodded through tears. Finding Psalm 150 and still kneeling, together we hummed:

Sing ye unto the Lord our God,
a new rejoicing song:
And let the praise of him be heard
His holy Saints among.

I read her poem as part of the service, adding, "'Twas you who were our brilliant lady fair, our shimmering flame through dark despair." Then I tucked the little book into her hand and closed her fingers around it. Tempie and I knew without saying so that we would keep her book in remembrance of Maggie—but we let her hold it just a while longer.

I turned to Tempie in sudden fear. "What will we do without her?"

She hugged me saying, "We will do as she did. Let our faith fuel our hope. However dim it may burn, it shall not extinguish."

At last, when we had busied ourselves with practicalities as long as we could and given her our own prayers of farewell, we knew it was the hour to part with her and call the soldiers. "'Tis time," I said, a catch in my throat. "But, oh, Tempie. Burial pit!" I felt ill even thinking of it.

She knew what I meant. How could we let them pitch her into a trench like so much refuse?

With heavy hearts, we summoned the soldier named Walter.

"Mistress Maggie Deale has died," Tempie told him with dignity, her voice quivering, her eyes red.

182

"Please," I said, impulsively grabbing the sleeve of his doublet. "Is there any way she can have a Christian burial?" He sighed and rolled his eyes impassively.

"I can't do that. Captain Percy's orders. We don't have the time or strength. You know that, Mistress Peirce, Mistress Yeardley. You see what we're up against. We've lost hundreds. It's just not possible with so many and us weak ourselves. I'm sorry." He leaned out the door and called to another soldier. "Help me, Edward. Another body here."

The thought of Maggie as a body made my stomach turn, and I grabbed my mouth thinking I might be sick.

"Here!" Tempie said suddenly, pulling her wedding band off her finger. "If I give you my ring, will you bury her right proper? Please! Do it for us, will you, Sir?"

Tempie's eyes pleaded, and I sensed he might relent. I jerked my ring off also. "One for each of you," I hastened to add, looking from one to the other.

They took our jewelry and then exchanged glances. Walter motioned us to wait, and he and Edward walked over by the garden. We could not make out the words. Tempie gazed at me. "What will we do if they say no?"

"We will pray now they say yes and not worry about no," I said in a trembling tone. My stomach still roiled. I put my hand across my mouth. *Lord, hear our prayer.*

A moment later, they returned. "This is the one who sang at eventides, isn't it?" Walter asked, pointing toward the bed where Maggie lay. There was no emotion in his voice.

We nodded. I tried to speak, but words would not come.

His weary soldier's face softened. "Many's the night I longed for home and heard her voice, 'cross the town, right quiet but sweet." I couldn't believe my ears. Had she, with her gentle song, touched this soldier who had thrust so many in trenches, himself half-starved?

"Aye," Edward added. "She sang Psalms, the only time I *ever* felt God move in this place. She sang ballads shipboard, and I remembered home." There was bitterness in his words.

A moment of silence ensued, and I held my breath, afraid to hope.

"I reckon we can bury her. It's the least we can do." They handed us back our rings. "Keep these, Mistresses. We want to bury Mistress Maggie. We'll come get her a little later, after we've prepared a spot. We can do it covertly in the corner of the fort. Then we'll let you know where." There was a trace of sad smile as they tipped their hats deferentially to us. "Trust us," Walter added.

We did, for we had experienced a miracle of hope in a moment of despair, just as Maggie's poem had predicted.

Like Wind I Go
Early February 1610

As I went down to the river to pray
Studying about that good ol' way,
And who shall wear the starry crown?
Good Lord, show me the way.

~ Appalachian folk song

Awake! for Morning in the Bowl of Night
Has flung the Stone that puts the Stars to Flight:
And Lo! the Hunter of the East has caught
The Sultan's Turret in a Noose of Light.

With them the Seed of Wisdom did I sow,
And with my own hand labour'd it to grow:
And this was all the Harvest that I reap'd—
"I came like Water, and like Wind I go."

~ Omar Khayyam

M aggie's death left a searing hole in my heart along with the echoes of her stilled songs. Tempie and I attended our chores silently for several days. Yes, we had to search the woods for whatever we could find and boil that up. We dipped water from the town's well and used it to produce a thin pottage. We went through our days as though nothing had happened.

And yet, everything had happened.

The outlook for the settlement had never been grimmer, and now Tempie and I had not even Maggie's keen insights to rely upon. Tempie was good hearted, it was true, and her sense of humor had cut through my misery many times in the nearly six months since our arrival.

But we had been as a stool with three legs, each providing balance and its own support. What happened to a stool with one leg chopped off?

Without Maggie, there would be no music and no one to help me steer our course. I loved Tempie dearly as I had loved Maggie. But she was young yet, still in her early twenties. She lacked the wisdom that I—and especially Maggie—possessed purely by having experienced more of life.

I slipped out of the house before sunrise and went down to the river. It was a little dangerous, but I could not care about that just then. I sought the river as I had sought the harbor in Melcombe so many times. It provided a consolation as nothing else could.

As I got closer, drawn in by the sounds of the moving water, I felt a sudden, crushing weight in my chest. Grief. My heart seemed to throb from all parts at once, and my insides tightened as though something were ripping me from the inside out. I slumped down, bowed my head, and pressed my hand against the dead ache. *Make it stop. Oh, please, make it stop.*

I realized at once that it was not just Maggie for whom I grieved, but also the stream of losses that had mounted and confronted me at once. My mother and father, Tom and baby Jack, Will and Sam—and now Maggie. I had not grieved them. Each time I had pushed the pain aside and gone on. Now that grief, like a dam bursting, had come for me. It was an anguish like no other.

I had delved into a well that had no bottom—a well I had not even known was there—and I began to cry as never before. I felt crushed beneath this weight, and its burden rendered me unable to breathe.

The tears came hard and fast, and my body released sobs rhythmically, painfully. I had never felt such agony, like a retching out of my own soul. And so I wept and wept and wept, my eyes flooding endlessly like the water rushing by, no beginning and no end.

I don't know how much time passed, but the sun began breaking in the eastern sky. With a final shudder, I realized my tears had subsided, leaving only a numbing grief. *What manner of journey is this?* I had suffered loss after loss, and, like the river's flowing, my life seemed to be one long, tragic march to the sea. Such a pilgrimage was futile.

Now I understood I was not only sad, but also desperately angry. Seeing a mussel shell beside me, I snatched it up and flung it as hard as I could. I enjoyed the feeling of sending it far away, listening to it crash helplessly into the river, knowing it was sinking down. That was me—pulled beneath the river, falling to the bottom, half carried, half swept under. Helpless and useless like the empty shell. Unable to swim, unable to rise and struggle against a hand larger than myself, lost in a rushing tide of water so deep I could not know what lay within it.

185

Yes, that was me. I even *felt* like an empty shell, and I began to cry all over again.

Then I reached for another shell, and as I was about to throw that one too—harder—something stopped me. I studied it for a moment. My eyes were so bleary from a thousand tears that the shell's glistening black image swam before them.

A hand throws a shell. Did God's hand throw me away? No, I had never felt that, not for any length of time. What would my father have said? What *did* he say?

Joanie, where the hand of God leads me, the hand of God saves me. He himself had fallen beneath the waves, but he had never considered the sea his destination. He had known his body was but a shell. His soul he had entrusted to higher journeys.

I pondered that a moment.

The bitterness of a February in Virginia was seeping into my bones, but I was unwilling just yet to walk away from the river. Besides, the aching cold seemed a fitting accompaniment for the numbness I felt inside.

Suddenly, the sun broke thoroughly, hopefully, over the water, casting spectacular rays onto the river, down at that place where it met the sea. A flock of geese passed overhead, and their noisy cries drew my attention upward. They soared in the shape of a wide *V*, the one in front no doubt taking the brunt of the morning air. Yet he pushed onward, the others trailing his lead.

The ones who come before always do that, I thought. My mother had faced death calmly, offering me chamomile while explaining how to concoct remedies for her cough. My father went into it with undiminished faith. Tom had carried love for his unborn child to the end, and by all accounts showed courage in his final battle. The baby, the baby. Poor little Jack. At that, I thought I should start to cry all over again. How efficiently I had cleaned the blood he vomited. His death was cruel by any standards. But Cecily had reminded me that Jack no longer suffered; instead, he soared with the angels.

Will and Sam would say, "You come from a fine bloodline. Carry on!" Had they rolled over and died in the hurricane, or charged it with their last ounce of strength? I knew them. I knew they fought 'til there was no hope left—only then relinquishing. Maggie, if she were here, would urge me on. "This is what we've got," she'd say. "Make the best of it. It's still an adventure, Joan!"

Like geese flying ahead of me in formation, they had blazed through the wind. These were gifts they left behind, and they asked only that I follow.

The journey would be alone for a while, but ultimate journeys always are. A man entered the world alone and departed it in the same manner. And all that fell between? *Perhaps this is what my father meant about all life being a pilgrimage. We have our companions, but the hand of God determines our beginnings and our ends.* God had not marked my end just yet. It was true I might not make it through the winter. If I accepted that—and gave it my best 'til then—what had I to fear? We were going to get very, very hungry, but our labors in late summer and fall had left us dried nuts and berries, and God might provide when least expected.

Again, as months before, I felt a hand upon my shoulder. I knew without looking it must be Tempie, for who else would care?

"There you are," she said gently. "I have been concerned for you."

Wordlessly I wrapped my arms around her neck and she wrapped hers about mine. I cried into her dress, and felt her tears upon my shoulder.

And suddenly I knew. She might not have the wisdom—yet—of a Maggie, but she had the heart of Temperance. When I cried, she knew when to make me laugh and when to cry along with me—and I was never quite sure how she could tell the difference.

At last she said, "I have some pottage with herbs and cornmeal simmering, and the fire is stoked. Are you cold?"

I was.

With arms about our meager waists, we walked in silence back to the house, as another flock of geese passed overhead moving onward down the river.

The Fall of a Sparrow
February 21, 1610

Not a whit, we defy augury.
There is special providence
in the fall of a sparrow.

~ William Shakespeare

B y early February, the cornmeal was completely gone.
All persons in the settlement had to fend for themselves, as there were no
food provisions of any sort left to dispense. As to leadership, Captain Percy remained dangerously ill, Captain Archer had died along with so many others, and
Captain Martin had not ventured back out of James Town. Captain Davis and his
group were still at Point Comfort, although no one knew how they fared. We'd had
no word from them since December, when the messenger had arrived with news of
the *Swallow's* mutiny and the birth of Annie's baby. Travel overland was treacherous
in the unyielding siege, while we had little means of water transportation—except for
one small boat and a canoe. These offered inadequate protection and firepower to
battle the enemies we knew lay in wait along the shores.

One morning in the middle of February, our only boat broke free its moor-
ings—or perhaps the Indians loosed it as they had the others. It drifted four
miles downriver before anyone noticed its absence. Captain Martin assigned
three soldiers to retrieve it, an order they refused to obey. No one, it seemed,
respected Martin's authority any longer.

Martin stormed into Percy's house, and the next we knew there emerged a
pale but enraged Captain Percy. We had scarcely seen him since he fell ill in September—but fury must be powerful medicine. Now he stood at the door of his
house, sword drawn and waving threateningly, his eyes narrowed in utter contempt toward the errant soldiers.

"You shall see that boat returned, or you shall see *yourselves* executed for treason before the sun this day sets!" The soldiers nearly knocked one another over

clambering into the canoe, recapturing the boat with remarkable speed. Captain Percy was responsible for the lives of the men, women and children who still survived, in a situation fraught with impossibility. He was in no mood to throw around our ever-dwindling resources, especially ones that might in any way help procure food—even the possibility of a few fish.

Meanwhile, desperation drove many to flee to the Indians, and we never saw nor heard from them again. Presumed dead.

Together, Tempie and I watched those around us take on increasingly odd behaviors—like the day an emaciated Hugh Price ran into the marketplace screaming, "There is no God! If there were a God He would not suffer his creatures to live such as this!"

Later that day, Price went beyond the fort seeking food, and warriors shot him through with arrows. At the same time, the Indians also killed a heavier man, a butcher, and his body lay only yards away from Price. Strangely, wild animals tore apart Price's thin body while leaving the fat butcher untouched. This event caused the whole town to speculate that God was punishing Price for his blasphemy. My initial reaction was that God would have forgiven him this outburst as the ranting of a man driven insane by hunger.

I had never thought of God as punishing and vindictive—but what if Price's unusual death were proof this were so? Deeply troubled by the possibility, I was unable to sleep that night. I had always believed that the God who created life led us through the parts of the road where we stumbled. I had never once considered that He Himself might be tossing stones into our path. Now it seemed the only conclusion was that He might indeed be punishing us.

With this paralyzing thought came a hopelessness. If this sense of abandonment pulled me in, would I be able to climb back out again? For if God were not in some unseen manner helping us—if He were not with us but against us—*what had we left?*

That night Tempie and Janey drifted off to sleep, but I could not. The fire crackled and burned, a small beacon of warmth against the winter chill. I remembered all we'd endured thus far and how the road seemed to wind downward interminably, always with a steeper valley beyond. We could easily anticipate three more months before any ships arrived. James Town had never seemed so remote from England and all that we had left behind. Sickness, murder, insanity, and famine had taken hundreds and left us all on a death vigil. So many gone, and so quickly they now fell. My mind spun in all directions.

Was God seeking retribution on us for coming here? Was this not the Promised Land as we had thought? Or suppose it were, but we had handled it so poorly God was taking it from

189

us again? Was He angry with us? Would He punish all for what a few had done? And if He were not angry, did He even know so many had died? Did He even see us here? Could he find us on the edge of this wild continent? My mind raced from thought to thought, each more disturbing than the last.

Calmly, a voice echoed in my head. *Let me take the wings of the morning, and dwell in the uttermost parts of the sea. Yet thither shall thine hand lead me, and thy right hand hold me.* My father's Psalm, the explorer and mariner's promise. At Melcombe Harbor, I had felt God reassure me of that. Had He?

I tossed and turned, my body sore and sleep eluding me. My stomach rumbled in hunger as always, but now I hungered for something further. I needed to know the truth. *Had God abandoned us here?*

Are not two sparrows sold for a farthing, and one of them shall not fall on the ground without your Father? The verse appeared in my mind, as if in response to my own question. *Yea, and all the hairs of your head are numbered. Fear ye not therefore, ye are of more value then many sparrows.*

"Do you truly know each sparrow?" I thought of my sparrow's voice, and the loss of our nightingale. "Do you truly count each one? If we are of more value than sparrows, why do we perish in such numbers? I do not understand," I murmured. "For, my Lord, *I am so hungry.*" This said as I drifted into a light and uncomfortable sleep, pain chewing my insides, as though my body consumed itself.

In the morning, I awoke after fitful dreams. I must have been crying, I thought, since my face and mattress were damp.

"Do you remember us?" I whispered to God. My despair and isolation, even from Tempie and Janey, had not improved during the night. They seemed, in fact, to be mounting. "Can You hear me, Lord? Are You there? Are You there? *Are You there?*" I was still speaking in a whisper so as not to awaken Janey or Tempie, but it was all I could do not to scream the words aloud, for the pitch in my voice rose with each cry.

"*Are... You... there?*" My last plea, hushed yet fierce and belligerent, echoed into the dim morning light of our cottage. I felt mocked, lost, betrayed. Forgotten. Tears streamed down my face as I rose. I was dizzy, and the room spun slightly. My vision was patchy and black, speckled with stars, and I thought I might faint. I steadied myself on the bed, the aching in my belly relentless.

It was no use. It was the twenty-first day of February, and how could we possibly endure three months—or more—of this? Hope was as distant as Dorset was from Virginia.

There was no reprieve from starving. We had our acorn meal and other rations from the fall, but the Virginia squirrels knew and we knew—there was little to find in the forests now. Even if there were, the Indians were out there. They watched with eyes like the night, wielding arrows of piercing accuracy.

Tempie was restless but had not yet awakened. She was also tossing, first one way and then the other, and I noticed again how thin she had grown.

Dawn was breaking, and a fiery sunrise topped the trees as I opened the door cautiously. All was silent, for the birds had been in hushed stillness this winter. Flown elsewhere, as we wished we could. The forests sounded as desolate as I felt.

And then—what was this? *Could it be?*

My heart raced, my eyes brimmed with tears—but this time, they were tears of gratitude. I knelt to get a closer look.

There lay a lifeless chickadee, the little sparrow with a black cap.

Delicate, perfectly preserved—had I been in Melcombe, I might have felt pity for the poor frozen creature. Here, in these circumstances, another emotion overwhelmed me entirely. God had provided our day's food! Such elegant answer to prayer, such kind demonstration of love in our suffering.

I dared not yell. I dared not raise my voice nor draw attention to it out of doors, for those who grew increasingly addled went to any lengths for the slightest morsel of food. In times such as these, a tiny perished bird might as well have been roast pheasant.

I carried it over to Tempie, who was just stirring. "See what I have? God sent us victuals today! He *does* remember the sparrow, and He remembers *us*. Even in the uttermost parts of the sea." My faith was not misplaced after all.

Tempie turned sleepily to see the little black and white bird in my outstretched hand. She squealed when her eyes opened enough to recognize it, a squeal of delight. We had seen so few birds this winter. Where had it come from? Especially during the night?

"Oh, Providence!" she whispered, her hands clasped prayer-like in front of her lips. "Praise God!"

Janey sat up, rubbing her eyes, as Tempie and I dropped to our knees in thankfulness at the hearth. Together we prayed, *"I was hungry, and you fed me."*

And never had I tasted a pottage as good as that little chickadee made.

The Breaking of the Shell
Late February–Late March, 1610

Your pain is the breaking of the shell
that encloses your understanding.
Even as the stone of the fruit must break,
that its heart may stand in the sun,
so must you know pain.

~ Kahlil Gibran

Accept whatever befalls you, in crushing misfortune be patient;
For in fire gold is tested, and worthy men in the crucible of humiliation.
~ Sirach 2:4-5

F ebruary had nearly given way to March, and yet the weather remained bitter. Men began ripping mats and bark from deserted cottages to use as kindling. No one wanted to venture far from the fort unless absolutely necessary, as it grew more dangerous daily. Now, the fort, the *pallisado*, and the homes around us were crumbling from neglect and abuse, just as the people themselves were. There was something tragic in watching the town deteriorate along with our hopes.

I did not know how long a Virginia winter lasted, but Tempie and I tried to glean what we could from men who'd survived the previous two years.

I had learned from Maggie the art of well-placed allies and informants. Walter, the soldier who had buried Maggie, had arrived with the initial expedition in April '07, so he understood Virginia better than we did. He was gaunt but reliable, and I continued to trust him more than most.

Bundled against the cold air, I approached him late in February, asking if he knew when milder weather might arrive. Virginia had been frigid since before Christmas and the cold showed no signs of abating. We had seen mild spells even in the harshest months, but these were the exceptions.

192

"Spring is nigh. Hold fast, she's coming!" he told me. By early March, we should see tips of buds on trees, yet the days would remain cold much of the time, he said. Spring would make a more formal arrival, it seemed, somewhere in April, when the days would be warmer while nights would remain chilly. Some days would be exceedingly damp, rainy and cold, like English weather. May, Walter said, delivered sultriness with a vengeance.

I dreamed of warm days, so even *sultry* sounded pleasant to me. May was a lifetime, an actual lifetime, away. Even then, it was uncertain how we would feed ourselves if still alive, but at least the wind would not blow through our bones.

I mentioned this to Tempie, who responded in two somber words: "Summer sickness."

Aye. And so the cycle of seasons would begin anew.

Regrettably, I could not offer Walter any herbs should he fall ill. That would have been dangerous. Herbs, even medicinal ones, we had to keep secret, so no one would harm us to obtain them. I had even hidden all my apothecary jars in the cellar with the acorns.

If the herbs were valuable, the acorn meal was precious. In a besieged fort, it might as well have been gold dust, and we had little way to protect it. Tempie and I told absolutely no one that we had a small store of acorn meal left. The trust between us, always important, had passed beyond critical into the sacred— for in extremes of hunger, what stopped one of us from eating more than her share? From slipping into the cellar at night and devouring part, or all, of the provisions stored there? But our deep regard for each other made this pact inviolate. If anything, the one serving spooned the other a more generous portion. We had a plan for rationing over a course of months, and our goal remained as much to keep the other alive as our own selves.

The acorn meal had helped us hold to our pact of not eating the worst vermin. I felt on instinct that God had not intended black rats or mice as victuals. There was something repugnant in their little faces, but beyond that, it made sense to me that the meat of filth-eating animals must itself be comprised of filth. Whether there was any truth to that I knew not, but with our stash of plant foods, I hoped never to test the idea. Forest vermin ate more wholesomely, so we considered these appropriate to eat—if we should be fortunate enough to catch any.

We could afford to be a little more particular because we had enough acorn meal to give us a base of sustenance. Not enough to keep us from withering, but enough to spare us, I hoped, from consuming the filth-eaters until we reached a last level of desperation. We were not there yet. Others that had no such minimal provisions considered house vermin a newfound delicacy—but we were holding out. Holding out for what, I did not know. Holding out hope that daily manna did not involve creatures with squinty eyes and whiskers, I supposed.

We did find a dead mouse in our cottage one day and carried him by his little tail out to the commons. Three men fought over him, and the biggest eagerly claimed his prize, the mouse. Tempie and I watched in disgust, I with my hands on my hips, she with her arms folded across her chest. Her eyes met mine knowingly. Well we remembered this man as one we'd seen playing skittles some days as we returned from the woods with our lowly acorns and our raw, aching hands.

Another day, Janey had pointed to a dead chipmunk in the garden. The cold weather had preserved him well, and we were quick to scoop him up and run him home for pottage. We considered him clean vermin—if there is such a thing—and were thankful to have spied him before anyone else.

While I felt plants to be far healthier for us overall, they still ran the risk of possessing poisonous properties. Yet, they might also possess the ability to heal. Our dilemma was that not all Virginia plants were familiar to us, so we often relied on what we knew from the Indians or Spanish, what others told us, and even sketchy reports from the previous settlement at Roanoke Island. Gerard's *Herball, or, Generall Historie of Plants* contained descriptions from the earliest English settlements. Then too we had learned a great deal from Annie before she left for Point Comfort—but there was so much more to know.

We started this day's search as we always did, with a prayer. We repeated Psalm 91 together and then I prepared to set out, remembering a cedar tree near the woods. "Tempie, what do you think of pottage made from cedar leaves?"

Tempie shrugged and replied, "I saw deer eating from it in the fall. Cedar pottage does sound a mite better than fried rat!" Our laughter was as bitter as we expected the cedar would be.

With a basket tucked beneath my arm, I approached the edge of the fort, taking a moment to look about or listen for anything unusual. *I will not fear the arrow that flyeth by day*, I reminded myself, quoting the morning's Psalm and adding, *God protect me from savages and fill my basket with cedar.* The cedar was close in—no longer would we go as far as the oak and hickory groves in the uplands.

Arriving at the tree, I snatched and broke the little branches, snapping off spiny fronds. I worked with all haste, except for tasting a sprig, thinking, *if it does not poison the deer, I reckon it will not poison me.*

194

It had a grainy, rough texture and made me cough, as some of it went down and some lay in the back of my throat. I swallowed again, hard and quickly. If the Indians were nearby, I did not want to attract their attention. They would not believe it was a deer coughing like that!

The flavor was not as bad as I might have thought. It was strong, but not unpleasant, and went into my empty stomach remarkably well. Cedar had a lingering taste, almost like mint. I picked and plucked and grabbed sprigs from the tree, filling my basket with as many small cedar branches as I could reach and whatever lay on the ground.

No savages appeared. Sometimes I thought I felt eyes boring into me from the dark of the forest, but not this day. Once done, I rushed back to the protection of the fort, feeling like a child escaping a goblin.

Tempie was waiting. I noticed her face grew gaunter, her cheeks more hollow, each day. As did my own, I was sure. Each day I tightened the apron cord and the tie around my waist—still my kirtle hung loosely about me.

"Did you find the cedar?" she asked eagerly. She picked up a small spray and smelled it. Then, as I had, she put a piece in her mouth and chewed. "Never thought I should see the day I would graze from trees like deer!"

Then, thoughtfully, she added, "But we are going to survive, Joan. I feel that if we can but make it until the spring…" She pushed the cedar into an iron pot filled with water. Many forest plants and roots were best boiled or roasted, we'd found. As the water began to rumble, Tempie gave the roiling kettle a stir. "Well, it's certainly coloring the water green—green cedar pottage! We can live off that for two or three days, I think," she said. She decided not to thicken it with acorn meal until we knew whether the mixture would be at all edible or not.

Suddenly feeling weary from my trip out of the fort, I sunk unto the bed. It was exhausting to take one's life in hand to fetch the poorest foods the forest offered—and even these barely edible.

As I sat, I studied this young woman earnestly mixing humble pottage and humming softly as she did so. Where were her complaints? Why did she not go running into the commons blaming God as others did? How was she able to maintain her wry humor? It stuck me suddenly what great admiration I had for her, how moved I was by her soul and her spirit and her character. Now that Maggie was gone, I was acutely aware of what Tempie's loss would mean to me. I prayed she were right about us surviving together.

"Tempie?" I spoke only the single word, and she paused stirring to look up. "The meal may be meager, but the company is fine."

Standing the spoon against the wall near the fire, Tempie walked over and placed a slender arm about my shoulders. "Fine company indeed, and a decent meal all-in-all, especially compared to what the others eat. If the men of this colony had been as diligent as we were in gathering—and not so ready to consume their own shoe leather—they might not be a-dying so fast," she said indignantly.

It was true we had seen people boiling anything made of leather, including shoes and even the sailcloth from the original church. Had anyone suggested to these men prior to arrival that they would consume a place of worship, I think they should not have believed them. Starch for ruffled collars—none left in the settlement now. We had even seen some lick blood from the ground in sheer desperation, starvation, and insanity.

She was right. By these standards, cedar pottage was indeed a feast.

I found that its taste lingered, which I welcomed. I savored it long after I took my last bite. It filled my stomach, and the hot broth calmed my body's shivering. The Virginia winter had made my bones ache and my hands numb, and I felt much older than before.

We only gave Janey foods we had tested on ourselves first and knew to be edible, so I waited until the next day to give her the cedar pottage. Instead, I fed her acorn meal. When I did give her the pottage, she ate it unquestioningly, even greedily. I hoped it did not make her ill, but I had no choice. Ill or dead—I had to choose ill.

Tempie and I remembered the holly berries and retrieved them from the cellar.

She mashed a berry and touched it to her tongue, making a face at its bitterness. "My fat squirrel loved these. Would that I could eat him instead! But I am not much a hunter, though gathering I do well. He would not count as vermin, would he?"

"If we could catch him, we could eat him. He's a little more appealing than his cousins in the rafters," I said. I placed a berry tentatively in my mouth and chewed, finding it gritty and bitter. "I suppose we should boil them, else we shall never get them down—unlike your friend the squirrel."

We boiled the berries and even considered adding them to the cedar broth. "But the cedar did not make us sick, so perhaps we shouldn't spoil it with the berries until we know they are edible. Let's prepare them separately," Tempie suggested.

This done, we two supped on the leftover cedar pottage and the rosy broth, giving Janey only the cedar.

Boiling had mellowed the berries' flavor considerably, although the supper of red pottage and green pottage, with floating berries and spindles, was strange to behold and stranger still to eat.

196

We had reached a point where hunger pains never actually left any more, and we stayed tired much of the time. It was early yet, but we three were growing drowsy. Janey yawned and curled up on her mattress, an arm wrapped around her doll. Tempie walked over and tucked her in, carefully bundling the doll, Bessie, as well. I kissed Janey's cheek, and she smiled as her eyes drooped.

How can the child smile, when she has eaten naught but green pottage? I wondered.

"G'night, Mama. G'night, Missus Tempie," she said sleepily.

"Good night, Lovey. And you too, Bessie," I added.

"She is a dear child," Tempie said to me.

"And a hungry one," I added quietly.

Something had been weighing on me, and I thought now a good time to address it. "Tempie," I began. "This is much to ask, I know, but if something should happen to me…" I looked at Janey, already asleep.

"Of course," she said, reading my thoughts. "I would have it no other way. You know that. I would love her as my own." She gave the child a tender glance. "I already do."

"It would be up to you, then, to determine whether she should remain here or return home if opportunity presented itself. I wrote an informal will to indicate my wish that she go to you. I will sign it tomorrow with Captain Tucker as witness. I would prefer she go where you go, but you have my permission to choose for her as you see most fitting and in her best interests."

She gave a serious nod.

"Would you also be responsible for Cecily? If she should disembark and find me…not here." My voice trailed off. "Or if you think it prudent, send for her if conditions at the settlement improve. Again, that would be your decision. She is living with my brother now."

"I am honored," she said, looking touched. "I would raise them as if they were my flesh and blood. However, you and I—and Janey—will see this through. I swear it."

I hoped this was true, but if not, it relieved me to know my girls would be in her capable hands.

Before we turned in each night, Tempie and I always ensured we had a plan for how to search the next day. "Any thoughts about tomorrow?" I asked.

"Tomorrow indeed. We can get more cedar, and there was a grass by the river we could try." We had been hoping the tuckahoe would appear in the swamp soon, but it was not up yet.

"We have not dug for roots in several days, either. There is that," I added. "Of course, the ground is so frozen, that becomes a nearly impossible task. Perhaps we dig by the right corner of the fort beyond the common grounds."

"We just keep digging and searching. That is what we shall do tomorrow. And leave the shoe leather and black rats to the *gentlemen*!"

It was a weak joke, but we laughed anyway.

"Never to give up," I said.

Tempie nodded, but her eyes were rimmed and weary.

The morning came, and Tempie did not rise early, as was her custom. I cocked my head and noticed her breathing roughly. She seemed drawn up in pain.

"Tempie!" In an instant, I was at her side. Squatting by the bed. I rested my hand on her clammy forehead. "What hurts you?" I said, my voice low and, I hoped, soothing.

"I know not." She paused. "Perhaps the berries are having a disagreement with my insides. I think," she said slowly, "the berries are winning." She made a weak smile and began to sit up, then lay back with a groan.

"No," I said, patting her arm and tucking the quilt around her chin. "No, stay put. I'll search for both of us today. I'll return as soon as possible, perhaps before Janey awakes."

Before I left, I gave each of us a tincture of rosemary, summer savory, chamomile, sage oil, and thyme. My belly had a cramp also, but hers was more severe as mine did not cause me to buckle in pain. I set the remaining berries aside, since they seemed to make us sick—but did not toss them out. Desperation might drive us to need these unhealthful berries in the coming months, and I was taking no chances.

She smiled wanly, took a deep breath and drew her knees close to her belly. Glancing back as I left, I thought how small she looked beneath the covers, how much of her had wasted away these last months.

If I should lose her—

But I would not think of that.

By March, Tempie had mostly recovered, though she often had stomach ailments after that. She would ache 'til she doubled over, kneeling by the bed. Sometimes she laid her head on the blanket and drew her arms across her belly. I tried various herb tinctures to see if any gave greater relief. Chamomile with sage seemed the most effective, but nothing removed her discomfort completely. Sometimes she went outside and vomited, and then I helped her into bed. Still she feigned humor.

"Blasted berries! They keep me alive or kill me, I cannot decide which."

After one daunting episode, she said, "Joan? I have changed my mind."

"About what?" We had not been in conversation, so I was confused. Was she losing her mind like so many others?

"About us being hunters," she said with a groan. "That squirrel that recommended me these berries? Shoot him. Bring me his little carcass and let us feast!"

I concurred with a laugh, "If I could but catch him, I should be most happy to."

The behavior we saw about us continued to deteriorate, as some went insane while others raged at God. A few blamed anyone near them. One man murdered his wife and unborn child, going so far as to consume a portion of his wife. Percy's men strung him up by his thumbs for a quarter hour until he confessed to the villainy. Then they put him to death.

A different kind of wild, Harrison had said. This was proving true, and one never knew what a day would bring.

Once Master Fleetwood ran from his cottage, screaming that his wife was a witch. Now Mistress Fleetwood kept to herself and we did not know her well, but we were certain of one thing. She was no witch.

Still, Fleetwood said she was due a ducking—that we should drop her into the icy river to see whether or not she floated. If she did, we'd know sure enough she was a witch and we could execute her. And, of course, if she drowned, we'd know then she was innocent. This was the accepted method of determining who was, and was not, a witch. But Master Fleetwood had no legitimate grounds for having his wife ducked. She had not cursed a woman with child, causing her to miscarry. Nor had she caused any animals to behave in an unnatural manner.

A crowd had gathered and pointed at her, whispering amongst themselves. Fleetwood's eyes were wild, and I felt Mistress Fleetwood's fear—would others believe him?

Fortunately, Captain Tucker stepped in on her behalf. He walked up to Fleetwood, speaking quietly, and put his arm around him.

"Now, now," he murmured. "River's too cold for a ducking today, Sir. And I see by her eyes, she's no witch." He continued speaking as he walked the slumping man back into his cottage. He smiled over his shoulder at Mrs. Fleetwood, who breathed deeply and appeared relieved.

"His hunger has made him foolish and insane," Tempie whispered to me.

"Pray that doesn't happen to us," I said quietly.

"Losing our senses?" she asked.

"Yes. *Or* someone accusing us of witchcraft." Two women alone, faring slightly better than the men because of hidden remedies and acorns...

We stood in silence, pondering that dark reality.

There were those like Master Fleetwood who crumbled beneath the harsh circumstances of the settlement. Yet others, like Captain Tucker, demonstrated that such struggles could bring out the best rather than the worst in them. Tucker reasoned that a Cape Merchant with an empty store had nothing to manage. Was there anything he could personally do to restock the settlement's supply of food? The brightest hope was to catch fish. Although they seemed not to be biting, we had little other manner of procuring food. As there were no adequate boats, Captain Tucker determined to build one. This not only gave his own hands work to do, but it put other idle hands to work as well. Each day, no matter how cold, we heard him pounding away as he and other men constructed a large boat. When he had completed it, he *did* manage to catch a few fish. Now and then, we all received a small portion.

The good from this endeavor spread to the rest of the fort in other ways as well. Percy swore having a project kept the distressed, hungry men from killing one another as the winter dragged on.

For every man or woman who lost his mind to hopelessness, there were still those among us preserving our sanity and dignity. By what means we were separated, I remained unclear.

The Beauty of a Receiving Hand
Late March–Early April, 1610

One would give plenty of almonds
if one had eyes to see the beauty of a receiving hand.
~ Johann Wolfgang Von Goethe

Be not forgetful to entertain strangers: for thereby
some have received angels into their houses unawares.
~ Hebrews 13:2

Heard a carol, mournful, holy…
~ Alfred Tennyson

"It's Master Fleetwood." Tempie stopped short upon the cottage threshold. Bucket in hand, she had been on her way to the well.

"Is he accusing his wife of being a witch again?" I asked with a touch of sarcasm. I came up behind Tempie, peering around her through the doorway. "Oh." I saw at once what she meant.

He was dead.

The soldiers Walter and Edward, bony and huffing white clouds of breath into the chill March air, carried his body from the cottage. Grace Fleetwood stared after them, the back of her hand to her mouth, her eyes distraught.

"The poor dear," Tempie whispered, dropping the bucket and rushing to her. She draped her arm around Grace, who embraced her fully with deep, long sobs.

"We're so sorry, so sorry," Tempie said, as we two glanced at each other. We knew what it was like to lose a husband and be on one's own in this harsh fort.

Her arms still wrapped around the grieving old woman, Tempie lifted her eyes to mine questioningly. We found we often understood each other's thoughts, sometimes through most subtle cues. I knew in a moment what Tempie was thinking. *She wants to bring her to live with us!*

It would be an act of true compassion, I knew. It would also take priceless food from our mouths and from the mouth of my daughter. Beyond that, Grace appeared ill and might need assistance. Surely, Mercy did not call us to do such a thing with ourselves so weak and hungry?

Tempie gave a helpless shrug and looked first to me, then at Grace and back to me again. *What do you think?* her eyes asked.

I shook my head, silently shaping the words, *"No. Can't."* I hoped the distressed expression on my face said what I felt. I had to think of Janey first.

Wordlessly, warily, Tempie lifted her eyes to the surrounding cottages, the palisade walls. She drew herself protectively around the woman's hunched form. Her motions said, *we have each other, but she is alone, vulnerable. Who will protect her?*

I shut my eyes and sighed deeply. She was right, I knew. I supposed we could make it somehow, pray God.

Nodding, I mouthed the words *go ahead.*

She raised her brows, silently asking, *you're sure?*

I nodded more firmly, *yes.* Actually, no, I wasn't sure at all. It might be a foolish move, especially on behalf of a woman we scarcely knew. But leaving her to her own devices seemed inhumane, perhaps even brutal.

Tempie spoke up. "Mistress Fleetwood…Grace, why don't you come to live with us? We are also widows."

Grace looked from one to the other of us with uncertainty. Her head hung low, her shoulders drooped. I thought, in a moment of hope, she might decline. However, she too recognized her helplessness and relented. "It is well. Thank you," she said at last. "Being alone here…" At this, her eyes filled with tears again and her face contorted. "Humphrey should have a better burial than that. He was a…a good man, before the vapors of the fort and the starving stole his mind. He…did not mean to call me a witch….he…." She stopped.

Tempie helped her. "'Tis a cruel place, Mistress. We all only do the best we can. To be so hungry affects everyone differently."

I looked at Grace and saw that her hair, streaked in grey, hung in strings about her face. It was dirty and her breathing uneven. Her apron had holes and her dress, once blue, was so filthy only parts of its original color showed through. She was probably in her late forties but appeared much older. Her skeletal thinness and jagged breaths concerned me, and I saw that she favored one leg. I wondered how much longer she truly might live. She would certainly be unable to contribute toward food.

I was hungry, and you fed me. I was sick, and you took me in, a voice murmured in my head. I remembered Tempie's delight when we'd found the sparrow with the little black cap, how we had prayed that verse when God fed us. *Well, Lord,* I said silently, *You'll have to find us just a bit more manna each day now that we are four again.*

We helped Grace gather her few possessions, and offered her Maggie's bed. Maggie would have liked that, I thought. Seeing how dusty the mattress was, Tempie shook it against the wind and beat it with a stick.

"Would that all our problems could fly as easily as this dust!" she said, bringing it in and laying it on the simple bed frame. Grace slumped upon it, and I promised her we would say special prayers for Humphrey that night. She was appreciative of this small effort.

"It would be his due," she said. "He was a fine man when he was younger, and he had such hopes for Virginia. He said we would share in mineral rights and have land some day..." Her voice trailed off. "Then he got so hungry and disillusioned, his dreams dashed by it being so different than we'd heard. He felt as if he'd failed me and failed at everything. When his mind started going, he'd imagine terrors in the cottage. Devils. Finally, he turned on me as if he'd never laid eyes on me before. He needed someone to blame, I reckon." She touched my arm from her bed and with a pleading expression said, "Don't judge him by his appearance."

I assured her I wouldn't.

"Do you have any children?" I asked her.

"I have two married daughters, and two boys who died as babes," she replied quietly. "If ever the chance comes to send a letter and you're able to do it, would you let them know we were not sorry we came? Will you tell them for me I love them?" She clearly did not expect to be around to do so herself.

In surprise, I asked, "But *aren't* you sorry you came?"

"'Twas not the way we thought it would be, that's true. But if we had never tried, we would always have wondered about this New World."

She did not regret. I patted her arm. "We will let your daughters know."

She told me they were from a Cornish village nestled high upon a rocky coast overlooking the sea, and her daughters lived there still. "The magical little town of Tintagel, birthplace of King Arthur and home of many a piskie." She smiled with a touch of wistfulness. "As for my daughters, perhaps they will decide to come to Virginia themselves one day or perhaps not."

"I'll keep an eye out for them," I said. She seemed to like this idea, and I wrote down their names.

"You're kind souls, sharing the little you have. Please forgive my burdening you."

"No burden," I said, trying to mean it. I thought I could probably afford to give her a small tincture of herbs and decided upon comfrey for her breathing and chamomile to soothe her grief.

By the time Grace had been with us for three weeks, her health was noticeably deteriorating. We were tending to her needs—helping her to the chamber pot, trying to keep her comfortable. And feeding her.

Some days serving four rather than three, I looked hungrily at the weak pottage, laced with herbs, roots, or nuts and stiffened with the little acorn meal we had remaining. Dividing it four ways meant a skimpy portion became paltry. At those times, I felt resentment burn with my hunger. Had the Fleetwoods been out gathering nuts until their hands were scratched and raw from the cold? They had no provisions at all, so I suspected not. *Besides*, I thought bitterly, *she is just going to die anyway*. Tempie and I had a fairer chance to survive, so sharing with Grace seemed a waste of the little we had left. *Maggie worked for this food and she is not here to have it*.

My aching belly urged me to give her less than a full portion. In fact, tomorrow we could eat while she was asleep, and she would be none the wiser.... I stood at the table, my back to her, she with her back to me on the bed. I looked at the bowls of pottage thinking, *she will never know*. I divided it unevenly, such that she had only a few spoonfuls. She would just believe we had less today. After all, it was right that those who had a chance of survival—those who had spent every day and night preparing this poor meal—should have it. I lifted the bowl and turned to carry it to her. She still faced the wall, and I thought she might be sleeping.

Wait! What was I doing? Here in this place under these vile conditions, we would have to make choices—were making choices—every day. Which path would we take? The selfish one turned us further into animals, and I had seen that effect on men's minds. Bitterness and hoarding, hatred and anger. I had only to look at the woman on the bed and my choice was clear. I did not choose to die an animal, or survive the winter knowing I had been one. I could not put her out, nor give her less than we ourselves ate. I set it down again and dished it fairly, even as my eyes greedily hungered for what was in her bowl.

Do her one better, I thought. I gave her an extra spoonful from my bowl. Two, for good measure. I stood there for a long moment, the last opportunity to change my mind. She definitely had more than I did now. A thought intruded again. *Give her less and she will never know.* Yes, I argued, that was so—but *I* would know. I brought the full dish to her.

Unaware of my struggle, she smiled when I fed her, a grateful light in her eyes.

"God will bless you and Tempie for your mercy and kindness." She made a circular movement with her finger, her grubby fingernail pointing upward. "All the world spins on good performed in secret, which sleeps like a seed in darkness and blooms with the dawn." She pointed her finger at me. "Health and prosperity to you in time. Remember that they who sow in tears shall reap in joy." She nodded mysteriously, repeating as though impressed, "Well done, well done."

Her eyes, a brilliant blue, shone with light in marked contrast to the rest of her unkempt appearance. Where had I seen this light before? Why was it familiar to me? Then I knew. It reminded me of my father's eyes, the way light seemed to radiate from deep within.

Yet this strange proverb about seeds in darkness baffled me. I could not recall it as a verse from the Bible. Was she losing her mind as her husband did? What if she truly *were* a witch? She smiled serenely and did not explain further. No, she could not possibly be a witch with eyes such as these. Why had I never noticed them before? I was certain she could not have known what just happened—yet I had the uncanny sensation she *did* know. And was conferring a blessing on me? I shook my head.

"Pardon, Mistress?" I asked, confused.

"Blessings be upon you both, and upon your children," she replied, and said nothing more.

She died several days later, but at least she had not been alone and afraid. Tempie had been right to suggest we take her in and share our food with her, I thought.

I washed her face, although I knew that soon enough soldiers would cover her with dirt. Yet it seemed somehow she should have the dignity of starting her journey with a clean face. Tempie lovingly ran a comb through Grace's hair, and as she did so, she hummed a lullaby.

> *Weep not, my wanton, smile upon my knee;*
> *When thou art old, there's grief enough for thee.*

I watched her eyes soften even as Grace's hair did. She tilted her head to the left and bit her lip, as tears ran down her cheeks. Then she began to sob, her shoulders shaking. I knelt beside her as she sat on Grace's bed and put my arm around her waist. I felt her pain, but there was little I could do to ease it.

Suddenly she threw the comb across the room. "It is useless to weep in such a place!" she screamed. "It is useless to comb a sorry old woman's hair and pretend it is all more than it is." She swung her arm back as though to strike Grace's still form.

"Temperance, no!" I cried.

She froze, a horrified expression on her face, her arm raised. "What am I doing? What am I doing? I hate this place—I hate what it does to people!"

I was uncertain how to respond to this outburst. Surely, I understood it. Then I offered, "Many have perished, 'tis true. And many have suffered as we ourselves have. That is undeniable. Many have been poor in health and then die to receive no prayers, no Christian grave. Some have resorted to eating things I cannot speak of, going to hideous means to obtain them. All of this is true. But while some have perished poor in spirit, others have not. Look at Maggie and at Grace herself. Their candles extinguished, but their memory lights us even now. And there are those living who yet inspire us. Captain Tucker struggled each day, starved, building a boat so that we all might have a few fish. This man could have taken more than his share of corn from the storehouse. But see that he is as thin as the rest of us, so he must have been honest. By his vigilance, the corn lasted as long as it did. And those who would steal from him hated him for this, but he persevered and he does so still."

Tempie sat, her head hung low, tears dried upon her face.

"And as for you, my dear and loving friend," I said more quietly. "You too are a light in this darkness of our Starving Time. My mother told me once, 'Never grow so hardened to life that you cannot cry.' Someone *should* shed tears over Grace's passing. You did, and that is a fine tribute to her. Kind words are never wasted. Maybe...maybe they go in some giant cauldron in heaven and one day we will *feast* off them!" I had not known where that came from, but of late, I'd noticed my thoughts were a strange concoction of God and food.

"Feasting off kind words, is it?" Tempie said, an edge to her voice. I wondered if I'd offended her. Neither of us spoke for a moment.

Then she murmured, "I like that, Joan. As though...as though it's not all for naught here. It feels like it much of the time."

I wanted to tell her that Grace had *already* blessed us somehow, but how would I explain it? Instead, I said, "Maggie's songs weren't for naught, were they? Remember how they touched the soldiers, and she died not even knowing that."

Tempie nodded as we looked over at Grace. Her cheeks now clean and her silvery hair lying in straight lines, she slept in perfect peace.

Before summoning the soldiers, each of us knelt by Grace's bedside holding a candle. This was an addition to our service we called *Maggie's hope*. We prayed and sang Psalms for Grace. Performing funerals was a task at which we had grown adept, we realized ruefully.

On ship, I had wondered if God could use a sparrow's voice. Now I saw that He had used this sparrow's voice not once but many times. And I felt oddly blessed by that.

A Faithful Friend
Mid-April to Late April, 1610

Oh, to be in England,
Now that April's there,
And whoever wakes in England
Sees some morning, unaware,
That the lowest boughs and the brushwood sheaf,
Round the elm-tree bole are in tiny leaf
While the chaffinch sings on the orchard bough
In England—now.

~ Robert Browning

A faithful friend is a strong defense:
and he that hath found such an one hath found a treasure.
~ Ecclesiasticus 6:14

Had Virginia not been so full of horror upon horror, I might have found the sight of the white-blossomed trees in the woods uplifting. Wildflowers— purple, yellow, and blue—danced on the edges of the forest and river. As the sky brightened, the ground had also become a rainbow of spring hues.

Animal life, playful and joyous, stirred in the forests and fields. Colorful birds returned after wintering, no doubt, somewhere far more comfortable than we had. We heard them whistling and singing in the trees, oblivious to the starvation in the town around them.

The only thing that kept Tempie and me rising each day was the hope that supply ships would arrive in a month or so. A structured day had always been important to us, but now it seemed crucial to have a reason to rise and a routine to follow to stave off despair.

We had carefully managed and rationed the foods we'd gathered, which was fortunate because there was little to find in the forest now. Besides the competition amongst starving survivors, the Indians grew more brazen in crossing Back River to get onto the island.

We had at least survived to see April, but the food deprivation had taken a toll on our bodies. Some days my limbs trembled just to walk. My hair fell out in clumps, as did Tempie's, and I could scarcely believe how much like poles my arms now looked. My fingers were skeletal and the veins in my hand stood out in ghastly fashion. Tempie's eyes had sunken and her skin had a grey pall. I supposed mine did too.

I had two sound reasons to live—my daughters. I had known Janey to be a sweet and uncomplaining child, but her quiet acceptance now amazed me. Of course, she could not truly grasp the situation. How could she? I could not grasp it myself.

Tempie, however, had less motivation to continue the struggle than I did. She had lost George, she had no children, and for her it would be easier to die than to live. In fact, many folks proved that every day. The numbers digging their own graves were greater than ever. We could see them from the well—shoveling in resignation, crawling in and waiting. How bitter; how sad and hopeless, that.

Tempie had an additional obstacle to overcome. She had a slighter build than I did and therefore had become thin as a wisp. Still, her sense of humor served her well. Her comments on things around her caused both of us and Janey to laugh. And laughter was as rare as food in James Town.

I noticed, though, that her shoulders sagged often and her belly troubled her more. The spark in her eyes grew distant, while her climb out of bed took longer each morning.

It was as though her soul were slowly slipping away with her weight. Must I stand by and watch? I felt helpless to intervene.

Late in April, I came in to find her sitting on the bed, staring into space.

"What are you thinking?" I asked, sitting beside her and placing my arm around her.

"Oh, I was just thinking about...my mother, about George, about my father. He died just a few years ago, and I was wondering how he was..."

This, my Tempie? Where was the smile, the joy?

Inspiration—I must find something. But what?

I struck upon an idea. "Temperance!" I cried. This startled her, and she jumped.

"Blazes, Joan, you frightened me! What? Did you hear something?" She was looking about as though she might see an Indian's eyes peering over the window.

"Tempie," I said again, more softly. "We have survived to see springtime in Virginia. The weather is turning milder. The birds that brought us such joy in August—remember them? They are returning. 'Virginia birds certainly like their fancy headwear.' Remember that?"

She smiled in spite of herself. "Mismatched Virginia birds. I sure would like to roast me one or two," she said, and chuckled. "Fancy headwear and all!"

"And the forests are coming back to life after a long and terrible winter. Why, soon you can take your sling out to the woods, and..." Now she was out-and-out laughing.

"Catch me that plump little squirrel? I do owe him a joust of some sort. Of course, he is probably fatter than I am these days and might just take *me* down."

Still bluffing somewhat and thinking quickly, I said, "I have a surprise for you!"

She raised an eyebrow skeptically. "If you boiled up your own shoe leather, I can wait."

I laughed and told her she would *have* to wait, but only for a few minutes. Then I hobbled down to the riverside where I knew some wildflowers grew. I plucked them, admiring the purple and blue petals and bright golden faces. I had never truly looked closely at them before. With my fingers, I stroked their velvety softness. I added some other greenery as well, and a few white and pink blossoms from flowered saplings we called *dog trees*. All of it humble, yes, but still perfect in their own way.

When I arrived back at the cottage, she looked at me curiously. I went to my chest and raised its lid, which creaked open. I lifted out the last bottle of *aqua vitae,* the remaining swig from England. I had cautiously rationed its use, and I suspected it to be the only left in James Town. "It is *finally* warming up. See, we have flowers," I announced, holding up the bouquet in one hand and the *aqua vitae* in the other. "Let us toast the arrival of spring!"

Tempie frowned with a protesting motion. "Joan, that is the last you have. Save it for yourself."

With further inspiration and ignoring her plea, I removed three bundles from the chest, rather than reaching for the pewter flagons hanging from the rack. I unwrapped one and held it for her to see.

"Delftware!" She almost squealed with excitement. It had been so long since we, or anyone, had enjoyed porcelain. I held a Dutch cup to the window and let the light play across its pattern. My eyes followed the painted windmills and houses, all blues and whites, and just for a moment, I was somewhere—anywhere—else. Anywhere but here.

I set one on the table, unwrapped the other, and was relieved to see they had both survived the storm, delicate and beautiful though they were. I arranged the tiny bouquet of wildflowers in one of them. The blue and white, purple, yellow, pink and green… *the color!*

Then I pulled out two more wrapped bundles. Inside were fragile wine cups. "From China!" I announced with a smile. Despite herself, Tempie's eyes sparkled as she admired its enchanting blue and lines on white porcelain.

Birds, I realized, were singing outside. It was as if we'd been deaf for months and now received the gift of hearing. "Listen to them all!" I said, marveling. So many chips and warbles called from the woods. "In a heaven above us, no one is starving. Imagine that! In a heaven above us, winter is past. Imagine that, too." My voice trailed off.

Tempie was admiring the Delftware. "Oh, it's lovely," she said softly, turning one of the cups over in the April sunlight that streamed through the window.

Ceremoniously, I poured the *aqua vitae* into the Chinese wine cups, giving half of what remained to each of us. It was little more than a swallow or two, but how festive it looked in the Delftware, sitting amidst the wildflowers and tree blossoms, all brightened by a ray of sun striking the table.

In our plenty in England, we would have found this celebration pathetic. A swallow of *aqua vitae?* We might have mocked it, even. Now in our want, it seemed grand beyond words.

Something akin to joy crossed Tempie's face, a remnant of the young woman she had once been. With a flourish, she raised her cup. "To friendship," she said simply but with great emotion. Then she added, "To things which never change, however mean the circumstance."

I raised my cup but found my voice choked. "Friendship," was all I managed to say. It lifted me to see her smiling. We clinked them together, and she added, "I suppose, Joan, that our friendship—and Maggie's—is the only treasure I shall ever find in Virginia. But I daresay no Spaniard ever found gold so pure."

She lifted her cup to mine, and we touched them again just for the joyous sound it made.

My Unconquerable Soul
Mid-May to May 23, 1610

Out of the night that covers me,
Black as the pit from pole to pole,
I thank whatever gods may be,
For my unconquerable soul.

In the fell clutch of circumstance,
I have winced but not cried aloud.
Under the bludgeonings of chance,
My head is bloodied but unbowed.

Beyond this place of wrath and tears,
Looms but the horror of the shade.
And yet the menace of the years,
Finds, and shall find me, unafraid.

It matters not how straight the gate,
How charged with punishments the scroll,
I am the master of my fate,
I am the Captain of my soul.

~ William Ernest Henley

He that hath no grave, is covered with the sky:
and, the way to heaven out of all places
is of like length and distance.

~ Thomas More

Tempie said my face looked like a skull with skin painted on. I would have been offended by that had I not known it was true, for she looked the same. We were pale, with tender bellies and withered legs beneath our kirtles.

212

At night, I placed folded linen between my knees so the knobby bones would not lie upon one another. It was hard to get comfortable in sleep for our figures were bony and all parts were angular. Making sleep more difficult was the piercing stomachache from a belly that had not known satiety since autumn and scarcely even then. Or the headache that never went away. Yet sometimes once I fell asleep, I had a difficult time awakening. My sleep was deep and restless, filled with strange nightmares.

Waking became a nightmare of its own. Every joint, every movement hurt with stiffness from the night. *Get up, search!* Find food—*anything*—to eat. Some days I lay there longer than others seeking that thing, that one thing, to make myself rise up with the morning, to face another day.

I found it lying in the bed next to mine, in the small, dwindling figure of my little daughter.

Much of Janey's hair had dropped out, and she now resembled an urchin from the streets of London, not my well-fed, well-loved little girl. Watching her caused my heart to bleed. In fact, even urchin children did not look as unnaturally gaunt as she did. Her eyes, always large, were nearly disproportionate to her face now that it was so thin, and her face seemed too broad for the thin body carrying it. Where were the full and rosy cheeks I so loved? Now the pallor of her face frightened me and drove me on. *Do it for her,* I told myself.

One morning late in May, I leaned into the stick I kept by the bed, pushing myself up. I needed it most days now to help me walk. It took me a few tries because my limbs were weak and trembled. The room seemed to sway—even the floor beneath my feet—and I knew this was another illusion of hunger. Yet its effects on my thirty-year-old body were real.

I took a deep breath and prayed silently. *God, thou art my refuge and my strength, a very present help in times of trouble.* I walked toward Janey's bed and noticed that her eyes were open but sunken and glassy.

"Janey," I said in a hoarse whisper, but she did not blink or move.

She is dead! I thought, and my feet found their strength as I rushed to her. The movement startled her and she turned her head in my direction.

She has not long, unless I find her food, I thought. I kissed her cheek, praying to God for manna, for a perished sparrow, for anything.

I noticed that, like Janey, Tempie lay very still on her bed and her breathing was shallow. My frame had always been sturdier than hers, and now that difference mattered. There seemed so little of her left.

"Tempie," I said hoarsely. "Tempie, I am going to dig us roots." She barely moved or looked my way. "Mm," she mumbled at last. I thought she was letting me know she had heard.

I went to the edge of the forest, where I had dug so many times before. I prayed, as I always did when searching, stabbed my spade into the ground and hacked at whatever I could find. A portion of sassafras and dog-tree roots. The James Town weed we had shortened to call *Jimsonweed* I avoided, as Annie had told me it was poisonous. I threw in a few snake plants. *Snakes! I could eat one of those about now,* I thought. Vermin no longer mattered. Outside of known poisons, I would eat anything I found.

The winter had taken its toll, and even the scent of fresh growth and colorful flowers in the woods seemed taunting. I had anticipated with joy every spring of my life, even those that brought sadness. But here I could only listen to the bird twitters and peeps, which though near sounded faraway and dreamlike. They did not sing for me, for us. If they did, it was a funeral dirge and nothing more.

We died at an alarming rate now, and there were few capable of burying the dead. Yet the dead could not stay in their cottages or on the ground where they fell, for that would only cause further disease, not to mention a terrible stench. Few men had the heart, much less the strength, to keep burying them. But most of these bodies made it to a grave one way or the other. We were trying to keep up.

I reckoned there were maybe forty of us left at James Town. We didn't know how many survived at Point Comfort, but they had started with thirty. So we could have no more than seventy still alive of the nearly five hundred that had started the autumn at James Town. So many hundreds perished of hunger, killed by Indians, or dead of disease. Prior to our arrival, two hundred or more had already perished, so we were the remnants of perhaps seven hundred settlers the Company had sent in the three years James Town had been a settlement.

Those of us living knew our time was short. Had any person more than ten days, I would be surprised. There were lean pickings in the woods, but worse than that, the natives—realizing the desperation of our situation—tightened the siege's noose. Anyone, man or woman, who ventured beyond the blockhouse was quickly pierced by a flying arrow. The Indians were such accurate marksmen that they could shoot a flying bird from the air, or pin both a man's arms to his body with a single shot. We had seen them do this. What they didn't accomplish with accuracy they made up for in quantity. We could not forget George Forrest with seventeen arrows protruding grotesquely from him, although he survived six days in spite of it.

Why the Indians did not overrun the blockhouse and fort and finish us off, I could not guess—unless they chose to waste none of their own lives doing what we could easily accomplish ourselves. Or perhaps our many illnesses kept them at arm's length.

214

Captain Percy, finally improved from his long sickness, had taken Captain Tucker's handmade boat and left on an expedition to Point Comfort the week before. This boat would still be dangerous and unprotected compared with the ship *Swallow* we had lost to the mutineers. But while river travel was hazardous, especially without ordnance, going overland past the blockhouse meant certain death. How fared they at Point Comfort? No one knew, as those settlers had not sailed up our way and we had little way of getting there.

I brought in the roots and plants and added to it the very last of the dried berries we had, using acorn meal to stiffen it. Thanks be to God for the acorns, for they more than any other single food had kept us alive. They truly had been our manna. After boiling, the roots became as tender as such things can be. I knelt by Tempie's bed and touched her shoulder. Her back was to me.

"Pottage?" I said softly. She felt like my own soul sometimes. What we had endured together would forever entwine our spirits, like the roots of the tree I had just found. Deep and buried, a treasure when least expected. We were like that. I felt the tears come, as I knew she had not long—days, maybe. A week?

She did not respond, so I tried once more. "Tempie, pottage?"

"Mm," she said again. She shook her head slightly and did not roll over. Too weak to sit up and eat, too hungry to put what little food we had in her mouth.

I sighed, stood up, and nodded. I had tried. Tempie was partially awake, but I would save her portion and offer to feed her again later. Janey still slumbered, so I decided to let her sleep longer so she would not have to endure hunger pangs as long this day. I would attempt to feed her after I ate. At five years old, her days of feeding herself were behind her—a skill she had lost, far too weak now. I would need to get my own strength up first, especially after my own fatigue from searching. Even the task of getting the little we had into our mouths had become an ordeal.

I sat at the wooden trestle table, my hand shaking as I tried to get the spoon to my mouth. Slowly I took one, two, three sips.

Tempie did not move.

Will you eat while your sister starves, a voice whispered in my ear. Perhaps it was my desperation; perhaps it was my extreme hunger, but the voice seemed to be louder and clearer than ever. I hoped by God I wasn't a witch, though who in this place would ever have the strength to duck me? I was not therefore afraid of punishment, except I did not want to be a sinner of such sorts that I would spend eternity in Hell. I looked around. Hell? Where exactly was I if not there?

Will you eat while your sister starves, the voice asked again, more insistent yet still without reproach. Now anger flashed through me, so sudden and fierce that my vision went red. I slapped the table with all my strength. My palm stung and the spoon jumped—and I nearly toppled the precious little pottage I had. Blinded by rage, I cared not.

"There is nothing I can do for her!" I yelled. "Don't You think if I could, I would? I cannot save her…if *You* are God, *You* do it!"

Tempie's limp body jumped. She had heard me, though she didn't seem quite conscious.

I shaded my eyes with my hand and began to cry. It was difficult to keep going, difficult to keep trying, difficult to keep believing.

"I can't save her," I said again, this time in a low and defiant voice, wiping the tears from my cheeks. "I can't. You can. *You* do it."

"Agnes, where's my mother? I'm so hungry. Fetch her, Agnes." That was Tempie, murmuring the name of a childhood maid. She was hallucinating. I sighed and my shoulders slumped in resignation. It was just as well that she did not know where she was.

"You do it, Lord. I can't," I repeated. There was no emotion now, for I was not sure I could feel anything.

"Agnes? *Where are you?* I'm so hot; it is the ague come upon me," she said, her words slurred. "Agnes? Mother?"

I took a deep breath and walked to her, sitting on her bed. I put my arm upon her shoulder. "Tempie, it is I, Joan," I said gently. "Agnes is not here, but I am."

She rolled ever so slightly in my direction, her eyes confused and glassy.

"Where is Agnes? She never leaves me." There was panic in her voice. Her cheeks were flushed vivid red while the rest of her face was pale as death. Her innocent confusion wrenched me.

"Agnes had to…" I thought quickly. "She had to fill your water pitcher, so I am here with you instead."

"Oh." She accepted this. Then, her eyes cleared slightly in recognition. "Joan?" she said weakly.

"Yes, Lovey, it's I."

I rubbed her arm. Then, with awkward and stiff steps, I made my way to the table. The pottage.

I steadied myself. Trembling, I slowly went back to her. In a movement that seemed one hundred small and painful motions, I sat upon the bed, still holding the pottage. It had not spilled.

"Time to eat," I said, offering her a spoonful. "Open and let me feed you."

She shook her head. "No…can't," she said simply.

Gently but firmly I said, "You can, and you must. It is the only way."

"I hurt." Her voice was plaintive, pleading, even childlike.

"I know." My voice was soothing now. "I know you hurt. But you must get something down. I did find some roots and plants, and these are the last of our berries. Come, you can do it."

She opened her mouth slowly and I realized that my trembling hand and her shaky mouth were not a good combination. We could not afford to lose any.

"Let's try you sipping it," I suggested.

Another long walk to where the flagons hung. Another long walk back. When had this cottage grown so large? When had my gait grown so unsteady and weak? As cautiously as possible, I poured the pottage into the flagon.

Propping her head with one hand, I helped her hold the cup, saying, "Sip slowly, aye?"

She did, and its warmth seemed to give some life to her. I was pleased that she drank most of it.

Her eyes met mine. "Psalm 91," she said with sudden conviction. I tilted my head uncertainly. Her words were firm, but I did not take her meaning.

"You want to sing? 'Tis not time for prayers, but if it would comfort you…" I began.

"No, Joan." She spoke without wavering, her gaze direct. There was a glimmer of the old Tempie in them. Where had this come from? What was she talking about?

"When it is my time, sing the 91st Psalm over me. I should like that very much." Her expression was frighteningly serious.

"No, no, you and I and Janey will see this through together, *no matter what!*"

She nodded patiently. "Yes, and this is part of seeing it through." She was showing me no mercy. "My legs are broomstick-thin," she continued. "I can count the bones in my hand and every rib. My backbone is but a bumpy ridge." Her eyes and her voice—as well as her wishes—were clear. "The 91st Psalm and the 23rd Psalm, and sing the Lord's Prayer as you do, if…if you are able. And read Maggie's poem." Now she was almost apologetic. Before I could respond, she added, "And if you are not able, I shall be your haunt until you are. I think you shall come 'round quickly then!" She gave a weak laugh, and I did also. Here was a reminder of the good humor I had loved so much.

"Let us not discuss such things," I said, with a touch of reproof. I did not expect her to defy me, yet she did.

Her gaze never left mine. "We must," she said firmly.

217

I wanted to protest. I wanted to say she was speaking foolishly. I wanted to tell her we would both live to see another summer in Virginia or in England. One more summer… But I knew she was not being foolish, but eminently practical.

"Well, if I should go…" I started, but she interrupted.

"Then I shall sing for you from heaven." She laughed again. "Oh!" She squeezed her eyes shut, gripping her side in pain.

I allowed this to subside, before I added quietly, "Please sing for me the same Psalms you requested. And…if you go first…I shall find a way to bury you." If we must speak of this, we must speak of it fully.

She took my hands in hers. "If you are able. I will not haunt you for that offense." Her eyes shone appreciatively. "If you…or you and Janey…" She could not finish, but I knew what she conveyed. I nodded, which seemed to give her courage. She continued, "I will do the same, if there is any way I can. You know I will."

"I know." I could not imagine what would become of the last one of us, but then my father's voice rang in my ears. *And if I die in the ocean, then away with me to another realm, for he who hath no grave is covered in sky.*

We may indeed be covered in sky, I thought.

We cautiously wrapped our skeletal arms in an embrace, loosely, so as not to cause the other pain. We dropped our heads upon one another's shoulders. Peace washed through me. I knew we had done all we could, and God would forgive us our mistakes. If our bodies *were* covered in sky, our souls would still be swept into heaven. It may be that this one promise was enough.

I felt the sleeve of my kirtle grow damp and realized that tears must be slipping from Tempie's eyes and I knew they were also dropping from mine. I had not been aware of them starting.

How long we sat that way, I do not know. A moment, or five minutes, or ten. It may have been an hour. Time seemed to pause, breathless, as though all else being taken from us, the only thing that mattered now was to love and be loved.

Perhaps we were saying goodbye.

I had thought it excruciating to let someone take my young son from me and bury him ceremoniously in the churchyard. How much more excruciating this. No one should have to bury, by her own hands, her closest friend or daughter—this was surely the cruelest blow Providence had yet dealt. But if this were what God called me to do, then this I would do, I thought, feeling a growing determination. With irony, I realized I hoped Tempie *would* go first, so this task would fall upon my shoulders, as her tears now did. And then she would not be famished any more—or Janey either. I could wish them no better than to sleep in peace without tossing and turning in hunger, in constant pain.

A sudden pealing of the town's bell rang out, startling us both, and someone shouted, *"Ships!"*

"What is that?" I asked, looking over my shoulder.

A scream seemed to be rising from the fort—voices were weak but I heard them.

Others took up the cry. "Ships!"

"Ships?" Surely, my ears were hearing only what they wanted.

Rustling, banging, moving—sounds of life spread across the fort.

"Tempie, I think he said, 'Ships!'"

"My Lord."

"Yes, our Lord, for who else can it be? We were lost, but now we are found...I hope." My heart thudded, pounding like Indian drums in my ears. I was afraid this might be a hallucination, so I dared not believe too much. Even if I saw it with my own eyes, how could I know it was real? Tempie slumped back down, her head on the pillow. She was too weak to walk, but I could make it.

From the doorway, I stared in amazement. Never had such life arisen from so many skeletal figures. A mass of bones raced toward the river that day, because, Praise God, there were ships' sails visible over the fort wall!

I turned around. "Tempie, I think I do see a ship! *Two* ships. They fly an English flag! They are not Spanish...they are our own!"

Tempie attempted to raise herself, but I called back over my shoulder, "Rest! I will bring news to you straight away."

We streamed out that morning—those of us still able to walk. Others peered on hands and knees from the doors of their homes. They could make it a little way, not far. Some, like Tempie, would have to wait from their beds—at least until we had a confirmed ship sighting. They conserved the remaining energy of their bodies as if it were a precious ore.

"We are starved! We are starved!" cried the emaciated throng about me. I did not yell...I only made my way down to the river as fast as I could push my legs, which no longer worked in steady coordination. Neither did I balance well. Beyond that, I trembled from excitement and weakness. I staggered, breathing heavily from exertion as well as pain. How I wished I had something to lean on. In my rush, I had forgotten my walking stick. Now stars danced before my eyes, a splotchy blackness speckled with lights. I blinked hard, trying to clear my vision.

My heart pounded wildly. These *must* be supply ships! The flags were unmistakably English. I could not catch my breath and gulped air quickly.

But what was this? Such odd-looking vessels, so strangely constructed. The earth seemed to pulse beneath my feet, reminding me of when I myself had first disembarked. The motion of the river lapping against shore increased my disorientation. I heard the echoes of the pealing bells, though I thought they might ring only in my head now. Louder and louder, they chimed.

I was near the river, and familiar faces gazed down at me from the ship's prow. I rubbed my eyes in disbelief and confusion. Now I knew I hallucinated because…these were ghosts. I saw *Sea Venture* passengers: John Rolfe, George Yeardley, Sam…and Will.

My heart crushed in disappointment. These were but phantoms of the mind as Tempie's nursemaid had been. I reeled with dizziness, while ringing and buzzing thundered in my ears. My mind struggled to piece these shattered shards of glass together.

Perhaps this was my father's ship and he had returned to the Port of Melcombe after all…he had found the *Sea Venture* passengers and brought them here. *Yes, that is something he would do.* I thought I saw him standing behind Will. Or did I? The ships were bobbing crazily, and the faces blended and blurred.

Now the blackness and stars were overtaking the light. The stars spun into a tunnel and in the center stood St. James, wearing a scallop of fire, holding Cecily's hand. He seemed to beckon me in, and I felt myself pulled down into the abyss. I could no longer remember where I was, until at last even the stars snuffed out, and there was nothing at all but darkness.

Such Stuff as Dreams Are Made on

May 23, 1610

We are such stuff
As dreams are made on; and our little life
Is rounded with a sleep.

~ William Shakespeare

I awoke in a bed, my body aching as never before. My eyes were foggy and the room seemed to pulse. I thought I might be sick. This pounding, raging headache. This dizziness.

If I could only see the room more distinctly, I might know where I was. My bedroom in Melcombe? My father's house? I thought I could make out another bed and a face. But who...?

James Town. The thought jolted me like icy water.

My eyes began to clear somewhat, and I heard myself moaning. At least, I thought the sound came from me.

A face pressed close in to mine and a trembling hand reached up to feel my forehead.

"Joan, it's Tempie."

Tempie? Tempie!

"And Janey—how is she?" I said at last, haltingly.

"She still sleeps."

It was coming back to me now. I tried to wave her away. "Go to bed. You are too ill..."

"I know, but it is my turn to check on you."

I squinted, trying to remember exactly why I was here and what day it was. I had a dream? A nightmare?

Tempie studied me. She took my hand and said cautiously, as though reading my thoughts, "It was neither dream nor hallucination, Joan."

I stared at her in amazement, unable to speak.

"You did see Will and George."

My mouth dropped open. Was I imagining this too? What *was* real?

"Why...how? They live?" I could not make sense of this at all.

She squeezed my hand. "Yes," she said deliberately, "but the *how* I do not know. Will came only long enough to bring you here and then rushed out to fetch us... *pork!*"

Now I knew I was hallucinating. Pork! My mouth watered at the image of it. Tempie stumbled back to her bed, and together we waited—for Will and for pork, but mostly, for answers.

They Say Miracles Are Past
May 23, 1610

They say miracles are past.
~ William Shakespeare

H e walked in the door looking hearty, carrying victuals in a small sack and coming to me straight away after tipping his hat to Tempie.

"You are awake." His voice quavered and reflected the words he did not say. *And you're alive.* He held me gently as though afraid he might crack my bony frame with his arms.

I tried to speak but words failed me.

"First things first," he said, dropping the pork into the still simmering kettle of roots, herbs, and acorn meal. The aroma that rose from it seemed to heal me with its promise of true food. He then sat back on the bed, searching my face as though unsure where to begin.

"I scarcely knew it was you when I spied you, so meager you've become." His eyes were dark with concern. I imagined how I must look to him, with my scrawny hair and the deep circles beneath my eyes.

"When you collapsed, Governor Gates allowed me off ship immediately. I lifted you from the ground and you did not stir, even a little..." His voice cracked, but he continued. "A soldier kindly showed me to your home."

"Walter," Tempie said to me. Of course. Walter.

"Gates tolled the bell for a meeting in the church for those who are able. You two don't qualify. No one from the fort does, actually. The Governor has given me special permission—ordered me, in fact—to attend to you both. Tempie's husband George is Gates's most trustworthy officer—has been since their time in the Low Countries. As Captain of the Governor's Guard, he must stay near Gates during this transition," he explained to me, while assuring Tempie, "He will be here as soon as he can. When I returned to the ship, I told him you were with Joan and I should stay at both your sides. You shall want for nothing now if it be in my power to provide it. Reverend Bucke has arrived with us, and

223

he said a blessing on behalf of the living and the dead. We are all…overcome with sorrow…to find you in this condition."

Then, Janey, so very weak by now, began to stir. She had slept through it all, so Will asked her gently, "Do you remember me, my little lass?"

She nodded solemnly.

"Not afraid of me? May I pick you up?" he asked.

She nodded again, so he bent down and lifted her.

"You came across the sea?" She looked at him with wide eyes, made wider by her gaunt face.

"I came across the sea."

"Jesus told me you would," she said simply.

I looked at Will and raised my eyebrows. I had not heard this before.

"I dreamed about Jesus. He said he saved you and all the men on the big ship." She yawned and nestled her head into his neck. "Father, I'm hungry." Her little legs hung in front of his chest like reeds with tiny, dirty feet.

"Of course, you are, my sweet girl," he said, his voice choked. "Let us eat, then." Gently, he laid her back down upon her mattress, and then ladled the pottage out in three small portions, bringing one to each of us in our beds. He sat beside Janey to help her steady hers, offering to feed us each in turn.

"None for you?" I asked him. "Aren't you hungry?"

"You all need it more than I do. It will be a pleasure to watch you eat. But," he cautioned, "you must take it in slowly or it will be too hard on your tender bellies. I put little pork in it, as you will have to grow accustomed to such things slowly. Small meals first, and you will build to larger ones."

Will went between the beds, patiently spooning it to us. The pork tasted like victuals from heaven itself. I felt some strength returning at once. Tempie, I saw, looked better too. Perhaps it was the *hope* we now had as much as the warm broth itself.

"Will? We have so many questions! *Where have you been for ten months?* Did the *Sea Venture* turn back to England? Did you shipwreck? Surely you were not floating aimlessly all this time?"

"Yes," Tempie put in impatiently. "Where *have* you been? *Tell us!*"

Spoonful by spoonful, Will fed each of us in turn. As he did so, he said, "If I had not lived it myself, I would not believe it."

The Fairies of the Rocks...
and All the Divils That Haunted the Woods
May 23, 1610

All is well, tho' faith and form
Be sunder'd in the night of fear;
Well roars the storm to those that hear
A deeper voice across the storm
~ Alfred Tennyson

These Islands of the Bermudos, have ever beene accounted as an inchaunted pile of rockes, and a desert inhabitation for Divels; but all the Fairies of the rocks were but flocks of birds, and all the Divels that haunted the woods, were but heards of swine.
~ Silvester Jourdain, *Sea Venture* castaway

Have courage for the great sorrows of life and patience for the small ones; and when you have laboriously accomplished your daily task, go to sleep in peace. God is awake.
~ Victor Hugo

"When the *hurricano* struck and separated all our fleet, we took a most dismal and terrifying beating from Monday until Friday..."

I recalled Maggie and me praying for the other ships in the days following the storm. Little did we imagine the *Sea Venture* was still battling the hurricane. "Friday? But for us, blue skies returned on Wednesday!" I could make no sense of this.

225

"I do not understand how it happened," Will continued. "Perhaps since we were at the front of the fleet we somehow got tossed in a circle while the storm cast you out to its side. Perhaps the currents and winds took you out. But we had no such fortune. At the beginning of the storm, we suffered a mighty leak. By Tuesday noon there was ten feet of seawater in the hold. We bailed and pumped furiously until Friday, through the storm, without food or water. We alternated sleeping and bailing in one-hour shifts with a partner. Every hour—*every hour*—during this time, we threw overboard one hundred tons of water, yet for all our effort we were only sinking deeper into the sea as the days wore on. Where was the great leak? We could not locate it, though we found many smaller ones as the seams of the ship spit out their oakum. Even Gates and Somers, God bless them, were bailing with us."

As he spoke, he gently spooned us pottage, going first to one bed, then another. For a moment, I was back in Melcombe—my father returned from sea, a warm meal and a story of his journey, all dangers behind him. Comfort washed over me, even as Will continued.

"St. Elmo's fire appeared mysteriously Thursday, and some thought this a providential sign. Yet come Friday morning, the situation's hopelessness became evident. Though we had bailed two thousand tons of water, the level in the hold kept rising. Some took toasts, if they could find unspoiled beer, and wished each other a happy meeting in the next world. We prepared to shut the hatches and await the end."

By this time, Tempie and I were rapt, scarcely breathing, until Janey asked, "Then what happened, Father?"

Settled on the edge of her mattress, Will held his little girl closely, gazing into her eyes. "A trusting child, you are. You knew Jesus saved us, didn't you?"

She nodded.

"Indeed He did, for it was a miracle. As we were giving up, Somers suddenly cried, 'Land! Keep bailing, men! *Lose not your heart now!*'

"Amazed and astounded, we returned to our positions, praising God with every new bucketful. By half past ten in the morning, the skies gradually cleared, and we could even see the trees moving in the wind. The Governor commanded the helmsman to bear up! The boatswain took a sounding and got it to four fathom. We were in smooth water and perhaps three quarters of a mile offshore of...*the haunted Bermudas!*"

"The Bermudas? The Devil's Isles?" I cried in disbelief.

"But...but they are filled with demons and are treacherously rocky!" Tempie said. "How can this be?"

226

"How can this be, indeed? But it was those very rocks that saved us, because the *Sea Venture* actually wedged between two rocks. This propped her upright and held her fast. By nightfall, we were able to bring all the men, women, and children safely to shore. This place that sailors avoid more than any in the world became the place of our deliverance. We found there some five hundred islands, an archipelago scattered like a half moon."

"But, Will, the screeches and howls and noise of demons…?" I asked. I still could not believe what I was hearing.

"The screeches were birds, Joan. We called them *cahows,* and they were as big as an English green plover—so friendly and abundant that we had only to stand onshore and whistle for them to land on our heads and shoulders. They *invited* us to have them for supper. During the dark nights of winter, cahows hover over the sea, making an eerie and harsh howling. That, along with thousands of wild hogs, is the sound that frightened so many sailors for a hundred years. All the fearsome noises were but living foods to sustain us so we could build two ships and come to you. And would you believe the only side of the island that admits a hope of safe landing is precisely where God brought us?"

"The Bermudas? The Bermudas," I said again, this time sleepily as the broth worked its wonders on my belly. "All this time, you were safe in the haunted Bermudas." Janey, I saw, had already fallen back to sleep.

Tempie spoke dreamily while stifling a yawn. "Joan, remember the day we stood at the river, and you said, 'Tempie, you know as well as I do miracles happen every day. If it takes a miracle, a miracle it will be.' I did not believe you then. I did not have the faith." Nearly asleep, her lids fluttered.

"*I* did not believe me either, dear friend. I only said it in anger and desperation." Her yawns were contagious, and I too felt sleep coming on.

"A desperate, angry vow of faith is a profession nonetheless. God hears," she said, drifting off. "He hears."

Her words blurred and I found myself slipping into a light sleep—the most peaceful of many months—even upon the words *He hears.*

All Strange Wonders That Befell Thee

May 24, 1610

God moves in a mysterious way,
His wonders to perform;
He plants his footsteps in the sea,
and rides upon the storm.

~ William Cowper

Thou, when thou return'st wilt tell me
All strange wonders that befell thee...

~ John Donne

In memory of our great deliverance, both from a mighty storm
and leak, we have set up this to the honor of God. It is the
spoil of an English ship of three hundred ton, called the Sea
Venture...

~ Governor Thomas Gates, etched
on copper, mounted to a cross
made of beams from the *Sea Venture*, and left behind on Bermuda

I drifted in and out of sleep, as the day slowly waned and night fell. As morning crept over the cottage, I opened my eyes to see a sweet, cherubic face gazing down at me. It took me a moment to place her.

"Sarah Rolfe," I said cautiously. "You have fared well in the Bermudas, I see. You have a lovely glow." *While I have the pallor of the near dead*, I thought without emotion.

She smiled sadly, and took my hand. "Indeed, we had victuals while you did not. For this, I am so sorry—sorry for your suffering. But I am sent to tend you now. While the men meet with Governor Gates, I am your nurse. Whatever you need, only ask, and I shall fetch it for you."

228

Someone to watch over me! The duty of caring for Tempie and Janey not solely falling on my shoulders. I noticed that they still slept.

"Thank you, Sarah," I murmured. I recalled my jealousy that she was on the *Sea Venture*. Yet God had saved her to care for us now, I thought. *How ironic the hand of God.*

"Each time you wake, I shall feed you a little. We will coax you three back to health." Her calm voice and gentle manner soothed me. Even as she spoke, I realized that something in the kettle had a tantalizing aroma. "That smells like poultry, not pork!"

She laughed. "That is the amazing Bermudan bird, the cahow, which we caught simply by calling to them. I have managed to bring you one from the ship. Governor Gates is allowing you and Tempie special privileges because George Yeardley is such a reliable officer. Your husband—and mine—also served well in the Bermudas. There were several mutinies there, but our husbands remained loyal to Governor Gates and the cause of coming to Virginia."

As she spoke, she brought some cahow pottage over. I propped myself up, and she spooned it to me.

I felt tears welling because of her kindness and the overwhelming circumstances that had preserved their ship and all their souls, bringing them to us in our time of greatest need. "You are an angel," I said in hushed tones.

"No, there is the angel." She glanced over at Janey, a tiny, pale bundle asleep on her mattress. "Praise God, she survived." Her eyes were wistful.

"It was the acorns," I said slowly. "They are a poor man's food, 'tis true, but they dropped in such vast quantities in autumn, like rain....We prayed for manna from heaven, for daily bread. They fell from heaven and thus we had bread. We gathered them, but not everyone did."

Sarah shook her head. "The men are suitably impressed by your survival, and, of course, saddened by such loss and devastation. The fort was nigh falling down around you," she said in amazement.

"We had to use other cottages as firewood when it became too dangerous to go into the forest." Suddenly I realized I did not want to speak of it any more. I wanted to begin putting it behind me, this day. "Tell me about Bermuda, then," I said to her. "What was it like? No devils, Will said!" We laughed.

"No devils. But many birds and turtles and hogs..." My mouth watered at the delicacies. "We found evidence of shipwrecks, so probably the hogs were left by the Spanish or Portuguese a hundred years ago. There were thousands of swine, and the ship's dog had no trouble running them down—fifty at a time—for us. In fact, we built a pen to hold them. The turtles were colossal—one could feed six men a dozen meals!"

How grand a turtle this must have been, I thought as I supped the cahow pottage, savoring every swallow.

"And the fish were plentiful," she went on. "They would nip at our ankles in the glassy blue water. A single *rockfish*, as we called one type, could feed two men. There were swordfish and whales and fish in every color of God's earth."

"Like Eden," I said in wonderment. "Was there no summer sickness as in Virginia? Did all survive?" I asked.

She looked down. "Not all survived. It is a...a poor place to have a baby."

I stopped eating as my eyes met hers. "You...did you...lose a baby?" I had not remembered her being with child at port in Plymouth.

She nodded. "Yes, my baby girl, named Bermuda, was born and died in February. Reverend Bucke performed her baptism as well as her funeral in a humble church built from cedar, thatched with palmetto. When we sailed away, I said goodbye to her little grave forever, abandoning it—and her—on the island."

"Oh, Sarah." I took her hand. We had all suffered in our own way, and a mother's grief must surely be the hardest to bear.

Her eyes were shining with tears. "Well, pray God, John and I shall have another child."

"Yes, I pray that is so."

Tempie was stirring, and Sarah obligingly went to her, introducing herself and offering her pottage.

As Sarah gently fed Tempie, I said, "It is unfortunate we did not know you were alive. How much heartache it might have saved us!"

"We did try. Henry Ravens and six men embarked on a longboat, hoping to reach Virginia. Ravens promised that if he survived he would return with a ship on the new moon. We kept signal fires on an overlook for not one but many moons, but he never returned." Later we learned that the Indians bragged of seeing this strange boat come from the sea and of murdering its occupants.

Sarah continued, "Therefore, our only hope was to *build* ships. Rocks held the *Sea Venture* afloat long enough for us to scavenge her wood and save our tools."

This explained the unusual construction of the ships I had seen. The larger one they had dubbed the *Deliverance* and the smaller one the *Patience*. They had used cedar from the islands, and the *Patience*, Sarah informed us, had only a single iron bolt in her, in the keel!

"We had Dick Frobisher, a master shipbuilder, as well as Nicholas Bennett and his carpenters. Gates directed the building of the *Deliverance*—all our husbands

230

helped in this task. The construction took months, and then we were disheartened to realize this ship could not hold all the settlers. That's when old Somers set to work on the *Patience*. Gates and Somers worked shoulder-to-shoulder with the men and encouraged them to keep going. Somers was particularly inspiring—up early and down late and no task too mean for him, despite his age and station. Our goal was always to reach Virginia. We never gave up hope of getting here."

I was interested in the plants on the *Devil's Island* and asked her to tell us about them.

"The *palmetto* tree was the most useful. When roasted, its fruit tasted like fried melon or cabbage. We peeled the bark, writing upon it like paper, and thatched our cabins with the leaves. Then there was a pea we named *prickle pear*. Blue berries there were similar to sloes and cured the flux caused by eating too many palmetto berries! And there was a fine cedar which bore fruit. When seethed, strained and let stand, these made a most pleasant drink."

Tempie's sense of humor flashed. In a weak voice, she volunteered, "Fancy that! They drank cedar as we did!"

Not Enough Darkness in the World
May 24, 1610

*England produces under favorable conditions of ease and cul-
ture the finest women in the world. And, as the men are
affectionate and true-hearted, the women inspire and refine
them.*

~ Ralph Waldo Emerson

*There is not enough darkness in the whole world
to extinguish the light of one small candle.*

~ Spanish proverb

There came then a knocking at the door, and Will entered the cottage with two gentlemen.

The first was my cousin Sam, who embraced me with a warm greeting. How I loved his robust grin. They lived! I had missed them and still could not believe they were here in our home at James Town. I kept asking myself if I were hallucinating after all.

The second one I knew as Will's comrade from the Low Countries—Maggie's husband, Hugh Deale.

Hugh held his hat respectfully, and hopefully, in his hands.

"Good day, Mistresses. I was wondering if…if you might know the whereabouts of my wife, Maggie." He bit his lip as though he already knew the answer.

I opened my arms to him. "Captain Deale…Hugh. I am pleased to meet you, at long last." He walked to where I sat propped in bed and took my hands in his. I motioned for him to have a seat on the edge of my mattress. When he had done so, an uneasy silence filled the room. All eyes were on me as I searched for words.

"I have heard such fine things about you from Maggie." I felt tears welling, as her loss remained both fresh and painful. "She was a wonderful soul, and we loved her so. She was a true gift to us—all of us—here at James Town."

232

Tempie nodded, encouraging me on. Hugh had noticed that I spoke of her in the past tense and an anguished sound escaped him. I hastened before I lost my nerve. "Her passing has affected us deeply, and we shall never forget her."

"She was our beloved friend," Tempie said gently.

He dropped his head, resting it upon his fingers. He looked down at his boots as he spoke. "I never should have brought her here. It is my fault that she suffered, and it was a terrible waste of her life."

I broke in. "No, Sir, not at all! I never heard her say she regretted the decision to come or that she blamed you for it." I glanced at Tempie, and she shook her head.

"Nor did I," she said.

I continued, "She was intent on making the best of what Providence presented her. Why, 'tis fair to say we might not be alive today without her friendship and foresight."

"We still eat from the labors of her hands. We were partners—working, planning, and sharing together," Tempie said.

He lifted his eyes, gazing from one to the other of us. We explained that it had been she who suggested we find an ally on ship, she who insisted we make a plan during the crucial late summer and autumn, and she who had unknowingly inspired many at the fort through her hymns and ballads. "Her sweet voice drifted out the windows of our home, and many across James Town heard her sing. How many might she have touched—as they were discouraged? Or dying? This, we will never know, but it is her legacy and a fine one at that. You've reason to be very proud of her," I finished.

"And forget not her poetry!" Tempie said.

We gave him her tambourine and book, and I added, "See that she described hope as a flame—but she was our light. She brightened and warmed our hearth through her very presence. I suppose, in fact, we were all lights for one another, against a darkness such as none could have imagined."

Tempie agreed, as again all fell silent.

At last, Will, looking thoughtful, placed a hand upon his friend's shoulder. "Hugh, we have all been comrades on the battlefield. But it sounds like our wives have been comrades in a war of a different sort. They have not buckled under mean circumstance but have endeavored to rise above it. They do us proud. No Captain in the Lowlands could have achieved more than they did with the little they had. And your Maggie seems to have gone down valiantly, a hero—or heroine."

Tempie and I both nodded, and I said, "Indeed she was."

Hugh thanked us, and as he and Sam took their leave, I saw Sam grip his friend's shoulder.

I remembered Maggie's words in church the day we had made our plan. *I do not expect to see my Hugh again. This side of heaven, I mean.* How right she would be, she could not have known.

When we met Elizabeth's husband, we would have to tell him of her loss too, but that would be a bit more challenging. Yet I still wore the ring she had given me. I would tell him that though she had been very ill, she had died peacefully and with great courage, for this was true.

This brought to mind those at Point Comfort, especially the Laydons.

"Will, how fared they at the other fort? We heard nothing through the winter and we could not get there."

Will glanced at Sarah. Was his expression troubled? Silence filled the room for a moment.

"Will?"

He drew in a deep breath. "When we arrived at Point Comfort, we learned to our profound and bitter sorrow of the famine here at James Town." He hesitated. "However, at Point Comfort, they fared a bit better than you did," he said cautiously, looking at the two of us as though wondering whether to proceed.

"Go on," I urged.

He nodded. "They had ample crabs, at least through part of the winter—and enough left over to feed their hogs," he said at last, a pained expression on his face.

A cry escaped from both Tempie and me as Will continued, "Percy had not been there long when we landed, and he, too, was furious! He accused Captain Davis of concealing their plenty from you and plotting to sail back to England. Percy said he had planned to send for half of those at James Town and then alternate the other half. While his orders were to keep James Town going, he felt men's lives, once lost, could not be reclaimed."

I was stunned. Crabs? We were eating cedar spindles and rotted chipmunks and they had crabs and hogs? I laid my head on the mattress. Strange, strange tales. I was too tired, too worn out, to be angry any longer. How did it serve me? But the question in my mind was *why?*

"Well we know about men's—and women's—lives being *unable to be reclaimed,*" Tempie said quietly. "We have seen so many perish—including our Maggie."

Again, the long, still silence. Who would speak? What words could quell this anger, this disappointment? My eyes fell upon Sarah Rolfe. I imagined a tiny

234

grave abandoned in the Bermudas, and the two baby boys who were born and died at sea last summer. I envisioned the little Parks boy who starved to death along with so many other small ones. A thought struck me.

"And little Ginny Laydon? The babe born in December?" I asked Will.

Will paused. "She lives. As does her mother, Annie."

In a startling burst, my heart leapt with joy for the young mother and the child. They lived! Virginia, for all its famine, illness, and siege, had not claimed its youngest, most innocent resident. "Then, praise God, in His mercy He has spared them. We have all suffered and endured enough. How would the starvation of Annie and little Ginny have served us here?"

Tempie nodded. "'Tis so," she murmured, her eyes full of tears as mine were.

Will, his voice choked, added, "I do have something for you, Joan. When I arrived, I asked Percy how you and Janey fared, afraid to hear his answer. He told me that when he departed for Point Comfort, you were both still alive, that you and Temperance had held up as well as any soldiers. He warned me you were all but skeletons. To hear that food was plentiful at Point Comfort, while you starved—I was enraged! I stood upon the beach and asked God why He had provided for us in the Bermudas, while placing food just beyond your reach. I knelt on the sand at the ocean's edge. I pummeled it with my fist, shouting, "She trusted You; I trusted You!"

When I lifted my head, I...I don't know how I missed it before, but this was laying before me," he stammered, reaching into his sack. "I know how you love them. Since it comes from the point we call *Comfort*, may it bring a measure of comfort to you."

His eyes filled with tears as held up a white scallop shell—larger, purer and more elegant than even the one I had found in Melcombe.

Things Beyond Our Reason or Control
May 25, 1610

The next day, Tempie and I were still absorbing all Will and Sarah had told us. The hurricane had nearly destroyed the ship, but yet they had survived. When all had finally seemed lost, land appeared magically, only to be the haunted Bermudas. Yet the Bermudas were not haunted at all, simply noisy with birds begging the men to eat them!

With all that had happened, surely God's Providence *was* with us, in spite of what we had endured. Now they were here—the head was back upon the body—and the devastating winter of 1609 to 1610 was behind us. There seemed so much hope. Perhaps all had not been in vain.

This was also the day that George finally had opportunity to spend time with his wife. When he came in, Tempie beamed her delight. Like me, she felt as if she were in an extended dream. He took his wife gently in his arms, afraid, as Will had been, that she might break. I felt a lump rise in my throat to see her happiness and his relief.

"Your suffering—the hardship you have borne—grieves me deeply," he said tenderly, his face distraught. Her condition must have shocked him, I thought, remembering how healthy she had been on the dock that day in Plymouth. Had it been only a year ago?

"You are here now," Tempie said quietly. "All is well."

Yet, despite relief at seeing his wife, a heaviness hung over George. He had just returned from a conference with Governor Gates, Percy, Newport, and

236

Somers. While George was not a leader himself, he was always privy to proceedings in his position as Captain of the Governor's Guard.

Tempie put her arms around him, a puzzled look on her face. "All is well now, George. Both you and Will are here. Joan, Janey, and I have survived, and, pray God, shall regain our health. We have heard the amazing adventure and strange wonders of the Bermudas. Despite our losses, surely, God is with us. Is it not so?"

He said nothing, his eyes cast to the floor.

"George?" It was Will. "You've been with Gates, Somers and the rest. Have you news? We can bear whatever you have to say."

Still nothing. George sighed and his eyes met Will's. He spoke slowly. "Gates thinks there is no way to make this work. At all."

Now it was we who were stunned.

Had all our suffering and struggling been for naught? Had the *Sea Venture* passengers worked months to build ships on a deserted island for nothing?

"What do you mean? You're here now! Surely there is cause for hope!" Tempie cried.

George shook his head. His expression of complete despondency caused my newly full stomach to sink. *What can it be now?*

Suddenly I felt nauseated. I drew a deep breath hoping I would not be sick. I had so many questions, so much I wanted to know.

"'Tis like a game of chess, and circumstance has checked us. It appears to be checkmate, but they're still studying it," George said finally. Will nodded soberly. The truth seemed to be dawning on him, as though he too were adding it up and seeing the deficit.

"First, we expected to find the town flourishing and with planted fields— not starved and under siege. One more has died since we've arrived, and there's likely to be others. Several are beyond saving, even with food. The surviving settlers probably had no more than four days left at best. We truly did arrive just in time for the sake of those like you—Tempie and Joan—who can still pull through with proper nourishment."

He patted his wife's leg and said to us, "I apologize for the bluntness, given all you have been through." He needn't have; it was no shock to us. We had seen so many die at an ever-increasing rate that we only praised God we ourselves might be strong enough to recover.

"Expecting to find things well here and having little room in the pinnaces, we brought only enough food for the voyage from the Bermudas," Will said in sudden recognition of George's dismay. His face was tight and drawn, as he added, "The ships were barely large enough for us as it was."

"Aye," George went on. "Second, the planting season is past. And even if it were not, we don't have time to wait for seeds to sprout into crops! We have two hundred mouths to feed. Third, the Indians are in no way amenable to trading. That much is evident. In fact, we believe their stores may also be low."

"An Indian princess, Pocahontas, told a woman last summer that Virginia has suffered great drought for four or five years," I put in. "Their storytellers say it is the driest they can remember across many generations."

George gazed at me with fatigued eyes. "That makes sense. It might help explain the hostilities as well as their reluctance to trade. But then again, our leadership has been so poor that they have perceived our weaknesses and exploited them."

He continued, "Add to that, most of our tools have been bartered to the Indians and the *pallisado* is falling down. It is sufficient to say hearts are heavy in the main house this evening. No one wants to own defeat, but we can see no way out."

"What about sailing back to the Bermudas to get more provisions?" Will asked. "Is Gates considering that?"

"They're considering it, but the hard truth remains. We have only a ship and three pinnaces to transport food. And though the sturgeon usually run here in the spring, they have not seen *one* this year. So we must rule out even this promising victual. There is only ten to sixteen days' worth of food here, and that takes into account strict rationing—two cakes per person per day. Not enough. And even on that beggar's portion, there would barely be enough time to get to the Bermudas, much less to restock and return. And how much could we transport?"

"Sixteen days means…" Will hesitated.

George met his eyes. "It means we don't even have enough food to sail back to England."

"We starve if we stay; we starve if we leave." Will shut his eyes and put a hand to his head. "Checkmate."

"That is the size of it. The blasted size of it. We are in a country of abundance and plenty, none of it accessible to us in time to feed so many. And still the siege continues."

The light dropped in the sky, and all around us, the sounds of the forest filled the room. We heard them because none of us spoke. No one knew what to say, though the word lingered in the air.

Checkmate.

The Path of Sorrow
May 26–30, 1610

The path to sorrow, and that path alone,
Leads to the land where sorrow is unknown.
~ William Cowper

The day after his landing, Governor Gates declared martial law under *The Laws Divine Morall and Martiall*, which the Virginia Company had given him authority to do if he deemed the colony in a state of emergency. He nailed these laws to a tree for all to read. There would be no further fighting over who would do what, no tolerance for laziness or filth. Homes were to be sweet and clean, we were to raise beds three feet off the ground to ensure proper hygiene, and we were to dump no waste outside our door.

In addition, Gates would tolerate no lying, embezzlement, profanity, or traitorous talk against the King. The laws ordered us to attend church twice each day and three times on Sunday. He set work times strictly from six to 10 o'clock in the morning and again from two until 4 o'clock in the afternoon, assigning each person—man or woman—a task. The only exceptions he made were for those still weakened from the Starving Time. Gates was authoritative, yet not inhumane.

Meanwhile, he continued to evaluate the food situation. A week passed, and the word from George, who was able to observe the Governor's decisions, was that Gates felt it remained hopeless.

Hopeless. One thought plagued me. *Why are we still alive? And why did the* Sea Venture *passengers not drown? Why did we starve, while they had provisions aplenty—only to have them arrive now for us all to perish together? If their late arrival was of no use, why save them at all? Why save us?* I could not put my finger on it, but something did not ring right. I understood God's ways were not my own, but this perplexed me. I shared my thoughts with no one at first. Finally, I approached Tempie, as I thought she would understand.

The *Patience* and the *Deliverance* had been in James Town a week. June was fast approaching and the season grew hotter each day. It brought to mind the

239

sticky August of our arrival last summer. Our strength had sufficiently returned so that we could feed ourselves and perform basic tasks in the cottage. Therefore, Sarah no longer nursed us but received a work shift with the other *Sea Venture* wives. We shared the same cottage as before—housing remained tight— and George and Will spent some nights there and some in the barracks.

This day, Tempie and I were on our way to the well, albeit slowly, each carrying a bucket.

"Tempie, why? Why is Providence with us, then against us? Why is the road so strewn with rocks?"

She shrugged. Her cheeks, though still as hollow as mine, were reviving their rosiness. It was a blessed sight. We relished every meal, and, as the only two surviving *Sea Venture* "widows," we ate well under specific orders from Gates—as well as possible under rationing, that is. We still moved like old women, but our strength and endurance returned a little each day with the addition of pork and fish to our diets. I found myself using the walking stick less often as my legs regained stability.

"Joan, you ask questions I cannot answer. We have survived. Isn't that enough?"

"For a week or two more, until the food runs out again. No, no, it doesn't seem just to me."

"God is always just, even when we don't understand." She pointed to the rope leading into the brick well, asking, "You or me?"

"Me. I'm stronger." I hauled the well's bucket up, and she dumped the water into our own bucket. It made me think of the thousands of bucketfuls of seawater the men had tossed overboard on the *Sea Venture*. Why?

A thought intruded. *The road to Compostela is always rocky.* I froze, still holding the rope, the well's bucket swinging.

"Joan, what's the matter? Are you ill?" Tempie was genuinely concerned.

"I…I don't know. I just had an odd notion," I stammered. Involuntarily I touched my chest where the scallop badge hung beneath my kirtle.

"What is it? Does it involve mutton?" Tempie had been saying lately that all she wanted was a good piece of mutton before she died. The joke broke the momentary hold the words had on me. I would ponder it later.

"See, that's what we get for starving you. Now all *your* notions involve food. How long will this go on?" I asked her, suppressing a smile.

"As long as I'm alive," she said slyly.

240

A Star to Guide the Humble

June 4, 1610

But we sit and weep in vain. The voice of the Almighty saith,
"Up and onward for evermore!" We cannot stay amid the ruins.

~ Ralph Waldo Emerson

Courage, brother, do not stumble,
Though thy path be dark as night;
There's a star to guide the humble:
Trust in God and do the right.

~ Norman Macleod

"Pack 'em up!"

The order was out, and Gates had devised a plan that might get us home to England without starving. In matters of strategy, Gates had no master. He had weighed all options before issuing commands to the men.

While there was not enough food to get us home, there might be enough to get us to Newfoundland. There, English fishing boats could feed us and provide us more seaworthy vessels than the homemade Bermudan ship and pinnace and the two pinnaces we already possessed, the *Discovery* and the *Virginia*.

Will, George, and Sam, along with Gates's other men, oversaw colonists as they caught and dried as many fish as possible, shot whatever game they could, and made all remaining flour into sea biscuits. None of this amounted to many provisions, however.

Gates continued the reprieve for Starving Time survivors. Therefore, Tempie and I only tended the house and cared for Janey, much as we had before—the only difference being we no longer had the burden of providing our own victuals. Our husbands brought them to us each day, and we rested as much as possible. The voyage would be hard on us, we knew, and we had not long to prepare.

From our window, we watched soldiers hauling whatever was salvageable from the fort, loading goods as they were ready, making lists, taking inventory. The ships grew fuller by the day, and everyone agreed Gates's plan was the only course that could see us safely home.

Everyone, that is, except Captain Martin, who felt we should stay longer. His bickering contributed to the strife and surprised no one.

"Does he want to stay so he can run away again?" Tempie asked with contempt. "I say the man looks a bit more *rotund* than the rest of us. Do you think he had a secret supply of food?"

I rolled my eyes in agreement. *Now* he had leadership ideas? Now that he was safely protected by Gates and all his men?

Standing at the window, we fanned ourselves against the heat. Summer's sultriness had already settled in, making the men's work grueling.

"I wonder how the digging's going," I commented.

"Lucky the ditch is already there," Tempie said. The men were using a trench put around the fort during John Smith's time, originally a barrier against the Indians. Now soldiers back-filled it after rolling in ordnance of various sizes. There was simply no way to carry these heavy weapons on the pinnaces to Newfoundland, and we did not want to leave them for the savages.

"Indians with ordnance—there's a frightening thought, isn't it?" Tempie remarked.

"Mm, I suppose *that* would surprise the deer all right. Not much left to make little fur doublets after that," I said.

We both laughed, but it remained tinged with bitterness at all we had endured beneath the natives' siege.

As for the fort itself, Governor Gates had reminded us all that we would leave it intact. "It will not be burned as some would like," he had said sternly at a church meeting the prior evening. "To ensure that, I myself will be the last to leave." In answer to the question on each adventurer's mind, he added thoughtfully, "It may be that some day, men as honest as ourselves will come to inhabit James Town."

Men as honest as ourselves. We had indeed given our all to this venture. We had endured hurricane, frigid weather, illness, siege, famine, and, if we were to believe the Indians, drought. The hand of Providence had smitten us soundly even while lifting us up. What did it mean? Still I wondered.

Abandoning Virginia meant not only the failure of this plantation but also perhaps the failure of any future English endeavors in the New World. The Spanish would grow more powerful, controlling this land and all its resources. It made everyone heartsick, but there seemed no other course.

Leaving brought a lump to my throat, though I was not sure why. The thought of England—and my Cecily—made my heart leap, to be sure. Yet leaving with nothing to show, failing, stung painfully. It was June 4. We would depart in three days, marking almost exactly a year since we had left the rocky shores at Falmouth. I remembered our hopes for this venture, our plans for the land and mineral rights we would someday own, and Cecily's courage when we told her she would stay behind.

Cecily! If there were one blessing remaining, it was that she had not endured the Starving Time. Thank God, she was in England, healthy and with a full belly, I hoped. We had planned to send for her in June. Instead, we would be sending ourselves home.

We Must Leave Thee,
Dear Desolate Home
June 7, 1610

Oh, weep for the living, who linger to bear
The renegade's shame, or the exile's despair.
One look, one last look, to our cots and our towers,
To the rows of our vines, and the beds of our flowers,
To the church where the bones of our fathers decayed,
Where we fondly had deemed that our own would be laid.
Alas! we must leave thee, dear desolate home...

Our hearths we abandon; our lands we resign;
But, Father, we kneel to no altar but thine.

~ Thomas Babbington Macaulay

A good person, striving dimly,
Is well aware of the right path.

~ Johann Wolfgang Von Goethe

June 7 dawned with all the fullness of a late spring Virginia morning. The trees and forests felt charged with life, while the fort grew more and more barren as men loaded the ships. It was time. There was no averting it, no hope of change. I had packed my few belongings, as had Tempie. Gates had ordered all Starving Time survivors to sail together in the Virginia pinnaces. So many were still unwell—in fact, two more had died—and the Governor hoped to keep the *Sea Venture* passengers from contagion. Again, I would sail separately from Will, even though we were so recently reunited. However, Tempie and I would be together this voyage. Our husbands had requested this and Gates gave his blessing.

244

"George has found considerable favor with Governor Gates," I said to Tempie, and she agreed. "What do you suppose his future will be in England?" I continued.

"More soldiering, I suppose. And Will?"

"The same, I reckon. We married military men, and there is always one more battle."

"After the battle with the ocean, the Spanish will seem harmless enough."

Suddenly, I remembered Maggie's grave. It was naught but dirt heaped in a corner of the fort, but at least she was not in the burial pit with so many others. I wanted to leave her something—anything.

"Tempie, I need to say goodbye to Maggie," I told her as I scurried out the door. The fort bustled with activity, everyone excited and nervous about the trip home. I hurried to gather a few flowers. There were always some near the river, just as the day Tempie and I had celebrated with our Delftware. A handful of purple, yellow, and blue wildflowers seemed a small token, but it was all I had.

I knelt before Maggie's grave. Tempie and I had marked it with several stones from the river. It would not be the same, taking a voyage without her lilting voice. Would there be another seaman like *Master* Harrison? And I, all but a *surgeon* in her telling. I smiled at the thought of how bearable she made that crossing.

"Your Hugh is here. Can you believe it?" I asked the dusty mound. "Well, they are packing. We gave it our all, didn't we? We miss you every day. God speed to you in your journeys," I said to the grave, laying the flowers on the dust.

Just then, a cardinal, festive in bright red feathers and plume, called from a nearby bush. *"Cheer cheer cheer cheer."* I looked over my shoulder at the stone markers as I returned home to the cottage. Again, the cardinal cried more faintly, *"Cheer cheer cheer cheer."*

"Farewell to you too, Maggie," I murmured.

Somewhere a drum began pounding a long, steady cadence, the signal to board.

The cottage felt deserted. I took Janey's hand, touched the badge around my neck, and gazed one last time around the home we had shared. I remembered it so full of women, Annie Laydon's visit, the endless grinding of acorns, Maggie's death. How we had taken Grace in. The starving and the striving.

"Somehow, it was all worth it," I said to myself. I was not sure why I felt that way.

"What's that?" Tempie came up behind me, a hand on my shoulder as we crossed the threshold for the last time.

"Just thinking back."

"Think forward now. Back is gone, good riddance!" She slammed the door behind us. Seeing my distress at her words, she added tenderly, "But I know what you mean. They weren't all bad times, were they?"

"We laughed a lot for two skinny women with a child."

"Just so." She draped her arm around me.

The breeze was gentle, easy. I didn't know why exactly, but I would miss Virginia. With all her hardships, I thought maybe I loved her still. But I wasn't sure. I squeezed Janey's hand and followed the others coming from their homes in a slow, trudging march to the ships. By noon, we were all onboard.

The guns blazoned a mournful farewell volley. The leaders had divided the knowledgeable mariners amongst the four ships. Each vessel would have a light crew, as the only mariners available were from the original *Sea Venture*.

Our husbands, gripping their muskets, marched from the fort last. Directly behind them came the masters of the four ships: Captain Davis on the *Virginia*, Captain Percy on the *Discovery*, Captain Somers on the *Patience*, and finally, Governor Gates who would be on the *Deliverance*.

If any curious Indian eyes peered from the forests, we never knew it. They had won. We were leaving now.

Spirit Supernal
June 7–8, 1610

Bind her, grind her, burn her with fire,
Cast her ashes into the sea,—
She shall escape, she shall aspire,
She shall arise to make men free;
She shall arise in a sacred scorn,
Lighting the lives that are yet unborn,
Spirit supernal, splendor eternal,
England!

~ Helen Gray Cone

The crew unmoored the ships, and we edged away from shore. The broken *pallisados* and the ruined town gazed as forlornly at us as we did at them that seventh day of June, 1610. Though there were those celebrating, it was hard to deny the defeat in the air.

Captain Percy, gaunt and still not entirely well, allowed us aboveboard in shifts since the weather was mild and winds light. Tempie and I stood on the *Discovery's* waist as it pushed further into the river, the sweeping James. Now closer to the middle of the river, we had a good view of the tree line on either side of the Virginia shore, as the fort slowly drifted from sight. It was strange to see places so long denied us by the Indian siege suddenly open to us, even if from the river.

There went Goose Hill, there the uplands where we had gathered so many bushels of acorns, down to Low Point, then to the place where the Thorofare branched off from the James River at Black Point. Woods and waterways encircled the palisaded area.

"James Town looks small from the water, doesn't it?" Tempie asked me.

I nodded. The rivers in Virginia were wide and deep, and the Chesapeake Bay was as fine as any in Europe. The four ships felt like a funeral procession as we slowly made our way with little wind and contrary tide.

"Even the tide runs against us!" Tempie said in disbelief. Did *nothing* go our way?

247

By evening, we had only gone as far as Hog Island, three miles downstream on the south side of the James. Even that was desolate, forsaken—all the hogs slaughtered by the Indians.

Our rations were light—dried pork from the Bermudas and a half cup of meal each. Janey and I shared a mattress as we had on the *Blessing* and settled in to the rocking of the ship, cradled by the river. The smallest of the three pinnaces, the *Discovery* was a fraction of the *Blessing's* size. There were about thirty of us onboard, mostly men, but also the Laydons and baby Ginny from Point Comfort. Gates had brought the Point Comfort settlers to James Town, leaving only a small contingent of soldiers there as sentry.

When dawn came, we set off again, the river growing ever more expansive as we approached the bay. We expected it to take a day or two before we arrived at Point Comfort where the James River met the Chesapeake Bay.

Governor Gates planned to wait ten days at Point Comfort on the slim possibility of a relief ship. Of course, no one in England knew the *Sea Venture* had survived or that we had starved. It was certainly possible one would come, but remote in the short time remaining. The ten days would also give us opportunity to catch and dry more fish for the journey north up the coast to Newfoundland.

By mid-afternoon, we were at Mulberry Island, a charming piece of land jutting into the river. Smith's men had named it several years back for its acres of native Virginia mulberry trees. The potential for silk was certainly there with all those mulberries. *Little silk worms would eat those hungrily*, I thought. So many dreams of prosperity…

"Beautiful little island, isn't she?" I asked Tempie absently as we glided past, and she nodded. We could see the mulberry groves from the water.

Here we anchored, waiting for the tide to turn.

"Hold up!" one of the crew cried upon a signal from the *Deliverance*. A lookout had spotted something on watch.

A longboat was making its way upriver. But where had it come from, and whose longboat was it? Surely it was Spanish? Percy quickly ordered the few of us standing above deck to go below until he knew what the situation was.

An hour or so went by and then Percy cautiously climbed down the scuttle into the 'tween deck. He steadied himself on the capstan, his expression giving little away. Was it astonishment? Disbelief? No one moved. Not a single passenger breathed. Yet the very air was weighted with something.

He looked about at the adventurers for a long moment, until the silence became uncomfortable. Finally, he announced slowly, "My Lord La Warr has arrived."

To Have Broke My Heart

June 8–9, 1610

*The 6 of June, I came to an anchor under Cape Comfort, where I met
with much cold comfort as, if it had not been accompanied with the most
happy news of Sir Thomas Gates his arrival, it had been sufficient to
have broke my heart and to have made me altogether unable to have
done my king or country any service.*

~ Thomas West, Lord De
La Warr, upon learning
of the Starving Time

"Captain Brewster on the long boat has brought Governor Gates a letter,"
Percy continued. He paused. "Governor De La Warr has just landed at
Point Comfort. He brings three ships, 150 new adventurers, and provisions for
an entire year. Governor La Warr hereby orders us to turn around. It would
seem this day, June 8, we may hereafter call *the Day of Providence*, for surely God
Himself has intervened to save James Town."

For a moment the crowd stood hushed, stunned by this latest development.
Lord De La Warr had arrived? With provisions for a year? My heart fluttered in
my chest, then dropped to my belly. The air was stifling in the 'tween deck and I
was damp with perspiration, yet I found myself shivering. Tempie took my arm
and we steadied ourselves. Our eyes met with a mixture of fear and incredulity.

The news fast enveloped the passengers—its implications clear. Some few
cheered, but the majority groaned. In any event, we were staying, so applauding
or grieving mattered not.

The ships that departed James Town in October had alerted the Virginia
Company that we were without charter or leadership. The presumed loss of the
Sea Venture, along with the return of the injured John Smith, meant that both the
colony and the investment were in danger. How much danger, Lord De La Warr
and the members of the Company in England could not have guessed. We had
suffered starvation and devastation on a scale unimaginable to Company

249

officials. No less amazing to them would be the unexpected survival of Sir Thomas Gates and all his passengers. This situation teetered so completely between extremes that my head reeled.

In April, De La Warr had set off from England. His original plan had been to sail at the end of 1609 or early 1610, but the task of raising new investors required three months longer than expected. Catastrophic losses don't sell much stock.

When De La Warr arrived at Point Comfort on June 6, Captain Davis told him of the Starving Time, the survival of the *Sea Venture*, and finally, the plan to abandon settlement. De La Warr had sent his longboat upriver with all due haste to tell us to *turn around*.

The old palisaded town welcomed us back that evening, with us having spent only one night on ship. We found no Indians and all just as we had left it.

Lord De La Warr made his grand entrance two days later.

The settlement bells pealed at first sighting of his ship, the *De La Warr*. He disembarked to colors flying and trumpeters heralding his arrival—Thomas West, third Baron De La Warr, the first ever Governor for Life and Captain General of Virginia. James Town, the ruined little fortification, had never seen such display of finery as it did on that day. There was no doubt about it. The Virginia Company had put Virginia on the map, and they intended to keep her there. A wisp of Providence saved her, and she was ready to start anew.

I sighed and set my cap. It appeared I might indeed be a *Virginian for life*, just as Lord De La Warr planned to be.

Stepping ashore with all looking on, the Governor fell to his knees and thanked God in a long, silent prayer. The content of his prayer was between him and his Maker. However, we were quite sure he thanked God for allowing him to arrive providentially to save the colony from extinction. No doubt, his prayer also included thankfulness for Gates's foresight in not burning the fort to the ground. After all, allowing it to stand was risky and meant Indians or the Spanish might occupy it. Gates gambled that De La Warr would come in time to be able to use the fort, even if we ourselves had returned to England.

Now, with nearly sixty survivors of the Starving Time, the 150 persons from the *Sea Venture*, and De La Warr's 150 passengers, we had some 360 people crowded into a falling down and smelly town. We needed new homes quickly and strong leadership to manage so many.

Governor De La Warr arose from his prayer and marched into the church, followed by his company of soldiers. All of us who were able attended as the

Reverend Richard Bucke preached a Sunday afternoon sermon. Then Governor De La Warr ordered one of his Captains to read his commission.

That done, My Lord himself took up the cedar pulpit. If we had expected any compassion for our suffering, none was forthcoming. De La Warr stared us down firmly, pointing his finger at the adventurers gathered. He rebuked us for being vain and idle, saying that our miseries were our own fault and that God had sought retribution on us. He was directing this, of course, at the Starving Time survivors. From where I sat, I could see Percy, Captain Tucker, and Walter the soldier. Janey sat next to me, a sliver of a child, eyes staring widely at the fancifully dressed man at the front of the church. *Easy for him to speak of retribution,* I thought. He had not lived the horrors as we had.

We certainly had not been idle! In fact, those of us here were the very ones who had been resourceful enough *to* survive. Fearing personal reprimand, I kept my gaze straight ahead on the Lord Governor, not wanting even to blink. I dared not exchange glances with Tempie. *He is not talking to the two of us,* I told myself by way of consolation.

After the formal condemnation came the cheerful news that he had enough provisions for a year. I believe he meant this to encourage us.

After the service, Tempie and I returned to our home. George and Will were now on active soldiering duty again.

"Did you know that Lord De La Warr and I have a passing relation by marriage?" Tempie asked idly. This was news to me.

"His aunt married Robert Dudley after my great aunt Amy died—was killed. Whatever the case may be. Actually, Dudley had a second wife in between whom he secretly divorced."

This was shocking. "Dudley sounds like a cad! Would the Governor know of this connection?"

"We have met," she replied with a shrug. "It may help George's promotions."

It appeared to, for both Gates and Governor De La Warr regarded George highly from the beginning as an able and honest soldier. This turned out to be a blessing for Will, Sam, and Hugh, for George felt he owed an allegiance to them as his comrades in the Low Countries—and perhaps more so for the role he perceived Maggie and I had played in Tempie's survival.

Governor De La Warr wasted no time in setting things right at the fort. The first order of business was establishing a Council, to which he appointed Gates, Somers, Newport, William Strachey, George Percy, and Sir Ferdinando Wainman.

Gates, Somers, Newport, and Strachey were all *Sea Venture* survivors. Wainman had come over with De La Warr, and the unfortunate George Percy had half-starved through the James Town winter with us.

De La Warr tightly organized his town from the beginning. Gates he made Deputy Governor, Wainman the Master of the Ordnance, and Percy Captain of the Fort. Strachey, along with our cousin Silvester Jourdain, had kept a meticulous record of the Bermudas. For this accomplishment, De La Warr named Strachey Secretary.

Next, he divided the men in the colony into fifty-man militias, each one under a Captain. No one was surprised when he made George a Captain, along with Argall, Percy, and two others. George in turn appointed Will, Sam, and Hugh to oversee squads of ten or twenty men.

Now James Town became a true military outpost in the wilderness, for all these leaders knew how to run martial campaigns in Europe—with a firm hand. Veterans of the wars in Ireland and the Low Countries became much-valued members of the colony, their chances for advancement great.

The Companies were to eat together when possible. Will's task was to oversee his men's work and to take account of it. Repairing and cleaning up James Town, experimenting with English vegetables, unloading ships, fishing, constructing housing, and setting up new outlying forts—the list seemed endless.

We women, while not assigned to a company, also had tasks to perform. These included spinning, sewing, working yard gardens, mending clothes, and even arranging flowers at the front of the church to keep it fragrant. It was no secret that the Governor thought James Town had such a putrid stench he slept on his ship most nights.

The laws were clear, and firm. Bells not only summoned all to work duties, they also called us to church twice each day and three times on Sunday. On Wednesdays and Sundays, Reverend Bucke preached. No one should utter any blasphemous word against the preacher, or make any treasonous statements, nor trade with the Indians without formal permission. Theft or embezzlement from the common store or from any individual was punishable by death. Gone were the days of the Starving Time when no man's—or woman's—food was secure. All of these, along with any crime against a person or the town as a whole, were death penalty offenses. Slandering Company leaders was a lesser offense punishable by whipping.

About a week after De La Warr's arrival, old George Somers sailed out on his vessel, the *Patience*, with Captain Argall on the *Discovery*. They were on their way to the Bermudas for six months provisions, but Argall and Somers lost sight of one another during the journey. Failing to find Somers, Argall sailed up to the northern waters instead, bringing us back fish.

However, it was the last we ever saw of the old lion Somers as he perished on Bermuda. His nephew buried his heart on the island, as Somers had wished. He pickled the Admiral's body to return it to England, never telling the superstitious sailors of their cargo. In this, his nephew did *not* regard Somers's wishes. Heroic to the last, Somers had asked that, if he died, his nephew return his body to *Virginia* so that we could have those live hogs. We never received them.

Come now the Indian wars.

Firebrands and Stones
July 4, 1610

Now firebrands and stones fly.
~ Virgil

*I don't know how long it has been since my ear has been free from the roll
of a drum. It is the music I sleep by.... I shall remain here while anyone
remains, and do whatever comes to my hand. I may be compelled to face
danger, but never fear it, and while our soldiers can stand and fight, I can
stand and feed and nurse them.*
~ Clara Barton

We had been back at James Town for nearly a month. George, Will, and
Sam gathered around our trestle table, as the air rang with evening sounds
of frogs and insects outside the windows. George was deep in discussion with
the men, while Tempie and I, not formally part of the conversation, nonetheless
took it all in.

The men had lit their clay pipes and the bitter smell of Indian tobacco filled the
room in the candlelight as we finished a light meal of fish and cornbread. An occasional breeze moved through the stultifying heat. Late June had been unseasonably
hot, or so the few original settlers told us. Early July was starting much the same way.
Tempie and I fanned ourselves with our hands as we listened to George.

"So Governor De La Warr sent a messenger to Powhatan, saying in effect,
'Return the hundreds of tools your men have stolen, and send us the braves who
killed several of our men at the blockhouse. You are an honorable king, and certainly remember that you are in subjection to His Majesty King James in
England.' You know about the coronation ceremony that occurred two years
ago, during Smith's tenure?" George asked the men.

They did. Powhatan had refused to get on his knees to receive his English-
made crown in the traditional fashion—the great chief dropped to *his* knees for

no one. Finally, however, Powhatan agreed to bend his head so Captain Newport could place it on him.

"I hear Powhatan is an Indian of immense stature," Sam commented.

Tempie interrupted the conversation. "Even by Indian standards? They are huge!" She had not forgotten our encounter with the braves in the fort last fall.

"Even by Indian standards, the grandest of them all," George continued. "Far taller than Captain Newport—that much is certain! That's why he had to bend to receive the crown, although the traditional king's kneeling ceremony would have been nobler. Anyway, De La Warr reminded him of the implicit agreement in receiving such a crown, something to the effect of, 'We believe you were not aware of the attacks made on our men and that these were the lowly sorts of Indians perpetrating them. Cease them at once, send us the stolen tools, and either punish the braves responsible or send them to us to punish.'"

"That seems reasonable," Sam said. "Has Powhatan yet responded?"

"Oh, aye! His response *infuriated* the Governor. 'Depart *my* country or confine yourselves to James Town only. Do not search the land or rivers, or I will have my braves kill you and do all the mischief they can,' he said. Oh, and the most insulting remark of all: 'Do not send a messenger to me again unless you bring me a carriage and three horses, as that is what all the great *werowances* in England have, according to my braves who have been there.'"

"He wants a *carriage?* Surely he does not believe he will receive one!" I put in.

"No, Joan, he does not in the least expect he will. But he is laying the foundation for…war," George replied. "The Governor reiterated that if his conditions weren't met, we would kill any savage we stumbled upon and burn their fields and towns. As they say, *'tis all an ill wind that blows nobody any good.*"

More war with the Indians? Would it never end?

"Gates and his companies are being sent to Point Comfort right away," George continued.

Will looked at me. "I suppose we are leaving you again."

I nodded. I had grown used to that. Tempie had as well.

The Chant of My Soul
July 4, 1610

Ut magna magnè desideremus, *that we may beg great blessings earnestly. Our hope is that our Sun shall not set in a cloud.*

> ~ Letter to the Virginia
> Company, explaining
> James Town's troubles,
> Autumn 1610

I know I have but the body of a weak and feeble woman; but I have the heart of a king, and of a king of England, too.

> ~ Queen Elizabeth I,
> prior to the Armada
> invasion

Lilac and star and bird twined with the chant of my soul,
There in the fragrant pines and the cedars dusk and dim.
> ~ Walt Whitman

The conversation turned to another topic, the imminent departure of Sir Thomas Gates for England. He would be leaving in a few weeks, after getting his troops situated at Point Comfort. Gates would then be able to recount his own version of events to the Virginia Company in person.

"They will not believe it when they see old Gates standing there!" Sam laughed. "They shall think him a phantom."

"'Tis frightening to think one sees a phantom," I said a bit defensively, remembering the arrival of the *Patience* and the *Deliverance*.

"Now, Joan. Sam is only jesting, and not with you," Will said. "The Virginia Company will throw down their hats and dance a jig about them with this news.

Of course, the tremendous loss of life here will temper that and will require a shrewd explanation." All eyes went to George.

"Aye, a most protracted explanation," George said. "I have seen the document. '*Ut magna magnè desideremus,*' it reads. Translated 'that we may beg great blessings earnestly.' It includes a list of reasons, and I must say they are convincing in the way of poor luck at every turn. It is almost as if God would have us suffer through the Starving Time and near-abandonment of the fort so that we would prove ourselves worthy to possess this land." He took a bite of fish and a swig of small beer.

I looked at Tempie and she at me. *Us?* The word went unspoken between us, but *we* had suffered through the Starving Time, while these men had lived off hogs and turtle in the Bermudas. Yet, I cautioned myself, God had brought them safely here, and for that, I must be grateful.

"What reasons, Sir?" Will asked, tamping down his tobacco.

"So many, Will. It opens with, 'Cast up this reckoning together. Want of government, store of idleness,' and goes on to talk about the traitors sailing away with the corn, the mariners undervaluing goods traded to the natives, the treacherousness of the Indians who chased the deer, killed our hogs, and destroyed our nets. It speaks of men fled, murdered or dead of sickness or famine; the brackish water of the James…"

Will stopped tamping, intent on George's words. "And all this shall be sent to the Virginia Company?"

"Indeed, for they should know what cards the hand of Providence dealt us, some of our own making and some sheer misfortune. We pledge to do better with what we now have in front of us. It is apparent the tide, at last, has turned."

Later that evening, Will called me to him. His serious expression caused a flutter in my heart. What now?

"Joan," he began slowly. I nodded and waited.

"George and I shall be leaving in the morning to accompany Gates. I do not know when we shall return. He may station us at Point Comfort, depending on what we find when we arrive."

"Surely you are not suggesting something might happen to you?" I broke in.

"Oh no, it is nothing like that. I am an optimist, after all." He smiled. "No, it is something entirely different. When we decided to make this journey, I consulted you as but an afterthought. I acknowledge this and apologize." He looked truly humbled. "You endured a far more treacherous turn of events than I did, as you survived both the hurricane *and* the Starving Time."

"Aye." It was a fact and no denying it. But I wondered what was on his mind.

"This time I ask you as one who has been in this country longer than I have—nearly a year longer—how do you feel about us staying, for the long run?"

There was a catch in my throat. I had come to love Virginia despite it all, even with her moody weather and Indian defiance. She had a pervasive wildness gone many a century from England. The *different kind of wild* described by Harrison could be—had often been, in fact—sinister. Yet it could also be exotic, enchanting, and intoxicating. We had seen Virginia at her worst—but with new leadership, well-stocked provisions, good husbandry of our stock...

Should we consider the past year a total loss, a regretful decision, and return to the known world? Or should we consider it but a hard road traveled—steps on the path toward a fresh start? The scallop badge weighted my neck as though asking, *what will you do?* When did the pilgrim's journey end? Where was the place one turned around for a return pilgrimage home? Had we reached it?

Lost in thought, I scarcely heard Will's tentative voice. "I ask for a reason in particular. The Company orders us to stay longer, but at some point, we will have the option to leave. If we are to stay, Gates could bring Cecily back with him when he comes."

Cecily? I jumped to my feet. "Aye, oh aye, my husband, aye! Bring her—I have missed her!" I had pushed thoughts of my daughter far away because there was nothing I could do for her, not even send a letter.

I threw my arms around his neck, but he pulled them away and put his hands out in warning. "Wait, Joan. Understand that if we bring her, she is destined to stay as we are, for an unknown span of time. It is farewell to England for her. The voyage, we know, is harsh, and she must survive seasoning here."

My words were firm and resolute. "I want her with us. I want my daughter with me. I have promised her, and *I will not forget.*" An image sprang to mind of a little hand, a scallop shell—and a garden in Dorset that seemed a lifetime away. A verse from Isaiah flashed through my mind: *I will not forget you! See, I have engraved you on the palms of my hands.*

Will's gaze met my own. "This is how I hoped you would feel. Virginia has much to offer us—all of us—if we but rise to the challenge and our hearts fail us not. Yet no one, least of all I, could blame you for choosing to turn back. You have suffered beyond suffering, and endured beyond enduring." He seemed to be offering me a last chance to retreat.

Still I wavered not. "It is precisely because of the *suffering beyond suffering* and *enduring beyond enduring* that my heart tells me, *press on.* We have come through too much to relinquish it now. We have invested much—only a small portion of it financial. We have truly adventured and invested ourselves. You ask what I say? This is what I say. *Press on.*"

Will's eyes shone, and he nodded. "Aye, and so it shall be then. I shall speak to Gates in the morning and arrange our daughter's passage."

I clasped my hands about my heart before throwing them upward in celebration. We would go on together. *Cecily, see I have not forgotten you!*

The True Harvest
July 12, 1610

[One day men here will support themselves] by planting their own vines, sowing their own corn, and brooding their own cattle, kine, swine, goats, etc., which would shortly be, and had been ere this, had the government been carefully and honestly established and carried here these 3 years past...

> ~ George Yeardley, *from a letter dated November 18, 1610*

And the soile is so fertile as by the industry of our people they may raise great crops of corne both Indian and English. Besides, all fruits, rootes, and herbes, out of England soe wonderfully prosper there.

> ~ Captain William Peirce, from his *Relation in Generall of the present state of his Majesties Colony in Virginia*

There is no Chance, no Destiny, no Fate,
But Fortune smiles on those who work and wait,
In the long run.

> ~ Ella Wheeler Wilcox

The true harvest of my life is intangible—
a little star dust caught,
a portion of the rainbow I have clutched.

> ~ Henry David Thoreau

Tempie and I were surprised when, in the middle of July, Lieutenant Governor Gates himself called upon us. George and Will had not returned from their mission to Point Comfort. For a moment, I felt my insides tighten. Did he bring us news?

"Sir!" I said politely, bowing my head but trembling somewhat. "May I get you a dram of beer?"

He removed his hat and shook his head. "That won't be necessary, Mistress Peirce. Thank you, kindly. First, let me assure you that your husbands have fared well in our recent skirmish with the Indians."

"Recent skirmish? We thought you were simply going to Point Comfort," I said.

"Well, that *was* the initial plan, aye. But we had complications *en route.*"

He went on to tell us that he had watched his man Humphrey Blunt brutally murdered by the natives. Master Blunt, he told us, was paddling a canoe across the river to fetch a longboat. A gale had carried it off to the south bank. "The wind drove him back to the north shore, where braves grabbed this honest soldier and carried him to the woods to be sacrificed." We flinched at his words and the pain on Gates's face. It was a fresh memory. "Your husbands, I regret to say, also witnessed this event. It was indeed horrific in its execution."

As we were ladies, he did not elaborate. He did not need to, since well we remembered other atrocities the Indians had committed. None that we had seen ourselves, however. If it shook a seasoned soldier like Gates, it must have also shaken our husbands, I thought.

Gates added, "I had believed until that moment that we could reason with or convert these natives, but I am of the opinion now that the only way to deal with a barbarous disposition is by the sword."

The thought of ongoing bloodshed made my own blood icy in the veins.

"I determined we must seek retaliation on the Kecoughtans," he continued.

"This was the tribe responsible for the murder?" Tempie asked.

He nodded. He went on to describe a clever ploy whereby he sent Master Dowse, a taborer, ahead to entice them from their homes. Tap, tap, tapping on the tabor, drumming and dancing, Dowse lured out the Kecoughtans, who were curious and expecting entertainment. "Then we fell upon them, killing about a dozen," Gates finished.

With a hint of admiration he added, "They didn't die easily. I was strangely in awe of the murderous wounds they suffered and how they yet held on. Nonetheless, the Kecoughtan land is ours now. The rest fled, leaving us the town with its vast cornfields. They are reputed to be the best farmers amongst all the tribes, and the land there is fruitful, healthy for vines and corn. The more I see of Virginia, the more convinced I am of its tremendous promise. I first glimpsed this country twenty years ago with Francis Drake, when we retrieved the earliest Roanoke adventurers. Seeing it then, I could only agree with Ralegh's vision. I thought, *the future of England lies in Virginia.*" He gazed away distantly, and then returned to the issue at hand. "My Lord La Warr himself will be off to Kecoughtan shortly. He has plans to erect two forts there, which he proposes to call Henry and Charles. George and Will are there now and will likely remain there throughout construction."

"We are grateful to have this information, Sir," Tempie said.

Clearing his throat, Gates continued, "Have I never commended you two on the courage you showed during the inconceivable Starving Time?"

We shook our heads. We were not sure we had ever spoken with him directly before.

"That, not my Kecoughtan battle story, is the reason I have called." He smiled. "I came to speak to you, Mistress Peirce." I was startled. Why would someone of Gates's stature need to speak with me?

"As you know, I am preparing to depart for England soon. Captain Peirce has told me you'd like for me to arrange your daughter's passage here."

I nodded firmly. I had not changed my mind on this. "That is so, Sir."

"I have come to tell you that when I return to Virginia, I plan to bring my wife and daughters with me. If it pleases you, I will have them visit with your Cecily, and she will be in their charge upon our return voyage."

My heart soared in excitement. "Aye, thank you, Sir! You are too gracious." No wonder this gentleman had earned the respect of all his men.

"It is my pleasure." He stood and bowed to us. "For all your valor and honor during the Starving Time. As the Bible says, *they that sow in tears shall reap in joy.*" This gave me pause. Wasn't that the same Psalm Grace had quoted? How peculiar. Grace! I suddenly remembered I must send a letter to her daughters.

Bowing courteously once more, Gates took his leave.

The Moving Finger Writes
July 18–20, 1610

For he shall give his Angels charge over thee: to keep thee in all thy ways. They shall bear thee up in their hands: lest thou dash thy foot against a stone.

~ Psalm 91:11-12

The Moving Finger writes; and, having writ,
Moves on: nor all your Piety nor Wit
Shall lure it back to cancel half a Line,
Nor all your Tears wash out a Word of it.

~ Omar Khayyam

While Gates was in England, he planned to ask the Virginia Company to send Sir Thomas Dale to act as Deputy Governor. De La Warr had fallen prey to Virginia illnesses, and, although he did not appear to be dying, the possibility remained that he might not be able to govern. Gates would ask that Dale embark immediately for Virginia in case De La Warr's health declined. Gates himself expected to be in England for perhaps half a year longer, tending to his business affairs, working with the Virginia Company, and resting up for the strenuous return voyage across the Atlantic.

The summer of 1610 brought heat unusual even by Virginia standards. Summer sickness struck the new arrivals swiftly, and deaths were mounting. A knight fell early—Sir Ferdinando Wainman, Master of the Ordnance, perished for lack of seasoning.

Many from the Bermudas fared better than those newly arrived from England—many, but not all. One who whose health deteriorated rapidly was Sarah Rolfe, perhaps because she had not fully recovered from childbirth. When she died, her passing reminded me of a pink or yellow tulip, its vibrancy withered away by sudden frost. Tempie and I consoled ourselves that she was now with her baby girl, but still we grieved. *What purpose in taking her so early, Lord?* Was there one?

263

We received this sad news just hours before I sat to compose a letter to Grace's daughters. I had promised Grace I would send them word on her behalf, and the ships were leaving within days. There was little time to spare.

Now I arched over our trestle table before a blank page, attempting to muster my thoughts. I waved the quill idly, as I considered what to say after introducing myself. *Words do fail me,* I thought. I felt disheartened, grief for Sarah mingling with uncertainty about the unpredictable, cobbled path upon which we all trod.

Tempie had commiserated with Grace that it was cruel here, and that was so. *Tis a strange quirk of fate. While Grace came seeking mercy, Sarah came offering mercy. Each was only with us a short time, and yet each ministered to us in her own manner and then moved on—like angels along the way.*

The white quill whisked along, like some angel feather itself, as I wrote:

It is with great sadness I convey to you that your parents perished during the Starving Time.

I struggled to remember Grace's own words.

Yet your mother wished me to tell you she loved you and that they carried no regrets. They desired to be Adventurers, she said, or they should always have wondered what lay beyond the bounds of the known in the New World. What fine parents you had. Your father suffered with Grace.

It was not altogether untrue. He *had* suffered with Grace, his wife. I recalled how she had told me he had once been a good man and of his battles with shattered dreams. It seemed kind to preserve the memory of him as he once had been, before his mind failed.

And as for your mother...

I paused, seeking the right words before finding them in the feather itself.

...she was an angel. God's blessings upon you both.

I bundled the letter and sealed it, then carried it to the Company Store. Grace had blessed me; now I hoped that I had blessed Grace.

As I walked back toward the cottage, I chanced to meet my cousin Silvester. A stately, educated man, he was nonetheless warm with bright eyes. He would depart on the tide with Gates to hand deliver his well-written travelogue of the *Sea Venture's* near loss, miraculous survival, and the splendor of the Bermudas. A friend of Somers, he would no doubt praise the Admiral's heroism to king and countrymen.

Silvester paused to greet me, wearing a broad grin. He appeared happy to be returning to his home in Lyme Regis, I thought.

"I shall recommend Bermuda for colonization!" he told me. He winked. "Won't they be surprised to learn the haunted Isle of Devils were heaven instead?"

"You recommend Bermuda to them, while I recommend *you* to God for safe passage to England," I said with a parting embrace. "God be with you, Cousin."

Sir Thomas Gates set sail on July 20. Along with his documents to the Virginia Company, he carried instructions and letters from many of the settlers. The most important of all, in my opinion, was the letter I had written Cecily, pouring out as much of my heart as I could. Dare I tell her all I had suffered? No, that would only cause her fear, which I would not do. In truth, I did not know if she was even alive, and even then, both she—and her ship—must survive the return voyage.

I felt much gratitude to Gates for seeing my husband through the hurricane and shipwreck and for his offer to place Cecily in his wife's charge. I had complete faith in him. If his wife and daughters were as conscientious as he was, Cecily should have a passable journey.

I might expect Cecily to arrive late the following summer. Each time I considered it, I was filled with joy. How tall would she be? How had she fared in her studies? By the time she arrived, nearly two years would have passed since last we saw one other.

As I watched the crew make ready for departure, I considered my decision. Today presented the last chance to change my mind about sending for Cecily. Bringing her here meant that, for Will and me, our stake in Virginia climbed even higher. What would the future hold for Cecily? Like Janey, she would grow up remembering little of England.

Mariners hoisted the rigging, pulled up the plank, and loosened the lines tying the ship to the James Town pines.

Last chance, last chance, the wind seemed to say to me as it whipped the sails.

Let it be, I thought suddenly. *Let her come.* I felt somehow it was her destiny as it had been mine. We had made this choice and would never be whole with half of the shell in England, half in Virginia.

Pray God, it is the right decision.

The ship drifted away from shore. It was done. There was no turning from it now. I realized fate had forced me to make this decision without even knowing how her health had been this past year.

Now, the waiting had to begin—one more fall, one more winter, one more spring. Into summer. We would watch again for ships on the horizon, and the one ship for which I yearned most would bring my healthy daughter, I prayed, upon its tides.

The Tide of Destiny
July 20, 1610–May 19, 1611

Serene, I fold my hands and wait,
Nor care for wind nor tide nor sea;
I rave no more 'gainst time or fate,
For Lo! my own shall come to me.
Asleep, awake, by night or day,
The friends I seek are seeking me,
No wind can drive my bark astray
Nor change the tide of destiny.
The stars come nightly to the sky;
The tidal wave unto the sea;
Nor time, nor space, nor deep, nor high,
Can keep my own away from me.

~ John Burroughs

Will and George remained stationed at Forts Henry and Charles, while closer to James Town, the Indian wars raged.

In August, Lord De La Warr sent three Captains to raid Indian villages. He ordered Captain Brewster to attack the Warraskoyacks, Captain Davis to the Chickahominy tribe, and Percy he set upon the Paspaheghs.

Percy sailed with seventy men to the mouth of the Chickahominy River, and then led his men overland for several miles. Surprising the Paspaheghs, they killed a dozen or so. The rest fled, while our men burned the houses and fields and carried off corn.

The soldiers decapitated the Indians they captured, except for the Queen and her two children. Percy suggested they spare them and take them back to De La Warr. "Have we not had enough of killing and blood for one day?" he asked. But before he could stop his men, they threw the children in the water and shot them in the head. They would have killed the mother too, if Percy had not put himself in front of her. "We will take her back to James Town!" he ordered.

News reached us that our men had murdered the children and that the Queen, held prisoner, would likely face the same fate. My heart ached for the needless bloodshed. "When does it end, Tempie?" I asked.

Tempie shook her head. "If only I knew. As George said, *'tis an ill wind that blows nobody any good.*"

De La Warr ordered the Queen put to death by burning, but again, Percy intervened, asking for a more humane method if she must die—rather than having her linger in pain.

"It is amazing that Percy can take any pity at all," Tempie said. "He has suffered at their hands just as we ourselves have."

"More so, as he bore the humiliation of leading us during the siege." Perhaps Percy could have done more to prevent our starvation, but I did respect him.

Captain Davis, himself just returned from his bloody mission to the Chickahominies, arrived at the fort in time to do the deed which Percy himself did not want to fulfill. Davis told Percy that De La Warr ordered the Queen put through to the sword, but Percy remained convinced that it was Davis's idea. Again, stories did not match up.

I was near the well when a grim-faced Davis and his men marched the forlorn but proud Queen to the woods. She was regal, in an exotic sort of way, with dark hair and eyes bearing a contemptuous expression. Barefooted, she wore a fringed deerskin skirt. Draped around her shoulders lay a mantle of skins decorated with bird and animal designs. Covering that was what appeared to be a turkey feather mantle, which I thought distinguished her as a queen. Her assortment of beads jangled as she walked, but that was the only sound she made.

The Queen's head was tilted upward, her eyes to the afternoon sun. For a moment—just a moment—she dropped her eyes toward me. I stood transfixed. I remembered seeing hatred in a brave's eyes, but how much more poignant were these eyes filled with grief.

She does not mourn her own death, but that of her children, I thought. In that brief melding of gazes, we were neither white nor red, English nor Paspahegh. We were but two mothers.

Would that I knew a native word for *grief* or *sorrow,* but, alas, I did not. Yet I understood a mother's heart. As Annie Laydon said, *the men folk fight and the women folk bear the brunt.* This woman had borne the burden of war between her people and my own and had paid the highest price any mother can pay—her children. My eyes filled with tears for her loss, and for the loss of all the children and all the mothers from these wars.

No, I had no word for *sorrow*, but I lifted my fist to my heart and let the tear run down my cheek. *Your sorrow, my sorrow. We are both women, and we are both mothers.*

In return, she gave the barest of nods, an acknowledgement. *Yes*, it said, *thank you.*

She had allowed me to share her concealed grief. She then turned her eyes upward to the sun once more—lest any soldier think her afraid or that *she* was any less warrior than they themselves were. I knew she would not cry out upon her death—natives never did.

My own eyes I averted, as I could watch no longer.

As autumn approached, De La Warr continued to suffer from a hot and violent ague, with flux, cramps, gout, and scurvy. He ordered George and his men back to James Town from the outlying forts in November, but we saw them only briefly before they embarked again.

This time their destination was the fort at the falls, the one De La Warr's brother Francis West had abandoned the previous October. De La Warr's strategy was to re-establish that fort in order to winter there. Doctor Bohun, who had accompanied him on his voyage over, suggested that the fresh air away from the marshes might be healing.

"What does this mean, Will? Might you be at the falls all winter?" I asked during his brief respite at our cottage.

"Aye, we expect so, and come spring My Lord La Warr plans to use that fort as a base to explore farther upland. He himself hopes to be well enough to go. The object, of course, is to find the route to the South Seas. Surely, the way to the seas cannot be too distant once we're that far west."

I nodded in understanding. When found, this route would ease English trading with China considerably, I knew. We hoped Virginia would become a thoroughfare for such trade.

"But you will have to go through hostile Monacan territory to search for the route," I said.

"Truthfully, Joan, the Monacans are no more our enemy than the tribes of Powhatan, whom the Monacans hate. It may be that the Monacans will actually help us in order to get back at Powhatan."

I had not thought of that.

"One troubling aspect remains, however," Will said thoughtfully. "Some natives claim that between us and the South Sea lie deserts and tall mountain ranges, the likes of which they themselves have not explored. Still, how far can it be? That is something we shall attempt to find out."

Deserts? Mountains? Exactly how vast was this country of Virginia, anyway, I wondered. What lay in the lands beyond the falls?

Several weeks after Will departed, we received a disturbing report. The Queen of the Appomattocs, with an eerily similar technique to Gates's at Kecoughtan, had lured fifteen men traveling to the falls with an invitation to feast and make merry. The foolish men went, and the Indians killed all but one. Ironically, it was the taborer Dowse who survived, the very one who had lured the Kecoughtans out by dancing. He used the rudder of the boat as a shield to fend off the arrows and made his way back to the other men, including Will, who was safe. Unfortunately for our efforts to build commodities, all of the Company's miners were killed in this incident.

For us in James Town, winter arrived and I felt an irrational fear, a rising terror. It was as though my mind had blocked much of the suffering, but somewhere in a hidden and cobwebbed corner, it knew. I knew. I remembered even as I thought I had forgotten. I knew logically that we would not starve and suffer as before, but I kept seeing quick images...the ghastly faces, the bodies dragged out of homes, the burial pit. Tempie too feared the oncoming cold, although we knew it was a new season, a new year, new leadership. The words came easy, but the waiting and holding on did not.

Fortunately, since our health had for the most part returned, we received Company duties. We passed the winter stitching shirts for the company, diverting ourselves that we might not remember the previous winter. Janey too began to plump up, and before I knew it, she was gaining apples in her cheeks again. *Now if only I knew how Cecily fared*, I thought wistfully, as I pumped the spinning wheel and ran the thread.

Gently, spring returned. With the break in the cold came a few blooming flowers and budding trees. Birds appeared, and all the wild creatures grew more active. We saw the occasional fox or raccoon, and the squirrels chased one another in seeming delight of the warm weather.

"I never found him, you know," Tempie said one day with a mischievous expression.

"Found who?" I asked, puzzled.

"My little friend that pointed me the berries that have left my stomach unsettled ever since! I still do desire me a squirrel pie made of him!"

"Fine for you!" I said, with mock seriousness. "I shall keep with wild strawberries or potatoes in my pies now that the Starving Time is past, thank you." Even our laughter was lighter, less bitter than it had been for many months.

269

We had stayed relatively well, as had Captain Tucker, George Percy, the Laydons, and Walter, who occasionally checked in on us to see if we needed anything.

"Well seasoned we are!" Tempie said to me, imitating Annie Laydon.

Many, however, were not as fortunate. The death tally had risen over the winter so that by March, nearly a third of all the adventurers had again perished. Of our 360 settlers, we now had perhaps only 170 remaining.

George and Will returned in the middle of March, after a miserable experience at the falls.

"We have a clearer conception now of what the Governor's brother suffered when he led the expedition at that fort last fall," George said. "We endured much and accomplished little, to paraphrase the Governor, through relentless, sporadic attacks."

"Besides his continuing illness and the deaths of soldiers, our Governor has suffered loss of a more personal nature as well," Will said. "The Indians slaughtered his nephew, Captain William West, during our stay. The natives took a sailor and boy prisoners. These braves were a cruel sort—they taunted as they killed," Will went on. "They derided us for crying out when we were tortured or even *saw* torture. They created songs with each slaughtered man's name and the weapon of his they desired, the reason for his death."

"They might steal his hatchet—they call it a *tamahuck*—or his bright sword, a *monnacoc,*" George explained to Tempie and me.

Will continued, "They call the English *Tassantassa*, and our firearms are *pocosacks*. They alter each verse to include the name of the soldier and his weapon." As he sang, the words and the brutality they signified gave me goose prickles:

> *Mattanerew shashashewaw erowango pechecoma*
> *Whe Tassantassa inoshashaw yehockan pocosack*
> *Whe, whe, yah, ha, ha, ne, he, wittowa, wittowa*

"Who can ever forget that chant?" Will looked at George, a troubled expression on his face.

"I never shall," George said with weary eyes. It had been a long trip home after a fruitless winter.

Perhaps the only good news the men heard in James Town was that some of George Percy's men had managed to kill the Paspahegh's *werowance*. *Paspahegh* meant *stranger* in the language of the Powhatan. The strangers now abandoned their home territory for all time.

At the end of March, Governor De La Warr's condition had deteriorated such that Doctor Bohun advised him to sail to the Bahamian Sea to recover his health. He had tried bleeding him, but the Governor's condition had not improved. Perhaps, Dr. Bohun suggested, the healing natural baths on the island of Nevis would cure him.

I wonder does My Lord La Warr think this is God's retribution on him for vanity and idleness, now that he has lived it as we have, I thought. Then I corrected myself. He had not actually *starved,* as we had. And we had not had doctors or island baths. *God forgive me,* I added hastily.

He set sail with his doctor and a company of fifty soldiers. Later we learned that ill winds had forced his bark, the *De La Warr,* on to England. This was a rather embarrassing homecoming for the Governor, one he would have to explain to the Virginia Company—much in contrast to Gates's arrival as a hero. However, to De La Warr's credit, James Town was certainly more sharply run and cleaner since his arrival and with the enforcement of Gates's martial laws. De La Warr himself was one of the Company's primary stockholders, and he had done a considerable amount to reverse its fortunes.

De La Warr left George Percy in charge as Deputy Governor, but only until Sir Thomas Dale could arrive to fill that position. We expected Dale by ship within a month or two, and Captain Adams returned in a familiar ship, the *Blessing,* to confirm that.

One morning early in April, Tempie was preparing our meal while Janey nestled on my lap with a thumb in her mouth. Suddenly, triumphant war screams rang eerily across the woods and marshes, echoing over the *pallisado* walls, the chant of what could only have been hundreds of warriors. Instinctively, at the first chilling cries, Janey buried her head in my shoulder and squeezed her eyes shut. I wrapped my arms protectively about her. She did not ask; she knew it was Indians. My pulse quickened as I heard Percy ordering troops out.

Tempie looked at me, alarmed. "I believe the shouts come from near the blockhouse."

The thought on both our minds—had they overrun the blockhouse? Were the sounds growing closer or farther away?

"Paspahegh! Paspahegh!" It echoed away into the still morning air, growing fainter as it did so. *"Paspahegh! Paspahegh!"*

Fainter, but leaving a handful of soldiers stationed at the blockhouse dead in its wake. Retribution for the killing of their *werowance,* their Queen, and her children.

The six hundred braves had fired so many arrows that the ground about the bodies lay littered in them—leaving no doubt that if the warriors had felt they could have taken us all, they would have.

"Paspahegh! Paspahegh!" Fainter and fainter.

Taking a deep breath and still trembling, we began eating our oatmeal. So began another day at James Town.

On May 19, a flotilla of three ships appeared in our river. I knew these would not bring Cecily, but their presence meant Gates had arrived safely back in England and sent Governor Dale here.

The three ships, once landed, brought three hundred new settlers—but most compelling to me were the letters they carried. Distance and circumstance had deprived us of news from England for so long.

"Mistress Joan Peirce," called the soldier delivering parcels. The young handwriting had to be…. I ripped it open, as Tempie looked over my shoulder.

> *Dear Mother,*
>
> *Lady Gates brings me your letter and happy news of your survival. Praise God, I knew He heard me as I prayed for you, my father, and little Janey each day and night you were away. I prayed all through the long winter, thinking you might be cold, you might be hungry, you might be sick. I prayed God spare you misery and preserve you, and then I touched my scallop shell and reminded myself you had promised we would be together again. I thought of St. James with his pilgrimage, and you with yours. I knew God heard me. I trusted Him always. Now I hear...*

I was reading the letter aloud, but at last, I could not dam the tears, so I handed it to Tempie and she read to us both.

> *...Now I hear you all three have survived, despite the Starving Time, despite the hurricane and the shipwreck. For nearly a year, we believed Father lost at sea with Governor Gates. How wondrous to hear the news from Lady Gates herself that this was not so! She said my father was an able Captain to her husband in the Bermudas, and that I should be proud of both you and Janey. She called your survival noble.*
>
> *Lady Gates said we shall depart here in several months, as I am to be an adventurer now too! Her daughters Margaret and Elizabeth were most gentle and kind.*
>
> *By the time this reaches you, I shall be at sea in their charge.*

I have much to tell you, but mostly that I have applied myself to my tutoring these nearly two years, hoping to make you and my father proud, and am in fine, strong, sound health. Thanks be to God for that and His many blessings.

I send my best love and kisses to Janey. How I have missed her warmth beside me at night, her sweetness and her giggles. I pray she has not suffered overmuch.

Pray me safely to Virginia, Mother. Pray me Godspeed. I will be courageous as you and my sister have been. I will make you proud. If it pleases God, we shall be together soon. Have your half of the shell waiting, Mother, and I shall have mine. We will make them whole once more.

While I am at sea, I shall not fear. This is my opportunity to adventure in Virginia, my own journey for which I have longed. As a tide washed our scallop ashore in Melcombe two years ago, watch for the tide that shall carry me to you.

I remain your loving daughter,
Cecily

"She is a bold one, that," Tempie murmured.

I nodded, touching the scallop badge beneath my kirtle. My little shell—not so little any more—was now at sea.

All my life I had been a doer, one who could weed the garden, grind the herbs, make everything right again just as soon as hard work could accomplish it. Well, not all the time. I thought of my little son's wrenching death, and how I felt I had failed him. The stilling of Maggie's sweet voice for want of nourishment, nourishment I could dream of but not provide. I remembered how I could not dissuade my father from his ship, so sure we could prevent his drowning— but no, because *he understood what I had not.* It was never meant that he avoid what lay before him. He must go about his days, making the best of them even while waiting for God to clear his path, to find the next milestone, and the next. How much of that path involved waiting—not doing, not fixing—I now understood. Waiting until one's stock of patience depleted, and then waiting more. And when that were done, waiting yet longer. Enduring beyond all reason. Only then came the miracle, if Providence deigned it. *Knowing this, that the trying of your faith worketh patience.* I saw at once that I had attempted to carry a yoke never meant for my scrawny neck, a yoke that fit the hand of God like a ring.

"Is it all about patience, Tempie?" I asked her suddenly. "Is that what all of faith is? You cast your lot into God's hand—and then you watch the river. You do not bring the ships here; you cannot. You only pray the hand of God will, and the rest is not your worry and never has been."

Tempie nodded, her eyes on the water. "I believe you have found an answer. I believe that is so. Your waiting, Joan, is nearly over. Soon, as your daughter says. Soon your days of watching the river—this time—will be over."

Like a fragile scallop shell, traveling miles upon miles through the ocean—at the mercy of every current and tide—yet by some miracle it lands unbroken on a shore, and a hapless woman like me picks it up. What preserves it? What keeps it whole? It survives its journey, its pilgrimage, and somehow, we had too.

Epilogue:
The Evening of a Well-Spent Life
August 1649

The evening of a well-spent life brings its own lamps with it.
~ Joseph Joubert

Such a pilgrimage were sweet.
~ John Donne

Now the evening shadows draw around us, and my visitor takes another sip of brandy. We have spent the better part after suppertime talking, while the servants tidy the kitchen. The dusk falls warmly, as it does here in Virginia in summer, and as it grows deeper, the buzzing bugs pitch louder, playing their own soothing summer music for us. It was never so noisy, nor so humid, during summertime in England. Never were the forests so full as here.

"You don't miss England at all, then?" my visitor asks. No, I say, I don't. Not truly. Oh, it's true that England has its own quiet charm, the little villages and towns, but there is a different sort of charm here. The charm is in the expansiveness of it, the purity of the land itself. From where we sit, I can see acres and acres of corn, about the height of a boy now. In another month, it will be ready to harvest. The tobacco leaves are broad-rimmed and growing to the left of the corn and behind it. The quiet shushing of the river reminds me it is nearby, too.

Tobacco, and land, has made us wealthy. We lived our dream and, God alone knows how, but by His grace, it worked. *Press on*, I had thought so long ago, *press on*. We had.

I smile at the irony of being an original planter—planter of a plantation, planter of a colony—when planting has always been my first love and it was my love of plants that kept me alive during that Starving Time. I am indeed an *ancient planter*.

"And Tempie?" my visitor asks, drawing another sip and looking at me as she does. "She died some time ago, as I recall. I was but a young girl."

Tempie. At the name, my eyes flood with tears, for I can never forget her. Who would have thought so many years, so many events, so many changes wrought by the growth of our own beloved colony could yet leave me with such fond memories of her.

In fact, since her death I have never been able to mention her name without tears.

"I'm sorry, Mistress Peirce," my visitor is quick to say. "I did not mean to upset you."

"I am not upset," I say. "You are only bringing to mind the loss of the closest friend I ever had, the friend of my heart. It is right to remember her." Thoughts of Tempie flood my mind and I see us there, toasting with Chinese wine cups, laughing even while we starved. Did we truly laugh? I know we did.

"She passed on in 1628," I say matter-of-factly, but my words catch on the year. She was but 38. George died the year before, and she married briefly Sir Francis West, the young Captain whose crew mutinied on him during the Starving Time. At the time of their marriage, West was the Governor. The risk this courageous young woman took paid handsomely: the wife of two Governors, with Sir George eventually becoming a knight and the wealthiest man in Virginia. Once she regained her health from the Starving Time, she bore three lovely children who survived. Like me, something drew her to stay. It was not wealth, nor land, but something about the place—Virginia—something that gets in your blood and will not leave it. Something that draws you back to it, even when you visit England, as Will and I did in 1629. You find yourself saying, "I must get home," and it is not Dorset you mean.

England was such to an Englishman who traveled elsewhere, but most Englishmen who traveled here found that same something here, too. I expect my grandchildren and my great-grandchildren will never know England but will think of themselves as Virginians only. Considering Cromwell's men beheaded King Charles in January of this year, Virginia is perhaps more devoted to the thought of the former king than is England herself.

"And Janey? She married John Rolfe after his second wife, the Princess Pocahontas, died. Is that not so?"

I nod. "Yes, it is so. Jane adopted two orphans after the massacre and bore two children, Elizabeth and John." My eyes mist again. My granddaughter Elizabeth did not live out her fifteenth year. And could Sarah Rolfe have known that her death would precipitate the longest peace we have yet known between the natives, when her husband John married Pocahontas. It was during this time we established ourselves as a colony and our roots spread and grew deep. I had wondered why God took Sarah early, but, alas, He had a reason after all.

My kind visitor interrupts my thoughts as she asks, "And Cecily? How did she fare? How was her journey?"

"Cecily had her own captivating story, too long to relay here as evening shadows creep in. But, do you know, we still have those scallop shells?" I smile. They are our family's own treasure, a memory of a long ago promise, a little girl—and faith.

In the falling twilight, my eyes sweep the corn, the mulberry trees—and the river. Always, the river. I am amused that I own an island as my grandmother Thickpenny and ancient grandmother Godgifu did. Will and I built Mulberry Island's first church, at Bakers Neck in 1627—and it is there, in the rich Virginia soil that I shall be buried, next to Will. God make it so.

Will has been gone these two years now, yet we were married forty-five years, an unheard of amount of time in wilderness Virginia. God spared us not tragedy but somehow preserved us through it, as He had promised. *Whole will I keep thee and thy family.*

Will had gone on to become Captain of the Governor's Guard, Commander of James Town, and even Lieutenant Governor of Virginia—days well past now. Most of his later years he spent in the Virginia Legislature and as caretaker of our lands and of our exports to England. He was active in the last great Indian campaign five years ago—always the soldier, even at sixty-four.

Now I begin to tire, not able to hold the conversation as sustained as I might have in my youth. "May we retreat indoors?" I ask.

My visitor nods graciously. "Of course."

I stand, and my hip creaks. Nearly seventy! But I still walk unaided, giving up my cane after the Starving Time. I cast it down and never came back for it. By my leave, I think gardening has kept me young.

The mosquitoes are coming out in little regiments now, but also the joyous lightning bugs. They give light to the music of the croakers and the frogs, and we have our own Virginia theatrics. It is not the Globe Theatre, to be sure, but it is relaxing, and, most of all, it *is* home.

Looking up, I see the moon is out now, and the stars. A bright one dominates the rest. "See there? The pole star, *Stella Maris*, the mariners star," I say, and my guest cranes her neck upward.

"So it is."

And around it, the entire Virginia sky is strewn with stars, from the river to the forest, across our corn and tobacco and beyond to the river.

Compostela. Field of stars.

I reach around my neck, and feel it. It is still there, still heavy, but I am used to it now. The pilgrim's badge. I wonder at my old grandfather who retrieved it on a journey so long ago. He could never have imagined it would ride to a New World, carrying its strange message with it.

I remember my father's vision: the winding journey I would take, my life as pilgrimage. *Indeed,* I think. Winding—and up hills and down riverbanks, and 'cross oceans, and here am I. An old Virginian, an ancient planter. *There are many ways to be a pilgrim,* he had said.

Yes.

The door shuts gently behind us, the lamps just lit for eventide, and I can hear my grandson playing his fiddle, a lively tune. It drifts into the night around us, softly and away, like the river, and I think, *this is why I came, and I knew it not.*

Author's Note:
What's Fact, What's Fiction?

In this book, historical and genealogical accuracy was my primary aim. I tried to understand the adventurers as *people* first, by tracing their family trees and migration patterns. The records are scant, but by mixing, matching, and cross-referencing, I drew certain conclusions in a "connect-the-dots" kind of way. Using old records, letters, and genealogies, I attempted to learn as much as possible about the background, tastes, and personalities of those who actually lived.

I have *not* played fast and loose with the facts. These people were real and, despite their flaws, they remain the earliest heroes and heroines of our country. The more I read, the more astounded I became by the raw courage of these men, women, and children. I was careful, therefore, not to malign any real people or create aberrant story lines except where the records indicated such events might likely have happened. It would be unfair and, worse, disrespectful to create wild story lines unless there was some basis in fact. In my opinion, deviating too far from known facts is unfair to those no longer alive to defend themselves.

In matters of religious convictions, I incorporated the predominant beliefs of those who settled Virginia—that is, Anglican. Virginia was *officially* under the Church of England (Anglican), although there were some who leaned toward other Protestant theologies such as Calvinism (John Rolfe, for example). A few held beliefs that were more Puritan. In fact, the Reverend Meese was known to be "too Puritan" for the tastes of most colonists in Virginia during his tenure of the Starving Time. However, church was important to the Virginia colonists. The Charters as well as *The Laws Divine Morall and Martiall* mandated church attendance at an Anglican service. The Charters and the King strictly forbid Catholicism in Virginia.

I tried to let the facts speak for themselves, making what I considered reasonable assumptions where facts were missing.

279

Real History, Real Politics, Real Timelines

The political leaders—both English and native—their personalities, biographies, and actions are based on fact. The history, timeline, and events are also factual, as are the genealogies. The hurricane, Indian wars, Starving Time, and the backdrop of events all happened. All of the Governors, Presidents, and Captains were real and the actions I wrote about, for the most part, I based on eyewitness accounts.

The Native American words used in this book are also authentic—at least, as authentic as they can be, considering they come to us from Englishmen of the time who copied down the sounds they heard. The Powhatans had no written language, so, sadly and ironically, most of what we know of the language is filtered through the English. William Strachey and John Smith kept vocabulary lists that are our best resources today. Tom Savage and Henry Spelman were fluent speakers, but if they penned such documents, they have not surfaced. Strachey was present at West's fort, and noted the chants used by the local Powhatan tribe included in the story.

Other Real People – The Cast of Characters

I remained as true to the life histories of these people as possible based on the research I uncovered. I have often used nicknames, such as Tempie for Temperance, because nicknames were popular during the time. The following people really lived:

REAL PEOPLE	RELATIONSHIP TO JOAN
Joan Phippen Peirce	
Thomas (Tom) Reynolds	1st husband (first name not definite)
William (Will) Peirce	2nd husband and second cousin to Joan's father
Cecily Reynolds Jane (Janey) Peirce	Daughters
William Phippen Jane Jordaine Phippen	Parents
Latatia (Lattie) Phippen	Stepmother
John (Jack) Phippen Robert (Robin) Phippen Thomas (Tom) Phippen	Brothers
John Thickpenny Anne Thickpenny	Grandparents
Henry Fitzpen Alice Peirse Fitzpen	Great-grandparents
Joanna Malet Lord William Malet Godgifu (Lady Godiva)	Other ancestors
Samuel (Sam) Jordan	First cousin
Silvester Jourdain	Distant cousin
George Yeardley Temperance Flowerdieu Yeardley	Friends
Sarah Rolfe John Rolfe	Friends
Anne (Annie) Laydon John (Jack) Laydon Virginia (Ginny) Laydon	Friends

[A note to genealogists: I apologize for the lack of sources, which would have been too cumbersome to notate and beyond the scope of this book.]

Who Was Fictitious?

The death of Joan's young son due to plague is somewhat fictitious. There *was* an outbreak of plague in 1603, and baby Jack represents the many children's graves that mothers left behind when they ventured to the New World.

Some sources indicate the Peirces may have had a young son named William who died in England, but I could not locate any records to confirm this. However, in allowing "Joan" to write her story, I found myself writing about how hard it was for her to leave "my mother's *and infant son's* graves behind." I was surprised! Until then, I had not written *anything* about an infant son, but my instinct told me he was indeed there and belonged in the story. I chose the name Jack rather than Will because of the confusion of having two characters named Will.

Harrison (Sailor), *Walter (soldier)*, and ***Grace and Humphrey Fleetwood*** were fictitious, although they represent the many unnamed mariners and adventurers whose stories we will never know. Some, like Walter, may have survived the Starving Time, but unless they lived fifteen years more until the 1625 muster or are mentioned in other records, their names are lost. Their contributions remain significant, however, and unfortunately we will probably never know the names of most.

Maggie Deal and ***Elizabeth Mayhew*** are fictitious but represent all those women whose names and stories are lost to time. Only men signed the Second Charter, and even that document only tells us who invested and not necessarily who *adventured*. We do know that women and children came, thanks to records like Captain Gabriel Archer's letter of his journey on the *Blessing* where he mentions the forty women and children. Also, William Strachey, writing about the *Sea Venture*, makes clear that of the 150 passengers, 140 men bailed for days "excluding women." That may indicate that ten women and children were on the *Sea Venture*. Only the few women fortunate enough to survive until 1625, like Joan, Temperance, and Janey, received mention in the 1625 muster.

Maggie's character emerged because Joan and daughter Janey are the only names surviving of the forty women and children's onboard the *Blessing*. I feel that, traveling alone for ten weeks, Joan no doubt befriended at least one other woman, who may also have been traveling alone. That these two women would have remained friends at Jamestown makes sense to me.

Having no record of so many women means their courage, their dreams, and their struggles are lost to us. And yet their contributions are not. Maggie is a candle I have lit in honor of those women and children who gave their lives to the adventure and were buried in unmarked graves, unmourned and unremembered. I feel very strongly they have not received their due. I offer the character of Maggie in honor of their sacrifices. Her presence is very real to me.

Interweaving Fact and Fiction

Joan, Temperance, Anne Laydon (and Thomasine Causey, not featured in this book) are unique because they survived until the 1625 muster, therefore their names come down to us today. This is the only census after the 1609-1610 Starving Time, so no doubt there were other women who survived the Starving Time who later died or returned to England, prior to the 1625 muster. There was a "List of the Living and Dead in Virginia" after the 1622 Indian massacre, but the best details are in the 1625 muster.

A majority of the women present during the Starving Time undoubtedly died during that time. Approximately 430 of 490 settlers died, according to John Smith's figures. It seems only fair to recognize those women whose names we do not know—and probably never will know—who did not make it through that horrible period. We can assume that some, like Maggie, showed tremendous courage, while others, like Elizabeth, were not too happy about their situation. In any event, Elizabeth and Maggie represent a cross-section of those women. Sadly, their names and stories are lost, but I hope this book has in some way paid tribute to all of them.

I studied time lines and events carefully. We know, for example, that Anne Laydon was the only woman at the fort (assuming Mistress Forrest died early on) for close to ten months. We also know Pocahontas's visits to the fort ceased around March 1609, when her father the *Werowance* Powhatan, moved to Orapax. Scholars believe he probably would not have allowed his daughter to visit the fort after that time—first, because of the distance and second, because she would have been a prime candidate for kidnapping. Therefore, Anne Laydon and Mistress Forrest were probably the only two Englishwomen to have met her until the English kidnapped Pocahontas and brought her to Jamestown in 1612. Anne and Pocahontas were similar ages; Anne was probably a year or two older.

Anne Laydon, a married, pregnant fifteen year old, would have needed women to help her through childbirth since this was the task of women. The new female arrivals were no doubt a great relief to Anne.

We know from the records that Joan was "an honest industrious woman" (according to John Smith's *General Historie*). She was later noted for the figs she grew at Mulberry Island, some of the earliest and finest figs in the country. She probably also had an interest in silk production, as silk came from silkworms devouring mulberry leaves, prolific on Mulberry Island. Her industry coupled with her knowledge of plants suggests a reason to me why she and her daughter survived.

Were Joan and Temperance Really Friends?

There is no definite proof of this but much circumstantial evidence. Cecily named her daughter Temperance, an unusual name for the times. Also, Joan and Temperance lived across the swamp from one another at Jamestown after the Starving Time until the end of Temperance's life. There is evidence that George Yeardley was considering buying land at Mulberry Island about the time of his death. Also, as two *Sea Venture* "widows," they may have bonded over that misfortune. Both of their husbands were soldiers and apparently comrades in the Netherlands as well.

Could Joan and Temperance Have Been at Point Comfort?

They could have been, but it makes sense to me that "widows" would have stayed at the main fort, closer in. I also chose to use the harsher setting of Jamestown because I feel on the *chance* they were at the fort, this accomplishment should not be underplayed. If there is definite proof linking them to one location or the other, I have not been seen it.

Did Joan and William Have Other Children?

There is some possibility that besides having a son William who died as a toddler, they may have had another son named Thomas. The naming pattern of

284

William and Thomas amongst this branch of the Peirce family is very predominant. This son Thomas would probably have been born around 1607, coming to Virginia with them in 1609. He may have returned to England to obtain his education, a common practice among the sons of the more well-to-do men, which could explain his absence in the 1625 muster. Thomas may have stayed in England to obtain military experience like his father. The first record we can find of him is when a Thomas Peirce, living at Mulberry Island, appears in the Virginia records in the 1660s with grown children. It is impossible to say whether this was William's son. However, Thomas Peirce's son-in-law Thomas Iken did dwell in the house formerly belonging to Captain William Peirce after William Peirce's death. This suggests a strong family connection.

When William testified in England in 1637, he petitioned to return to Virginia and mentioned his "children," so obviously more than one child was alive at that time. Unfortunately, he did not list their names.

Were Temperance and George Married When She Arrived in Virginia?

I spent many weeks researching this question, as it was so central to the story. Although many second-hand sources refer to them as being married in "1613 in Virginia" or "1618 in England," I ultimately discarded both of these as incorrect. I concluded they were married in 1608 or 1609 in England for the following reasons:

1. It is unlikely that a woman of Temperance's station would have come to Virginia unmarried as some servants did.
2. It is possible that she had a husband before George, but there is nothing to document this.
3. An obscure letter from her cousin George Pory states that his "relative Temperance" married George Yeardley *in England.*
4. In a letter written while he was in England in 1618, George thanks someone for entertaining him and his wife. I believe this is where the misconception originated that they were married in 1618. The letter does *not* say they were just married.
5. Temperance arrived on the *Falcon* in 1609 (according to the 1625 muster).
6. George Yeardley was in Virginia from 1610 until 1617.

7. One scholar concluded that Temperance's first child was born in 1615, and that the year (1619) listed in the muster was incorrect. The muster states that the child was born in Virginia. I believe this is where the misconception enters that the Yeardleys were "married around 1613 in Virginia."

Therefore, if they were married in *England,* if their first child was born in 1615 in Virginia, and if George was in Virginia from 1610 until 1617, it only follows that they were married before the ships sailed in 1609. I think it is plausible that Temperance had to recover her health from the Starving Time before she could bear children.

A frequent conclusion is that Temperance arrived unmarried in 1609 and soon "scurried back" to England, then married George Yeardley on his return trip to England in 1618 after the King knighted him. There is a subtle (or sometimes not-so-subtle) implication in this conclusion that Virginia was not good enough for Temperance unless she had a knight at her side. Studying the extant facts, I believe this is grossly unfair to her, as she apparently was a Virginian from 1609 onward, even after the horrific Starving Time. This, to me, indicates extreme fortitude.

Where Are the Peirces and Yeardleys Buried?

Although the knight's tomb at Jamestown Church is missing its inscription, many believe this is George Yeardley's grave. After George's death during his second term as Governor, Temperance married Francis West, who succeeded George as Governor. Temperance died within a year of that marriage. I believe she would have been buried near George at the church in Jamestown.

As for the Peirces, I suspect they are probably buried on Mulberry Island. In 1627, William Peirce paid for a church to be built at Mulberry Island near his property, according to some sources. Had the church not been so near his home, I believe the Peirces would have been buried at their plantation, as was common practice at the time. However, due to the church's proximity to their home, they probably selected a church burial. This church no longer stands, and the Federal Government has owned most of Mulberry Island since 1918. Fort Eustis is located there today.

In Tribute to the Long-Term Survivors
of the First Jamestown Adventurers

GROUP	ARRIVE JAMES TOWN	SHIP	# to ARRIVE	NOTES
Initial 3 Ships	May 1607	Susan Constant Godspeed Discovery	105	There were 144 men on the ship, but only 105 were left behind at Jamestown.
1st Supply	April 1608	John & Francis	120	
	July 1608	Phoenix		
2nd Supply	Sept 1608	Mary & Margaret	70	Including Mistress Forrest & her maid Anne Burras, first women.
3rd Supply	--	(Sea Venture -lost)	290-420 (est.)	Passengers included perhaps 100 women & children. The *Sea Venture*, with 150 passengers, did not arrive with other ships & ketch was lost in the hurricane.
	--	(A ketch – lost)		
	Aug 1609	Falcon		
	Aug 1609	Unity		
	Aug 1609	Lion		
	Aug 1609	Blessing		
	Aug 1609	Diamond		
	Aug 1609	Swallow		
	Oct. 1609	Virginia		
Total to arrive by October 1609			**585-715**	

When I study the dusty old records, now computerized, I am astounded.

Can it really be that so few of the men, women, and children who arrived during the first years of Jamestown, from 1607 to 1609, survived 15 years later?

287

It is a story in itself.

Altogether, by October 1609, approximately 600 to 700 adventurers had come to Virginia with high hopes of making Jamestown home. Of these, about 490 still survived in October 1609, just prior to the onset of the Starving Time, according to John Smith.

The winter of 1609 to 1610 would wipe out most of those who had not already perished, leaving only 60 gaunt survivors when help arrived in May and June 1610.

Some researchers question the figure of 60 survivors, feeling it does not take into account those living at Point Comfort. I disagree, for these reasons:

1. All primary documents refer to 60 ("three score") survivors being present upon arrival of the *Patience* and *Deliverance* from Bermuda. (Percy, Strachey, Jourdain, Smith.)

2. Percy would have been motivated to show as many survivors as possible, since he was President and very troubled by the large number of deaths.

3. All the writers were investors. Bad news is bad news in terms of investments, so they had no reason to make the scenario appear worse than it actually was. I believe they gave the highest possible number of survivors in the colony.

4. It is unlikely that all the writers "forgot," overlooked, or failed to include the Point Comfort survivors.

5. The figure most relevant to the Virginia Company would be the total number of those alive. Where the settlers were living was less important to them than the total count.

6. It is true that Percy sent 30 to Point Comfort in the fall, but while not starving, they were unlikely to be bursting with health. It would not be surprising if half of those settlers died over the winter. Illness and Indian attack, not just starvation, were a huge factor for all.

7. Silvester Jourdain, an unbiased but reliable reporter of the events from the hurricane through De La Warr's arrival, corroborates the fact that there were about 60 Starving Time survivors plus 150 from Bermuda. He gives the number "of all those people that were living being in number two hundred persons."

Silvester Jourdain's account (original spelling):

"...At James towne...wee found some threescore persons living. And...some three weeks passed, and **not hearing of any supply,** it was thought fitting by a generall cosent, to use the best means for the preservation of **all those people that were living, being al in number two hundred persons.** And so upon the eight of June one thousand six hundred and ten, wee imbarked at James Towne, **not having above fourteene dayes victuall,** and so were determined to direct our course for New-found-land, there to refresh us, and supply our selves with victuall, to bring us home; but it pleased God to dispose otherwise of us, and to give us better meanes. **For being all of us shipped in foure pinnaces,** and departed from the towne, almost downe halfe the River, we met My Lord de la Warre comming up with three ships, wel furnished with victuall, which revived all the company, and gave them great content."

Calculating Jourdain's Population Figure, June 1610

"All those people that were living, being al in number 200 persons"

Starving Time Survivors	60
Sea Venture castaways	150
Sent from Bermuda to Virginia in a long boat (lost)	-7
Executed in Bermuda	-1
Left on Bermuda to hold island for England	-2
Starving Time survivors dying once Gates arrived (est.)	-3
Total number of persons Gates must feed, June 1610	**197**

Nowhere do any of the sources indicate the leaders planned to transport *all but* the Point Comfort survivors or that they planned to leave *anyone* behind. The actual breakdown of the portion of the 60 survivors at Point Comfort and at Jamestown remains conjecture. We can only know that there were no more than 30 at Point Comfort, as that was the original number sent in the fall. We also

289

know that, without famine, a much higher ratio of those at Point Comfort survived than at Jamestown.

Assuming, then, that 60 settlers survived the Starving Time, what became of them?

For the next twelve years, thousands more settlers, including the 150 surviving *Sea Venture* passengers, came into the somewhat stable colony.

However, in March 1622 the colony suffered another major setback, a massacre executed simultaneously on all the settlements up and down the James River. Thirty-five hundred more settlers perished that day, some of them from the original group of 600.

In the year following the massacre, many more settlers perished from famine due to the interruption of the spring planting. The injured and grieving were in little position to plant, and the Governor called most back to the main fort at Jamestown.

Added to that was severe illness sweeping the colony the same year. The misery would be unbelievable to us today. In December 1622, a ship landed carrying what some said was plague. Others blamed a man called Dupper and his "stinking beere." To these occurrences, many massacre survivors fell.

In January 1625 (listed as 1624 in Old Style Calendar), the alarmed Virginia Company had a colony-wide muster taken. Today, this muster provides us a snapshot of the colony during that month.

I studied the muster and attempted to account for errors (such as John Laydon's arrival in "1606"—no one arrived before 1607). Another error, for example, was the listing of a few passengers on the *Starr* as arriving in 1608; the correct year was 1611 with Sir Thomas Gates.

Using the more conservative figure of 600 arrivals (instead of 700): Of the **original 600 who came by 1609**, 15 years later only **14** still survived or had not fled the colony, equaling only **2** of every **100** persons. While some did leave the colony when they could, the majority succumbed to famine, illness, or Indian attack.

In comparison, of the 150 *Sea Venture* passengers 11 survived and were residing in Virginia for the January 1625 muster (or 8 of every 100). This suggests the extremely harsh conditions in which the first 600 found themselves.

I compiled a list of the 14 survivors of the original 600 who had come by the time the Starving Time commenced in 1609. The accomplishment of these individuals, first living through the Starving Time, then having the fortitude to stay and hardiness to survive (including the devastating Indian massacre), remains as impressive today as it no doubt was then.

Of these 14, five are women. This is disproportionate to the small number of women who had actually come by 1609. Of those initial 600, there were no more than 92 women and girls. (The third supply included approximately 100 women and children, but it appears 10 were on the ill-fated *Sea Venture*.) So although only 15% of the initial 600 were women, 35% of the long-term survivors were women. Jane ("Janey") Pierce was the youngest, being only about five when she survived the Starving Time.

This book is my tribute to these 14 long-term survivors, and to the hundreds more who perished.

#	PLANTER	SHIP	Arrival Date	Age 1625	Residence at January 1625
Survivors from the Original 105 Settlers - arriving 1607					
1	John Dods (or Dodson)	*Susan Constant*	May 1607	36	Neck-of-Land, Charles City
2	John Laydon	*Susan Constant*	May 1607	44	Eliz. City, Eliz. City
Survivors from the First Supply – 120 Settlers - arriving 1608					
3	Thomas Savage	*John & Francis*	April 1608	36	Eastern Shore over the Bay, Eliz City
4	Nathaniel Cawsey	*Phoenix*	July 1608	–	Jordan's Journey, Charles City
Survivors from the Second Supply- 70 Settlers—arriving 1608					
5	Capt. Thomas Graves	*Mary & Margaret*	Sept 1608	~ 44	Eastern Shore over the Bay, Eliz City
6	Anne Laydon	*Mary & Margaret*	Sept 1608	30	Elizabeth City, Elizabeth City
7	Richard Taylor	*Mary & Margaret*	Sept 1608	50	Neck-of-Land, Charles City
Survivors from the Third Supply - approximately 350 arriving 1609					
8	Robert Partin	*Blessing*	Aug 1609	36	West & Shirley Hundred, Charles City
9	Thomasine Cawsey	*Lion*	Aug 1609	–	Jordan's Journey, Charles City
10	Edward Barkley	*Unity*	Aug 1609	–	Hog Island, Jas. Cty
11	John Powell	*Swallow*	Aug 1609	29	Eliz.City, Eliz.City
12	Temperance Yeardley	*Falcon*	Aug 1609	~ 34	James City, James City
13	Joane Peirce	*Blessing*	Aug 1609	~ 44	James City, Jas. City
14	Jane Peirce Rolfe Smith	*Blessing*	Aug 1609	~ 20	James City, James City

What Happened to the Survivors?

John Dods (or Dodson) came to Jamestown originally as a soldier and laborer in 1607 on the *Susan Constant*. One Dodson family tradition says he married an Iroquois, Jane Eagle Plume, daughter of Chief Eagle Plume. The 1625 muster lists him as 36 years old and his wife Jane as 40. Although his ship is given, no ship or year of arrival is listed for her, so perhaps the Iroquois family tradition has merit. (The nearest Iroquois to Jamestown were the Nottoway Indians, just west of Jamestown on the Nottoway River. They were not in the Algonquin Powhatan Confederacy.) John and Jane lived at Neck-of-Land in Charles City and reputedly had a son Jesse, born between 1620 and 1623.

John and Anne Burras Laydon, who lived in Elizabeth City, had four daughters on record in 1625: Virginia, Margrett, Katherin, and Alice. Virginia, born around Christmas 1609, was the first white child born at Jamestown. John received 200 acres by patent in Henrico, and patented an additional 1,250 acres with Anne's brother Anthony Burrows in 1636 in Warwick County. Some sources give John's date of death around 1650.

Thomas Savage, traded to the Powhatan Indians as a boy in January 1608, lived to adulthood and became an interpreter in colonial dealings between the natives and the colonists. A chief of the Eastern Shore granted him an estimated 9,000 acres, and here is where he made his home. His wife Anne, or Hannah, came on the *Sea Flower* in 1621. Thomas died sometime between 1631 and 1633. He has one son of record, John Savage, born around 1624.

Nathaniel and Thomasine Cawsey (or Causey) were living at Jordan's Journey when the 1622 Indian massacre occurred. The natives wounded Nathaniel badly. Yet, surrounded by Indians and despite his wound, he grabbed an ax and drove it into the skull of one so that the rest fled. In 1620, the Cawseys patented a 200-acre plantation, near Kimages Creek in Charles City, named Cawsey's Care. During 1623, Nathaniel was a member of the House of Burgesses from Cawsey's Care and Shirley's Hundred. John Smith reports in his *Travels of Captaine John Smith*, "Now the most I could understand in generall, was from the relation of Mr. Nathaniel Cawsey, that lived there with mee, and returned Anno Dom. 1627." The Cawseys apparently deeded their land holdings to their sons, Thomas and John, who came over around 1620.

Captain Thomas Graves, who started his adventures at Jamestown as a gentleman and not a Captain, apparently earned that rank over time. He was one of two representatives from Smythe's Hundred to the first Representative Legislative Assembly, which met in July 1619, and he later held other positions of prominence. By court records, it appears he died in the latter part of 1635. He lived on the Eastern Shore, near his friend **Thomas Savage**, who once saved his life at the hands of an Indian attacker.

Richard Taylor was fifty and living at Neck-of-Land in Charles City at the time of the muster. Some genealogists believe he died shortly after the muster was taken.

Robert Partin was about 21 when he arrived with Joan and Jane Peirce on the *Blessing*. He was 36 years old at the time of the muster, as was his wife Margrett, who arrived in 1619 on the *George*. At the time of the 1625 muster, their daughter Avis was five, Rebecca was two, and son Robert was four months old. As immigrant ancestor of the Partin and Parton family and given Virginia migration patterns, Robert Partin is *probably* an ancestor of musician Dolly Parton. In the story, Robert seemed a good choice to play his lute (similar to a guitar) on the *Blessing!*

Lieutenant Edward Barkley lived at Hog Island with Mrs. Jane Barkley and a daughter, also named Jane. There is no arrival information for his wife or daughter, or their ages. Lieutenant Barkley reportedly died sometime just after the 1625 muster.

John Powell was about 14 when he survived the Starving Time. He is believed to have died after 1638. The muster lists him along with his wife Kathren, 22, who had arrived on the *Flying Hart* in 1622. He had only one son, John, born at the time of the muster. Some sources list Richard, William, and Henry as probable younger sons. John and Kathren owned land in Elizabeth City, Virginia. His son John is probably Colonel John Powell, a Burgess from Elizabeth City in 1657.

Temperance ("Tempie") Flowerdieu Yeardley lived to bear two sons and a daughter in Virginia. Her husband, Sir George Yeardley, was Governor from 1619 to 1621. During his administration, the colonists held the first democratic governing body in the New World, the Virginia General Assembly, in 1619.

Connie Lapallo

Yeardley became Governor again in 1626. In his lifetime, George was the wealthiest man in Virginia. He also built the first windmill in the New World.

Following a brief marriage to Governor Sir Francis West, Temperance died in 1628, just one year after George's death. George is probably buried in the "knight's tomb" at Jamestown, inside the old church. We can believe Temperance lay there too. As the wife of two Governors, she had the honor of being Virginia's First Lady twice over.

Joan Phippen Peirce survived to perhaps as late as 1650.

By 1622, Joan and her husband William had two large tobacco plantations in conjunction with John Rolfe: one across the river from Jamestown and the other at Mulberry Island.

Joan, her daughter Jane, and Temperance Yeardley were neighbors in New Town on Jamestown Island, although the Peirces had significant holdings at Mulberry Island as well. According to *Virginia Carolorum*, the Yeardleys' home was an enclosure of seven acres, which abutted the river to the north. To the south was the home of "Janey," Jane Peirce Rolfe Smith, on four acres. From Jane's house, a bridge led across the marsh to the home of her parents, the Peirces.

During 1623, George Sandys, then Treasurer of the Colony, lived with the Peirces while he raised silkworms and completed his celebrated translation of Ovid's *Metamorphoses*. In April 1623, Sandys wrote to England of *"my own chamber at Lieut. Peirce's, the fairest in all Virginia."* All of the homes in New Town at that time were wooden structures.

In 1629 Joan and Will visited England. John Smith wrote of her: *"Mistress Pearce, a honest and industrious woman hath been there near twenty years, and now returned, saith she hath a garden at Jamestown containing three or four acres, where in one year she hath gathered near a hundred bushels of excellent figs and that she can keep a better house in Virginia for three or four hundred pounds than in London, yet went there with little or nothing."*

In 1641, Mr. Anthony Barham left Joan a bequest in his will. Barham, a former Burgess of Mulberry island, was married to Elizabeth, Joan's grandniece: *Mrs. Joane Pierce, wife of Mr. William Pierce, 50 shillings to make her a ring.*

Joan and Will had the distinction of being one of the few early Jamestown families where both husband and wife survived together. They were each close to 70 years old when they died, after being married for 40 to 45 years. Joan and Will lived to see their grandchildren born on Virginia soil.

Jane ("Janey") Peirce Rolfe Smith, the youngest arrival to have survived long term, married John Rolfe around 1619 after Pocahontas died. John Rolfe had a son, Thomas, by Pocahontas, and a daughter, Elizabeth, by Jane Peirce. Elizabeth was born in 1620 and died in 1635 at the age of 15.

After John Rolfe died in 1622, probably of disease following the Indian massacre, Jane married Captain Roger Smith and lived at James City near her parents and Temperance Yeardley. She took in two additional children, Sara Maycock and Elizabeth Salter, apparently orphaned in the Indian massacre. It appears Roger and Jane had a son, John Smith, who was born around 1625 (just after the muster). Their son John may have survived until 1674, marrying Hannah Daft.

It is unclear when Jane died or if she had any other children.

Jamestown Personalities

ARCHER, Gabriel **(c. 1575–1609/10)** — Archer, a Cambridge-educated lawyer, was a part of the 1602 exploration of what is today New England. In 1607, he arrived in the first expedition, but Indians wounded him before the ship even reached Jamestown. By 1608, Archer had returned to England. He sailed to Virginia once more in August 1609 as Master of the *Blessing*. No record exists of his death during the Starving Time, but it appears he perished then. He is not heard from, or of, after a letter he wrote home on August 31, 1609, describing his voyage on the *Blessing* and conditions in the settlement.

ARGALL, Sir Samuel **(1580–1626)** — History is mixed in its assessment of Argall. He pioneered the more direct route to Virginia and also well understood its fishing grounds. His kidnapping of Pocahontas, by enlisting her aunt and uncle to trade her for a large copper kettle, seems harsh. Yet Pocahontas's rejection by her father Powhatan, her embracing of the colonists' ways, and her marriage to tobacco pioneer John Rolfe, led to the long-term success of the colony. None of this would have happened without Argall.

DALE, Sir Thomas **(d. 1620)** — Apparently of lowborn status, Dale yet rose to heights in military circles prior to Jamestown that in those days (where privilege was everything) shows he must have had remarkable military ability. His strict, even harsh, enforcement of *The Laws Divine Moral and Martiall* was a positive turning point for the colony.

GATES, Sir Thomas **(c. 1559–1621)** — Gates traveled with Sir Francis Drake when Drake attacked Spanish settlements in the Caribbean and was also present at the rescue of the first Roanoke Island settlers in 1586. A veteran of the wars with the Spanish and in the Lowlands, Gates was a strong leader and a good organizer. He and Somers made a powerful team of naval and military prowess. His take-charge manner on Bermuda and at Jamestown demonstrates a phenomenal leader, particularly when coupled with compassion unusual for a 17th century military man.

MARTIN, John **(d.c. 1632)** — Martin was a commander under Sir Francis Drake and one of the seven original Councilors in April 1607. He returned to

296

England and then sailed back to Virginia in August 1609, finding himself at odds with Capt. John Smith. Both George Percy and John Smith refer to incidents where Martin seemed afraid to venture his own skin but left his men and others to venture theirs. Percy and Smith don't agree on many things, and both men support this assessment by naming actions Martin failed to take and excuses he gave which neither Smith nor Percy believed. Unfortunately, we do not have Martin's version of events. In 1616, Martin received one of the first permanent land grants, a vast tract of 4,500 acres on the south side of the James River. Here he founded Martin's Brandon Plantation, which held a special charter putting it outside of the Virginia Company's authority. Martin died in Virginia around 1632.

NEWPORT, Christopher (1565?–1617) — Newport's reputation as an expert mariner and privateer flowered when he brought in the *Madre de Dios*, the largest-ever Spanish prize, in 1592. With one arm lost to battle, Newport yet led the preliminary expedition to Jamestown in 1607. He also commanded the first three supply expeditions during 1608 and 1609. Newport was among those shipwrecked in Bermuda from 1609–1610 as part of the Third Supply. In 1611, he made his final voyage to Virginia when he commanded Sir Thomas Dale's three ships. The Virginia Company granted his widow lands, and his three sons subsequently lived in Virginia.

PERCY, George (1580–1632) — George Percy was the eighth and youngest son of the eighth Earl of Northumberland. He came to Virginia with the first colonizing expedition in 1607 and stayed until 1612. We tend to view him as weak due to his failures in leadership during the Starving Time, but this may not be fair. Percy was seriously ill during the fall and winter and stepped into the Presidency in an already volatile situation with the natives. He had planned to return to England in October 1609 due to poor health, but Smith's unexpected gunpowder accident thrust him into the Presidency instead. Although he did not care for John Smith, Percy appears to have been somewhat neutral in the battles between Archer, Martin, and Ratcliffe against Smith. All four men seemed to agree on Percy as the next president. Percy did many of the right things that critical fall of 1609, but he had poor luck and lacked imagination—critical factors in averting the oncoming siege and famine. His lack of knowledge of the food available at Point Comfort is perhaps his most glaring failure.

RATCLIFFE, John (alias Sicklemore) (157?–1609) — Why Ratcliffe used an alias remains unclear, but this charge surfaced at Jamestown. He was one of the seven original Councilors in May 1607. He served a one-year term as President of the Council from 1607 until 1608, handing his Presidency over to John Smith under duress from the Council. He returned to England in January 1609 but arrived in Virginia once more in August 1609, where he and John Smith, still President, clashed immediately. Around November 1609, the Indians ambushed and killed Ratcliffe on a trading expedition.

ROLFE, John (1585–1622) — John Rolfe was on the ill-fated *Sea Venture*, which shipwrecked on Bermuda. His first child was born and died on the island, and his first wife Sarah died soon after their 1610 arrival at Jamestown. A pious, industrious man, Rolfe's innovations in bringing Caribbean tobacco to Virginia to replace the bitter tobacco of the Powhatan peoples turned the Virginia economy around and gave it its first mass-marketable commodity. His love for and marriage to Indian princess Pocahontas—a wrenching decision based on his Calvinist beliefs about marriage to "heathens"—demonstrates a man who nonetheless acted on his conscience. By uniting the colonists and the natives, the Rolfe's marriage brought "the peace of Pocahontas" to the settlement until her death in 1617. Rolfe later married "Janey," Jane Peirce, the young daughter of Joan and William Peirce. Jane bore him a daughter, Elizabeth in 1620. Rolfe died soon after the 1622 massacre.

SMITH, John (1580–1631) — Arriving in 1607, Smith was one of the original seven Councilors. The son of a yeoman farmer, he quickly made enemies of the highborn members of Council—John Ratcliffe, John Martin, George Percy, Gabriel Archer and Edward Maria Wingfield. Was it because he spoke his mind, was highly egotistical, or both? His record of turning around the Jamestown settlement is hard to argue with, and his knowledge of the native peoples and their language served him well. Had Smith not been seriously injured and forced to return to England, there may not have been a Starving Time. Whether the injury was a true accident or an assassination attempt is unclear. Smith maintained that one of the other Captains—he did not name names—attempted to shoot him in his bed as he recovered from the gunpowder injury. The Captain, Smith said, lost his nerve or the gun misfired. However Smith was also "near bereft of his senses" from pain, so might it have been an hallucination? No one knows.

SOMERS, Admiral Sir George (1554–1610) — Somers became a knight in 1603 and a founder of the London Company. A naval hero and Admiral of the

Third Supply expedition, he was known as a "lamb on land and a lion at sea." His bravery during the hurricane shows why. He claimed Bermuda for England and died there from "a surfeit of pork" in the fall of 1610 in attempting to bring hogs back to Virginia to aid the colony's food supply. His nephew buried Somers' heart in Bermuda but returned his pickled body to England. However, Somers had requested his heart be in Bermuda but his body be interred in Virginia.

WEST, Francis (1586–1634) — Younger brother of Lord De La Warr. It appears he was the victim of mutiny with a shipload of corn at a crucial time just prior to the Starving Time. The loss of this corn and their best ship increased the colonists' famine and dimmed their hopes of survival. He returned to Virginia shortly thereafter and later became Governor upon the death of Sir George Yeardley in 1627.

WEST, Thomas, Lord De La Warr (1577–1618) — A strong leader, member of nobility, and pious man, health issues nonetheless prevented De La Warr from accomplishing all he would have liked at Jamestown. Still, his firm hand following the Starving Time and strict enforcement of the code of martial law enacted by Gates initiated the turnaround in Jamestown's fortunes.

YEARDLEY, Sir George (c. 1577–1627) — As Gates's right-hand man in battle at the Lowlands, Yeardley learned with the best. He was Captain of the Governor's Guard and later Governor. Yeardley was Governor during 1619, when adventurers patented their first land and the Virginia General Assembly met for the first time. His actions show him an ardent supporter of self-government and free enterprise. He was the wealthiest man in Virginia in his time, building the first windmill in the colony at Flowerdew Hundred. The Knight's Tomb at Jamestown Church may be his grave.

A Relation in Generall of the Present State of

His Majesties Colony in Virginia (1629)

By Capt. William Perse,

an antient planter of twenty yeares standing there

[This is fascinating in that these are Captain William Peirce's actual words and gives us insight into his voice and opinions. Captain Peirce apparently penned this on his return trip to England in 1629. I reproduce it here with his original spelling. Source: *Virginia Carolorum*, Edward D. Neill, originally obtained from the Public Record Office in London.]

First, for quantity ye people, men, women & children, there are to the number of between fower and five thousand English, being generally well housed in every plantation, most plantations being well stored with head cattle, as likewise with goates and swine in abundance, and great store of poultry, the land abounding all the year long with Deer and wilde Turkeyes, and the rivers in winter with many sortes of wilde fowle, and in summer with great variety of wholesome fishe.

And the soile is so fertile as by the industry of our people they may raise great crops of corne both Indian and English. Besides, all fruits, rootes, and herbes, out of England soe wonderfully prosper there.

The Colony under the favor of God, and of his Majesty hath bine raised to this heighth of people, and provisions especially by the means of Tobacco, by which also they must subsist for awhile untill by degrees they may fall upon more stable comodities, as upon salte, fishe, hempe for cordage, flaxe for linnen and others.

And as touching timber for building of ships of all sortes, and mastes I have heard many good Masters and Shipwrights affirm there can not be found better in all the worlde, the Countrey affourding also great quantity of pine trees for making of pitche & tarre, and so may in short time abound with all materials for building & rigging of ships.

For our defense against the natives every plantation is armed with convenient number of muskettiers to the number of two thousand shott, and upwards, but against a forrein enemy there is no manner of fortification (which is our greatest wante) wee of ourselves not beeing able to under take the chardge thereof.

As for the natives Sasapen is the chief, over all those people inhabiting upon the rivers next unto us, who hath been the prime movver of all them, that since the massacre have made war upon us. But nowe this last Somer, by his great importunity for himselfe, and the neighbouring Indians hee hath obtained a truce for the present, from the Gov'r and Councell of Virginia being forced to seeke it by our continuall incursions upon him, and them by yearley cutting down, and spoiling theire corne.

This being the summe of the present state of thinges in Virginia.

Virginia Indian Tribes

Native American tribes in Virginia fall primarily into three linguistic groups: **Algonquin, Siouxan,** and **Iroquoian.**

The tribes of eastern Virginia were for the most part **Algonquin.** In the central portion of the state, they were mostly **Siouxan. Iroquoian** tribes tended to be located more in the southern and western parts of the state.

Algonquin Tribes: The Powhatan Confederacy

There were about 35 Algonquin tribes surrounding Jamestown. These tribes, living in approximately 160 scattered villages throughout eastern Virginia, were all part of the confederacy of the great leader, or *mamanatowic*, whom the English called **Powhatan** but whose given name was **Wahunsonacock.** Powhatan himself was a member of the powerful Pamunkey tribe, which had recently conquered most of these tribes. These tribes paid tributes of corn to Powhatan while keeping their own *werowances*, or lesser chiefs. Powhatan referred to his empire as *Tsenacomoco*. John Smith estimated there were 3,000 bowmen and so perhaps the total native population was about 8,000 in these tribes.

The table includes the tribes mentioned most frequently in primary documents of the era.

Algonquin Tribes

Algonquin Tribes	Location
Accomac	Eastern Shore
Appomattock	On the Appomattox River
Arrohattoc	Henrico County
Chesapeake	Princess Anne County
Chickahominy	On Chickahominy River
Chiskiac (Kiskiack)	On York River
Kecoughtan	Elizabeth City County
Mattaponi	On Mattaponi River
Moraughtacund	On the Rappahannock River
Nansemond	Isle of Wight, Nansemond, Norfolk Co.
Pamunkey	King William County
Paspahegh	Charles City and James City Counties
Potomac	Stafford and King George Counties
Powhatan	Henrico County
Warraskoyak	Isle of Wight County
Weanoc	Charles City County
Werowocomoco	Gloucester County
Wicocomoco	Northumberland County
Youghtanund	on Pamunkey River

Iroquoian Tribes

Meherrin	On the Meherrin River
Nottoway or Mangoac	On the Nottoway River

Siouxan Tribes

Manahoac	Primarily on the Rappahannock River, but also through much of Northern Virginia
Monacans	On the James River from the Falls to the Blue Ridge

Glossary

Ague	Fever with chills, shivering, and sweating.
Aqua Vitae	A type of fermented drink, such as brandy.
Barricoes	Kegs holding 6 to 8 gallons of water each.
Brightwork	Polished metal on a ship.
Bulwark	At Jamestown, the rounded corners of the fort which extended outward from the fort's walls. The bulwarks contained platforms with cannon to allow better defense of the fort.
Burthen	Archaic for "burden," or amount a ship could carry.
Calenture	Fever and delirium, formerly believed to be caused by extreme temperatures.
Coney	A European rabbit.
Culverins	Heavy long-range cannon, used in the 15th to 17th centuries, with a weight of about 4,500 pounds and shot weighing 17 1/3 pounds.
Curat	An armor breastplate.
Delftware	A style of blue and white glazed pottery from the town of Delft in the Netherlands.
Falconets	An ancient form of ordnance, with a weight of about 500 pounds and shot weighing 1¼ pounds.
Firelock	An alternate name for wheel lock, an early form of flint weapon.
Fo'c'sle	A contraction of *forecastle*, a raised and fortified platform on a ship's bow.
Hogsheads	A large cask or barrel holding from 63 to 140 gallons.
Horologer	Clock maker.

Impost	A tax levied on goods brought into a country.
Knot garden	An herb or flower garden with plants arranged in patterns to give a woven effect.
Lute	A musical stringed instrument with a body shaped like half a pear, a bent neck, and fretted fingerboard.
Minion	An ancient form of ordnance, weighing about 1,000 pounds with shot weighing about 4 pounds.
Morion	A kind of open helmet somewhat resembling a hat.
Narrow Sea	An old term for the English Channel.
Oakum	Hemp or fiber, possibly treated with tar, used to caulk a ship's seams.
Ordnance	Cannon.
Pinnace	A small ship.
Recorder	Type of flute.
Shallop	A light boat used for shallow waters.
Snaphaunce	The earliest form of flintlock firearm.
Taborer	A player on the tabor, or small side-drum.
Tercio	The elite infantry forces of the Spanish military during the 16th and 17th centuries, combining firepower with pikes.
Trencher	A wooden plate used to serve food.
Tres escallops	Heraldry term meaning "three scallops."
Tuckahoe	A nearly aquatic plant with arrow-shaped leaves.
Vittler	A person who maintains the food stocks (*victuals* or *vittles*).
Werowance	Algonquin word for chief.
Whipstaff	Nautical term; a vertical lever attached to a ship's rudder for steering.

305

18 Generation Descendency Chart
From William Phippen to the Lapallo Children

William PHIPPEN 1551-1596 Of Melcombe Regis, England m. Jane JORDAINE	**Joan PHIPPEN** 1580-1650 Born in Melcombe Regis Arrived in Jamestown, 1609 m. Thomas REYNOLDS	**Cecily REYNOLDS** b. 1600, Melcombe Regis, Arrived in Jamestown, 1611 Jordan's Journey Plantation m. Thomas BAILEY
William COCKE 1674-1717 of Henrico, Virginia m. Sarah PERRIN	**Thomas COCKE** 1639-1697 of Malvern Hills Plantation m. Margaret POWELL	**Temperance BAILEY** 1617-1651, Henrico, Virginia m. Richard COCKE of Bremo Plantation
Sarah COCKE 1696-1750 Henrico, Virginia m. William COX	**John COX** 1710-1793 Prince Edward, Virginia Furnished supplies to the Continental Army m. Lucretia WYNNE	**Thomas COX** c. 1743-c. 1794 of Bluestone Creek, Mecklenburg, Virginia m. Obedience
Hester A. NASH 1836-1911 Mecklenburg, Virgina m. William R. RICKMAN	**Mary COX** b. 1814 of Halifax, Virginia m. William P. NASH	**Archer COX** of Halifax, Virginia m. Polly HATCHELL in 1802
Mary Elizabeth RICKMAN 1872-1931 Mecklenburg, Virginia m. Charles H. BURGESS	**William Garner BURGESS** 1897-1972 Mecklenburg, Virginia m. Annie Etha TUCKER	**Hazel Lee BURGESS** b. 1918 in Richmond, Virginia m. Peyton Rudolph CHRISTIAN
Sarah A. LAPALLO, b. 1990 Michael C. LAPALLO, b. 1991 Kerry A. LAPALLO, b. 1994 Adam C. LAPALLO, b. 1996 Born in Richmond, Virginia	**Connie Maria MAIDA** b. 1962 in Richmond, Virginia m. Christopher LAPALLO	**Marie A. CHRISTIAN** b. 1942 in Richmond, Virginia m. Michael MAIDA

Preliminary source: Cockes and Cousins, Virginia Webb Cocke, 1974

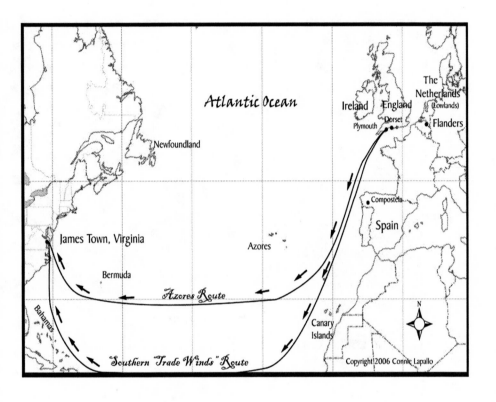

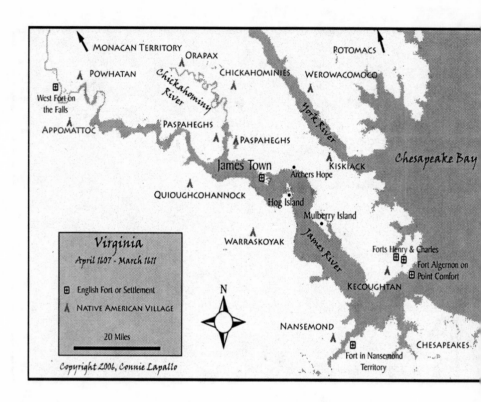

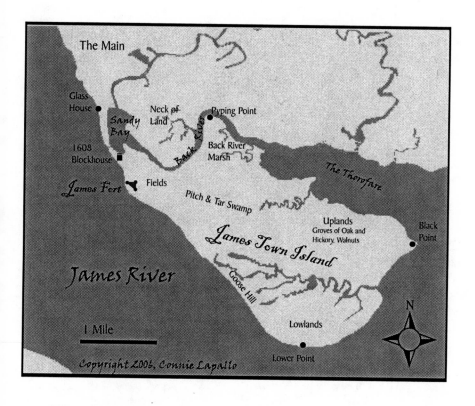

The Main

Glass House ●

Neck of Land

Pyping Point ●

Sandy Bay

1608 Blockhouse ■

Back River Marsh

James Fort

Fields

The Thorofare

Pitch & Tar Swamp

Uplands
Groves of Oak and Hickory, Walnuts

Black Point ●

James Town Island

James River

Goose Hill

N

1 Mile

Lowlands

Lower Point ●

Copyright 2006, Connie Lapallo

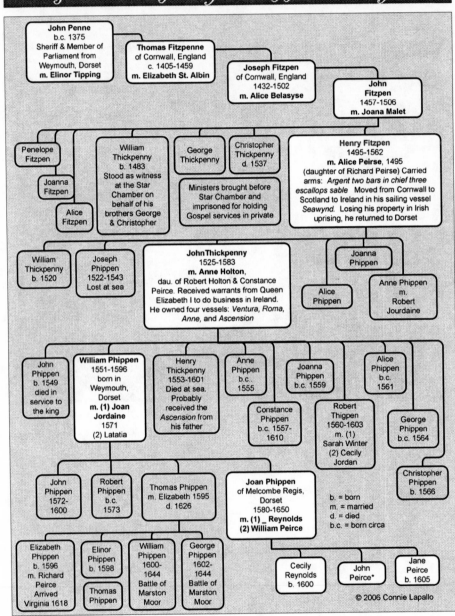

Fitzpen – Thickpenny – Phippen Family Tree

John Penne
b.c. 1375
Sheriff & Member of Parliament from Weymouth, Dorset
m. Elinor Tipping

Thomas Fitzpenne
of Cornwall, England
c. 1405-1459
m. Elizabeth St. Albin

Joseph Fitzpen
of Cornwall, England
1432-1502
m. Alice Belasyse

John Fitzpen
1457-1506
m. Joana Malet

Penelope Fitzpen

Joanna Fitzpen

Alice Fitzpen

William Thickpenny
b. 1483
Stood as witness at the Star Chamber on behalf of his brothers George & Christopher

George Thickpenny

Christopher Thickpenny
d. 1537
Ministers brought before Star Chamber and imprisoned for holding Gospel services in private

Henry Fitzpen
1495-1562
m. Alice Peirse, 1495
(daughter of Richard Peirse) Carried arms: *Argent two bars in chief three escallops sable* Moved from Cornwall to Scotland to Ireland in his sailing vessel *Seawynd*. Losing his property in Irish uprising, he returned to Dorset

William Thickpenny
b. 1520

Joseph Phippen
1522-1543
Lost at sea

John Thickpenny
1525-1583
m. Anne Holton,
dau. of Robert Holton & Constance Peirce. Received warrants from Queen Elizabeth I to do business in Ireland. He owned four vessels: *Ventura, Roma, Anne,* and *Ascension*

Alice Phippen

Joanna Phippen

Anne Phippen
m. Robert Jourdaine

John Phippen
b. 1549
died in service to the king

William Phippen
1551-1596
born in Weymouth, Dorset
m. (1) Joan Jordaine 1571
(2) Latatia

Henry Thickpenny
1553-1601
Died at sea.
Probably received the *Ascension* from his father

Anne Phippen
b.c..
1555

Joanna Phippen
b.c. 1559

Constance Phippen
b.c. 1557-1610

Robert Thigpen
1560-1603
m. (1) Sarah Winter
(2) Cecily Jordan

Alice Phippen
b.c.
1561

George Phippen
b.c. 1564

Christopher Phippen
b. 1566

John Phippen
1572-1600

Robert Phippen
b.c.
1573

Thomas Phippen
m. Elizabeth 1595
d. 1626

Joan Phippen
of Melcombe Regis, Dorset
1580-1650
m. (1) _ Reynolds
(2) William Peirce

b. = born
m. = married
d. = died
b.c. = born circa

Elizabeth Phippen
b. 1596
m. Richard Peirce
Arrived Virginia 1618

Elinor Phippen
b. 1598

Thomas Phippen

William Phippen
1600-1644
Battle of Marston Moor

George Phippen
1602-1644
Battle of Marston Moor

Cecily Reynolds
b. 1600

John Peirce*

Jane Peirce
b. 1605

© 2006 Connie Lapallo

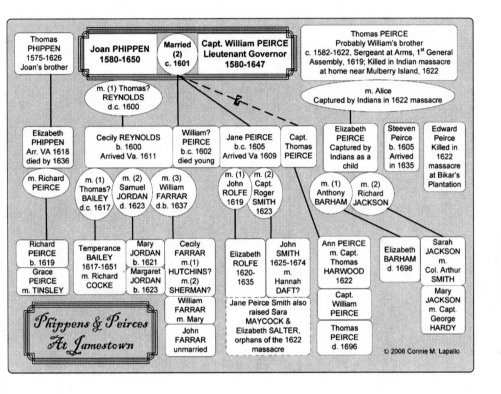

Thomas PHIPPEN 1575-1626 Joan's brother | Joan PHIPPEN 1580-1650 | Married (2) c. 1601 | Capt. William PEIRCE Lieutenant Governor 1580-1647 | Thomas PEIRCE Probably William's brother c. 1582-1622, Sergeant at Arms, 1st General Assembly, 1619; Killed in Indian massacre at home near Mulberry Island, 1622

m. (1) Thomas? REYNOLDS d.c. 1600

m. Alice Captured by Indians in 1622 massacre

Elizabeth PHIPPEN Arr. VA 1618 died by 1636 — m. Richard PEIRCE

Cecily REYNOLDS b. 1600 Arrived Va. 1611 — m. (1) Thomas? BAILEY d.c. 1617 / m. (2) Samuel JORDAN d. 1623 / m. (3) William FARRAR d.b. 1637

William? PEIRCE b.c. 1602 died young

Jane PEIRCE b.c. 1605 Arrived Va 1609 — m. (1) John ROLFE 1619 / m. (2) Capt. Roger SMITH 1623

Capt. Thomas PEIRCE

Elizabeth PEIRCE Captured by Indians as a child — m. (1) Anthony BARHAM / m. (2) Richard JACKSON

Steeven Peirce b. 1605 Arrived in 1635

Edward Peirce Killed in 1622 massacre at Bikar's Plantation

Richard PEIRCE b. 1619 Grace PEIRCE m. TINSLEY

Temperance BAILEY 1617-1651 m. Richard COCKE

Mary JORDAN b. 1621 Margaret JORDAN b. 1623

Cecily FARRAR m.(1) HUTCHINS? m.(2) SHERMAN? William FARRAR m. Mary John FARRAR unmarried

Elizabeth ROLFE 1620- 1635

John SMITH 1625-1674 m. Hannah DAFT? Jane Peirce Smith also raised Sara MAYCOCK & Elizabeth SALTER, orphans of the 1622 massacre

Ann PEIRCE m. Capt. Thomas HARWOOD 1622 Capt. William PEIRCE Thomas PEIRCE d. 1696

Elizabeth BARHAM d. 1696

Sarah JACKSON m. Col. Arthur SMITH Mary JACKSON m. George HARDY

Phippens & Peirces At Jamestown

© 2006 Connie M. Lapallo

Printed in the United States
91225LV00006B/52/A

9 781595 264213